Hear No Evil

by

Suzanne Rossi

Hear No Evil

Cover Art by *Kim Mendoza*

The Wild Rose Press, Inc.
PO Box 708
Adams Basin, NY 14410-0708
Visit us at www.thewildrosepress.com

Publishing History
First Crimson Rose Edition, 2012
Print ISBN 978-1-61217-007-7
Digital ISBN 978-1-61217-248-4

Published in the United States of America

Andy took a deep breath, muttering, "Damn you, Renee. You're going to get yourself hurt or worse and I don't want that to happen." He pulled me into his arms, his lips crushing mine.

I stood in shock for all of a nanosecond before parting my lips and clinging to him like a limpet. Searing heat radiated from the pit of my stomach and rolled throughout my body. My heart thudded in my ears and I didn't care whether or not I breathed. My hands slid up his shoulders to his nape where I tangled my fingers in his silky hair. The scent of his cologne made me throb in all the right places.

His lips traveled down my cheek to my neck and his hands wandered under my t-shirt.

"God, Renee, stop me."

"No way," I said, panting.

Nimble fingers unsnapped my bra and pushed it out of the way.

We careened around the kitchen banging off the cabinets and the table. I jerked his shirt from the waistband of his jeans and slid my hands up his rippled chest. I'd been dreaming about this moment from the day I'd seen him ninety percent naked in the pool and spa room at the gym.

I moaned and wrapped my leg around his—anything to get closer. He sucked at the pulse point on my neck, sending a zing along my nerves and a strong throb to the one place it belonged.

Suddenly, glass shattered in the living room.

Praise for Suzanne Rossi

"I found [*ALONG CAME QUINN*] entertaining and a quick read. It's a fun road romance with a twist on the treasure that I think is different yet believable. And it just goes to show that sometimes you can't see what's right under your nose."

~Jayne, Dear Author

~*~

"*NEARLY DEPARTED* is a wonderfully written and entertaining romance that will please readers on many different levels."

~Long And Short Reviews

~*~

"Just when you think you know the answer to the mystery, in come some more suspects, leaving you on the edge of your seat and keeping the pages turning."

~LynnMarie, GoodReads

Dedication

This is tough. I'm running out of people to mention.
I've already gone through family, editors,
critique partners, and friends.
That leaves my dogs, Lucky and Liza.
Unfortunately, they can't read, so what's the point?
Instead, I dedicate this to the reader.
Without you buying my books, I wouldn't be here.
I hope you all enjoy the adventures, the mayhem,
the love, and the actions I try to provide.
My humble thanks to all of you.

Other Titles by Suzanne Rossi

Along Came Quinn
All in the Family
A Tangled Web
Nearly Departed

Chapter One

Let's get something straight. I am not paranoid—a little suspicious, a tad obsessive, and possessed with a burning desire to know everything that's going on around me, but I'm *not* paranoid.

Take my boyfriend, Joel Wainwright. His sudden interest in jogging made me suspicious. He'd never given a damn about physical fitness. Now, he rose at six o'clock every morning to sweat up a storm in the City Park of Palm Lake, Florida. Two hours later he'd return, shower, dress, and leave for his almost-an-office-with-a-view at Banks and Banks Advertising.

Naturally, I had to know what—or who—caused this change in attitude.

"I'm concerned about my lifestyle," he'd said. "Exercise is good for the cardiovascular system."

"Then why don't you quit smoking?" I pointed out one morning.

He finished tying his still unscuffed Adidas running shoes and hit me with a stern look. "One thing at a time, Renee."

"Maybe I should start running, too."

A look of alarm crossed his face. "Not today. I'm late and haven't got the time to wait on you." He jogged in place for a second. "Gotta go. Be back in a little while."

The front door slammed. My suspicions shot to red alert. I drummed my fingers on the kitchen table. *What the hell is he really doing, and who's he doing it with?*

Once fixated on an idea, I follow through with

1

the thoroughness of a military commander planning an invasion. Later that day, I pretended to work, maintaining the illusion of being busy for my immediate boss who was out to get me. I'm sure he pictured his shapely girlfriend behind the reception desk.

However, I am *not* paranoid.

That night, a TV commercial advertising a listening device called Lend An Ear gave me an idea. The thing resembled an iPod complete with headphones and was touted as an inexpensive hearing aid, but the ad stated conversations could be heard from two hundred feet away.

Perfect—just what I needed. I'd follow Joel, keep my distance, and hear anything he said to anybody he met.

I ordered one, requesting fast shipment. Lend An Ear arrived two days later. I tested it on my front lawn and had no problem hearing my next door neighbor refer to *his* next door neighbor as an ass, then wondered if he meant *me*. He hadn't lived there long enough to make that determination yet. I'd barely spoken to the man.

At any rate, the machine's performance pleased me. When Joel left the next morning, I followed at a discreet distance.

I parked, slid out of the car, then slid back in again and ducked my head below the dashboard when I spied a familiar face. It was Detective Andrew Jackson. Yeah, I know, just like the seventh president. He took a lot of ribbing about his name as a kid. His younger sister, Katie, had been a high school classmate and my best friend.

I held my breath and waited, then lifted my head and peeked out the window. Damn, he'd stopped right next to my car. My movement must have caught his attention because he looked over.

"Renee, is that you? What are you doing here?"

"Uh, hi, Andy. I, um, walk in the mornings. I take it you jog."

"Whenever I can." He glanced at his watch. "Oops, I'm running late." He smiled a charming, lopsided smile. "Nice to see you."

That smile was distracting, holding me tongue-tied for a moment. He cocked his head to one side, and I snapped out of it. "Uh, yeah. Same here."

Through the rearview mirror, I watched as he trotted over the pavement to the guardrail separating the parking lot from the trails. His thigh and calf muscles resembled ropes—hard, sinewy ropes. The tank top he wore revealed equally well-muscled shoulders and biceps. For a moment, I mentally drooled, and then remembered why I was here—that son of a bitch, Joel. I got out of the car, and giving Andy a wide berth, took off down the trail my so-called boyfriend had taken, finally spotting him not far ahead. I closed in before moving to the side of the path in case I had to make myself scarce and slapped the Lend An Ear headphones on my head.

My boyfriend didn't jog. He walked, paused on a footbridge, and gazed up the path, then squirted his face from his water bottle. A moment later, a female runner appeared. I dodged behind a bush.

"Sherry, hi," Joel said, huffing and puffing as though he'd run a marathon.

Jerk.

The woman stopped. "Looks like you've been working hard."

I sized her up—tall, slender, and very fit. Everything I wasn't. Her brown hair was tied up in a ponytail and hung down her back from the opening at the back of her red baseball cap. The rest of her ensemble was typical jogging clothes. She looked great in them. Damn.

Joel leaned over, bracing his hands on his knees

3

and said between panting breaths, "Big day at the office. Partnership interviews. Needed to work off excess energy."

Joel's company had recently gone through a merger. Old partners had retired and new partners would soon be selected. He wanted that partnership—bad.

"Don't worry. Brad Holcombe likes you. I whispered a few good words in my uncle's ear, too. And you know you have my vote."

"You're the best. I knew it the first day you walked through the door. You can be my boss any time." He leaned over and kissed her. "Dinner tonight?"

Well, that explains the 'working late at the office' excuses I've been getting for the last two months.

"Of course. Easy Breezes as usual?"

"Sounds good. I signed the papers on the condo yesterday. I'll move in this weekend. No more borrowing a co-worker's apartment. It'll be just you and me."

I'd heard more than enough. Was the miserable son of a bitch going to sneak out under the cover of darkness, or did he plan on setting up two households? My bet was on the former. He didn't make enough money for the latter. I trembled with rage, and tears of humiliation coursed down my cheeks.

I broke from my hiding place, ran the hundred feet to the bridge at full speed, lowered my shoulder, and rammed into Joel with the intent of sending him over the rail into the water. Only a last second desperation clutch saved his sorry ass.

"What the hell's the matter with you?" his companion screamed. She leaned over and made a grab for his arm, but missed.

Joel floundered and grunted, trying to gain a foothold on the bridge supports. For a moment he

4

dangled like bait over an alligator pit. I liked the analogy, visualizing a big one emasculating him.

"You bastard! Setting up a second home?"

"Renee! What the hell are you doing here?" Joel found a purchase and with Sherry's help finally crawled over the rail.

"Do you know this crazy person?" she demanded.

"I'll say he does. He lives with me."

"What? You told me you lived with two roommates because you'd just gone through a divorce." Her eyes narrowed.

"He did—a couple of years ago. That's how he ended up at my place."

Her hands fisted on her hips. "Oh, yeah?"

"Look, Sherry, I can explain." The sweat on his face was real this time. "It's true I've been living with Renee, but as a friend. I was going to tell her about us. Just didn't get around to it yet."

"You slug," I retorted with contempt in my voice, before turning to the girl. "What's your connection to Banks and Banks?"

She stared, her expression both confused and suspicious. "I'm one of the owners of New Horizons Advertising. We just merged with Banks and Banks. My uncle is the CEO. Joel, what's this all about?"

"You need to ask? He's ambitious as hell and can taste that partnership."

"Honey, if I'd known Renee was this obsessed, I'd have walked out a long time ago. She means nothing to me, and is obviously unbalanced."

He shot me a look that should have curled my hair, but I glared back. Various forms of revenge flashed through my mind. Coating his body with honey and shoving him into the bear enclosure at the zoo? Jamming fire ants down the crotch of his pants? That one appealed. How about just pummeling him into jelly?

"Maybe I should go and let you and your—ah—

friend work out your problems," the woman said. "I want no part of a triangle."

"And he doesn't jog. He just squirted his face with water. If he's lied about all of this, what else has he lied about?" I enjoyed watching Joel's face turn white.

Sherry gazed at him with a speculative look. "Yes, I wonder."

"You can't be buying this, can you?" Joel cried, a note of desperation creeping into his voice.

"Of course, she can. Look at her face." I pointed my finger.

"Sherry, no! Honey, you mean the world to me." His voice turned whiney, and he reached out as though to touch her.

Sherry stepped back. "Yeah, so much so that you forget to tell me you're living with another woman. In fact, you called your roommates Bill and Al. In my book, that's a lie. I'm outta here. I need to talk to my uncle and Brad."

Without another word, she whirled and ran back the way she'd come. Joel turned on me.

"Thanks a lot, you fat pig! You just screwed three months of hard work. Now, I'll be lucky to keep my job."

His insulting words hurt like hell and added to my anger. "Good. I hope you end up living in a cardboard box and chowing down on fine cuisine in a soup kitchen. And get your shit out of my house. If it's still there when I get home tonight, I'll dump it on the lawn and burn it. It'll be the biggest bonfire on the east coast."

I turned and ran down the asphalt path, leaving Joel standing alone in the middle of the bridge. I had no idea where I was going and didn't care. Humiliation and blinding rage fueled my flight.

I finally stopped running and leaned over, my hands braced on my knees, gasping for oxygen. I was a little lax in the exercise department, too.

Regaining my breath, I straightened, gazing around. City Park was pear-shaped, surrounded by woods and nature trails on three sides. I looked toward the narrow, northern end of the pear. The parking lot lay just beyond. Somewhere along the line, I had dashed off the jogging path and stood alone in a large grassy area. In the distance, a man tossed a Frisbee to his dog, which caught it and trotted back to its owner. I spied a park bench situated near the tree line several yards away.

My legs trembled and burned. I clasped one hand against my still pounding heart and the other over the stitch in my side. I walked to the bench, sitting down with a thump, and then clapped my hand over my mouth to stifle the sobs bubbling in my throat.

Damn Joel Wainwright to hell and back.

How could I have been so freaking blind—so consummately stupid? He didn't love me. Never had. He just needed a place to stay until something better came along—like Sherry and the promise of a partnership. I'd cooked for him, cleaned to his specifications, and was always there whenever he needed a little slap and tickle. The sob burst from behind my hand. I swallowed the others threatening to follow.

Bastard! Miserable, low-down, stinking bastard.

I whacked the heel of my hand against my forehead. "Renee Ryan, what the hell's wrong with you? Are you really this needy?"

Of course I was or I wouldn't be sitting here listening to the sounds of nature scream in my ears. I still wore the Lend An Ear device headphones. The twenty-four ninety-five I'd shelled out had proven worthwhile. I fumbled for the off button, and then stopped when I heard human voices.

"This is a down payment—twenty-five grand as

7

discussed. You'll get the rest when everything's over," a man said.

"So, how do you want it done?" a female asked.

"It's got to look like an accident or a mugging gone bad. Anything except what it is."

The woman laughed. "You mean murder. Tell it like it is."

My flesh crawled and my breath caught in my throat, threatening to strangle me. I cast my eyes toward the woods, but saw no one. I was alone—very alone. A tremor, starting in the pit of my stomach, quickly made its way to my extremities.

"Okay, murder."

"Got a picture?"

"Yeah, here."

"Nice looking," the woman said.

"That's about three years old. Her hair has grown. It's shoulder length now with blonde streaks in it."

"Any set routine?"

"Yes. Jogging here starting between eight and eight-thirty every weekday morning. Sunday is a sleep in day. She rarely leaves the house. We spend every other Saturday with her parents at their Key West condo.

"She also stays busy with a ton of volunteer work—all for what she calls worthy causes. Lunch is usually at some trendy restaurant with either a friend or someone she's trying to talk into donating money."

"What kind of car does she drive?" the woman asked.

"A black Lexus, 300 series. Here's the license plate number."

Paper crinkled in my ear through the headphones.

"Any other activities she does on a regular basis?"

"Yeah, yoga and the gym, but the times vary depending on how much she has to do in a given day. I know she tries to do the yoga thing three times a week. She visits the gym only if it's raining and she can't jog." He paused. "If the bitch had stayed home and paid half as much attention to me as she does to the rest of her life, we wouldn't be having this conversation."

The man spoke in a bitter, hate-filled voice. My heart squeezed tight in my chest like I was having a heart attack. I had tapped into a conversation not meant for my ears, and didn't want to hear.

Once again, I clapped my hand over my mouth to stifle a sob. If I had any sense, I'd get up and run like hell, but I sat, my butt glued to the bench with the headphones solidly in place. My muscles refused to obey my brain.

"There's no reason to mug someone on a jogging path. Joggers don't carry anything worth stealing. And Key West on Saturday has too many people. Ditto for the gym and yoga. What about the Saturday you don't go to the Keys?"

"It varies. Nothing is set in stone on that day."

"When do you want it done?"

"As soon as possible. But it has to happen when I'm out of town. I'll be the first one they'll suspect."

"I thought you wanted this to look like an accident?"

"I still want an alibi—just in case. I'm due to fly to Chicago next week." His voice sounded hopeful.

"Don't rush me. I like to take my time. Is she observant—conscious of what's going on around her?"

"In spades. Getting close will be a bitch."

"Leave that, and the how, to me." Her voice turned hard.

A sudden rustling in the leaves or bushes made me flinch. Sickness clogged my throat.

"What's that?" the man said in a sharp voice.

"Relax. It's just an animal. We have plenty of time to melt into the woods if someone comes. By the way, this is our one and only face-to-face. When the job's done, bring the remainder of the fifty grand to this address."

Paper crinkled in my ear again.

"Gainesville?"

"Just hop in your cute little Porsche and drive on up to campus."

"How—how do you know I drive a Porsche?"

"I know a lot of things about you, but let's get back to Gainesville. The house is easy to find. Drop the envelope through the mail slot and leave. If I see you or your car hanging around, your future will not be bright—or long. Understood?"

I shivered at the menace in her voice. This woman meant business.

"I understand," the man answered. "I won't stiff you. I just want her gone."

I not only heard, but could almost feel his fear.

"There is such a thing as divorce, you know."

"She controls everything. I'm not about to go back to living in a two bedroom apartment and driving a Ford."

"I understand. Your new girlfriend wouldn't be nearly as enamored of you without all that money— your wife's money, I mean." The woman laughed again. "I don't care why you want her dead, so don't bother to justify hiring me."

More voices in the distance came through the headphones.

"Someone's coming. If you change your mind, call the cell number I gave you. But don't forget, I'll need a six hour notice of cancellation along with delivery of half the remaining money. I'll be angry if I don't get it—and you don't want me angry. Clear?"

"Clear," the man echoed.

"*Adios, amigo,*" she said.

I listened to the sound of two sets of footsteps, one jogging and one walking, fade into silence.

I yanked the headphones from my ears and leaped to my feet, whipping my head from side to side. Where had they been? On the nature trail, or just around the bend on the jogging path? I had to find a cop and fast. Andy! I took off at a dead run. I didn't stop to think, but ran as though *my* life depended on it.

Chapter Two

"And you say you heard a murder for hire plot through *this* contraption?"

Here I sat, an unwilling witness to a potential crime, and this stupid cop gazed at the Lend An Ear like it was a kid's toy and at me like I was nuts. I wanted to kick him in the shin. Or higher.

Andy was long gone by the time I got back to the parking lot. I'd jumped in the car and driven straight to the police station.

"I just told you that—twice. So, what are you going to do about it, besides play with that thing I mean?"

He shrugged and set the instrument on the table. "Don't give me a hard time. We could have come to the park if you'd given us a call. Whoever you heard is nowhere near by now." He picked it up again as if fascinated.

"I forgot my cell phone this morning, so I drove here."

My earlier actions had been centered on proving Joel an asshole. I'd never even thought about the phone or my purse for that matter. Both remained on my kitchen counter. And I certainly hadn't anticipated a trip to the police station, unless, of course, I'd actually killed Joel. I avoided the police as a rule, and only overhearing that damned conversation had sent me driving like Jeff Gordon through the streets of Palm Lake.

When I couldn't produce ID, the cops had shoved me in a room until verifying I was who I said. Why bother? They knew me. I'd been here before. It only took a couple of minutes for an officer to confirm my identity. The fact that he'd chuckled while doing so didn't make me feel better.

"Can you identify the voices you claimed to have heard?"

"No, but it was a man and a woman. What do you mean by claimed?"

He ignored me. "And she's the hit person?"

"Yes. How many times do I have to tell you?"

The policeman, a detective by the name of Santos, inspected the device again, turning it over in his hands, and fiddling with the volume control.

"And this picks up conversations two hundred feet away?"

"So the ad says."

"But you don't know if the people you heard were ten feet away or two hundred, right?" He asked the question with raised eyebrows, therefore causing *my* temper to rise.

"No, I don't. It's not a GPS. All it does is amplify." Irritation at his attitude bubbled in my chest. I'd lost patience long ago. Fortunately, I held my temper in check—no easy task. "Look, Detective Santos..."

He held up his hand, cutting me off. "You know, I have to wonder at the legality of this thing. It could be construed as an invasion of privacy."

I stared in disbelief. "You've gotta be kidding. I was in a public place. Who has the expectation of privacy in a park, for crying out loud? And I didn't record anything. I just listened. What part of this don't you get? I overheard a *murder* being planned."

"I don't know, but I'm sure a good lawyer could get testimony based on an eavesdropping device tossed out of court in a New York minute. Uh, why do you have it in the first place? I mean, were you listening to someone's conversation?"

Heat radiated from my cheeks, and I shifted in

the chair. Busted. Gritting my teeth, I answered with as much dignity as possible.

"Of course not. I was communing with nature."

The interrogation room door opened. A uniformed policeman entered and handed Detective Santos several folders. I sat silently while he read. Finally, he lifted his head and smirked. I wanted to smack him in the worst way.

"I see you were arrested on a disorderly conduct charge three months ago. According to the report, you created a disturbance in a fast food restaurant when you accused a patron of trying to steal your purse."

"He did," I retorted. "I hung my purse over the back of the chair. Next thing I knew it was in his hands."

"He and several witnesses claim the purse fell to the floor."

"Witnesses are sometimes wrong."

"And when he tried to return it, you called him a thieving bastard, tossed a soft drink in his face, and then kicked him in the knee. You're lucky he didn't sue."

I glared at Detective Smart Ass, and swallowed the angry words threatening to erupt. I should have known they'd pull my file.

He set the folder aside and opened another. "Nine months ago you were brought in for pepper spraying a seventy-year-old man in the parking lot of a local discount store."

"He followed me throughout the store and to my car."

"So, you whipped out your spray and let him have it, huh? Turns out the man had the bad luck to have parked his car next to yours."

I leaned forward. "Then explain why he was in the lingerie aisle at the same time I was."

Santos glanced at the report. "He says he was

buying his wife a birthday gift."

"Seventy-year-old men don't buy their wives lingerie. They take 'em out to dinner."

He closed the file and grabbed another. I wanted to scream with frustration. Santos didn't take a word of what I'd told him seriously.

"Last year, you filed a complaint against one of your neighbors for not picking up after his dog with a pooper-scooper."

"Hey, that one's legit. He also never has that mutt on a leash. Both are city ordinances."

He opened the last folder. "I remember this one!" His voice had a gleeful tone, and he chuckled. "You called the Department of Homeland Security on your next door neighbor and accused him of being a terrorist."

I wanted to sink through the floor in humiliation, but defended my actions.

"He had strange people coming and going at all hours of the day and night. I heard them talking. Not a one of them spoke English without a Middle Eastern accent. And they'd look around to see if anyone watched as they slunk into the house. I was suspicious and did what any red-blooded, patriotic American would do."

"According to this report, the guy was a U. S. citizen of Moroccan descent. He held classes on American culture in his home for recent Moroccan immigrants so they could assimilate into their new country faster." Santos closed the file. "Tell me, does he still talk to you, or just run in the opposite direction when he sees you coming?"

"He moved."

"Miss Ryan, you seem to have a history of, shall we say, erratic and bizarre behavior. Are you under a doctor's care or on medication?"

That did it. I leaped to my feet and snatched the Lend An Ear from his hands. *Damn all men to hell.*

"No, I am *not*, and everybody has a right to be different. It's in the Constitution or something. Now, what are you going to do about the murder plot?"

He sighed. "We don't know who, where, when, or even if this is a legitimate threat."

"What? You're going to wait until a woman shows up dead before you do anything?"

"Has it occurred to you that someone may have seen you in the park this morning—someone who knows you or who's been on the receiving end of your accusations? Maybe they decided to have a little fun at your expense." He rose. "Go home, Miss Ryan."

I whirled, stalked from the room, and through the police station. What bullshit! I was the only one who knew I had, and intended to use, the Lend An Ear. And with my record of complaints, I could see why they didn't take me seriously. The whole thing reminded me of some childhood story about a little boy crying wolf.

With my anger barely under control, I shoved the door open, running headlong into Andrew Jackson. His hands clasped my shoulders.

"It's you! Not again. Twice in one morning is a surprise. Why are you here? Pepper sprayed anyone lately? Please, tell me you haven't filed another complaint against an innocent citizen," he said with a grin.

Andy was an okay guy. He possessed a rugged face with a square jaw, and a wicked sense of humor. Other than a couple of hours ago, I hadn't seen him since the old dude in the parking lot incident.

"Go to hell," I snapped, twisting free. The grin infuriated me even more.

He clasped my arm. "Whoa. What's got you so riled up?"

I jerked away. "Ask that asshole Santos."

I left him staring after me and strutted to my car. He'd gone inside by the time I looked back. In

16

spite of my irritation, I wished he'd come after me. He might have understood. After all, he knew me as a kid. And even though his words had been teasing, he wouldn't poke fun at me when he heard my story.

Settled in the driver's seat, I smacked the steering wheel with my fist. Damn. I couldn't just sit around and wait to say "I told you so" when a body appeared. If I'd used my brain earlier, I'd have stayed in the parking lot to see if a man drove off in a Porsche.

I should have watched for a black Lexus arriving, too. Why don't I ever do things logically at the moment? Why do I always come up with these gems after the fact?

My dash clock read eight-forty. Shit. No way would I get to work on time. I put the car into gear, headed to my house, a quick shower, and probably a lecture on the virtues of arriving at nine o'clock instead of nine-twenty from my boss—the one who wanted me gone.

****

I simmered all day, almost as angry with myself as at Joel. I'd allowed him to use me, and the fact I didn't feel one iota of remorse about the break-up said a lot about the relationship.

I arrived home to find Joel carting my very expensive, super-great sound quality, radio/CD player out to his car.

"Thief! Put it back now. That's mine."

He skidded to a halt, glaring at me. "Since when?"

"Since I paid for it with my tax refund last year."

"We both wanted it. It's a joint purchase."

"Like hell. You never paid for squat. Put it back."

Joel smiled and dropped the radio on the sidewalk. "There, you can have it."

I wanted to kill him. My daylong, festering

17

anger erupted like Mt. Vesuvius. His golf bag stood next to his car in the driveway. I dashed over and grabbed a club, raising it over my head. Joel turned and ran. It was a great decision.

For a guy who smoked and had only pretended to jog for the past few months, the son of a bitch was nimble. I chased him across the yard calling him names at the top of my lungs, while taking the occasional swing as he dodged through the landscaping. Neighbors stopped and stared, including the one with the unleashed dog that moseyed over and left a deposit while I had Joel cornered behind a bush.

I swung and hit a small tree. The golf club bent.

"That's my nine-iron, you stupid bitch!"

I swung again, hacking at the foliage. He sidestepped, his gaze darting from side to side, no doubt seeking escape.

"So what? Use another. You've got more." I had him trapped and moved in for the kill.

Before I had a chance to swing, someone plucked the club from my hands. A pair of strong arms encircled my body, holding me still. I kicked backward and made contact with a shin.

"Ouch! Stop that!"

The grip didn't lessen, yet somehow I turned around and stared into Andy's face.

"Let me go!"

"She tried to kill me. I want to press charges," Joel hollered from the safety of the bushes.

"He's a thief!"

"Bitch!"

"You're a liar, a cheat, and an asshole!"

"Both of you calm down. What's going on?" Andy ordered.

"I caught him cheating and threw his ass out."

"She's a nut case. When I decided to leave she went ballistic."

I squirmed in Andy's arms, but the grip didn't lessen. Instead, his attention swung back to me. "Why are you taking practice swings at his head?"

I pointed toward the sidewalk and told him what had gone down, besides the radio.

"You," he said to Joel. "Have you got all your stuff?"

"More or less."

"Then leave."

"I want her arrested! Look what she did to my golf club."

"Mister, I wouldn't be so anxious to see her in jail. This is a domestic dispute, and they always get nasty in court."

"Yeah! I'll tell the judge all about your little partnership plan. Sherry'll probably be on my side, too."

Joel looked like he wanted to hurl something at my head. Instead he shouted his favorite epithet. "Bitch!"

I struggled to break free, but Andy's arms tightened again.

"Forget about your golf club. Buy a new one. Just leave—now."

"Not until I see what else he tried to steal," I said.

"You gonna behave?" he asked.

I nodded. Andy released me and picked up the mutilated nine iron. In a way, I was disappointed. I liked his arms around me. Why, I had no idea.

"Open the trunk," Andy said.

Joel complied, tossing the golf bag in. I saw his clothes and other assorted junk. At my nod, he slammed it shut, then slid behind the wheel and peeled out of the driveway, making sure to give me the stiff middle finger in place of a goodbye wave.

I stalked back to the sidewalk and scooped up the radio. Andy examined it.

"Just a little crack in the bottom. You're lucky. It partially fell on the grass. When are you going to control that temper of yours?"

"I took anger management classes several years ago. Today was an exception. What are you doing here?"

"I came to see you. Let's go inside."

He followed me into the house, sitting on the sofa. I set the radio on the coffee table and settled into a chair across from him. I felt better. Swinging that golf club had been therapeutic, easing my anger.

Maybe I should take up the game.

He drew a deep breath and frowned. "I talked to Santos and read the report. Renee, could you have misconstrued the conversation you heard?"

"What's to misconstrue about murder?"

"That device you used picks up all sounds, doesn't it?"

"Yeah."

"Maybe you overheard a man and a woman meeting—like a tryst—and only got part of the conversation because of the other noises. I'm sure birds chirped, insects buzzed, and leaves rustled in the wind, not to mention other joggers. This thing would also pick up their footsteps, wouldn't it?"

I rubbed my forehead, and then twined my fingers together in my lap. He humored me, like a five-year-old. He also pissed me off, but I refrained from letting it show. I didn't want him to think of me as a basket case. Why I cared was a mystery.

"Andy, I know what I heard, and it was no tryst. Where did you learn such a word anyway? That's not a guy word."

"Never mind my vocabulary. The fact is, we have nothing to go on—no names, no descriptions, no times, or places the so-called crime will happen. You have an active imagination—always did. Got you

and Katie into trouble on more than one occasion."
He smiled as though recalling a fond memory.

I sighed. "I know I can be a little erratic, but not
this time. I'm not..." I didn't continue. Once again
for reasons I couldn't fathom, his doubting me hurt.
I'm not a nut case. I'm really not.

"You're not your mother," he finished for me. "In
spite of what happened out front, you haven't tried
to kill anyone."

"It was an accident. Daddy came home drunk as
a skunk, reeking of cheap perfume. Mama got mad
and grabbed the thirty-aught. She didn't even know
it was loaded."

"She still shot him."

"The bullet just grazed his head."

Andy took a deep breath. "Yeah, but then there
was the road rage incident that got her where she is
today. By the way, how is your mother?"

I shifted my gaze around the room happy he
cared enough to ask. "Fine. She actually likes it at
the sanitarium. The doctors say she might be
released in a few more months."

"And your father?"

"The last I heard, he's living somewhere in
Texas. Why do you ask?"

"Renee, between your father's drinking and your
mother's temper, you didn't have the best of
childhoods. Have you ever considered therapy?"

Oh crap, he does think I'm a nut case.

"I went for a while after Daddy's little accident
five years ago. I usually handle things a lot better
than I did today. Yes, I was angry at Joel, but that
still doesn't mean I didn't hear what I heard."

Andy rose. "All right. Believe what you want,
but I suggest you toss that listening device in the
trash. It'll only get you into trouble."

I walked with him to his car parked at the curb.
In his own way, Andy sounded concerned about me

and it struck a chord. God knows, my parents hadn't cared much. My last visit to Mom six months ago lasted a whole thirty minutes. We'd had nothing to say to each other.

"Look, Andy, thanks for coming by. I appreciate it. Maybe you're right, and I didn't hear what I thought."

He smiled, his eyes crinkling at the corners. He resembled his sister with dark hair and hazel eyes. It was an attractive face. Why hadn't I noticed that before? Because he was Katie's obnoxious older brother? I did some quick math and put his age at thirty-seven.

Funny, I'd known him for years. At eight, I'd considered him just a yucky boy. At ten, I developed a massive pre-pubescent crush. They say puppy love never goes away, but by the time I was thirteen, his status had changed back to being an irritating pest. Then, he'd gone to college and I forgot about him— well, almost.

"Goodbye, Renee." He eased behind the wheel and closed the door. "Try and stay out of trouble, okay?"

I waved as he drove away, and then strolled into the house. In the kitchen, I picked up the Lend An Ear and messed with the controls.

Had I misheard? In spite of my words of a moment ago, I didn't believe them. Somewhere, a woman's life was in danger, and other than the killer, her husband, and me, no one else knew—or at least thought it possible.

I set the instrument back on the counter. No, I couldn't let it go. If the police wouldn't do anything, then I would.

Chapter Three

I awoke the following morning determined to help this unknown victim survive her cheating husband's deadly plot. During the evening, I'd come up with a plan. I decided to hang around the parking lot until a woman with shoulder length hair and highlights got out of a black Lexus. Then, I'd warn her of the danger. With any luck, the husband and the killer would be in jail before they knew what hit them.

The Lend An Ear didn't find the trash can as Andy had suggested. Instead I tucked it inside the console of my car, ready in case I needed it. Even though not a recorder, the device might still play a role.

Before I forgot, I wrote down most of the conversation I'd inadvertently overheard, and wished I remembered more details. The husband's words remained fresh in my mind, no doubt because of Joel's actions, but the killer's comments stayed elusive. I'd been more horrified by her cold as ice tone than the words. And I wasn't sure if I'd recall the voices if I heard them again. Andy had been right about background noise. It fuzzed my memory.

I jumped out of bed, showered, dressed for work in record time, then grabbed a travel mug of coffee and drove to City Park, slipping into a parking space near the jogging path. I sipped the aromatic, life sustaining liquid and waited—and waited, and waited. A quick glance at my dashboard clock told me that if I didn't make contact in the next ten minutes, I'd be late for work—again.

Neither had I expected so many joggers. Since the time I arrived, the lot had almost filled. At least a dozen people warmed up by the guardrail separating the cars from the paths.

I tapped my fingers against the steering wheel impatiently. What if she didn't show? Then what would I do? How could I warn someone whose name remained a question mark? A horrible thought crossed my mind. What if the killer had already struck?

No, Renee, don't think that way. It's not true.

The news hadn't reported the untimely death of a woman I assumed was stinking rich. And I remembered the hit woman saying something about taking her time.

I was about to leave when a black car drove in and parked in an end slot. A woman with a pony tail emerged. From this distance I couldn't tell if the automobile was a Lexus, or if she had highlights.

Scrambling from my Honda, I walked toward her while she braced her foot on the guardrail and stretched. As I passed her car, I checked the make— a Lexus. Relieved I approached the woman.

Tall and slender, she looked to be in her early thirties and very fit. Maybe there was something to be said for jogging, the gym, and yoga. I'd look into it later. At the moment, I had a mission.

Sunglasses hid her eyes, but as I got closer, I had no trouble seeing the golden streaks in her medium brown hair. This was my victim. Had to be. I approached cautiously.

"Um, excuse me, but I was wondering if I could have a word with you?"

The woman looked up. "About what?"

"Well, your safety." I hadn't expected this to be so hard. How do you tell someone her husband is out to kill her?

"My safety?" She stopped stretching. "What

about my safety? I heard this park is very secure."

"Oh, I'm not talking about the park. This is kind of complicated, but yesterday, I overheard a conversation. A man and woman were—well, there's no easy way to say it, but they were plotting to kill you."

She backed up a few steps, ripping the sunglasses from her face. Brown eyes stared at me with an incredulous gaze, which shifted from side to side as though seeking help.

"Uh, look lady, I don't know who you are, but you've obviously got the wrong person."

"No, please, I know it sounds farfetched, but it's true. Your husband wants you dead so he can have all the money to himself. He has a girlfriend. And he was hiring someone to kill you—even made a down payment."

She backed up another couple of paces. I followed. This was not going as I had hoped.

"Stay away from me," she said in a loud voice. Other joggers stopped what they were doing and stared.

"But, it's the truth. I swear it. I'm only trying to help. Your life is in danger. I heard them. He gave her twenty-five thousand dollars."

"Lady, you're nuts!" She edged sideways and cast another glance toward the parking lot. The crowd of curious onlookers grew. My frustration increased.

"Why won't anybody believe me? What is it with people? I try to be a good citizen, and all I get in return is scorn and suspicion."

"You are seriously unbalanced," the woman declared backing up further.

Her accusation struck a little too close to home. I bit my lip to keep my temper under control.

"Sounds drunk to me," a jogger said to a friend.

"Drunk and nuts, if you want my opinion," the

friend replied.

An arm suddenly draped over my shoulder and hugged me to a lean masculine body. I looked up at Andy. Oh damn, just what I needed. I tried to ignore the warm glow in the pit of my stomach.

"Hi, sis, how's it going? Mom's worried about you. Have you been taking your medication?"

"Medication?" the woman asked.

"My sister's harmless, really. She just has an overactive imagination. Please forgive her."

I tried to pull free, but Andy's arm tightened. A thrill of awareness rippled along my skin. Then the thrill was gone and my temper came through loud and clear.

"Let me go, you asshole! I'm trying to—"

"I know, honey, you're trying to warn the lady about danger, but just because you and Joel broke up doesn't mean that this lady's husband is out to get her. We've had this discussion before. Remember?"

Anger management be damned. I attempted to stomp on his foot, but he moved just in time. I stomped the grass instead. He locked his leg around mine to prevent a repeat, grabbing my wrist before my elbow made contact with his stomach.

The woman slapped her sunglasses back on. "And to think Delores told me this park had lots of friendly people."

"I take it you've never been here before?" Andy inquired.

She shook her head. "I usually jog in Wolf Park, but it's become too crowded. A friend of mine suggested I come here. Didn't realize I'd be accosted by a lunatic. Your sister kept going on and on about my husband wanting to kill me. I've been divorced for four years. My ex wouldn't have the guts to do something like that, and I don't have enough money to convince him otherwise."

Oh, shitburger on a bun, I'd warned the wrong woman. I went limp in Andy's grasp and couldn't ignore the heat burning my face. The morning sun had nothing to do with it. I was humiliated down to my toes in front of over a dozen curious onlookers.

"Don't you have something to say to the lady, sis?"

"I—I'm sorry. I mistook you for my ex-boyfriend's newest recruit. I heard she was married. I—I just wanted to scare her, that's all," I stammered.

"I'm sorry, too," Andy told her. "Please, enjoy your run."

He led me away from the now dispersing crowd back to the parking lot and his car. Opening the door, he shoved me into the passenger seat, and then climbed behind the wheel.

"What the hell did you think you were doing?"

Embarrassment, an emotion I should be getting used to, held me mute. No words could have slipped past the lump in my throat anyway. Tears filled my eyes.

"Never mind. I know what was going on. Jesus, Renee, I'm beginning to think you *are* a whack job. This was way out of line, even for you."

I swallowed. His words stung and demanded an answer. "I thought I was helping. The police weren't going to do anything about it, and I can't let an innocent woman be murdered by her greedy, philandering husband, so I decided to warn her."

"What would you have done, if I hadn't come along?"

"I—I don't know. Try to convince her, I guess."

"But you cornered the wrong woman."

"I didn't know that! She drove a black Lexus, had highlights in her hair, and was a jogger. I thought it was the intended victim."

"A black Lexus, huh? Kind of like that one over

there?"

I craned my neck and followed the direction of his thrusting chin. Three spaces down someone had parked a black Lexus.

"That wasn't there earlier. I swear it."

"I know. It arrived a few seconds before I got to you."

Oh, God, how could I have been so stupid—and impulsive. That had always been my problem. I frequently acted before I thought. Patience may be a virtue, but it was a virtue that ran under my radar.

Now, however, another thought crossed my mind. For the first time since getting in the car, I turned my gaze onto Andy noticing he wore jogging shorts, a t-shirt, and very sophisticated running shoes. A coincidence? At this particular time? He'd been here a lot earlier yesterday.

"Wait a minute, why are *you* here?"

He ran a hand over his face. "Satisfying my curiosity."

It took a moment for the nickel to drop. "You— you believed me?"

"I re-read your report. Even though you have obvious problems—"

"Put a sock in it, Jackson."

"Though you have a past—is that better—I decided this was stranger than usual. I didn't think checking it out would hurt."

"How would you have warned her?"

"I wouldn't until I knew for sure the woman was in danger. I'd run her license plate, get a name, and investigate to see if she does any of the activities— jogging, the gym, and yoga—you say you heard."

"I kind of screwed things up, didn't I?" I hung my head. The word contrite doesn't often surface in my vocabulary, but somehow, Andy made me feel it.

"No shit, Sherlock. I drove up just in time to see you crossing the parking lot. But since she isn't the person you had pegged for the graveyard, I can still do what I have to do. Stay put. I'll be back in a minute."

He grabbed a small notebook out of the console and exited the car, then strode to the recently parked Lexus where he copied the license plate number. Curiosity damned near burned a hole in my stomach.

When he returned, I had to ask, "Andy, will you let me know the woman's name?"

He shot me a look I could only describe as outraged. "Not in a million years. Now, if you don't mind, I plan on jogging. I suggest you go to work and forget this ever happened. If I see you stalking another poor woman, I swear on my mother's grave, I'll arrest you. Is that clear?"

"Your mother's alive," I pointed out.

"Renee!"

I saw his point and gave in. "Oh, all right, but if what I heard turns out to be true and you catch them, you will let me know, won't you?"

His face softened. "Yeah. I'll let you know. Now scoot."

I glanced at my watch. Shit. I was going to be super late. I bailed out of Andy's car and ran to mine. My boss would have a field day placing another black mark for tardiness next to my name.

I slid behind the wheel and fastened my seat belt, then looked up when someone rapped on my trunk lid. It was Andy's way of waving goodbye.

Better than Joel's. I raised a limp hand in reply as he trotted down the path and out of sight.

My gaze wandered to the other Lexus. Before stopping to think, I unfastened the seat belt and casting an eye around the parking lot, got out. I ran to the black car, memorized the license plate number, then dashed back to my Honda and scribbled it on an old bank deposit slip I found on the floor.

There! Tomorrow when I came I'd know one Lexus from the other. And of course, I intended on returning. I just had to figure out a way so Andy wouldn't see me.

Pleased with myself, I drove to work.

****

The next morning I pulled into the parking lot and this time found a slot as far away as possible from the entrance. A new plan had hatched while I tried to look busy at work the day before. If Joel had pretended to jog, then why couldn't I? I'd scrounged around in my closet and finally found a pair of gym shorts and some old tennis shoes. At least I'd blend in.

My boss, a charter member of Assholes-R-Us, had read me the riot act again yesterday including the stern warning that I was on probation. One more late arrival and I was history. He hadn't bought the flat tire bullshit any more than the traffic excuse of a few days ago. So, today, I called in sick. Half the office did that on Friday anyway.

I exited my car, grabbed a bottle of water, slapped on a pair of sunglasses, and pulled my hair into the regulation pony tail. There! Now, I looked like a jogger.

My next move involved warm-ups. I scanned the parking lot, but seeing no black Lexus, made my way to the guardrail and hopped over. Not the most coordinated person in the world, my foot caught the top edge of the metal and before I could stop the momentum, fell flat on my face.

"Lady, are you all right?" a man asked.

Another ran up to me. "Are you okay?" He placed his hand under my elbow and heaved.

Half a dozen people stared. So much for blending in. My entire body flamed with embarrassment.

"Thank you. I'm fine. Just misjudged," I mumbled when upright again.

I surreptitiously looked around to see how warm-ups were done. I used the woman next to me as a guide and braced one foot on the guardrail and the other out behind me. Then, I leaned forward.

Pain shot up the back of my leg from ankle to ass. This was no good. I cast my gaze onto a man seated on the ground, his legs spread wide. He grasped his foot and pulled without bending his knee. I couldn't do that in my thin and active high school days.

I stepped back, scanned the parking lot again, and jogged in place. Two minutes later I was sweating and gasping for air. My heart hammered away at ramming speed. Maybe this hadn't been such a terrific idea after all.

Then, a black Lexus pulled up. A tall woman sporting blonde hair with multicolored blonde highlights stepped out and made her way to the guardrail several yards away from me.

Acting casual, I stepped over the barrier and jogged to the back of the car. The license plate number I'd jotted down the day before matched. My doubts vanished. I had the right woman this time. Now, how did I approach her?

Yesterday was subtle for me, but obviously not subtle enough. I'd decided to play it by ear—strike up a conversation, and then jog behind her. I'd be like a bodyguard. I also had a plan. I'd follow her home, get an address, and then use tax records on the Internet to find out a name.

I strolled over and stopped next to her, assuming the slashing pain to my ass position.

"Hi. Jog here often?" I asked.

"Five days a week unless it's raining."

"This is my first time. A friend recommended it. Said it had lots of friendly people."

I found using the same words as the woman yesterday ironic, to say the least.

"Yeah, they are as a rule. Although I heard some fruitcake scared the pants off a woman yesterday."

I swallowed. So far, no one had recognized me as the fruitcake. "No kidding? Hope she outran him," I said with a laugh.

"Let's hope so."

She switched legs and so did I. Damn, the warm-up was killing me. *How do these people stand it? Must have a masochistic gene. I'm ready to call it a day.*

"Is there any particular path you'd suggest I use?"

"Depends on how far you're going. What's your distance?"

"Uh, I'm not sure. I've never done this before."

"In that case, I'd combine walking with jogging until you get your wind. Use that path over there," she said nodding her head to the right. "It's only a mile and a half."

Only a mile and a half? She had to be kidding. "How far do you jog?"

"Three miles. Used to do five, but had to cut back when I strained a calf muscle a couple of months ago." She did a few deep knee bends. "Well, I'm off. Have a good run."

"Yeah, thanks," I said as she adjusted her sunglasses and took off.

I now saw the flaw in my plan. Three miles? I couldn't *walk* that far without getting a cramp. Well, I'd just have to try. At least I'd made contact. Then a thought occurred to me.

You idiot, why didn't you introduce yourself? It's common courtesy to reply. That way you wouldn't have to follow her.

I mentally kicked myself for not doing the logical thing and prepared to walk very fast when a familiar arm draped over my shoulder. Oh, no! I didn't need my eyes to know Andy stood next to me.

"And you are here because..." he said in my ear.

I compressed my lips and breathed hard through my nose. The thrill I'd experienced yesterday at his touch returned, both pleasing and dismaying me. I reminded myself I was no longer ten years old. It didn't help.

"Come on, Renee, finish the sentence and win a prize."

"I jog," I snapped back. The amusement in his voice pissed me off almost as much as my reaction to his arm.

"I see. You wouldn't be planning to jog behind the tall blonde I saw you talking to, would you?"

"Certainly not! We were just chatting." I didn't know why I bothered. Andy had me figured.

"I have an idea. Why don't we jog together? I do five miles. How about you?"

I finally looked up wanting to slap that silly grin from his face. His lips twitched, barely containing the laughter.

"Not that far, I'm afraid."

The laughter erupted. "My guess is you wouldn't last five feet. Renee, go home or go jogging. Make up your mind—which is it?"

I set my jaw and raised my head defiantly, furious he found me amusing. "I'll jog!"

"Suit yourself. Let's go."

I didn't want to give him the satisfaction of being right again, so I followed knowing it could only end in disaster. Andy set a brisk pace. For a few brief moments I had an excellent view of a very nice ass along with those impressive legs.

Then reality set in. By the end of the first three hundred yards, I wheezed like an asthmatic. At five hundred, my legs and thighs burned as if my blood had turned to fire. I threw in the towel at eight hundred.

"All right! You win," I said, gasping, bent over, my hands on my knees, sweat dripping from my chin and nose.

Andy, several yards ahead of me, jogged back.

"Are you all right? Here, sit down." He led me to a stump at the side of the path. "Don't faint on me now, honey."

Honey. He called me honey. His kind tone and the endearment did me in. I plopped my fanny down and burst into tears. He crouched next to me.

"Aw, Renee, come on, no need for that."

"Look at me, I'm a mess. I'm thirty-two years old, can't run even a half a mile without oxygen, and—and I'm—I'm fat. No wonder Joel left me," I wailed, blubbering.

"So, you're a little out of shape—so what?"

"I'm—I'm ugly! Fat and ugly!" God, I hated whiny women, but couldn't control the self-pity.

Andy tucked a stray strand of hair plastered against my cheek behind my ear and smiled. I tried, but couldn't quite suppress a shiver of delight.

"No, you're not."

"I'm not?" I sniffed and used the end of my t-shirt as a tissue.

Okay, this bordered on pathetic. Now, I invited soothing compliments he didn't believe, but would make anyway because he was a nice guy.

"Of course not. You've got gorgeous hair. Did Joel ever tell you that? It's kind of brown with reddish-blonde streaks in it. I think they're natural. I'm a guy and don't know about stuff like that. And personally, I find brown eyes and upturned noses very attractive."

"But I *am* fat."

"Not really. More like…"

"If you say pleasingly plump or healthy, I swear I'll hit you."

He chuckled. "Okay, so you can stand to lose twenty pounds, it's..."

"What!" Nothing like a guy who never heard of the phrase "little white lie" to break up the pity party.

"Hey, do you want the truth or platitudes?"

Outraged, I glared at him. "Platitudes!"

He rose, laughing. "I have an idea. Why don't you come to my gym on Sunday? I'll show you how to work out with machines and weights. You might want to join. And if you're game, we can meet here two or three mornings a week and jog."

"Five miles?" I asked in a horrified tone.

"I'll do five miles. You run until you're tired. Eventually, you'll be up to my speed."

"Sunday?" God, was this a date?

"Yeah. I'll even buy you brunch afterward. When was the last time you saw or talked to Katie?"

I hadn't seen his sister in forever. "I don't know."

"I'll invite her to brunch, too. The two of you can catch up on old times. She'll tell you all about her latest boyfriend. Is it a date?"

My heart thumped and I swallowed the lump of anxiety forming in my throat. A date with Andy? Sounded like fun, even if it was to a gym.

"They have a Jacuzzi at this place?"

"Several."

"Okay, it's a deal."

"I'll pick you up at eight, or is that too early?"

"Eight works for me."

"Good." He pulled me to my feet. "Now, I suggest you head for home and let me finish my run."

"Thanks, Andy."

I turned and walked to a bend in the path where I paused and looked back. Andy had already disappeared down the trail. I had a date with Andy Jackson. *Who'd have thunk it?* I strolled on, willing Sunday to come quickly.

Chapter Four

Embarrassed, I stared at my reflection in the mirrors surrounding the exercise area in the Fitness Forever Spa, a five pound barbell in each hand. *Oh, God, when did I develop chipmunk cheeks, a blubber butt, and thunder thighs?*

But more importantly, *why* had this happened? I didn't need a whole series of mirrors to answer that question, but envisioned the bowl of salsa and the bag of chips I'd devoured last night. Thank God, I'd had the sense to climb into baggy gym shorts and an oversized t-shirt. A hard-bodied woman walked by wearing a skin tight leotard. My chin quivered.

"Don't you dare cry," Andy ordered. "And stop feeling sorry for yourself."

My gaze met his in the mirror. His biceps bulged and flexed as he easily curled fifty pounds per arm. I'd never seen muscles like his on any man. The pleasant distraction eased my self-pity. I lifted my chin. "I have no intention of crying."

"Good, now do what I do. One arm, and then the other ten times each."

Gritting my teeth, I hefted the shiny steel to my left shoulder and lowered, then repeated the action with the right. I cut my eyes to the perfect size-two-not-an-ounce-of-fat-on-her redhead who stopped for a sixty second flirt with Andy. I wanted to hit him with the damned weight when he smiled and watched in the mirror as she walked away.

I continued curling. "Ten! There, that's done!"

But Andy had more forms of torture in mind for me. Some included those stupid barbells, while others involved machines and apparatuses straight out of a medieval dungeon.

"This'll work your abs," he said steering me toward a machine that resembled a cage.

I straddled the narrow bench and laid back. "Now what?"

He threw his leg over the bench and stood over me while positioning my hands on the bar. I couldn't take my eyes off his hard muscled thighs three feet from my face, and refrained from reaching out to touch them. Much to my disappointment, he withdrew his body from over mine and moved back to my side.

"Brace your feet on the footrest and pull down on the bar above your head."

That sounded easy enough and imagined having six-pack abs by tomorrow morning. I gripped the bar and pulled. Nothing happened. I set my jaw and tried again. This time the bar moved two inches, and then snapped back like a bungee cord. The descending weights banged together with a loud clang. I thought I'd broken my back.

"You've got to be kidding."

"Renee, you've only got five pounds worth of weight. Are you that out of shape?"

"Of course, I am, dummy, or I'd be home doing something constructive like downing a pint of Ben and Jerry's. If it's all right with you, I'll just do sit ups." He scrunched five more times on the machine next to me. "How much weigh are you using?"

"Fifty pounds," he grunted.

That figured. I heaved a deep breath, held it, and pulled for all I was worth. The bar moved a whole six inches. Screw ten reps. I quit after three.

The Spanish Inquisition had nothing on Andrew Jackson—the treadmill, the stationary bike, and some thigh machine guaranteed to enable me to crush cinder blocks with a simple squeezing together of my legs, left me sweating and silently cursing. Some date. Boy, could I pick 'em or what?

Just when I was certain my legs had fallen off, he escorted me to the chin-up bar.

"Grip it with your fingers curled toward your body and pull."

The horizontal rod lurked a good three feet above my head. I raised my arms. "I can't reach it. I'm only five-four."

"Use this." He grabbed a footstool next to the apparatus.

Facing the inevitable, I stepped up and grasped the bar. He whisked the stool out from under me.

"Why not just put a rope around my neck?" I said with a gasp, hanging limp like a rag doll on a clothesline.

He laughed. "Come on, give me ten."

"You'll be lucky to get three."

I tried; I really did, and even surprised myself by doing four before losing all sense of coordination. In an effort to pull my body upward, I swung wildly, my foot nearly decapitating another torture aficionado as he walked past.

Andy grabbed my legs and sighed. "Okay, that's enough."

"Are we done?" I asked in a hopeful voice.

"No way. Now we walk the track, and then start the rotation over."

"What!"

"I usually do it five times, but because this is your first visit, we'll go for three."

"Three! Andy, are you trying to kill me?"

He chuckled. "All right, I'll take pity on you. We'll only do it twice."

"And I should be grateful for that how?"

The second rotation wasn't any better than the first. It was worse. While on the treadmill, I tripped over my own feet and almost fell. I finished never so happy to see the end of something in my life.

"Ready for the whirlpool?" he asked.

"I'm so tired, I'll probably drown."

In the locker room, I peeled my sweat drenched clothes from my body and wiggled into my swimsuit. The mirror was not kind. At least in the exercise room my clothing had hidden some of the defects, but the swimsuit revealed every bulge and roll. I shuddered. What would Andy think? Wrapping a large towel around my torso, I turned and followed the signs to the pool area.

I opened the door, poked my head through, and peered inside. Great—empty. I hurried to the nearest of three whirlpools, slipped free of the terry cloth armor, and slid in, turning the timer on for fifteen minutes. Jets of forced air gushed, churning the water into a froth of bubbles. I leaned my head against the rim of the tub, closed my eyes, and sighed in bliss. This almost made up for the past two hours—almost.

"Water warm enough for you?" Andy asked.

"H-m-m-m."

I opened my eyes and stared. I had never, and I mean never, seen a human body like his. He wore one of those tiny spandex swimsuits that left absolutely nothing to the imagination, including mine. Six feet, a hundred and eighty pounds of straight out, sculpted muscles from neck to ankle. Forget six-pack abs—he'd bought a whole damned case. I imagined bullets bounced off of him.

He dropped his towel onto a nearby bench and adjusted a pair of goggles over his eyes.

"I'm just going to do a few laps, and then I'll join you."

He dove into the pool while I shoved my tongue back into my mouth. My hormones had ratcheted up several notches. I gazed in fascination while he swam. Did he know I salivated like a rabid dog? I leaned my head back again and stared at the ceiling.

Get a grip, fool. You've been drooling over him all morning. What is your problem? This is Andy Jackson, for God's sakes. You've known him most of your life. And remember Joel—the asshole you just threw out.

I'd salivated then, too. Given my judgment regarding the male of the species, I figured Andy must have some major, although as of yet undiscovered, character flaw.

I heard Andy get out of the pool and pad toward me, but kept my gaze fastened on the intriguing sprinkler system overhead. The door to the room opened.

"Hi, Andy," a female voice called. "How's it going?"

"Hi, Marylou. I'm fine. Yourself?"

"The same. Just finished a hell of a workout. Been out of town for a week and didn't have time. Now, I'm ready for the whirlpool. Care to join me?"

I finally opened my eyes, and then wished I hadn't. The newcomer was as buff as they come—not an ounce of fat anywhere. I slid deeper into the bubbling water.

Isn't there one other fat, out of shape female in this stinking gym other than me?

"Thanks, but I'm with a friend. It's her first time here. Renee Ryan, meet Marylou Barton."

We both murmured greetings. How well did Andy know this woman?

"Why don't you join us?" Andy invited.

I inched further down in the tub. The water swirled just under my chin.

"Oh, no thanks, I don't want to intrude. Besides, I have to leave in a few minutes."

"It's no intrusion, is it, Renee?"

"Of course not." Just what I needed. A gorgeous blonde with perky boobs and a perfect body sitting next to my flab.

"Well, okay, if you don't mind." She slid into the water. Andy followed. "Are you a new member, Renee?"

"I don't know yet." To salvage my pride, I lied. "I used to work out, but got off track. I'm paying the price now."

Andy snorted. I tossed him a glance daring him to contradict me. He leaned against the rim of the tub, his arms outstretched. The water frothed against his hair covered chest. Damn, he was sexy as hell. I swallowed hard.

"I know what you mean," Marylou said with a smile. "That happened to me a few years ago after the birth of my son. I let routine slide. The next thing I knew my husband had a girlfriend, and I had thirty pounds of fat. I threw the bum out and got serious."

"Your hard work certainly paid off."

"Thanks." She turned to Andy. "So, what have you been up to?"

The timer dinged. Andy turned it back on before the concealing bubbles dissipated and showed too much of me. I liked to think he'd done it deliberately as a kindness. I remained seated. No way would I get out with her in the same room. I'd become a prune first.

I listened to their conversation about each other's work, but offered none. *She* was buff. I was flab. *She* was an executive for a software company. I was a receptionist.

I'm admiring his body and viewing this as a date, while Andy obviously sees it as helping a friend lose a few pounds. Dumb ass. I wasn't sure if those last two words were directed at him or me.

My self-esteem hit rock bottom. I'd never thought *that* was a problem, but with Joel's recent cutting remarks still fresh in my mind, I'd discovered I wanted Andy to think of me in the best possible terms.

Finally, Marylou rose. "Guess I'd better call it quits. Nice to have met you, Renee. Hope you join us."

She exited the room with a wave of her hand, and I sat up allowing the water level to hit me in mid-chest.

"How long have you been in the tub?" Andy asked.

"I don't know. Twenty, twenty-five minutes."

"That's too long." He reached over and turned off the timer. "Let's grab a shower, dress, and meet Katie for lunch. I let her choose the restaurant. Is The Venetian all right?"

The Venetian was an upscale trattoria on the beach, known for fabulous martinis and sensational food.

"That sounds wonderful. I could eat a cow."

He laughed, climbed out, and extended a hand. I grabbed it. He hauled me onto the tile floor where my foot slipped hurling me into Andy's arms. He held on tight, preventing a fall, my nose buried in his chest sending my hormones to a whole new level. And I was right—he had the body of Superman.

I leaned back and looked up. He had the strangest expression on his face—a cross between surprise and awareness. He took a deep breath and released me.

"Careful."

"Thanks," I muttered. The gush of heat had nothing to do with the hot water I'd just vacated. I swathed myself with the towel while he dried off.

"Now, that's what I call a great end to a good workout," he said.

Yeah, I kinda thought so, too, but decided to keep the conversation light. "You've discovered the perfect crime, haven't you? Death by exercise." I knew I shouldn't, but had to ask anyway, "Did you find out the name of the woman in the Lexus?"

"Yes, I got a name."

"Wanna share?"

"No. I thought we agreed you weren't going to involve yourself in this?"

"I never agreed to any such thing. I said I wouldn't accost any other women. That doesn't mean I can't chat while I walk or jog."

"Renee," he said in a warning tone.

"You might as well tell me. All I have to do is strike up a conversation at the park and introduce myself."

"Then that's what you'll have to do." He headed for the men's locker room.

I stuck out my tongue at his retreating back. So, he thought he had the upper hand, huh? He had absolutely no concept regarding the depths of my tenacity.

****

The Venetian was packed with Sunday brunch lovers, but we had no problem finding Katie at an outside table. She stood and waved.

"Renee!" She embraced me in a bear hug. "God, it's good to see you. It's been way too long."

"I know." I hugged her back, swallowing a lump in my throat. We'd been best friends throughout our school years and somehow had let time slip away.

"What about me?" Andy asked.

Katie laughed. "I just saw you last week at Mom's, but I'll hug you anyway."

We sat, and a waiter glided up to take our drink order.

"I suppose it's too early for a martini," Katie said with a smile. "What do you suggest?"

"*Una Pesche Bellini*—a Peach Bellini. Is *molto stupendo* for brunch."

"That's made with champagne, right?" I asked.

"*Si, signorina.*"

Katie and I indulged in the bellinis, while Andy ordered a beer.

Katie hadn't changed much over the years. Her dark brown hair was now cut in a hip, jagged style, but her slim figure told me she probably hadn't gained so much as an ounce since we were seniors. I immediately lapsed into our old ways of conversation.

"So, Katie Jack—getting any?"

"You betcha."

"Geez!" Andy said, rolling his eyes. "I don't need to hear this."

"Okay, let's keep it clean for the prude. He's picking up the tab." She shot a glance at her brother, and then winked.

I laughed. "I heard you got divorced from what's-his-name, Dan?"

"Yep, five years ago. Then I had the bad luck to marry Sammy. He played bass in a local band. Dumped his ass when I caught him screwing one of the waitresses in the bar where he performed. That was three years ago. I'm done with marriage. Now, I just have boyfriends. How about you? Didn't you get married and divorced also?"

"Yeah, Brad Simmons—a major prick."

I gave her the lowdown on my lack of judgment concerning men, too, including Joel. The waiter brought our drinks and we ordered food. Katie and Andy chose pasta dishes. I was about to do the same when I remembered the workout I'd just gone through and settled for a chicken Caesar salad instead.

"So, have you got a new guy on the line?" she asked.

I shot a glance at Andy who sipped his beer and gazed out at the ocean. Why hadn't I noticed his great profile before? The straight nose and strong chin was damned attractive. When I looked back, Katie's gaze danced between me and her brother. She grinned and raised her eyebrows with a speculative look. I hastened to answer.

"Are you kidding? I just tossed Joel's sorry ass out a week ago. How about you?"

"I'm seeing a terrific guy named Barry."

"Barry?" Andy said with raised eyebrows. "I thought his name was Taylor."

"Oh, good grief, that's been over for ages. I met Barry six months ago during a showing I'd arranged at one of the art galleries."

Katie was part owner of a firm specializing in setting up shows for artists in the area. She and her partner had started the company just out of college. It was a huge success.

"And what does Barry do?" Andy persisted.

Katie sighed and sent him you're-being-a-big-brother-again look. "He's a motivational speaker. Travels all over the country giving seminars. In the past month, he's been in New York, Los Angeles, and points in between. Right now, he's speaking in Miami, but has gigs in St. Louis, Chicago, and Philadelphia over the next few weeks."

"So, when do you get time to see him?" I asked.

"Whenever I can. That's the beauty of the relationship. Absence makes the heart grow fonder."

I sipped my drink and savored the sweet peach flavor with that of good, dry champagne. For the next several minutes Katie waxed poetic on Barry's virtues. The arrival of our food brought her monologue to an end. I realized Andy hadn't said a word.

"Are you bored?" I asked.

His right eyebrow rose. "With Barry? Yes."

"Aw, poor Andy," his sister said, patting his arm. "Okay, your turn. Are you still seeing that busty brunette?"

"Janet was a very nice lady who happened to have a great figure."

"Oops, past tense. She dump you?"

"No," he answered in a patient voice. "We drifted apart. She liked to hit the nightclub district until the wee hours, and I didn't."

"Well, whatever became of that blonde at the gym?"

"Marylou?" I asked.

"You've met her?"

"This morning. Andy took me for a workout and introduced us." So, he did have a history with the woman. Damn!

"Really? You going to join?" she asked with an eager expression.

"Already did. Must have been lightheaded from the whirlpool. Next thing I knew my checkbook was out and I now have a membership card to Fitness Forever."

"Great! I belong, too. Maybe we can work out together. When's the best time for you?"

We spent the rest of the meal and two more peach bellinis organizing time schedules and poking lighthearted fun at each other—and Andy. By the time we left, it was like old times.

"Katie hasn't changed a bit," I said to Andy on the drive home.

"I worry about her."

"Why?"

"The first divorce crushed her. Dan came home from work one night, packed, and said 'I don't love you. I never did.'"

"The bastard."

"It tore Katie up. She married Sammy on the rebound. That lasted eight months. Now, she drifts from one guy to another. You notice she didn't mention Barry's last name. She knows I'll check him out."

"There is such a thing as privacy, and Katie's a big girl. I'm sure she's developed a shell."

"That bothers me, too. I want to see her settled down, married with a couple of kids."

"This from Mr. Blonde-At-The-Gym and Busty-Brunette?"

He grinned. "I'm a guy. It's different for guys."

"How, you sexist pig?"

He laughed outright. "Okay, it's different for me." He sobered. "I have a dangerous job, and being a cop's wife is hard. I've never met a woman who understands why I sometimes get so damned angry and depressed at what goes on out there."

"I guess we all have our moods. Let's make a deal—you tell me the Lexus driver's name, and I'll pump Katie for Barry's last name."

"No way. When was the last time Katie ever kept a secret? She'll tell me sooner or later. Besides, you wouldn't tell me anything my sister confided to you."

Andy was right, but it had been worth a try.

Back at my place, we got out and walked to the door. He made a fist and brushed it lightly across my chin. The action ignited that warm glow again in my stomach. *Why am I suddenly so aware of his every move and touch?*

He smiled that funny lop-sided smile. "You did good today, kid. I know those machines aren't the easiest to use when you're out of shape. I'm glad you joined the club. Katie and I will help. It's not as painful with a friend around to cheer you on."

I couldn't tear my eyes away from his mouth. "Believe it or not, I'm looking forward to it."

"Give your body a couple of days to rebound." He paused and gazed at me with a serious expression. "I suppose you're going to the park tomorrow morning."

"Did you really think I wouldn't?" I chided.

"No, I guess I didn't. I have to be in the station

at seven, so I can't be your back up. Just promise me you won't do something stupid or impulsive."

"You mean like warning her?"

"That's right." His voice took on a patient tone.

"Are you doing anything about the situation?"

"I'm checking out her and her husband. You know, there's no guarantee this woman is the right one either. Lots of people drive a black Lexus."

"I know, and lots of women have highlights in their hair. But can't you understand? I have to make sure."

He rolled his eyes. "God, you're obsessive."

I sighed and shrugged. "That's only one of my virtues."

"I'd have said shortcomings. I've got early duty all this week. Will I see you at the gym on say, Wednesday evening?"

"Yeah, I guess so."

"Good." He leaned down, kissed my cheek— again with that kind of surprised look on his face, then turned and walked back to his car. "Be careful."

My heart rate had sped up considerably as his lips contacted my skin. "I will. I'll be very subtle— oh, thanks for lunch and taking me to the torture chamber, ah, the gym. I had a great time."

He laughed and drove away.

I wandered out onto my patio, plopping my weary body into one of the lounge chairs. I'd been right. Andy didn't view this as a date or he would have given more than a peck on the cheek. Still, I couldn't erase the image of his body from my mind, and hoped I wasn't setting myself up for another misjudgment. In spite of my inner turmoil and the physical pain I knew I'd feel later, I'd had a terrific day.

Erotic thoughts concerning Andy flitted through my mind. His body was to die for, and oh my God, I wanted to feel it against mine, naked. A throb from deep within set my hands to shaking.

What the hell is the matter with me? This is Andy Jackson, for crying out loud. My best friend's brother! I've known him since grade school.

Maybe my fantasies had to do with the gym, especially the hot tub and him in that almost there swimming suit. Idly, I wondered what shoe size he wore. *Is it true? Is a guy's...uh, equipment somehow related to foot size?*

Then, I remembered reading somewhere that a penis is three times the size of its owner's thumb. I tried to visualize Andy's hands, especially his thumb, but failed. I'd check it out the next time I saw him, although that skimpy swim suit gave me a pretty good idea of, well, things.

Suddenly, it was much too warm for March in Florida. I flapped the front of my t-shirt to cool off. I needed to get my mind off of Andy and onto the blonde whose husband wanted her dead.

****

Raindrops splattering on my face awakened me. The peach bellinis along with the workout had taken a toll. The deepening darkness told me I must have been asleep for a long time. Struggling to sit up, I winced as pain stabbed my left calf. *No pain, no gain.* The gain had better begin soon.

I hurried inside, glancing at the clock on the stove. Seven-thirty? I'd been asleep for almost five hours? The grumbling from my stomach confirmed it.

Too tired to bother with cooking real food, I was tempted to order in Chinese, but instead opted for a low-fat, low-cal, low-taste frozen dinner I'd unearthed from the back of the freezer, popping it into the microwave. Maybe massive amounts of iced tea would ward off terminal hunger.

I rescued the Sunday paper from where I'd tossed it in the foyer when Andy had picked me up and carried it back into the kitchen. If I read between bites, the food would last longer. I made a salad and sat at the table.

The Palm Lake Courier wasn't much of a newspaper. But then, it had to compete with the Ft. Lauderdale, Palm Beach, and Miami papers, so it tended to report local news. I rarely read much more than the headlines and comics anyway. If I wanted real news, I watched cable or got it online.

I finished the first section when the microwave timer dinged. Pulling the plastic wrapper off, I sniffed the lasagna. At least it smelled Italian. Would extra cheese be a no-no? I didn't care, and shook more Parmesan from a can, transferred the three inch square delicacy to a plate, then carried it to the table like crown jewels to the king.

While I ate, I leafed through the paper until coming to the society section. I didn't really care about the adventures of the ridiculously rich, but a grainy picture stopped me cold.

I narrowed my eyes and leaned closer. I wasn't sure, but damned if that didn't look like my lady. She stood in a group of people, smiling for the camera. I quickly read the caption.

Elizabeth Gray-Gorman and her husband, Todd Gorman at the fundraiser for The Home for Friendless Animals held last week in Palm Lake. Also pictured with the Gorman's are Mr. and Mrs. Robert Shay, and Alyssa Hamilton.

Elizabeth Gray-Gorman just sounded like a rich person's name. I peered at the photo again. Since it was Sunday, the *Courier* had used colored ink, and the print quality sucked.

She wore a floor length blue dress and I assumed the jewelry around her neck was the real McCoy. My gaze immediately swung to the man standing next to her. He had half turned from his wife and looked into the eyes of the woman next to him. Since the other two people were older, I figured the recipient of the rapt attention was Alyssa Hamilton. Even though I only had a profile, and a slightly out of focus one at that, he looked like a weasel.

I crammed the last bite of lasagna into my mouth and stared hard at Elizabeth's picture again. Was it the same woman?

There was only one way to find out. Tomorrow, I'd ask.

Chapter Five

The alarm buzzed in my ear jerking me from a solid slumber. I reached over and banged my fist on the noisy contraption silencing it. How could the damned thing be going off? I'd just gone to bed.

I opened one eye and tried to focus on the clock. Seven on the nose. Shit, I'd slept the night through. I hadn't done that in years. I snuggled deeper under the covers not wanting to get up. Uninterrupted sleep or not, the sun peeking through the slats of the blinds didn't inspire me to greater things. A garbage truck rumbling down the street noisily dumping overfilled trash cans convinced me the party had ended.

With a sigh, I tossed back the covers, sat up, and then tried to stand. My muscles let me know they weren't happy. I hurt everywhere. The remnants of sleep fled.

Maybe I should skip the park today. The picture in the paper flashed across my mind. *No, I have to see if she's the same person.*

I'd appointed myself as bodyguard, and by God, I'd keep my promise. Hobbling to the closet, I donned my shorts, t-shirt, and sneakers, then made a small pot of coffee. I can't operate without caffeine.

While waiting for it to brew, I studied the picture in the paper again. The image hadn't improved overnight. Armed with my trusty travel mug, I hit the road, pulling into the parking lot at seven-fifty.

The woman I hoped was Elizabeth had already arrived. I scrambled as fast as my protesting muscles would allow and slid into a spot next to her at the guardrail. I assumed the position, leaned forward, and bit my tongue to keep from screaming.

"Hi, again," I began. Not brilliant, but an opening.

She glanced over. "Oh, hello."

I couldn't decide if her tone was disinterested or a polite brush-off. It didn't matter. Immune to stuff like that, I plowed on.

"I want to thank you for showing me the right path to take last week."

"No problem. Did you have a good run?"

A little thawing—that was good. She ceased stretching and raising her arms above her head, bent from side to side. I followed her example trying not to cry.

"I took your advice. I walked more than I ran."

"Good for you."

She spread her legs and grasped her ankles. I couldn't do that sitting, let alone standing. I continued bending.

"I also joined a gym."

"Wise move. Helps to exercise when it rains. Which gym did you join?"

At last, a direct question. "Fitness Forever over on Sunshine Parkway."

"I've heard of them. They're supposed to be good."

"Do you belong to a gym, too?"

"I belong to the Palm Lake Country Club. I use the one there."

The Palm Lake Country Club occupied a large chunk of very expensive property on the west side of town not far from the Everglades. Its membership was deliberately kept small to ensure only the richest could join. Being voted in to the most exclusive club in South Florida signaled you'd made the financial grade. The only way I'd ever see the inside of the place was if I cleaned the johns or served the food.

She quit stretching and jogged in place, signifying she was about to bolt. I needed to act now.

"By the way, my name's Renee—Renee Ryan." I held out my hand.

I thought it was a smooth move. She stopped jogging, smiled, and had no choice but to shake it or appear rude.

"Liz Gorman."

Bingo! A match. *Who needs Andy Jackson?*

I pictured his face when he learned I had the name. Maybe I should become a detective.

"Well, I'm off. Have a good one."

Liz trotted down the path. I watched until she rounded a bend and disappeared from sight. A good bodyguard would jog along, but until I could keep up, I'd have to figure out other ways to protect her. Besides, if I remembered right, the killer didn't want to strike in the park.

"So, how do you like Fitness Forever?"

I turned to look at a man next to me. "Uh, it's fine."

"I heard they have a terrific personal training regimen," a woman next to him added.

"I'm just beginning. I can't even jog yet," I replied.

The man chuckled. "I just started a few months ago. Woke up one morning, got on the scale, and decided two-hundred twenty was too much for a five feet, ten inch man. Also went on a diet. I've lost fifteen pounds so far, but need to tone up. I may check out your gym."

"The machines rank right up there with the Rack and the Iron Maiden."

The woman laughed. "I take it you're still on the walk-run routine."

"Yeah, I guess so." I had no idea.

"So am I. I broke my leg last fall. I finally got out of the walking cast two weeks ago. The doctor just released me to run again, but I have to start from scratch. Care to join me?"

I glanced at my watch. By walking a short distance, I could still make it to work on time.

"Well, the workout yesterday left me pretty sore, but I can go for a short while."

"Good." She looked at the man. "How about you? Care to join us?"

"Sure. Name's Jeff McCarthy."

"Renee Ryan."

"Corinne Vassar. Are we ready to go?"

We stepped off at a brisk pace. I hadn't expected to pick up jogging buddies. The prospect didn't displease me and might even force me to jog on regular basis.

I covertly gave each of them a sidelong look. Once Jeff dropped a few more pounds, he'd have to fight the women off. His dark hair and blue eyes would be a chick magnet. I judged his age as between twenty-five and thirty.

Corinne's curly, chin length, light brown hair was held back by a headband. I put her age at around forty with a trim figure.

Probably one of those women who looks slender as a thread, but can bench press a boat.

Maybe I could incorporate Jeff and Corinne into my plan—introduce them to Liz. Get them to run with her for a while until I came up to speed. Jeff looked like he could hang for at least a little while, and I suspected Corinne wouldn't take long to regain her old form.

At the end of half a mile, my legs didn't protest as much as earlier, and I was tempted to go further, but if I wanted to keep my job I had to leave now.

I heaved a deep sigh. "Guys, my legs are killing me. I guess I have to ease into this gradually."

"Sure, no problem," Jeff said with a smile.

"I'm about to hit running mode anyway," Corinne told me. "See you tomorrow?"

"Yeah, tomorrow."

I returned to the parking lot tempted to call Andy and crow about my success at discovering the intended victim's name. *Come on, admit it, you just want to hear his voice again.* No matter how much that might be true, he wouldn't be happy at my continuing actions. Instead, I dashed home, showered, and then headed for work.

****

I arrived ten minutes late. Luckily, my boss, Richard James, was nowhere in sight and didn't see me race through the front doors. I fired up my computer and clocked in, then answered the three ringing phone lines.

"Carson Electronics," I said, only slightly out of breath.

After directing the calls to the extensions, I sat back. The object of my boss's affection walked past with several folders. She was supposed to be a file clerk and why she strutted through the reception area, I didn't know.

"Oh, you're finally here," she said, brushing a lock of long red hair over her shoulder.

"Of course I'm here. Where else would I be?"

"You weren't here a few minutes ago."

So, the bitch was checking up on me. "I dropped my pencil under the desk and leaned over to pick it up. You didn't see me. Aren't you supposed to be in the file room?"

She shot me a nasty look and stalked out. The bimbo didn't need to tell me where she'd been. My boss's office was just down the hall where she had no doubt reported my absence. Cattily, I wondered what else they'd been doing.

Just another day in paradise.

I spent the next twenty minutes taking calls until my boss finally emerged.

"Ms. Ryan, I see by your sign in that you were ten minutes late again."

"No I wasn't, Mr. James. I got here on time, but the phones were so busy I didn't clock in until later." I gave him my most innocent voice. Since he didn't see me arrive, he had no proof I lied.

"From now on, clock in first, and then answer the phones." He scurried back down the corridor like a rat.

Twerp. Bimbo boinking twerp. The customer comes first, or did you forget that?

I pushed him out of my mind and concentrated on Liz. Jogging was only part of her routine. I had no idea how she spent the rest of the day. I needed to think more on this.

At the same time, a sense of urgency prodded me in the backside. The killer hadn't wanted to be rushed. I hoped that bought me a few weeks. Certainly, the husband didn't have the balls to dispatch Liz himself. Regardless of believing nothing would happen on the jogging trail, I still worried. Building rapport with an intended murder victim during jogging warm-ups could take longer than the time available.

Then, a sudden thought sent chills skittering down my spine. What if the killer had already begun surveillance? What if the killer had been in the park this morning? Had Andy thought of that? Liz might well be in danger at this very moment. The time frame shortened.

****

I rolled out of bed the next morning. My muscles still protested movement, but had to admit I had more energy, and discovered that while my appetite had increased, I didn't mind eating healthier food. If necessary, I could live on salad and fish or chicken.

On that positive note, I headed for the park.

Once again, Liz had arrived early. However, I had a plan. I might not be able to keep up with her, but that didn't mean I couldn't chat and pump her for more information.

"Hi, Liz. Gorgeous morning." I promptly warmed up, gritting my teeth in the process.

"Hi, Renee, right?" At least she remembered my name—a positive sign.

"That's right. Don't you just love this weather?" The sun shone brightly and a light breeze further cooled the morning air. "I'll bet jogging in the summer is tough."

"It's not so bad as long as you keep hydrated and do it early in the morning or in the evening near sundown."

"Morning, Renee," Jeff called out, placing his foot on the guardrail next to mine.

I might as well get the ball rolling. "Hi, Jeff. Have you met Liz?"

"Can't say that I have."

I introduced the two just as Corinne walked up, so I included her in the group. Liz didn't look like she cared one way or another, but I'd achieved my mission. Two other people could identify Elizabeth Gray-Gorman and maybe eventually run with her. Now for the next phase of my campaign.

I bent from side to side. "Wow, am I ever tense."

"How come?" Jeff asked.

"My boyfriend and I broke up. We had this huge fight and he called me a fat pig."

"Hope you punched his lights out," Corinne said, bending at the waist and grasping her ankles.

"I tried, but missed. That's why I decided to lose weight."

"Never mold your body into what someone else thinks it should be," Liz said.

"That's right, do it for yourself," Jeff added.

"At any rate, I need to indulge in some inner peace, and I was thinking about yoga. Any of you ever try it?" I asked.

"It's wonderful," Liz told me. For the first time I heard enthusiasm in her voice. "I've been involved in yoga since college. It really helps."

"Where do you go?"

"Barnard's School of Dance and Exercise. It's over on Zephyr Springs Drive. They teach ballet and tap, and have classes in jazzercise and yoga."

"Is it expensive?" Given the country club thing, I was almost afraid to ask.

"No, I don't think so. A friend of mine runs it."

A friend, huh? She probably got a discount, which meant I'd likely go broke. Maybe I could get a reduced rate if I mentioned Liz and I were good friends. A dollar saved here and there couldn't hurt.

"Yoga," Corinne murmured. "I never thought of that. I've been a wreck since my divorce last year. Maybe I should give it a try. We could go together, Renee. How about you, Jeff?"

"No, thanks. I can't see curling myself into a pretzel with a bunch of women."

Liz actually laughed. "Men do yoga, too. I have three in my class."

"When do you go?" I asked.

"Mondays, Wednesdays, and Fridays. I haven't been in a couple of weeks." She ceased stretching, did a few deep knee bends, and then jogged in place. "Well, I'm off. Nice to meet you."

"I'm about ready, too," Corinne said. "Jeff? Renee?"

I glanced at my watch. Damn. If I stayed any longer than twenty minutes, I'd be late for work, but had to keep up the pretense of exercising. Somehow, I had to fulfill my duties as jogging bodyguard and retain my job.

Work on it later.

"Hi! Do you guys mind if I join you?"

I turned, staring at a tall, rangy blonde with a toothy grin and a perky attitude. Her over-permed hair stuck out from her head like a brassy halo.

"No, but I think I should warn you, we're on the walk-run routine."

"Far out. So am I. I think jogging is way cool, don't you? I mean, I can get exercise and be in the fresh air all at the same time."

"Uh, yeah, I guess so," Corinne said.

"Nothing like it," Jeff answered with a smile.

"Is that the trail you take?" the newcomer asked, indicating the long way around the park.

"No, we do the short run," Corinne said.

"Oh, well, I saw you, like, talking to that other lady and just thought, like, maybe you all jogged together. She looked familiar. Who is she? Do you know?"

"Her name is Liz Gorman," Jeff said.

"Liz Gorman...Liz Gorman. That name's familiar, too."

"Speaking of names, mine is Jeff McCarthy. This is Corinne Vassar and Renee Ryan."

"Hi, I'm Freddy Lane."

"Freddy?" I asked.

"Short for Frederica. I used to hate my name, but now I kind of like it. It's different, you know, and people, like, remember it. So, what do you all do?"

"Uh, I'm in advertising," Jeff said.

"Oh, like, wow! I mean, do you do like TV commercials and stuff like that?"

"No, I'm in print media."

"I'm a receptionist," I said.

She turned her wide smile to me. "Cool. I'll bet its fun answering phones all day and meeting new people."

Little did she know. "It has its moments. What do you do?"

"Oh, I work in a bookstore at the mall." She turned her gaze to Corinne. "How do you pay the rent?"

"I'm divorced and do as little as possible," she said in a sharp tone. "Are we ready? I have a butt load of things to do today."

I glanced at my watch. Damn, time was ticking away.

"I'm all set," Freddy said with a laugh.

To the best of my knowledge, she hadn't warmed up one iota. Jeff set the pace with our new partner, while Corinne and I held back a few yards behind.

"Well, I guess we, like, have another, like, new friend to, like, jog with. It'll be so cool," Corinne said with raised eyebrows and a sardonic expression.

I stifled a laugh. Okay, Freddy didn't have much in the line of dazzling conversational skills, but the more people to watch over Liz, the better.

"Let's go, but don't worry if I fall behind. I'm still kind of sore from the other day. Just go on without me."

"Uh, Renee, please don't think I'm being critical, but your shoes are all wrong," Corinne said.

I looked at my feet and the simple canvas, lace-up sneakers on them. "Wrong how?"

"You need something more supportive along the sides and with more cushioning for either walking or jogging. You might want to consider a pair of cross-trainers. They're good for both."

"I never thought of that. Told you I was new at this," I said with a laugh.

Mental note—if I want to look like a jogger, I need to dress the part.

We walked while I wondered how big of a dent yoga classes would make in my checkbook. I shrugged. No matter. I had to make Liz my friend. What I really wanted, however, was a good look at her husband. The newspaper photo hadn't been clear. As soon as I could, I'd check the Internet. Being socialites, their photos had to be all over the place.

Corinne, Jeff, and Freddy broke into a trot. I tried to follow, lagging behind a small distance. I breathed heavily when they slowed to a walk again. Another peek at my watch confirmed I'd have to hustle to make it to work on time.

"Guys, I have to call it a day. At least, I ran this time," I said with a laugh. "I'll see you tomorrow."

They waved, continuing down the path. I turned and hurried to my car suddenly realizing I'd made three new friends. Maybe I would soon add Liz to the list.

****

I burst through the doors of Carson Electronics at nine-oh-seven and skidded to a halt. My boss stood next to the reception desk, his arms folded across his chest and bearing a satisfied expression. The bimbo sat in my chair. Not a good sign.

"Well, Ms. Ryan, late again I see. I warned you last week about your tardiness."

"Gee, Mr. James, I can't help it if the traffic sucks. It's tourist season and the roads are crowded."

"You've lived here all your life. You know the drill. Leave ten minutes early or take a different route to the office during the winter. Come with me."

I was toast. I knew it, but followed him down the hall to his office all the same. The redhead shot me a smug smirk as I passed. I'd kick her ass later.

"Sit down, Ms. Ryan." I sat in the straight backed chair in front of his desk. "I've been more than fair about this. The constant late arrivals, and your flip, insulting attitude toward Miss Peabody can no longer be tolerated."

Miss Peabody—a/k/a The Bimbo. Of course I insulted her at every opportunity. A lot of people did. Everyone knew why she was employed. But because she wanted *my* job and boffed *my* boss, he picked on me. On this I was not paranoid.

"I'm sure Miss Peabody misinterpreted what I've said in the past. I didn't insult her any more than anybody else." Why did I fight to hang on to a job I hated?

James glared. "I can assure you Miss Peabody is held in high esteem by her co-workers."

I struggled to hold onto my temper, and then quit fighting. He was going to fire me anyway, so I might as well make the best of it.

"Are you kidding? She's a joke. The stupid bitch can't file worth a damn. Last month, one of the secretaries spent an hour looking for the Johnson Fire Alarm file. She finally located it under 'F' for fire."

He scowled and curled his lip. "I have no intention of discussing Miss Peabody with you. She is a valued member of the company."

"Yeah, right. She does her best work on her back or on her knees, but then that's what *you* value most."

He leaped to his feet, his face a deep red. "Out! Now! You're fired! Go to Human Resources and fill out the termination papers. Then clean out your desk."

"My pleasure, asshole."

I stood, kicked the chair over, and stalked from his office. Passing the reception desk, I refused to look at my replacement. I had an absurd urge to cry. I didn't give a damn about the job, but hated getting canned.

Human Resources was located in the building next door, a minute away. The papers were ready and waiting when I arrived, telling me my first hunch was right. James had probably called them at nine-oh-one if not the night before. I wasted little time signing on the dotted line and when finished, sailed back to my old desk.

The bimbo stood and shoved a box my way with her foot.

"Here. Maintenance brought this up for you."

"Blow it out your ass."

She laughed and tossed her head, setting the red hair to swinging. "It's about time the company had something attractive sitting behind this desk."

I yanked open a lower drawer scooping stuff out and into the box. Some of it was mine, some wasn't. I took all the staplers. She'd need those.

"And have a nice day, Renee." Her smile widened.

"I've quit better jobs than this, and you won't last long. Have you checked out possible employment at the Chicken Ranch in Nevada? I hear they're looking for hookers."

That wiped the smile off her face. Before she could reply, the phone rang. Glaring at me, she answered in a low, sexy voice.

"Carson Electronics. This is Angie. How may I help you... Uh, Mr. Comstock? Just a minute, please."

She put the caller on hold, checked the alphabetized list of extensions, and then pushed the wrong button to transfer, thus disconnecting the call. A moment later, the phone rang again.

"Carson Electronics. This is... Oh, I'm so sorry, sir. Just a minute."

This time she transferred the call correctly, but to the wrong extension. The customer was immediately re-routed back. I slowed my movements, not wanting to miss a second of this. Two of the eight lines rang simultaneously.

"Carson Electronics. Can you hold please? Hello, Carson Electronics... Mr. Welsh? One moment." Another line lit up. "Carson Electronics... Oh, I'm sorry, sir. You didn't speak with Mr. Comstock? I'll try again."

I set the box on the edge of the desk, enjoying the show. Incompetence always rises to the top or something like that. I think it was called the Peter Principle, and Angela Peabody was rising fast.

I laughed. On Tuesdays, the out of town salesmen checked in, usually around nine-thirty. The lines sometimes flashed for close to half an hour. According to my watch, it was nine-thirty-five.

By now, all eight lines glittered like the Vegas strip. Angie frantically punched buttons, most of which were wrong. Finally, James appeared.

"Angie, why am I talking to Howard, and why is Maintenance getting calls meant for Sales?"

"I'm sorry, Richard, but I'm not familiar with the extensions yet. And I'm not getting much help." She shot me a filthy look.

"Ms. Ryan, stay here until Miss Peabody understands how the system works."

"You should have thought about that before you put Miss Inflatable Tits on the job."

"Carson Electronics... Just a moment... Oh, shit!" She'd disconnected another caller.

A woman from Technical Services walked into the reception area. She looked confused, gazing between me and my replacement.

"Uh, excuse me, but I've had three calls in the past two minutes from our out of town sales personnel."

"Hang on! I'm doing the best I can, goddamn it." Another line rang. "Hello, Carson Electronics... Keep your shirt on. I'll reconnect."

"Help her!" my ex-boss ordered.

I hefted the box. "Cram it up your wahzoo. I don't work here anymore. Have a nice day."

I'd have loved to stick around and see how she screwed up the company president's weekly overseas call, but decided to leave before someone called security and escorted me off the property.

I kicked open the front doors, laughing all the way to my car where I tossed the box into the trunk. I'd go home, apply for unemployment benefits online, and take a few weeks off before looking for another job.

Then, I realized I already had another job, so to speak. The good part of getting fired was that now I could devote all my time and effort into protecting Liz.

Once again I was tempted to call Andy, and once again held off. This absurd desire to hear his voice was so...so high school. I needed to focus on my mission. Besides, Andy wouldn't be pleased to hear I now had more time to devote to my self-proclaimed bodyguard duties.

Still, I couldn't get him out of my mind. *I wonder if he'd like a home cooked dinner.* It was something to think about.

Chapter Six

I gazed around the spacious lobby of Barnard's School of Dance and Exercise. A scent redolent of India or the Far East permeated the air. Sandalwood? Eucalyptus? Something more exotic? I wasn't sure. Posters of ballet, tap, and ballroom dancers adorned the walls along with those of impossibly supple women in leotards bending into unlikely positions. Protecting Liz may now have been my number one priority, but I saw no way in hell I'd ever get my ankles around my neck.

"That's a very advanced position," a woman crooned from behind me.

"No shit." I turned, surprised to see a woman in her late forties smiling at me.

"My name is Yvonne Kennedy. How may I help you?"

"Hi, Yvonne, I'm Renee Ryan, a friend of Liz Gray-Gorman's. When I told her I was thinking about taking some yoga classes, she suggested you."

"Oh, please call me Vonnie," the woman said with a smile. "Liz has been coming here for years. What do you know about yoga?"

"Very little, other than there's no way I'll ever be able to assume *that* position," I replied, indicating the poster on the wall.

She walked over to a seating area, picked through some brochures on the coffee table, and handed them to me.

"These should help. Yoga originated in India. The word means 'union,' we like to think between the mind, body, and spirit. I won't bore you with the

67

whole philosophy. I assume you are interested in the asanas."

"Uh, I guess so."

"The poses," she said with a laugh. "I'm sure what you seek is more strength and flexibility." I nodded as if agreeing. What I wanted was to keep tabs on Liz. "Come with me, and I'll show you our studios."

She led me down a hallway and opened a door. Inside, about twenty people, mostly women, stood on one leg, arms outstretched, inhaling and exhaling slowly.

"This is a beginning class for those with more mellow personalities," Vonnie explained.

"Mellow personalities?"

"Our workouts are based on what you expect from the class. For instance, these people want to take it slow and easy."

I'd never passed up slow and easy in my life, but had to ask anyway, "What does Liz do?"

"Liz is in one of our highly advanced classes. She's what we call a gym rat with a bit of the free spirit thrown in. She likes to work up a sweat."

Well, nuts. I'd assumed everyone just got together, bending and twisting into interesting shapes. It never occurred to me that Liz and I might not be in the same room or on the same program. I'd had no idea yoga came in different sized packages.

Vonnie closed the door and showed me another room. This must have been an advanced class. The ten women inside lay on mats with their legs bent over their heads. I backed out into the hallway. The human body—at least my human body—was simply not prepared do to that.

"How does this work? I mean, if I come in, say two times a week, do I keep doing the same thing? How do I advance to more difficult positions?" What I meant was how can I get in Liz's class.

"Over time. When you are bored with a routine, you move on to a higher level. Some people are very happy with their practice and never change. Let me ask—do you consider yourself competitive?"

"I don't know about competitive, but I do have an anger problem. It's under control most of the time, but occasionally..." I let the sentence hang.

Vonnie nodded as if in understanding. "Yoga is very liberating. Once you can ignore the ego, an inner peace replaces it. Some yoga studios dwell on the spiritual, but we focus on the physical—the positions and breathing."

The tour continued and as she gave me the sales pitch, I had to admit just being in the place made me relax. The wall colors varied from cool blues and greens to the more neutral beiges and grays.

Even relaxed, I still had the problem of protecting Liz. She was advanced, and I was a beginner. It would be like jogging all over again. Maybe I could still do my job if I managed to come on the same night or day. I doubted the killer had a death by yoga plan.

"Tell me, when does Liz come? It would be nice if we could carpool."

Vonnie shot me a strange look. It occurred to me that the Elizabeth Gray-Gormans of this world didn't carpool. Or perhaps my tour guide thought that I should know, since I proclaimed friendship with Liz.

Vonnie answered anyway. "It varies. Her classes are held twice a day Monday through Friday—once in the morning and once at night. It depends on when she has the time. I haven't seen her in a couple of weeks. However, beginner classes may not coincide with the advanced. I'll check. Shall we go to my office?"

We re-entered the lobby, and I stopped to stare at two women standing off to the side talking and leafing through brochures.

"Corinne, what are you doing here?" Why do people always say that when the answer is obvious?

"Renee! Checking out yoga classes. I got to thinking about our conversation this morning and realized it sounded like a great idea. What are you doing here? I thought you'd be at work."

"It's a long story. Are you going to take classes?"

"I think so. How about you?"

I turned to Vonnie. "Uh, I'm on a budget. How much will this set me back?"

She named a price that only made me cringe a little, but if it helped save Liz, it was worth it.

"That sounds reasonable. When does the beginning Mellow class meet?"

"Monday through Friday at ten o'clock and again at six in the evening."

"Are you a Mellow, too?" Corinne asked. "Maybe we can do this together."

"Sure, why not?"

"Wonderful," Vonnie said, beaming. "If you'll just follow me, we can do the paperwork now."

Corinne followed her sales lady, while Vonnie led me into an office.

"Could you check when the advanced classes meet for me? It would be nice if Liz could join Corinne and me."

She consulted a printed schedule on her desk. "The class Mrs. Gray-Gorman takes meets at noon and six. I guess that means you'll be attending the evening session."

"I guess."

She handed me three pages of instructions. I answered the questions and signed my name, then reached for my checkbook.

"Oh, no need to pay now. Just pay your instructor before each class." She checked over my replies. "The only thing you'll need is a mat. Wear loose fitting clothing or leotards to get the full range of movement. I see you occasionally take Xanax. See your doctor in six months. You may no longer require it. This will change your life. It did mine." She pressed a forefinger to the middle of her chest. "How old do you think I am?"

I hate these games. If I guess way under it sounds like pandering. If my estimate is over, then it pisses people off.

"I'm not very good at this, but I'd guess maybe forty-five?" I held my breath half expecting her to come across the desk to throttle me. Instead, she laughed.

"I turned sixty last month."

"Holy shit! You look fabulous."

"So will you. I started yoga ten years ago. The more inner peace I achieved, the more wrinkles disappeared." She rose and held out her hand. "Goodbye, Renee. I'll see you soon."

I made my way to the ladies room and stared at my image in the mirror. I didn't see much in the line of wrinkles, just a few around the eyes and mouth. Then placing my fingers on my cheekbones, I pulled upward. The skin smoothed and most of the wrinkles disappeared.

Maybe all I need is a good plastic surgeon.

The door opened. Corinne walked in and laughed. "Thinking about plastic surgery?"

"How did you know?"

"I stand naked in front of a full length mirror every morning checking to see what's sagging. Surgery is faster, but yoga is cheaper. Are you free for lunch?"

"As a matter of fact, I am. Where did you want to go?"

"There's a nice little Mexican restaurant on the beach called El Toro. Know it?"

"I've passed it a couple of times."

She glanced at her watch. "It's only eleven. Can we meet in an hour? I have a couple of errands to run first."

"Noon works for me."

We reentered the lobby when a voice called out.

"Wow, fancy meeting you here."

I whirled, facing Freddy standing just inside the front doors.

"Good grief, what are you doing here?" Corinne asked.

"Oh well, I, like, overheard you talking with someone this morning about yoga and, like, decided to give it a shot. Which classes are you taking?"

"We haven't decided yet," Corinne said in a crisp tone.

I shot her a glance, puzzled by her answer.

"We're both beginners," I said, not wanting to be rude.

"Groovy! Maybe, we can, like, all come together. Wouldn't that be fun?"

Vonnie walked up to Freddy, introducing herself and ready to give her spiel. Corinne headed for the doors.

"I'll see you at El Toro in a little while."

She exited while I fished for my car keys. Vonnie whisked Freddy down the hallway.

I sat in my car, tapping my fingers on the steering wheel. My idea of incorporating Corinne and Jeff into helping keep an eye on Liz now had another set of teeth with yoga classes. I had the impression that until she broke her leg, Corinne had been active. She'd probably move on to the advanced classes ahead of me. Perhaps *she* could be my surrogate. I didn't want to involve Freddy in this. With her mouth, there was no way in hell she'd ever keep a secret, especially one concerning life and death. Corinne fit the bill much better.

Assuming there's time to protect before the killer

strikes.

****

I arrived at El Toro a few minutes early and snagged an outdoor table with a view of the ocean. A sailboat bobbed past, and on the horizon where the deep cobalt blue of the water met the lighter blue of the sky, a cruise ship slid up the coastline, no doubt headed for The Bahamas. The breeze rustled the palm trees along the sidewalk, and I breathed in the refreshing salt air.

A waiter stopped by the table and I ordered a margarita. After leaving the yoga studio, I'd gone home and changed into shorts and a tank top. Maybe after lunch, I'd walk on the beach or sit in the sun. Why not? I had nowhere to go.

My drink and Corinne arrived at the same time.

"I'll take one of those also," she said, pulling out a chair. "Am I late?"

"No. I was early." I sipped the margarita, savoring the combination of sweet, sour, and salty.

"So, are you playing hooky today?"

"Got fired this morning."

"Oh, I'm so sorry," she replied with a sympathetic expression.

"Don't be. I hated the job and my boss." I gave her the lowdown on my work environment.

The waiter brought her drink and she raised it in a salute. "Here's to finding a better job, with a better boss, and no bimbos!"

"I'll drink to that."

We both sipped and set our glasses on the table.

"Why is it ordinary women who are good at what they do have to put up with bimbos and the idiots they target?" she asked.

"You sound like you speak from experience also."

"I'll say—my ex-husband. He had bimbos on the side for years before I discovered it."

I winced and took another sip. "Ouch! That must

have hurt."

"Know how I found out? The mistress of the moment called and asked why I wouldn't give Mark a divorce when he so obviously didn't love me anymore. When I informed her he hadn't asked for one, she didn't believe me."

"Did you dump him?"

"Damned right I did. If I hadn't been blinded by his smooth talking, I'd have done it years ago. After the divorce all my so-called friends told me he'd been boffing other women for most of our fifteen years of marriage. I took him to the cleaners, too. He's a developer and made a killing in the real estate market." She laughed and sipped more of her drink. "That is until the market went south. Now he wants the alimony payments lowered. My attorney told him to cram it."

I laughed with her. The waiter came and we ordered lunch—cheese enchiladas for her and a taco salad for me.

"Have you always been into jogging?" I asked.

"My husband was a sports freak. When he wasn't working, he played squash, tennis, golf, and jogged. In order to spend time with him, I jogged, too. It was the only thing I enjoyed. He used the other pastimes for conducting business. What about you? Are you married?"

"Not lately. I had a very brief marriage when I was twenty-two. It lasted a whole eighteen months."

"Was he a scumbag?"

"Not really. We just fought all the time."

Other than the other day with Katie and Andy, I hadn't thought about Brad in a long while. My temper and his drinking was a hideous reminder of my childhood, and rather than let history repeat itself, I'd bailed. The last I heard, my ex had quit boozing and lived somewhere in Georgia with a new wife and a couple of kids. I wished him well.

"Got any boyfriends on the horizon?"

"Nope. Just unloaded a scumbag." I gave her the details on Joel and how I caught him.

"You eavesdropped on him?" She crowed with laughter. "Oh, God, I'd have loved to have been there. I know that bridge. Too bad you didn't send him into the water."

She laughed harder when I told her about chasing him with his golf club. "Renee, you are priceless. What prompted you to take up all this activity?"

I had no intention of revealing what I'd overheard in the park—not yet. Nor did I want to admit I had a plan for protecting Liz, although eventually I'd have to if I wanted her and Jeff's help. After all, it was a strange situation, and God knows the police, other than Andy, didn't take me seriously. I was tired of looking like a fool.

"Joel made a nasty comment about my weight, and I decided to do something about it."

"That's right. You mentioned that the other day. Good for you." She raised her glass and licked some of the salt from the rim before sipping again. "Do you live close to the park?"

"Over on Palmdale."

"That's a nice area."

"The house belongs to my grandparents. They traded in the tropics for the mountains of North Carolina five or six years ago, but didn't want to give up the place. I'm kind of a caretaker. I live there rent free and pay the utilities, while they take care of everything else." I wiped some of the condensation from the glass with my fingertip.

"Sounds like a good arrangement."

Our food arrived and we spent the next couple of minutes enjoying the meal. I eyed her enchiladas with envy, but found the taco salad better than expected.

"What about you? Where do you hang your hat?" I asked between forkfuls of lettuce and spicy ground beef.

"We had a house in Darnelle, out near the country club, but it went in the divorce. I bought a condo near the park. It's far enough inland, so hurricanes don't force me to evacuate."

We talked about how hurricane seasons of the past had affected us while we ate. I liked Corinne. She had an easy going manner, and I imagined the more we got to know each other, the more we'd find in common. *Like friends. Like with Katie.*

We were almost finished when a voice called out, "Yoo-hoo! Mind if I join you?"

Corinne laid her fork on the side of her plate. "Oh, Jesus, not her again. Is she stalking us or something?"

I had to admit that Freddy showing up at the dance studio and the restaurant was odd.

Freddy rushed up. "Hi, isn't this too wild! I love this place, don't you? It has the coolest margaritas in the city. Mind if I join you?"

"Actually, we're almost finished," I said.

She ignored me and pulled out a chair, then plunked her skinny butt into it.

Corinne's jaw clenched. She pushed her plate away and rummaged in her purse, laying fifteen dollars on the table.

"I have to be somewhere." Her curt voice along with the sudden color in her cheeks told me she was pissed and ready to pop a blood vessel.

"Oh, too bad. I just figured out where I heard the name Liz Gorman and why she looked familiar. She's, like, a socialite. I've seen her picture in the paper lots of times. Do you guys, like, know her?"

"Casually," I replied.

"Wow, that is way cool. I've, like, never met a socialite before. Is she snobbish?"

"I've only just met her, and she seems perfectly nice. She minds her own business," Corinne said, pushing back her chair. "I'll see you tomorrow, Renee."

She left as the waiter arrived. Freddy gave her order before turning back to me.

"I am so glad I met you guys. Jeff and I had a great time this morning. He's, like, so cute, don't you think? Have you known him long? What about Corinne? She left suddenly. I didn't, like, interrupt anything, did I?"

"Uh, no, not really. So, did you sign up for yoga classes?"

"Sure did. When are you going?"

"I'm not sure. Whenever I have the time, I guess." I didn't want to lie, but too much time around Freddy would send me around the bend.

"Maybe we can ride together. Where do you live?"

Not telling her seemed rude, and while I'd never let that bother me in the past, I didn't want to hurt her feelings, and told her.

The waiter brought the check, and I added fifteen bucks to Corinne's. Freddy seemed nice enough, but a little went a long way. I imagined her speech patterns wore thin after a while.

"I hate to run, but I have another appointment. See you later."

"Oh, okay."

I felt guilty at the dejection in her voice. I walked a few yards down the sidewalk, and then turned to wave. Freddy sat alone, a cell phone plastered against her ear. I made a mental note not to give her my number.

I lost myself in the crowd on the sidewalk and, crossing the street indulged in the promised walk on the beach, before sitting on the seawall watching the waves come and go. In spite of having lost my job, and not to mention Liz and her situation, I was calm. I had a new friend and a new outlook on life.

I had turned a corner.

****

Not used to being at home in the middle of the afternoon, I paced around the house restlessly. The television held no interest unless I wanted to listen to political pundits, endless news repeated over and over, soap operas, or movies. The latter didn't sound so bad, but the schedule bore nothing that interested me.

I finally fired up my computer, logged onto the unemployment benefits site, and added my name to the list. I'd made decent bucks at Carson Electronics and had been there for almost four years, so my weekly allotment was the maximum allowed. It would pay the utility and grocery bills, but sooner or later I'd have to get a paying job.

I pulled up a local job finder website and searched for receptionist opportunities. The list wasn't all that impressive. Most of them were for entry level positions with the salary to go with it.

Discouraged, I logged out, read a few blogs, made some comments, and bored to tears, decided to Google Joel Wainwright. That took all of ten seconds to read. I Googled myself next. Equally dull and short.

"Let's try Andrew Jackson," I murmured, and pulled up tons of info on the seventh president of the United States. "Oops." I modified the search.

Andy had an impressive listing. I'd had no idea he'd received several commendations and awards over the years, but it didn't surprise me. Andy was the kind of person who succeeded at whatever he chose to do. The last item showed he'd recently been accepted at the University Of Miami School Of Law. Andy? A lawyer? That did surprise me.

I killed the next hour Googling most of my

acquaintances, including my boss and the bimbo, before typing in Elizabeth Gray-Gorman. It wouldn't hurt to know more about the woman I'd sworn to protect.

Her activities were numerous and I soon discovered the full range of her charitable contributions. She not only donated time, but money to The Home for Friendless Animals, The Shelter for Abused Women, and the Palm Lake Home for Unwed Mothers, along with The Library Association of Palm Lake, and Stop Illiteracy Now. Liz also worked for and donated to The American Cancer Society. Last year, she'd placed fifteenth in the 10K Mini-Marathon for Breast Cancer Awareness.

"Geez, is there anything she doesn't do?" I muttered. Compared to her most people, me included, were a bunch of slackers.

I scrolled down, reading about the various fundraisers she'd hosted and attended over the years. My admiration grew. Here was a woman who had genuine interest in and compassion for her fellow human beings.

And her shit heel husband wants to kill her?

If I lived to be a hundred, I'd never understand. Any normal husband would be proud of her dedication, but no, this asshole had to take out a contract on her life because it wasn't all about him.

I read on to the end of the article.

"Elizabeth Gray-Gorman is the founder and CEO of the Susan Richardson Gray Foundation. Originally focusing on breast cancer, the Foundation expanded three years ago to include all types of cancer, and has to date distributed millions of dollars toward cancer research. It also aids families of cancer victims. Gray's Hospice provides comfort and housing free of charge for the terminally ill and their loved ones."

Susan Richardson Gray? Gray-Gorman—a

mother or grandmother?

I immediately searched for the foundation online and pulled up the website. It had been formed twelve years ago by Liz and her father, Stanford Dean Gray, when Liz's mother succumbed to breast cancer at the age of forty-three. Last year alone, the foundation had raised over twenty-five million dollars with the majority of it earmarked for research. The hospice supplied rooms, meals, and counseling for families all free of charge. Doctors donated time and in some cases money. The nursing and administration staffs were salaried, but CEO Liz didn't accept one thin dime for her work.

Running a hospice must eat up a huge amount of bucks. No wonder Liz worked like a beaver.

And no wonder she jogs and does yoga. She's got major league stress.

Stanford Gray had retired from the Foundation four years ago, leaving Liz in charge. Then I remembered something from that fateful overheard conversation about her parents' condo in Key West. Parents?

I pulled out of the Foundation and looked up Stanford and Susan Gray. Stanford had inherited a bundle from his father, a boat manufacturer.

Of course, Gray Boatbuilding and Shipyards. Located a few miles up the Mangrove River, it had been an institution, not to mention an employer, for hundreds of Palm Lake residents. I remembered driving past once with my parents and weaving fantasies about the sleek yachts moored there. He'd sold the business some fifteen years ago for an indecent amount of money.

Susan Richardson had also come from money— old money in Boston. According to the bio, she and Stanford met while attending a regatta in Newport, Rhode Island one summer and were married a year later. Elizabeth Dianne Gray made her appearance two years after that.

"Wow, Newport. If the blood got any bluer..." I said out loud.

The article went on to mention Susan's death and the last line gave me the information Stanford Gray had re-married five years ago to a woman from Palm Beach.

Hmm. So Liz had a stepmother. I wondered if they got along and if she was the reason her father had retired from the Foundation. If she and the asshole journeyed to Key West every other weekend, then the relationship couldn't be too uncomfortable.

I'd snooped into the lives of everyone in the family except one. Might as well make it a clean sweep, I thought typing the name of her malevolent husband, Todd Gorman.

His bio wasn't as storied, but still impressive. He came from a Mainline Philadelphia family and had attended Harvard, graduating with a degree in Business Administration. He'd married Liz ten years ago after what must have been a whirlwind courtship. The nuptials had taken place in Las Vegas two months after they met.

A Philadelphia Mainliner? Harvard? That spelled money. So, why did he need Liz's? Was he that greedy? I remembered his comment about a two bedroom apartment and driving a Ford.

"Lineage does not necessarily translate into money," I murmured to myself. "Suppose old Todd had the breeding, but not the bucks?"

He lived the high life and didn't want to give it up. Why bother with killing his wife? Rich people who didn't pay their bills, never had problems obtaining more credit. Lots of restaurants and stores were only too glad to have them as patrons. It helped the establishment's image.

I scrolled down further, staring at the final paragraph.

"Mr. Gorman is the Director of Donations and Distribution of the Susan Richardson Gray Foundation."

Holy shit! Liz is his boss? He handles the money? Oh, Lizzie, you'd better call for an audit—quick!

Chapter Seven

I pulled into my usual parking spot near the jogging trails early, and stopped to breathe in the fresh air before heading for the warm-up area. I almost called Andy to tell him the news about Todd Gorman working at the Foundation, but then stopped with the number half-dialed. If I did that, I'd have to admit I knew the intended victim's identity. And *that* would further shove the burr up Andy's butt regarding my participation in this whole thing. I could visualize the exasperated look he'd give me now.

I could handle exasperated looks—just not from Andy.

Of course, sooner or later my knowledge would come to light, along with my newly found interest in yoga. I disconnected the call. Save the information for later.

The sun caressed my shoulders with a light touch. By afternoon the temperature would reach into the low eighties—a perfect South Florida winter day.

Now that I was unemployed, I could jog at my own pace without concern about being somewhere else at a specific time. Liz had already arrived and was in the midst of her pre-jog stretching. Surprised, I hurried to stand next to her.

"Hi, Liz, you're up with the birds this morning."

"Good morning, Renee. I'm scheduled on a noon flight to Los Angeles. I have an affair to attend tomorrow night and a couple of business meetings."

"I've never been to California. What's it like?"

"Don't look at the license plates, and you can't tell it from South Florida."

"Is that good or bad?"

Liz laughed. "I'm not sure.

I stretched my left hamstring and worried. A smart hit person would follow Liz to L. A. and fulfill the contract there away from people close to her. I had no hope of protecting against that. I wondered if this had been on the agenda for a while. I recalled nothing about Liz being out of town from the conversation through the Lend An Ear. A little probing couldn't hurt.

"You don't sound too happy about going. Is the trip sudden?"

"Yes and no. It was on my personal assistant's schedule for months, but she forgot to include it on mine. She didn't discover the error until yesterday," she replied in a peeved voice.

"Doesn't sound like a very good personal assistant."

"She isn't. One more screw up and she's history. My husband's due home from a business trip tonight. We'd planned on celebrating his birthday. I had to leave a message in his voice mail."

I wondered if Scumbag Central had planned on celebrating his birthday or his wife's unfortunate demise.

"Maybe you can celebrate when you get home. Will you be gone long?"

"I'll be back Friday afternoon."

She bent over and grasped her ankles. By now I recognized this as the end of her warm-ups.

"Maybe I'll see you at the yoga studio Friday night. Corinne and I joined yesterday."

"Good for you." She straightened, jogging in place. "I'll probably be there. After trips like this I need the relaxation. Well, gotta go. Be seeing you."

She trotted out to the asphalt path, turned,

smiled and waved, then jogged out of sight. It was the first overt sign of friendship I'd seen her make. I returned to my warm-up.

Okay, maybe she'd be all right in California. If this was a last minute thing and the husband just found out, he probably hadn't had time to inform the killer. And the *killer* probably hadn't had time to come up with a plan.

The impromptu trip solved a problem for me as well. I'd had a hard time deciding whether to keep my appointment at the gym with Katie or go to the yoga class. I couldn't decide which torture sounded worse.

"Hi, Renee, how's it going this morning?"

I looked up. Jeff planted his foot on the guardrail next to mine. In spite of my irritation with Andy, I wished it was him. I thought about the possibility of a home-cooked meal again. *Won't hurt to ask.*

"Morning, Jeff. Pretty good. Yourself?"

He shot me a smile. "Great. I got on the scale and found I've lost another three pounds. That's a total of eighteen even though I backslid with beer and pizza last weekend. Today is an all salad diet."

"Good morning, everyone," Corinne said in a cheerful tone. "Enjoying your first day of leisure, Renee? I'd have thought you'd sleep in."

I shrugged. "Force of habit."

She turned to Jeff. "Did Renee tell you she got fired yesterday?"

"No kidding? I'm sorry to hear that."

"Believe me, I'm not." I finished my half-assed warm-ups.

"You going to yoga tonight?" she asked.

"No, the gym. I'll start yoga on Friday." Since Freddy hadn't shown up yet, I decided to take off. "If you guys don't mind, I'll press on. I'm sure you'll catch up to me."

I waved and took off at a brisk walk. I needed the time to think. The more time passed, the more Liz was in danger. Surely by now, the killer had a handle on Liz's routine. The park was too public, and her daytime schedule too varied. That left yoga. *If Liz attends classes at night, then the parking lot is the most likely target area. Or the drive home.*

I remembered reading about some businessman in Ft. Lauderdale who had been killed in his car on a dark side street by hit men while leaving his office one night.

Maybe if I'm careful, I could follow her. I'd be a potential witness, and the killer won't want witnesses.

Footsteps pounded from behind me.

"Gotcha," Jeff said, puffing. Freddy was with him.

"Boy, you are so, like, in another world. How come?"

I ignored Freddy's question and looked around. "Where's Corinne?"

"She got a phone call and had to leave. She was pissed. Kept muttering something about an ex-husband and alimony payments," Jeff explained.

"Yeah, he's been trying to get them reduced."

"I guess he succeeded because I heard her scream, 'son of a bitch' to whoever she was talking to," Freddy offered.

"That doesn't sound good."

We walked for another couple of minutes, and then Jeff said, "Ready to jog?"

"I have to sometime."

I broke into a trot and kept pace with Jeff and Freddy for another three minutes before my tortured lungs demanded I cease.

"I'm slowing you down," I panted, grabbing at the stitch in my side. "Go ahead. I'll see you tomorrow."

"Okay, have a good one." Jeff waved as he and Freddy moved on.

I stopped, bent over, and placed my hands on my knees for a moment. All this exercise shit was killing me. When I had my breath back, I walked. As I approached the bridge where I'd almost dumped Joel into the water, a figure with dark brown hair had just crossed it, jogging toward me. I recognized Sherry, Joel's boss.

I hadn't heard from Joel the Asshole since our encounter on my front lawn, and couldn't resist taking advantage of the opportunity. I had to know what had happened.

"Hello," I said as she neared.

"Hello," she said with a smile. Then she did a double take and stopped, jogging in place. "Oh, it's you."

"Look, I really want to apologize for last week. I was upset and acted before I thought."

She took a swig from the water bottle she carried. "Don't be. It's better to find out the lay of the land before you start the hike."

"So, did Joel get the partnership?"

"Are you kidding?" she replied with a snort. "I called a meeting with the rest of the board when I got to the office. Joel was already there trying to mend the fences. Swore you were a lunatic, but the decision on the partnership was put on hold. My uncle hired a private investigator to check out Joel's background beyond the personnel files. We should get the results any day now."

"Well, I may be a lunatic, but I wasn't lying."

"The funny thing is I believe you. I asked a few discreet questions around the office and discovered Joel didn't always represent his own work."

"He stole other people's ideas? That doesn't surprise me. Once a liar, always a liar."

She nodded. "You got it. I'd better be going."

I watched her disappear down the trail, and then continued on my way. If Joel didn't get that partnership, the blame would fall squarely on my shoulders. Didn't bother me a lick. Not my fault he was a liar.

****

"And you called your boss's playmate a bimbo to her face?" Katie asked from the stationary bike next to me.

"Not quite, but I was insulting enough to piss her off," I puffed, pedaling my ass off to nowhere on a medium setting. "Felt good, too. Getting fired has its upside."

"Slow down on that thing. This isn't the Tour de France."

"I know, but for some reason, I feel energized."

"Did you jog this morning?"

"Sort of. I walked and jogged. Guess who I ran into—Joel's boss."

"Please tell me he got fired, too."

I shook my head. "Not yet, but I plan to pop the cork on a bottle of champagne when he does."

The timer on Katie's bike dinged signifying the end of twenty minutes. Mine followed a few seconds later and we wandered over to the barbells. I tried not to stare at our reflections in the mirrors. Katie was sleek and fit. I still resembled a chipmunk on steroids.

"So, are you looking for a job?" she asked, grabbing a couple of ten pound weights.

"I've got a small window of grace time. I'll collect unemployment and take it easy for a couple of weeks, maybe even a month or so." I picked up the five pound barbells and did two or three curls before my muscles told me to knock it off. "Your brother is a liar."

"In what way?"

"He told me this would get easier. My biceps are

not happy."

Katie laughed. "Give it two weeks. When you don't hurt, that's the time to increase your reps."

"And you do how many?"

"I do ten per rotation, but that's the limit. I don't want to look like a bodybuilder."

We moved on to the Stair-Stepper. "So, how's your business?" I asked.

"I've got another show at Rendell's Art Gallery next week. The artist is Beauregard. He's a minimalist."

"What's that?"

"You know, he paints a few brush strokes in purple on white canvas, calls it an Iris, and then sells it for a bundle."

"Weird stuff."

She chuckled. "That about sums it up. I just book the showings. I don't have to like the art. Why don't you come? There's free champagne and hors d'oeuvres."

This Stair-Stepper was killing me. My legs burned and my conversation turned breathless. "I might. I've never attended an art showing. Too high society for me."

"How about lunch tomorrow? Just you and me this time."

I noticed Katie climbed imaginary steps with little effort. "Sounds like fun. Where?"

"You pick—just don't make it too trendy. I've only got an hour or so to spare."

"How about The Golden Hummingbird at noon? Its vegan, but I'm into salads at the moment."

Katie agreed, and we moved again to the concrete block thigh crusher. At least I could sit down on this one.

"Seen your mom lately?" she asked.

"No, thank goodness."

"She's still at the sanitarium, isn't she?"

"Yeah, the last time I went we talked about the weather, the flowers growing in the gardens, and oh, how can I forget, about what an ungrateful child I am. She still has issues, but the doctors think she may be able to leave in a few months."

"So, she still blames you?"

I shrugged. Between this machine and the step thing, my legs had about had it. I exerted more pressure and increased my speed to keep up with Katie.

"My testimony put her in The Palm Lake Rest Home for three years taking anger management classes and having every psych evaluation known to man."

"Honey, she tried to solve a road rage fender bender with a gun." Katie paused. "Was it the same gun she shot your father with?"

"No, she kept the thirty-aught at home. She used a twenty-five caliber semi-automatic. The cops also found a thirty-eight revolver, a twenty-two Saturday night special, and a nine millimeter stuffed under the front seat."

"Geez. I take it they confiscated them."

"Oh sure, but what they didn't know was Mom had more at home. God only knows what would have happened if I hadn't been with her that day. Can we change the subject? I get all depressed talking about my mother."

I not only got depressed, but scared also. My mother was a nut case—a real lulu from the cheap seats. And sometimes I broke out in a cold sweat wondering if the limited gene pool affected me in the same way. My past wasn't exactly littered with calm reactions.

We moved on to the chin-up bars. I sneaked a peek at my best friend after three, relieved to see her face contorting with the exertion. At last! I felt much better.

"How's your dad—or is that subject taboo, too?"

"I haven't seen him in over five years. He divorced Mom after the thirty-aught incident and went back to Texas. The last time I talked with my grandparents, they said he had stopped drinking and was working in Odessa. I never even heard from him when I passed on the information about Mom getting three years on the funny farm. I guess he doesn't give a shit about her or me."

I wanted to say "nobody does," but resisted the urge. It sounded pathetic. I'd been taking care of myself since I was fifteen, even learning how to pay the bills. Dad was too drunk and Mom too looped on the medication of the month—or sometimes not—to handle things. It was a miracle Child Protective Services never got involved.

"Well, if he pulled his act together, maybe your mother can, too."

"Maybe, but I'm not holding my breath." I quit the chin ups after only seven and wiped perspiration from my forehead.

Katie finished out her reps and dropped to the floor. "Whew, glad that's over. I hate chin-ups."

We completed the first set of exercises along with the cool down walk, and approached the bikes again when a familiar figure walked up.

"Good evening, ladies," Andy said with a grin. "Getting all buff?"

"You should talk," I said before thinking. My mind was busy processing those biceps.

"Liked what you saw the other day, huh?"

My cheeks radiated warmth, while Katie chuckled. Andy winked, threw his heavily muscled leg over a bike, cranked the difficulty level to high, the time to twenty minutes, and pedaled with what looked like little effort. I covertly checked out his thighs. They bulged and flexed with each stroke. His shorts covered his derriere, but my imagination

Suzanne Rossi

made up for it. I mounted the bike next to him.

"So, whose reputation were you shredding when I walked up," he asked, still grinning.

Katie got on the bike next to me and wrinkled her nose. "We were about to start on yours. And how was your day?"

The grin slipped from his face. "Just peachy. Spent most of the day on a double homicide in the projects. Drug related, of course." He shook his head. "The sons of bitches killed each other in front of a couple of kids."

No wonder he worked out so hard. His stress levels must have been ten times mine.

"Is that why you're going to law school?"

Katie stared at her brother with wide eyes. "Law school? Where? And when did you decide this? Do Mom and Dad know?"

"Not yet. I was going to announce it at the next family get together. I've been accepted to the University of Miami, School of Law. I start in June."

He shot me a look, part suspicious, part amused, making me squirm inwardly. Oops. Major flub. I gulped and pedaled faster.

"How did you know about it? I just found out a couple of weeks ago."

I didn't answer.

"You Googled me, didn't you?" He laughed. "That interested?"

"Don't flatter yourself. I was bored to tears yesterday afternoon and looked up a lot of my friends."

"Sure. Come on, admit it, you find me fascinating."

"Hey, give Renee a break. She got fired yesterday," Katie said. She turned to me. "At least you'll be able to jog whenever you want for a while."

Andy's pedaling slowed, and he turned his head to stare. I kept my gaze focused straight ahead.

"So, you're still jogging? Dare I ask what brought on this interest in physical fitness?"

A dart of guilt stabbed me in the chest. I'd meant to tell him. Really, I did. "I'm concerned about my health."

Hadn't I just had this conversation with Joel last week? This time Andy was the skeptic, and I the liar.

"And how often do you jog?" he asked in a quiet tone.

"Every morning around eight o'clock in City Park."

"Make any new friends?"

I stared straight ahead. I couldn't bring myself to look at him. "As a matter of fact, I have. There's Jeff, Corinne, a woman named Freddy, and Elizabeth Gray-Gorman. I jog with them." He didn't need to know I only warmed-up with Liz and walked most of the time. "And to set the record straight, I've also signed up for yoga classes."

"At the Barnard School, I suppose."

"That's right. It came highly recommended by my new friend Liz." I finally made eye contact. "How do you know about the Barnard School?"

"I said I'd check things out. Renee, I thought we agreed jogging wasn't your thing." His voice had taken on an exasperated quality.

"Why is it I have the feeling this conversation isn't about jogging?" Katie asked. "What's up?"

I snapped off the timer on the bike and slid from the seat. "Nothing. Your brother's being a pain in the ass."

I strode over to the weight rack and grabbed one. I ignored my protesting muscles and curled. A few minutes later, Andy materialized next to me. In the mirror I saw Katie talking to a woman who had taken my bike.

"You promised me you wouldn't accost any more

women," he said in a low voice.

"I haven't. I simply learned her name and did some research."

"And how did you do that?"

"I saw her picture in the paper, along with that of her sleazy husband. When I went to the park I introduced myself."

His forehead furrowed, but whether with worry or irritation, I didn't know.

"Renee, for God's sake, we don't even know for sure if she's the target."

"It's her," I said ungrammatically. "She jogs, works out in the gym when it rains, and does yoga. Did you know she's the head of a foundation?"

"The Susan Richardson Gray Foundation is heavily into cancer research, and other charities. Mrs. Gorman is a big time social activist with the money to back it up."

"What else has your investigation found? I'm sure you discovered her husband also works for the Foundation."

"That doesn't automatically make him a killer, although, I can see any husband of yours taking that step," he said.

"But Andy, he's in charge of donations and who gets what. Don't you find that suspicious?" I demanded, ignoring his verbal jab.

"No. Someone has to do it. It might as well be him—he's her husband and has a business degree from Harvard. He comes from old money."

"He has an impressive pedigree, but I have to wonder how much of that old money is still around." I finished my curls and dropped the weights back into the rack with a clang. "Look Andy, I know what I'm doing. If I can stick close to her, then maybe the killer won't get a chance to fulfill the contract."

"So, you've appointed yourself as her bodyguard?"

"More or less."

Andy replaced his weights and frowned. "God Almighty, Renee, don't you realize how dangerous that is? A hit man..."

"...woman," I interrupted.

He closed his eyes, took a deep breath, and then opened them again.

"A hit woman won't care if you're around. A contract is a contract. What's the difference between one dead body with a missing purse and two? She'd have to take you out. You'd be a witness."

I walked over to another apparatus. A chill, like an icy feather, tickled the back of my neck. I'd never looked at it from that perspective, or considered that my actions might put me in danger. Andy followed and grasped my shoulders, turning me around.

"You're not playing some game. If what you heard is true, then let the police handle it. This isn't TV where the bad guys are rounded up at the end of sixty minutes."

I twisted free, as much in irritation as from the searing heat his fingers had produced even through my t-shirt, and took my place on the Stair-Stepper. "I know that. I'm not a fool. Are you at least considering the possibility I might be right in all of this?"

"I said I'd check it out and I am."

He stalked away, his face set, straddling the ab machine and crunching those sculpted abs with more force than necessary. I climbed furiously, finished out the set, and headed for the whirlpool to think.

I slid into the warm water and set the timer, letting the frothing bubbles ease my sore muscles. I leaned my head on the rim of the tub and closed my eyes.

His comments about my being in danger left me uncertain, but I didn't see any other way to protect

Liz. I didn't worry about the park, but the parking lots at the Foundation and the yoga studio concerned me.

Maybe I should tell Liz what I heard. She'd probably think I'm a candidate for The Palm Lake Rest Home, but on the other hand, she might take precautions and have her husband followed or something.

I scrapped any thoughts about asking Jeff and Corinne to help. I had no business putting them in danger, too. And maybe playing it by ear about informing Liz made more sense. Besides, she didn't strike me as the kind of woman who'd park in the far reaches of a parking lot at night. She sounded smarter than that.

Is she conscious of what's going on around her?

In spades.

That snippet of eavesdropped conversation eased my mind somewhat. The killer would have to take precautions herself. What would be the weapon of choice? A silenced gun? A knife? Both required getting in close. A rifle fired from a distance? Perhaps. Suddenly, the park didn't sound so safe after all.

Someone slid into the water next to me. I opened my eyes. It was Andy. I wished the hot tub was in a more secluded area, and then wondered why. *You know why, dummy, and don't pretend the water isn't getting hotter. Calm down.*

"You're finished early," I commented to hide my confusion.

"I cut my work out short. I don't suppose there's any way to talk you out of this bodyguard crap, is there?"

"Not really."

A frown marred his face. Good Lord, was he actually worried about me? Nobody had worried about me in a long time. I liked that it was Andy.

"Then for God's sake, be careful. Try to stay in a crowd. Keep your cell phone charged and with you at all times. Be aware of your surroundings, and stay out of isolated areas. What time do you jog?"

My heart rate sped up at his caring tone. "Anywhere from seven forty-five to eight, but I won't be there tomorrow. Liz had to go to Los Angeles unexpectedly. She left on the noon flight and won't return until Friday. Her husband's due back in town tonight. Are you joining us for morning jogging, too?"

"When my schedule permits. I take it Mrs. Gorman runs further than you."

"She always takes the long trail."

"I'll follow her. Introduce me as a friend. If she'll let me, I'll jog with her and try to strike up a conversation."

"All right." I paused. "You think she's in danger, too, don't you?"

"I don't know, but there's something about your bullheadedness that makes me wonder."

Katie entered the pool area and slid in next to her brother.

"I'm surprised you haven't drowned each other."

I laughed. "I thought about it, but decided he has his uses. It's always nice to know a cop."

"And you've gotten to know so many of us over the years."

I refrained from smacking him, choosing instead to assume he meant it in a teasing manner.

"Are you suggesting Renee needs a keeper?" she asked with a devilish grin.

Andy stretched out his arm and tugged my pony tail. "That and a lot more."

"Smart ass."

The gentle movement and his tone brought a glow to the pit of my stomach. I got a lot of those lately.

"Hey, I've got an idea. Why don't you bring

Renee to the Beauregard showing next week?"

"The what?" he asked.

His sister sighed. "The Beauregard showing at the Rendell Art Gallery. I told you about it a couple of weeks ago. How could you forget?"

"Very easily. Who's Beauregard?"

"I understand he paints weird things," I offered.

"Swell, like I'd really look forward to that."

"Andrew Beverly Jackson, you promised."

"Beverly?" I sputtered with laughter.

His head turned toward me. "Shut up! It's an old family name."

"Please tell me you haven't asked some airhead to come with you," Katie said.

His head swiveled to her. "Might liven this affair up if I did." He turned back to me, scowling. "Dammit, quit laughing."

I couldn't. It was just too funny. Andy placed his hand on the top of my head and pushed me under. I popped up, spitting water and still laughing. Without another word, he exited the tub and stalked to the locker room.

"It was our grandmother on our mother's side's maiden name," Katie informed me in all seriousness.

I roared again.

****

I arrived home still in a good mood from the teasing Andy had taken. Beverly. God, if the kids at school had known, he'd have never lived it down.

I flipped on the lights in the living room and walked to the kitchen. The workout had given me an appetite so I popped a pre-prepared meal into the microwave and made a salad. Ten minutes later, I sat at the kitchen table sipping a glass of Chardonnay, and enjoying Chicken Teriyaki. I'd bought a better grade of frozen dinners.

Finished, I poured another glass of wine and turned on the TV, settling on a movie about a woman whose husband wanted to kill her. Maybe I could pick up some tips on how to help Liz. I watched about fifteen minutes before deciding Liz being bedridden wasn't an option.

I switched off the TV and thought about Andy, a much more pleasant subject. My daydreams envisioned passionate embraces and kisses to making love so hot, the sheets caught fire. I'd known him forever, it seemed, and yet had never had these crazy sexual fantasies about him. I didn't count when I was ten. That was kid stuff and the most my imagination had conjured up was holding hands or a chaste kiss.

Renee, you're losing it. He's just being nice. If he knew what you were thinking, he'd be horrified and embarrassed or worse yet, die laughing.

I hoped the latter wasn't true and wondered for the umpteenth time if maybe, just maybe, he could think of me as something more than his kid sister's best friend. I liked being around him, and although he could be irritating as hell, he also made me laugh—something I'd not done a whole lot of with Joel. Andy Jackson was slowly worming his way under my skin and into my heart.

I was about to call it a night when my phone rang. Caller ID told me it was Dr. Reynard, my mother's shrink and the head of the sanitarium.

"Hello?"

"Good evening, Miss Ryan. I hope you're well."

"Yes, I'm fine. Why are you calling at ten-thirty at night? Is something wrong?"

"I'm calling to let you know you mother had a little episode this afternoon."

"Episode?" I sighed heavily. "Why can't you people ever come right out and say what happened? What kind of an episode?"

"She's been testy with some of the other patients in group the last couple of days, so I called her in for a private session."

"And?"

"We discussed the incident that led to her being sent here. Naturally, I can't give you specifics."

"Naturally, but you don't have to. I know she's still angry about it. I thought she was making progress."

"Oh, she is, most of the time."

"Will you just get to the point?" By now, my anxiety level had risen to stratospheric heights and I was impatient.

"Your mother had a serious setback. She raged and made threats against you and threw several items around the office. I had to sedate her."

I relaxed. "So? It's happened before. Why call me?"

"According to the nurse on duty, she had a long nap and woke up much better. The problem occurred during shift change."

Forget relaxing. My stomach tightened. "The—the problem?"

"Yes. You see, your mother was left in the conservatory watching TV, and I'm...I'm afraid she's gone."

My heart lurched. "My—my mother's dead?" Tears welled in my eyes.

"No, no, Miss Ryan. I mean she's gone—missing. She's escaped."

Chapter Eight

Mother's escaped? Oh, shit! Just what I need to hear. Are these people stupid or what?

"Miss Ryan, are you there? Did you hear me? I said your mother is missing from the sanitarium."

I took a deep breath to control my anger. "Escaped? Missing? No, Dr. Reynard, my mother didn't escape. You assholes lost her. You left a highly emotional and irrational woman alone in a TV room with outside access. I thought all those doors were supposed to be locked."

"They're open during the day when staff can supervise outdoor activity, but locked at five o'clock in the evening. There must have been a security breach."

"What the hell do you people use for brains?"

"Miss Ryan, I understand that you are upset—"

"Upset? No, I'm beyond upset. You're lucky I'm not in your office, because I really want to kick you in the nuts so hard they get stuck in your throat. Did you notify her lawyer or the police?"

"Uh, no, not yet. I wanted to inform you first."

"Why? What the hell can I do about it?"

"Uh, Miss Ryan—"

"And why haven't you called the cops?"

"As soon as we missed her at bed check, we searched the grounds. So far, we haven't found her."

"Of course, you haven't found her. Did you think she'd be sitting under an oak tree contemplating the meaning of life? I assume you've also searched the road."

Isolated in a rural setting, The Palm Lake Rest

Home sat on thirty acres on the northwest side of town not far from The Everglades. One two lane road led to it with eight foot deep ditches along either side. Anyone walking in the dark would have a tough time.

"Yes, we did. The road was empty. Beyond the ditches, the vegetation is saw grass—very difficult to navigate without a machete."

"Oh? Does she have one of those, too?"

"Uh, no, Miss Ryan. There are no weapons here at the sanitarium." His voice held a mixture of resignation and censure.

"Since you've searched and come up dry, do you have any idea how she left?"

My anger waned and a strange sense of doom crept over me. My mother could be anywhere.

Dr. Reynard cleared his throat. "It seems one of our orderlies was late to work this evening and forgot to lock his car. It's missing from the parking lot, too."

"The idiot didn't also leave his keys in the ignition, did he?"

"No, he had them with him."

"She probably hotwired it. Mother used to do that whenever she found Daddy's pickup at a bar. She'd hot wire the damned thing, and then drive home leaving him to walk as punishment. Look, call the cops and her lawyer."

"I don't suppose you have any idea where she'd go? Would she come to you?"

"Not bloody likely, and I have no clue where she is. You lost her, you find her."

I hung up on Reynard and kicked a chair, ignoring the pain radiating from my toes. Damn and blast. Not only had Mother escaped the rest home, but had stolen a car as well.

"That'll set her release date back," I muttered.

Maybe her lawyer could talk the guy into not

pressing charges, provided I paid for any damages. I didn't want the cops brought in, but someone who knew what they were doing had to look for her. God knew Reynard and his bunch of terminal idiots operated in blind ignorance.

I poured another glass of wine and sat in the abused chair. Why me? Had I somehow pissed off or offended God *in utero* and been born to a screwball as punishment?

Wouldn't surprise me in the least.

I gulped half the wine and yelled, "Ah, shit!" I didn't care if the windows were open and half the neighborhood heard me.

Then, a chill skittered up my spine. The hair on my arms rose. Mother walked away during or right after shift change, which if my memory served, occurred at six o'clock. Dinner seating wasn't assigned, so her absence would go unnoticed until the bed check at nine. If she hotwired the car and took off a little after six, then she could have pulled into my driveway by six forty-five.

And I wasn't home!

I rushed to the back door. Dammit to hell. It was unlocked, and I remembered locking it before I left for the gym. I tipped over a small potted plant on the patio and felt for the emergency key hidden there. It was gone.

Mother had been here, but obviously not to see me or she would have stayed. So what did she want? I had nothing of hers except...

Oh, no! Please God, not that!

I ran into the house, tore through the living room to the spare bedroom, yanked open the closet door, and rummaged around on the top shelf. After her arrest, the police had confiscated the guns in her car. Even though legally registered to Mother, they'd been destroyed. To keep her calm, I'd gone to her house and removed the other guns she owned before the police could get them. They were now gone, as was all the ammunition.

I knelt next to the bed and pulled up the bed skirt. Clean as a whistle. She'd gotten the husband-shooting thirty-aught, too. She really liked that rifle.

I went into my bedroom and searched the closet. A large duffle bag and some of my clothes had disappeared.

Wonderful, just fucking wonderful. My mother's escaped, stolen a car, is armed, and dressed like me.

I had no choice but to call the police, Dr. Reynard, and her lawyer.

Back in the kitchen, I picked up the phone when words I had spoken earlier in the evening ran through my head.

It's always nice to know a cop.

I dialed Andy.

****

"And other than the hunting rifle, what else did she take," Andy asked. He'd arrived less than fifteen minutes after I called. Just having him here made me feel protected. For once someone else could bear some of the responsibility. He listened and took me seriously. Believe me, my mother armed was not something to brush off.

"She got a thirty-eight revolver, a nine millimeter, and a couple of twenty-twos. Pretty much the same as the police found in the car. Mother tended to buy in bulk—one for the car and one for the house. The thirty-aught is like a family heirloom. It belonged to my grandfather."

"Plus the ammo?"

"Plus the ammo. Not a box left."

He wrote the information in a small notebook. "Did she know you had all of this?"

"Yeah, when she was arrested she made a big deal about the cops taking or someone stealing them, so to shut her up, I went to the house and rescued them. Seemed to satisfy her. She never mentioned the damned things again."

"Did you call Dr. Reynard?"

I nodded. "And her lawyer."

"What did the doc have to say?"

"Not much. Just a bunch of mumbo-jumbo about being careful, since I was the subject of her wrath twelve hours ago."

"That makes sense. Anything else I should know?"

"I don't think so. Oh, she also found my emergency stash of money—close to three hundred dollars. I kept it in an old teapot on the window sill in the kitchen. Do you think it'll take long to find her?"

He shrugged. "Hard to tell. Depends on where she's going. What about your father? Would she go to him?"

"I doubt it. He's in Texas somewhere, and as far as I know she hasn't been in touch with him since the divorce. I guess I should notify my grandparents their daughter is up to her old ways again."

"Where are they?"

"Asheville, North Carolina."

"Maybe she's on the way to see them."

"God, I hope not. They're in their eighties and in no shape to deal with Mom."

"Any other relatives she might seek?"

"The usual assortment of aunts, uncles, and cousins, but I have no idea where they live. She was an only child, so that lets out brothers or sisters."

He snapped his notebook shut. "I'll call this in while you pack a bag."

"Pack a bag? What for?"

"You can't stay here. Bunk in with Katie for a few nights until we find her."

"Of course, I can stay here. Mom might rant and rave, but she'd never hurt me. If she wanted to do that, she'd have hidden, and then nailed me when I walked in the door. And she's not hiding under my bed. You checked the place out. Besides, Mom's outbursts are short lived. She explodes, and then goes on to other matters."

"That doesn't mean she might not think about it and have a go at you later for testifying against her. And remember, she does have a key."

I sighed and ran my hand through my hair. I was tired and had no intention of leaving.

"Andy, I'll be fine. I doubt she'll come back here."

"All right, if you won't go to Katie's, then make up the sofa. I'll spend the night—and no arguments. Call a locksmith and have the locks changed. I can't remember the guy's name, but he's in the phone book and has a twenty-four hour service."

I opened my mouth to protest, and then shut it again. According to Reynard, Mom had shown improvement, but my mother was good—damned good. She'd conned more than one doctor into giving her prescriptions she imagined she needed. She might have conned Reynard into believing she was making progress, while all the time just waiting for an opportunity to bolt. When it comes to sneaky, Mother has the patience of Job.

Maybe having Andy spend the night wasn't such a bad idea. For once my mind was on safety, not sex. And the locksmith made sense, although I suspected Mom had simply acted from long ago memories. The key had always been kept under a flower pot, even when she was a teenager.

"All right, you win."

I snatched sheets, a blanket, and a pillow from the linen closet, spreading them on the sofa. Andy was talking on his cell in the kitchen, but I couldn't decipher the words. He returned just as I finished.

"What's going on?" I demanded.

"Dr. Reynard called it in about an hour ago. I told them what happened here and that I'd be staying with you."

"But what are they going to do?"

"A BOLO is out. Sooner or later, we'll find her." He frowned. "I just wish she didn't have those damned guns."

"That worries me, too. I can just see her reaction to being arrested again. If she points a gun at a cop..." I shuddered at the possibility. My eyes filled with tears.

Andy pulled me into his arms and held me close. "Don't think about it, Renee."

I let the tears fall onto his shoulder. His hand smoothed my hair. The warmth from his body seeped into mine, calming my frazzled nerves. I'd never felt this safe and secure with any man. A brief vision of us cuddling on the sofa every night flashed through my mind. I wanted to stand in this position forever. He finally backed away, but kept his arms loose around me. His smile was lopsided and that strange, almost surprised expression returned to his eyes.

"Don't cry, okay?"

I dried my cheeks with the back of my hand. "I can't help it. Why does everything happen to me? Mothers aren't supposed to do things like this. She's my mother, for God's sake. I love her, but..." I sniffed and let the sentence fade. Loving Mother had been hard. She hadn't allowed it. Yet, she was my responsibility.

Reluctantly, I pulled away from the comfort of his arms and wiped my eyes. "Never mind. I'm bone tired and rambling."

He smiled and kissed my forehead. "In that case, go to bed. Get a decent night's sleep. I'll call the locksmith."

I nodded and headed for my bedroom. "Oh,

there's a new toothbrush on the vanity in the bath, and Joel left some toiletries. I transferred them to the guest bath. They're in the medicine chest."

"I'll find them. Now go to bed."

"Andy? Thanks for staying."

"No problem." He pointed down the hall. "Bed, Renee."

I closed the bedroom door, undressed, and slid under the covers. For the first time since learning about Mother, I was calm. I credited Andy's presence as the reason.

****

"Here are the new keys. Both the front and back doors are the same. I tried them. They're a little stiff, but shouldn't give you any trouble. And for God's sake, don't put one under the damned flower pot," Andy admonished the next morning, handing me two shiny brass keys.

In spite of Andy on the sofa, I hadn't slept well. The locksmith arriving at one in the morning had me sitting upright listening to my heart pound in my ears. I'd finally drifted off around three. It was now five.

"I have to go home, change, and get to the station by seven. Are you going to be all right?" he asked with an anxious looking frown.

"I'll be fine. I wasn't going to jog today, but I think I need it. I'm all wound up. Katie and I are having lunch later."

"Good."

"Any word on Mother?"

"Not yet." He strode to the foyer and hesitated before opening the door. "I have to go to the University of Miami later this afternoon and get my registration packet. Want to come along?"

"Sure. I've never seen the campus. What time?"

"I'll pick you up at three. Here, catch." He chucked the morning paper at me. I caught it and tossed it on the floor with the rest of this week's news. I hadn't had time to read any of them.

Andy left. Missing him already, I wandered into the kitchen to put on a pot of coffee, and then attached one of the keys to my key ring. I lifted the spare set kept by the garage door and attached the other one. With Mother on the loose, putting another key outside or by the door where she could find it made no sense.

With the coffee pot burbling, I walked into the laundry room and dug a hole in the powder of a box of detergent. Dropping the keys in, I shook the box until the ring was buried. Even if Mother smashed her way in, at least she wouldn't find a key for future easy access, although knowing her warped mind this might be the first place she'd look.

I poured a cup of coffee, retrieved the latest paper, and carried it back to the kitchen. It was too early to go to the park, so I got my Doonesbury and Garfield fixes, read the society pages—no mention of the Gormans—glanced at the editorials—everyone had an opinion about everything—and skimmed the front page headlines.

I refilled my cup and wondered if a piece of toast would be in order. I didn't think jogging and breakfast mixed, but since I didn't really jog it probably didn't matter. When I finished, I dressed and headed for the park.

It was still early, but the sun had risen, and I was restless. A few cars dotted the parking lot. I spotted Jeff at the guardrail.

"Wow, this must be the day for early running," I said, taking a place beside him to warm-up.

"I have to be in the office for an early meeting, so that's my excuse. How about you?"

"I had a lousy night's sleep and decided to get it over with. Seven isn't too far off my schedule. I wonder if Corinne will be here today."

"She was sure ticked off yesterday," he commented.

I thought about Joel. "Yeah, ex-husbands and boyfriends have a way of doing that."

Jeff chuckled as we warmed up, and for once, my muscles didn't protest.

"You ready?" he asked.

"You go on ahead. I think I'll wait a few more minutes for Corinne." I was curious about her phone call. "Where's Freddy this morning?"

"I don't know."

I couldn't face the "likes", "you knows", and "far outs" this morning. I had too much on my mind.

"Are you all right, Renee? You seem really tense."

"I'm fine, Jeff. Just a bad night."

He nodded and moved off. I waited a full fifteen minutes, but when my new friend didn't show, I headed for the path, walking the first hundred yards, and then breaking into a trot.

I lasted longer this time before slowing, and got my breath back faster. Before I knew it, I once again jogged. I'd never completed the mile and a half loop, and once I crossed Joel's bridge—as I now thought of it—found myself in unfamiliar territory. The vegetation grew denser and close to the path. The cooling foliage would be a blessing in the hot summer months.

I walked a second time, and then stopped to listen. Leaves rustling in the light breeze sounded like a person pushing through the bushes. Somewhere in the woods to my right, a twig snapped, as if broken by a careless step. I looked around. I was alone on the path. Very alone. I shivered and gazed into the surrounding trees.

"Is—is anybody there?" I called out. No one answered. I rubbed my arms to warm them from the sudden coolness and erase the goose bumps.

I remembered my concerns about Liz's safety in the park, even though the killer had dismissed the idea of a hit here. I bit my lip and walked on.

Don't be an idiot. There's no one there. It's just some animal—a dog or a cat on the prowl. My mind's in overdrive, that's all.

Still, I walked faster. The rustling sounds continued to keep pace with me. I broke into a jog and looked over my shoulder. No one was there, but I had the strangest, most insane urge to run like a jackrabbit. I forced my legs to maintain a steady pace. I heard a sound as though someone had tripped and fallen. I stopped and peered hard into the greenery.

Get a grip. It's probably some guy who had to take a leak and is too embarrassed to answer.

It seemed like a plausible explanation to me. Then another, more sinister, one crossed my mind.

"Mother? Is that you?"

Silence. Not even the smallest sound of movement came from the woods. I couldn't see, but definitely felt, someone watching me. My pissed off mother? With all those guns?

My breath caught in my throat, and I abandoned all sense of being in control. I ran. The path twisted and turned until finally merging with another track. I spied two joggers about a hundred yards in front of me. I brought my pace down to a walk, breathing heavily. Ahead, the trail ended near the parking lot. I wasted no time and took off, throwing myself into the car and locking the doors.

I closed my eyes and tried to bring my ragged breathing and pounding heart back to normal levels, then leaned my forehead against the steering wheel.

Mental note—do not jog alone again.

A loud rap on the window almost gave me a heart attack. I yelped and jerked my head toward the left. It was Jeff. Heaving a sigh of relief, I rolled down the window.

"Are you all right? You came flying down the path and jumped in the car so fast, I thought maybe you were sick."

"No, I'm fine. Thanks for asking."

He backed away with a slightly embarrassed expression. "Well, if you say so. Sorry. Didn't mean to scare you."

"You didn't. I was thinking and the knocking startled me, that's all."

"Oh, okay. See you tomorrow?"

"Sure, tomorrow."

I started the engine and pulled out, remembering to wave goodbye.

Had there been someone in the woods? If so, who? My mother? Someone else? A rapist? Or was it simply an animal? That made more sense. Or...was I paranoid?

I drove home, refusing to answer the question.

****

"I think Andy's right," Katie said. "You should move in with me until your mother's back in custody."

We were halfway through our lunch at The Golden Hummingbird. For vegan, it was a popular spot. The restaurant was packed, but the high ceilings allowed most of the conversational noise to float upward. Located on a side street just off busy Webster Avenue, the large plate glass windows let in abundant light, and the modern décor gave the place a sleek look. The price was slightly out of my comfort zone, but the food was good.

I'd filled Katie in on Mother's escape and the pillaging of my house, but didn't mention my heebie-jeebies in the park. I'd finally convinced myself I had overreacted.

"The locks have been changed, so I'll be fine. Like I told your brother, Mom would never hurt me."

"I don't know about that. She was pretty pissed at the trial, and the doctor said she cursed you earlier in the day. Offhand, I'd say the Palm Lake Rest Home hasn't been much of a help in curing your mother of anything."

"I know. Once she's back in custody, her lawyer will petition the court for a new sanitarium." The subject matter depressed me, so I changed it. "Let's talk about you. How's Barry? Does he have a last name?"

She laughed. "Of course, he does. If I tell you, are you going to tattle to my brother?"

"Hell no—cross my heart and hope to die." I made a big X on my chest with a finger.

"His name is Barry Blackledge, and I met him at a showing six months ago. God, he is so gorgeous—tall, dark hair, blue, blue eyes, and the sexiest smile this side of heaven."

"You told me that the other day," I reminded her.

She wrinkled her nose and laughed. "Plus, he just got a brand new cherry red sports car. Don't know what kind. Cars confuse me. Guess I should bone up, since Barry loves them. His last one was British or German or something like that. At any rate, we hit it off immediately."

"You said something about him being a motivational speaker and traveling a lot."

"He just got back from a week on the road—somewhere in the Midwest. He called every night."

"When do I get to meet this paragon of manly virtues?"

This time Katie stuck her tongue out before laughing again. "Soon. He said he'd try to come to the Beauregard showing next week. He's out of town again next week, but we had dinner last night at his penthouse condo. Tonight I'm going to dazzle him with my culinary skills."

"Hit the sheets yet?"

"Of course, silly. How about you? Made it yet with my brother?"

I choked on a bite of apple from my fruit salad. "Katie! There's nothing going on between Andy and me. Where would you get that idea?"

"He stayed over last night, didn't he?"

"On the sofa, and because he was worried."

"He could have assigned a patrol car to sit out front or drive by every few minutes." She forked some kind of Spring Roll concoction into her mouth and smiled. "I think he kind of likes you."

Oh, really? Sudden heat warmed my heart. "I think you're kind of nuts."

"I don't know about that. Andy doesn't take just anybody to the gym on a first date."

"Oh yeah, a date at the gym—how romantic." In a weird way, it was. I'd enjoyed myself in spite of the ensuing pain. And I still couldn't shake the image of him in that skimpy swim suit. "I'll let your imagination run wild. He asked me to go with him to the University of Miami today to pick up his registration packet."

"Whoa, baby! A hot time on campus. My brother sure is a smooth operator." She pointed her fork at me. "You owe me a fully detailed report the next time we meet."

"I'm sure it'll have you sitting on the edge of your seat."

She chuckled and glanced at her watch. "Oh, shit, I have to get back. I've got a new client coming in at one-thirty."

Katie finished her meal and tossed down the last of her Chardonnay, then fished in her purse before extracting her wallet and three twenty dollar bills. The Golden Hummingbird was not cheap.

"I'll get it, Katie."

"Nonsense, you're the one who's unemployed.

Have another glass of wine and tell the waiter to keep the change." She rose, slinging the strap of her purse over her shoulder. "Give me a call if you change your mind about bunking in with me, and have a wonderful date with my brother this afternoon."

"Are you aware that it takes forty-two muscles to frown at someone who's pissing you off, but only four to shoot that person the bird and say bite me?"

Katie grinned and exited with a hurried stride. I finished my fruit salad, paid the bill, and sat enjoying a second glass of wine, all the while thinking about this afternoon.

Why had Andy invited me to Miami? And why had I agreed to go? I knew I found him attractive, and being a healthy female, had speculated on his prowess in bed, but that's as far as it went—sheer speculation. Besides, he was Katie's brother—the teasing pain in the ass who'd try to scare us during sleepovers by rapping on the bedroom window and making moaning sounds. Then he'd gone to college, and I'd forgotten about him. God knows, except at the age of ten, I certainly never entertained romantic thoughts about Andrew Jackson way back when.

Andy and romantic thoughts? Lustful, definitely, but romantic? To me romantic always brought to mind, well, romance—as in flowers and candy. I couldn't see Andy presenting me or anyone with a bouquet of daisies or a Whitman's Sampler. Was I breaking new ground here?

Unsure, I finished my wine in a single gulp. The large, boisterous noontime crowd had diminished, and the waiter kept glancing in my direction. Time to go.

A man rising from a table across the room caught my attention. I didn't see his face, but he walked toward the exit, his back ramrod straight, as though angry, and swinging his briefcase. Then, his dining companion also rose. It was Corinne. I did see her face and the furious expression on it.

I grabbed my purse and hurried after her. "Corinne!"

Another couple leaving blocked my path, and by the time I got to the door, she was gone.

Probably just as well. She looked hot enough to fry bacon on her forehead. I'll see her tomorrow at the park.

Seeing Corinne reminded me that Liz was due home tomorrow, and I hoped she'd show up at the yoga studio. Maybe I would suggest having a drink afterward. She'd thawed a little on Wednesday, and I needed to know her—and her routine—better.

I pulled into the driveway and fumbled at the front door with the new key, sliding it in and out several times to file off the rough edges. I moved faster when I heard my land line ringing inside. The door finally opened, and I staggered through. Maybe it was news about Mother. Andy would have called my cell, but the police, Mother's lawyer, and Dr. Reynard didn't have it.

I dumped my purse on the sofa and picked up. "Hello?"

Silence greeted me. "Hello, is anybody there?"

The caller hung up with a soft click.

Chapter Nine

"Damn this traffic," Andy said with a growl. "I should have known late afternoon was a bad time to drive in Miami."

I commiserated with him. The trip down had taken a little over an hour, but now on the way home I-95 crawled with vehicles. In the past hour, we'd moved maybe twenty miles closer to Palm Lake.

"We should have stayed and had dinner while this mess cleared out." Andy looked at me. "I know a nice place in Ft. Lauderdale just off the interstate. Want to give it a try?"

"Sure. I had a fruit salad for lunch. Doesn't last a long time."

He aimed the car for a gap in another lane, making the transition smoothly.

I'd strolled around campus while Andy picked up his paperwork. Located in Coral Gables, the university was a monument to the South Florida culture and atmosphere with palm trees and tropical foliage. The buildings weren't anything special, but students loved it along with the winning athletic teams.

I flinched when Andy's cell phone rang. A ringing phone put me on edge. I'd had several hang-up calls before leaving for Miami.

"Jackson... I'm not surprised... No, I'll tell her. She's with me now... Right." He snapped the phone shut.

"Mother?"

"Patrolman found the stolen car—undamaged except for the hot wiring—parked a block from the bus station."

"The bus station? So, she *has* taken off. God, I'd better call my grandparents if she's headed that way."

"I doubt if she got on a bus."

"Why not?"

"Because she has a hunting rifle. Someone would have noticed. Was it in a case?"

I nodded. "A nice canvas one with lots of padding and a carrying strap." I had a mental image of Mom sauntering down the sidewalk in downtown Palm Lake, carrying a duffle bag loaded with guns and ammo, and a thirty-aught slung over her shoulder. "And no one in the surrounding area noticed this armed woman strolling down the street?"

"Depends on when she did the strolling. Noon, yes, someone would have seen her and remembered. Midnight? Not likely."

We inched our way toward the Golden Glades interchange. At this rate, it would be tomorrow before we got home.

"This is ridiculous." Andy flipped on the turn signal and eased into the far right hand lane. "I'm getting off. Surface streets can't be any worse."

We made much better time and finally pulled into the parking lot of the restaurant a little after seven-thirty. The hostess showed us to a table and handed out menus. When the waiter came by, I ordered a glass of wine, while Andy had a beer.

"Are you all right?" he asked. "You've been uncharacteristically quiet the entire afternoon."

"Just thinking about Mother—wondering where she is, and if she's safe. Hope she hasn't pulled a gun on anyone yet."

"You know, I never knew exactly what your mother was diagnosed with. Is it schizophrenia?"

I bit my lip and nodded.

His hands covered mine sending a zip of energy along my nerves. "We'll find her, Renee. She probably doesn't even realize what she's done. At this moment, your mother may be in the supermarket acting like any other shopper."

"At least she won't have to go to a gun store." The attempt at humor didn't work. My eyes filled with tears and I blinked to drive them away.

"What is it, honey? This is more than just your mother, isn't it?"

The endearment made my heart flutter. "I'm scared. Scared to death I'm just like her. When I was a kid, she either had screaming rages talking to people who didn't exist or walked around like a zombie. It depended on the medication of the month, which didn't leave a whole lot of time for being a wife and mother. Half the time she lived in her own little world. I don't think she was even aware we were in the same house. No wonder Daddy drank. I should have bailed years ago, but stayed for reasons I can't understand."

"You stayed because she's your mother, and you're a nice person." He drew my hand to his lips and kissed it. The flutter intensified. "Honey, if you were schizophrenic, it would have manifested itself by now. The onslaught shows up in the late teens or early twenties."

The waiter brought our drinks. I took a sip of the cool, dry Chardonnay to soothe the frazzled nerves his warm lips had produced. The smooth liquid eased my aching, tear choked throat. We ordered our food, both of us indulging in burgers and fries.

"I'm as messed up as she is, Andy. Look at my track record—all the weird stuff I've done and accused other people of doing. You can't seriously call that normal, can you?"

"You're not at all like her. Your mother has a

disease and a fixation with guns. You recognized you had an anger problem and did something about it. You entered therapy. Both are positive moves."

"Mother never thought she needed help. As far as she was concerned, her actions were perfectly normal. Honest to God, sometimes I think half the world is on Prozac, and the other half should be. There are too many like my mother floating around society."

"What do you do for fun?"

"Fun? Up until last Tuesday, I got up, went to work, came home, ate, watched TV, then went to bed and started the whole thing over again the next day."

He tilted the beer bottle and drank. "No, I mean fun. You know, going out with your friends, having a few drinks, dancing at a club."

I shifted my gaze to my glass, refusing to meet his eyes.

"You do have friends, don't you?"

"Who can have friends when your mother tries to kill your father and does six months in the slammer for domestic violence? What kind of friends could I face when during a minor accident on the interstate, my mother clamors onto the hood of her car brandishing a gun, squeezes off two rounds into the air, and threatens some poor schmuck who made an improper lane change? God only knows what would have happened if I hadn't gotten the gun away from her. Traffic was backed up for miles, and motorists terrified. And don't even start on my high school years. It was just too embarrassing to bring anyone home to meet the folks."

His sister was the lone exception. She'd smiled, acknowledged Mother in zombie state and Dad in a drunken stupor before suggesting we go to her place to study.

"You have Katie." He picked up my hand and

drew it to his lips again. "And you have me."

He knew. He understood. A gush of warmth spread from the pit of my stomach to the tips of my fingers and toes. I had Andy. Did I? Or was he just being nice? Suddenly, I wanted with all my heart to believe I did have him.

I squeezed his hand. "Don't forget the new friends I made through jogging, Jeff and Corinne, maybe Liz, too. I don't know Freddy very well, but I guess I can include her. I find it ironic that it took Joel Wainwright, a total loser, to get me out of the house. If I hadn't been suspicious, I'd have never moved my ass off the sofa, heard a murder planned, and done new things. I enjoy working out at the gym, and will find out about yoga tomorrow night. With the exception of today, I actually like jogging."

"What was so different about today?"

I told him about my attack of nerves in the park.

Andy frowned and released my hand. "I know the spot. To the best of my knowledge, no one has had any problems. I hate to ask this, but are you sure?"

"The whole thing seems so silly now. I let my imagination get the better of me."

His forehead still furrowed. "I wish you'd give up this notion of being a bodyguard. It's going to get you into trouble. So far, there's not one shred of evidence Todd Gorman is trying to kill his wife. If you keep hanging around her like this—especially if she finds it annoying—your actions could be construed as harassment or worse, stalking."

"In other words, my behavior could be classified as that of an irrational, mentally unstable person?"

"I didn't say that!"

"No, you didn't. I did."

"I just have this feeling you're biting off more than you can chew. I don't like it. Something's in the air."

"Like murder?"

He hesitated and tilted the bottle again. "I don't know. I just wish you'd drop it, that's all."

"It's not like I'm hiding in the shrubbery in front of her house with binoculars. And in the long run, you can't keep me from jogging or attending yoga classes with Liz."

"No, I can't. Damn, you're stubborn."

"I know," I said with a laugh.

Our food arrived and we spent the next few minutes eating. I was sick of discussing my problems. I'd come off sounding whiney and a tad pathetic. I didn't want anybody, especially Andy, feeling sorry for me.

"Why law school? Don't you like being a cop anymore?"

"I love my job, but it's taking a toll. I take a giant leap forward by catching the crooks, and then get shoved back two steps by the court system. Overcrowded jails, overworked public defenders, backlogged courts, and trials held as long as two years after the crime drive me nuts. There aren't enough prosecutors, witnesses move or die, and half the time I can't remember details of why I arrested the sons-of-bitches in the first place."

He popped a French fry into his mouth and chewed hard, the muscles of his jaw flexing with the action. I'd never heard Andy sound so angry and dejected.

"Is that why you work out so much?"

"It helps relieve the stress. A lot of cops do it. Still others are in therapy and anger management." He wiped his mouth with a napkin. "Some never do cope and try to find the answer in a bottle."

Anger management—finally a subject I understood. "One of the things I learned in anger management class was that anger leads to anxiety, which leads to more anger, which leads to more anxiety, et cetera. It's a vicious cycle."

He shook his head. "It's the frustration level. We work our asses off to protect and serve, and the courts too often let the bad guys go, so we have to start over again."

"Will you still be in law enforcement after law school?"

"I'd like to be a prosecutor. I could certainly never defend the scum I arrest now."

I hadn't kept up with Andy once he had graduated. "Where did you go to school? Seems Katie told me ages ago, but I can't remember."

"University of Florida. Got a degree in Criminal Justice. Took my Master's, and was thinking about a doctorate, when I applied at the Police Academy."

I finished off my burger before asking, "Did you always want to be a cop?"

"Thought never entered my head until I hung around police stations while researching my master's thesis. Always figured I'd teach. How about you? You go to college?"

I snorted. "You've got to be kidding. I graduated from high school and went straight into the work force. I couldn't leave my parents alone—together. When Daddy finally left, I was the only one making any money, and not much at that. Mother certainly couldn't hold a job longer than a few hours. As long as she was doped up, I didn't worry. All she did was sit on the sofa and watch TV. It was when she went off her meds that trouble came knocking.

"That's part of what worries me now. She took her medication at the sanitarium. She's off them now, and it'll take a few days, but sooner or later, Mother will sober up and get mad."

I crammed the last of my fries into my mouth and washed them down with the remaining wine. Andy did the same and finished his beer.

"I thought of that, too. The first person she

might be mad at is you. Why not stay with Katie for a few days? What can it hurt?"

"Her love life for a start. She's making a romantic dinner for Barry tonight."

He groaned. "Barry—I still haven't checked him out."

I laughed. "Don't bother. If Kate runs true to form, he'll be history in a couple of months."

Andy paid the bill and we left. Traffic flowed on the interstate at a normal pace, and he pulled into my driveway a little after nine-thirty. He insisted on giving the house a quick once over before allowing me to enter. I thought it unnecessary, but liked that he cared.

"Coffee?" I asked, dumping my purse on the kitchen table.

"No, I'd better be heading home. Early duty in the morning."

The phone rang and I jumped. It rang again. I glanced at the answering machine. No messages had been left. I wet my dry lips.

"Aren't you going to answer?" Andy asked on the third ring, shooting me a strange look.

"Oh, yeah, sure. It might be about Mother."

I picked up the cordless receiver. "Hello?" The familiar silence on the other end both scared and pissed me off. "Hello? Is anybody there? This isn't funny! Who's there?"

The caller hung up with the same soft click. Andy yanked the phone from my hand.

"Hello, who is this?" he said in a sharp tone, and then replaced the receiver in the stand. "What was that all about?"

"Oh, someone keeps calling and hanging up."

"Do they say anything?"

"Not a word, dirty or otherwise. No heavy breathing or sinister sounds of any kind. Whoever it is just hangs up."

He frowned. "I don't like this. Could be someone checking to see if you're home, trying to find out if you have a routine. Tomorrow, I'll set up traces on your phone. Make up the sofa. And I'll take that coffee."

"Andy, you don't have to stay. And forget about tracing my calls. I'll unplug the phone, and that'll take care of it."

"Don't argue with me. Has it occurred to you that your mother's meds may have worn off already? In fact, it's possible she concocted this escape and stopped taking her pills days, even weeks ago."

I gave in. Besides, having him in the house sounded like a good idea. "I suppose you're right. When Mom got to feeling better, she'd claim she didn't need them."

"How many of these calls have you had and when did they begin?"

The thought that it was Mother calling had crossed my mind. "That was the fifth. They started about two or three this afternoon when I got back from lunch with Katie."

"Wait here. I'll be right back." He left and returned a minute later with his gun and a penlight, tossing them on the coffee table. "I'll make the bed, you do the coffee."

"This really isn't..."

His expression had changed from concerned to angry and he grasped my shoulders. "For once, would you please just do as I ask without giving me a bunch of shit?"

I gulped, realizing Andy Jackson could be just as stubborn as me.

"Renee, you're driving me nuts. Have you ever considered for one moment, that I might be concerned about you?" His fingers dug into my shoulders, and then he pulled me into his arms. "Dammit, I care. I care a lot. You're a little bit crazy, but that's part of your charm."

Charm. No one had ever used that word in connection with my personality. Safe and secure in his arms, I wanted to cry. Then, he tilted my chin up with his finger, lowered his head, and kissed me.

I responded in the only way possible. I kissed him back. Heat gushed from head to toe.

He broke off the kiss and stepped back, running his hand through his hair.

"Just go make that coffee. Please."

I pointed to the sheets and stuff from last night still folded on the end of the sofa, then headed for the kitchen. I needed a couple of minutes to calm my churning emotions. The kiss had been damned good.

When the coffee was ready, I brought him a mug. He had made up the sofa, and now sat in a chair, watching TV.

"Are you going to sit up all night?"

"No. I'm going to have a couple of cups of coffee to guarantee I won't fall too deeply asleep."

"Do you really think it's Mother and that she'll come back?"

"I have no idea, but refuse to let you stay alone. Now, go to bed unless you have a burning desire to watch *Cops*."

I opened my mouth to send a pithy reply when the phone rang.

"Let it ring," he said.

"But it might be about Mother."

"Then they'll leave a message."

The machine picked up after the fifth ring. A soft click followed my announcement. The caller had hung up. Andy flipped open his cell and dialed.

"This is Detective Jackson. I want any messages for Miss Renee Ryan concerning her mother to be forwarded to this number." He waited a few seconds. "Thanks, Sergeant."

He closed his phone, rose, and unplugged mine.

"There. Now maybe we'll get some rest tonight."

"You certainly do take over." I still maintained Mother would never harm me, but admitted to having doubts.

"I certainly do. Now, go to bed."

I flounced into the bedroom and shut the door, then undressed and slid under the sheets. I was only a little irritated with him. Did his brusque tone indicate he regretted the kiss? Had he acted out of impulse or true desire to plant one on my lips?

I tossed and turned for over an hour, unable to still my racing mind. Through the closed door, I heard the muted TV, and then it went silent. The sliver of light from the living room peeking under the door finally disappeared. Andy had gone to bed.

I dozed fitfully, until awakening with a snap. My clock read two-fifteen. Had I heard something? I propped myself up on my elbows and listened. My bedroom overlooked the back yard with its lovely old hydrangeas, oleander, and citrus trees. I'd left the window open, but only the sound of the wind rustling through the foliage came to my ears. All was quiet. I lay down again, mentally chastising myself for being a ninny.

Then I heard it—the soft scrape of a footstep on the patio followed a moment later by a scratching noise near the back of the house. Was it Mother trying to get in?

My heart pounded and my breath threatened to choke me. I flew out of bed, grabbed a robe, and ran into the living room. The glow from the streetlight outside showed Andy was already up, gun in hand and shoving the small flashlight into his jeans pocket.

"Andy?"

"I know, I heard it, too. Someone's at the back door. Call 9-1-1, and then lock yourself in the bathroom."

I called in the emergency, giving the operator the pertinent information, and then headed for the kitchen. I had no intention of hiding from my own mother. The LED clocks on all the appliances gave off a surprising amount of light allowing me to see. The back door stood wide open, and Andy was nowhere in sight.

I hesitated, and then stepped over the threshold and onto the patio. The backyard was lit with muted tier lights in all the flowerbeds.

"Andy? Andy, where are you?" I whispered.

He appeared from behind a clump of hydrangeas.

"I thought I told you to stay inside."

I ignored him. "Did you find anyone?"

"No. By the time I got out here, whoever it was had left. I found some footprints around those bushes next to the fence. Maybe the prowler came and went that way. How agile is your mother?"

"Are you kidding? That fence is six feet high. Nobody's that athletic."

"There's also some kind of stone bench nearby to give her a boost. Did you call?"

"Yes."

"Then we'd better get back inside."

Two squad cars arrived, minus sirens, thank God. I sat in the kitchen sipping a bottle of water while Andy filled them in on the details. The policemen searched the yard and surrounding area, but found just what I expected—nothing. They finally left a little before three-thirty.

"Go back to bed, Renee. I'll stay up. I doubt if she'll return, but if she does and sees lights on, she may think twice."

"There's no way I can go to sleep now. What's on TV?"

"Bad movies and news."

"I'll take bad movies for two hundred, Alex," I

quipped, curling up on the sofa. I could play the game of lightening the mood.

"Bad movies it is, and don't forget to put your answer in the form of a question." He sat next to me.

His feet and chest were bare, and there was something about his jeans hanging low on his hips that was sexier than hell. And of course, who could overlook those ridged abs? Certainly not me. All that exercise had paid off.

He reached over and pulled me close to his side, cupping my chin in his hand. Without so much as a word, he kissed me, his lips soft, and briefly demanding on mine before lifting.

"Try to get some sleep. I'll be here."

Get some sleep? Was he kidding? The urge to grab him by the hair and bring those lips back to mine raged. Instead, I nestled my head into his shoulder, licked my tingling lips, and wrapped my arms around his waist. Never had I felt so safe.

****

I awoke to the sounds of sizzling bacon and coffee churning through the machine, along with the mouthwatering aromas accompanying them. I lay on the sofa, covered with the blanket. My watch told me the time was six-thirty. I pushed the covers off and sat up, rubbing my hands over my face. I couldn't believe how soundly I'd slept.

Guess having Andy as a pillow helped.

I rose and padded out into the kitchen. Andy stood at the stove draining the cooked bacon on a paper towel. He looked up and smiled.

"Good morning, sunshine. Didn't mean to wake you."

I sniffed appreciatively. "That smells fabulous. I'm starving." I poured a cup of coffee. "Can I eat and still jog?"

"You're going after yesterday?"

"I only jog a little. Most of the time I walk."

"That's not answering my question." He cracked four eggs into a bowl and whisked.

"I won't be alone this time. If Jeff and Corinne don't show, I'll come home. I doubt if my mother was anywhere near the park. How would she know I've taken up jogging?" I waved a hand. "I was just imagining things."

"I don't suppose anything I say will change your mind, so be careful and stay with someone." He poured the eggs into the pan and used a wooden spatula to stir them. "Toast?"

"No, thanks." I glanced at the clock. "Aren't you running late?"

"I called in and requested a later shift. I have some things I want to check out. Are you also going to the yoga class tonight?"

"Of course. And I won't be alone. Even if Liz doesn't come, Corinne probably will, and I doubt I'll be the only one in the class. Lighten up, Andy. Mother doesn't know about this either."

He spooned the eggs onto two plates along with the bacon. I grabbed a fork and sat at the table. He set the plate in front of me, and then seated himself.

"By the way, I'll need your spare key," he said biting off a piece of bacon.

I stopped with my fork halfway to my mouth. "Why?"

"Short memory? I told you last night, if you won't move out until your mother's back in custody, then I move in. You were damned glad to have me here at two in the morning."

Sighing, I realized this was not an argument I'd win nor did I want to. Having Andy around for the long haul sounded like a damned fine idea.

"It's on a key ring in a box of detergent in the laundry room. I didn't like leaving it outside so Mother could find it and figured if she did break in, she'd never think to look for a key there."

He shook his head. "I must be sleep deprived, because in a weird way that makes sense."

I finished my breakfast, then did the dishes and donned my jogging clothes, including a new pair of cross-trainers. I left Andy reading the paper and enjoying a third cup of coffee.

"Don't forget to plug my phone back in before you leave," I called from the foyer before heading out the door.

I daydreamed about Andy, last night's kisses, and those warm arms surrounding me all the way to the park, and breathed a sigh of relief when I saw both Jeff and Corinne warming up. In spite of my confident words to Andy, I harbored an uneasy feeling.

"Hi, everyone," I greeted.

Freddy exited a dark gray Toyota Camry and joined us. "Hi, Renee! Isn't this a groovy morning? There's not a cloud in the sky. I, like, just love early mornings, don't you?"

From the other side of Jeff, Corinne made choking sounds.

"Adore them," I said quickly. "Missed you yesterday, Corinne."

"Yeah, I was in a funk and slept in. Looks like my stinking ex-husband is going to get his way," she answered in a bitter tone.

"Why? What happened?" Once my curiosity is piqued, I have to know the facts.

"The son of a bitch declared bankruptcy on me, and is petitioning the court to lower the alimony payments to damn near nothing. If he wins, I'll end up living in a cardboard box."

"What a bummer," Freddy said in a high-pitched tone. "I've never been married, so I can't, like, sympathize, but I'd be mad, too."

"Yeah, whatever," Corinne replied in a tight voice.

"You could always get a job," Jeff said.

"Doing what? I'm not trained for anything, and refuse to have my employment mantra be, 'you want fries with that?' Besides, the asshole and I had an agreement when we got married, he'd make the money, and I could spend it. I'll be damned if I let him get by with screwing me now."

"Wow, no wonder you looked so damned mad yesterday."

She paused in her warm-up routine to gaze at me, frowning. "Yesterday? When did you see me yesterday?"

"I was at The Golden Hummingbird. You were with some guy and looked furious. By the time I got up, you'd disappeared."

She resumed stretching. "Oh, yeah, that was my lawyer. He bought lunch in the hope food would soften me up for the bad news that Mark could win this round. Are you guys ready to roll?"

"I am," Jeff said. "Renee? Freddy?"

I could have used a little more time, but wanted to make sure they were with me in the woody area.

"I'm ready."

"Me, too," Freddy chimed in.

She hadn't done a single warm-up.

I hung with them most of the way, including the woods. I finally slowed, only slightly winded, to a leisurely stroll when the parking lot came into sight.

Our newest jogging companion stopped a few feet away and answered her ringing cell phone. She jerked it off the clip at her waist, listened for a couple of seconds, and then frowned. She lowered her voice, but I heard her say, "I said I'd deal with it. These things take time."

She snapped the phone shut. "I've gotta run. See you Monday." Freddy turned, trotted toward her car, and waved goodbye as she drove off.

During the cool down exercises, I asked Corinne,

"You going to yoga tonight?"

"Sure am. After the week I've had, I need all the relaxation I can get. And you?"

"I'll be there. Sure you don't want to join us, Jeff? I really did see men there the other day."

He laughed. "Not my thing. I relax in front of the TV watching a good ball game." He glanced at his watch. "Damn, I've gotta go. See you on Monday."

"See you," Corinne said with a wave, and then turned to me. "What's on your agenda for today? Up for lunch?"

As much as I liked Corinne, I wasn't in the mood to listen to her slice and dice her slimy ex-husband. Besides, in a way I agreed with Jeff. Corinne might not be able to make a fortune, but she could help herself.

And of course, there was Mother. Eventually, new friends ask about family. I didn't want to talk about her. Mental illness, even a generation removed, drives friends away.

"Wish I could, but I have a bunch of personal stuff to do today. I'll see you tonight. Maybe we can have a drink afterward."

"Suits me." She walked to her car, got in, and drove off with a wave of her hand.

When I returned home, Andy had left but heeded my request to plug the phone back in. My answering machine showed three messages. I wondered how many hang-ups had occurred. I punched the button and listened to message number one.

"You fucking bitch! I not only didn't get the partnership, but got fired this morning, too. I hope you're satisfied. I swear to God, you won't get away with this. You'll be sorry! Just wait!"

I rocked with laughter. Finally! Joel got what he deserved. His threats didn't scare me. He was nothing more than a bag of hot air. I went on to the next message.

"Miss Ryan, this is Loretta Downs from the Human Resources department at Carson Electronics. Your final separation package is ready and may be picked up at your convenience. Please give me a call at 555-6045 so I might know when to expect you. Thank you, and have a good day."

Have a good day? Was she serious? Was that the standard message given to recently fired or laid off people? *Have a good day?* I snorted and punched the button again.

"Good morning, Miss Ryan. This is Dr. Reynard. We have no news of your mother, but wonder if you would be so kind as to come to the sanitarium today. I've been informed by Mrs. Ryan's attorney that she will not be returning to this facility when she is finally—ah-that is, she won't be returning. Her personal effects must be packed under the supervision of a relative or a surrogate. Thank you."

Swell, now I'd have to go all the way out to the Palm Lake Rest Home and cart Mother's crap back here. And what the hell kind of personal effects did he mean? She only had a few clothes and some books. As far as I was concerned, the other inmates could have them. I sighed and decided to go. I wanted to give Reynard a piece of my mind anyway.

I called Carson Electronics and told them I'd be there in an hour or so, then grabbed a bottle of water from the fridge. I gulped the cold liquid and went outside to view the flower beds where Andy had seen the footprint.

I peered at the sandy soil, barely able to follow the faint outline of a shoe. Damn, Andy must have the eyes of an owl to see it even with the flashlight and in the meager glow given off by the tier lights.

Returning inside to a ringing phone, I hesitated and bit my lip, then snatched the phone from the holder. I refused to be intimidated.

"Hello?"

Click!

I slammed the phone down.

Chapter Ten

All visitors to Carson Electronics report to the receptionist who then informs the employee they have a guest. No way would I allow Angie to smirk while I waited. I intended to bypass the bimbo and slide directly into Loretta's office in Building Two. What were they gonna do—fire me?

I gazed toward the main doors ready to flip my replacement the bird, when I stopped. Angela Peabody was not at the desk. My friend Susan answered the phones. She worked in what I called the total-waste-of-talent department officially referred to as Administrative Services, sorting and delivering the mail, and keeping the break rooms full of supplies. I changed direction and walked in.

"Hi, Renee, here for your package?"

"Forget the package. Where's you-know-who?"

Susan grinned and cast her eyes down the hallway toward my ex-boss's office. She leaned forward and lowered her voice.

"Gone. Yesterday. Canned like a tuna."

I laughed. Angie was dumber than a box of rocks, but even this had to be some kind of record.

"Details, I crave details."

"It started the minute you walked out the door. About ten o'clock I got a frantic phone call from Mr. James asking me to come over and help Angie with the phones. Said you'd refused to cooperate and had split. That's how I discovered you'd been fired."

"Damned right I didn't cooperate. Why should I? What happened?"

The phone rang. Susan answered and

transferred the call efficiently, then turned back to me.

"Well, I spent all freaking day with her, and I swear to God she never did understand that she had to put the caller on hold before hitting the transfer button, and then the number. Half the time she routed the person to the wrong extension. In between calls, she cursed you up one side and down the other. And then there was the incident with the delivery gate."

The driveway to the shipping and receiving department was gated. All traffic was supposed to stop by reception, sign in, and get an authorization slip before continuing to the warehouse. The drivers spoke through an intercom to the receptionist who activated the gate. It was a recent addition after a thief made off with a bunch of electronic gizmos last year.

"Let me guess—she told them to just go on back?"

Susan nodded. "It was after office hours Tuesday evening, and I guess she wanted to leave. If it hadn't been for the security guard asking to see authorization, Carson Electronics could have been minus a few more components."

"I'll bet the big guy wasn't happy about that," I said, referring to the owner of the company.

"Furious." She stopped to answer three phone lines.

Angie's actions should have been grounds for immediate dismissal, but since she'd held on another twenty-four hours, I guessed James had intervened.

"What next?" I asked.

"The final straw came yesterday. Mr. Carson had a conference call scheduled. He asked Angie to set it up. She didn't have a clue, so called me, but I was re-supplying one of the break rooms and didn't talk to her. She tried doing it herself. Botched it.

"Mr. Carson was livid. Came charging down here wanting to know what she used for brains, who had decided *she* was your replacement, and on and on."

I chuckled. Mr. Carson had liked me, always smiling and saying good morning when he came into the office. "How did you find out about all this?"

"Security shift change at noon. One was clocking in, the other out. They heard and saw everything. At any rate, Angie shed a few tears, pouted, and suggested to Mr. Carson that if she could speak with him privately in his office, she'd make it worth his while."

My mouth dropped open. "She propositioned him in the lobby?"

Susan nodded. "Yep. He fired her on the spot. She started yelling, and James came out of his office to see what the hell was going on. There was nothing he could do, of course. She was history. Rumor has it James was reprimanded and written up for hiring outside channels."

I crowed with laughter. HR had the last word on hiring and all prospective employees had to go through the process even if it was just for show.

"This is too funny. Do you have the job permanently now?"

"Not yet, but I have the feeling if you want it back, it's yours." She answered the phone again, hung up, and then hesitated before saying, "The security guard also said that when he escorted Angie from the building to her car, she kept up a foul-mouthed litany against you. She'd get even; you'd get yours—that sort of thing."

Even though her words echoed Joel's, I waved a hand still chuckling. "Phooey! That silly bimbo doesn't scare me. What's she going to do? Beat me to death with her silicone tits?" Then an uneasy thought occurred to me. "Sue, when did all this go down?"

"I'm not sure. It was sometime after lunch. I was in the middle of delivering the mail when I got word to man the phones. Somewhere around one or two, I guess."

And a little while later my hang up calls began. Maybe it wasn't my mother after all. Maybe it was Angie—or my ex-boss—out for a little revenge.

"So, do you want to come back?"

"Not really, but I'll talk to HR. A raise would help."

Susan announced me to Loretta, and I walked to Building Two. Sure enough, she offered me my old job back with a dollar an hour raise.

I was tempted—very tempted, and a few days ago wouldn't have hesitated, but that was then. Somewhere along the line, I'd changed. I could do better than this. Perhaps it was seeing the campus or listening to Andy explain how at age thirty-seven, he wanted to send his life in a new direction. I couldn't pinpoint it, but realized I wanted more.

And then, there was Liz. I'd made keeping her safe a priority, and could only do that by not having a nine-to-five job. Besides, I'd still have the same asshole for a boss, and he would probably make my life a living hell.

I thanked Loretta, but turned it down suggesting Susan was the best candidate for the job, and then left Carson Electronics for the last time. Never had freedom felt so good.

****

I ate an insipid salad at a fast food restaurant before heading to the edge of the Everglades and the Palm Lake Rest Home. The building was utilitarian. The three stories rose in boring stucco walls punctuated by windows too small for patients to climb through. I entered through a large door with top to bottom shatterproof glass. The staff had emphasized the feature when mother was admitted. I approached the reception desk and told the woman attending it my name.

Dr. Reynard saw me immediately, no doubt worried I'd sue over my mother's disappearance. He should. The thought had scurried through my mind.

"Miss Ryan, how good of you to come so quickly."

"Your message specified today. What's the rush? Running out of room?"

He tried to laugh as though I'd made a joke. Ha-ha. Nothing funny about the situation. I had a hell of a lot more to say.

"No, we just thought that since your mother will not return to us, that you'd like her belongings. The longer they're left here, the more likely they are to become lost."

"You mean stolen."

"I mean lost, Miss Ryan." His voice turned frosty.

"All right, lost if that pleases you. This place has a habit of losing things—like my mother."

"I can assure you this is the first time such a thing has happened. Other than the outburst I discussed with you the other night, Mrs. Ryan had shown marked improvement."

"Mother is good. She told you exactly what you wanted to hear. My guess is she went off her meds a long time ago and just waited for a chance to split."

"That's not possible. The nurses reported she took her medication as scheduled."

"She conned them, too." I leaned forward in my chair. "And why the hell was the Goddammed door open? All outside doors are supposed to be locked. The Palm Lake Rest Home accepted funds from the state to house and treat my mother. You fucked up. I plan to report this sanitarium and you to whatever state agencies I can and get your licenses revoked."

Dr. Reynard rose, a scowl on his face. "Please

don't do that, Miss Ryan. It could ruin my reputation and that of this institution."

"Yeah? On just one letter? Or am I merely the latest in a long line of complaints?"

"Miss Ryan, I'd hate to see this get ugly. And I have very good lawyers."

"And if I were *you*, I wouldn't bring up the subject of lawsuits."

"What happened was a grievous mistake, but as a professional, I think my opinion on your mother's progress will be upheld by the various boards." He picked up the phone and punched in a number. "Mrs. Shafer, would you escort Miss Ryan to room three-oh-four? Thank you."

He hung up and we glared at each other, speechless until a woman entered his office a few seconds later.

"Good day, Miss Ryan," he said in a crisp tone, dismissing me.

"Nothing good about it, *Dr.* Reynard. Oh and, remember that Mother broke into my home the night she escaped and took her guns back. She may have been angry with me, but I'll bet there's a special place in her heart for you, too. If I were you, I'd walk real fast to my car after work."

I whirled leaving him open-mouthed and followed the woman down the hall to the elevator. I doubted if Mother skulked in the 'Glades waiting for an opportunity to drill Reynard, but it gave the fraud something to think about.

If he's such a great psychiatrist, let him deal with his own high anxiety for a while.

The ride to the third floor was silent. We turned left when the doors opened and passed a nurse's station. Mrs. Shafer stopped, unlocked the door to Mother's room, and walked in.

"As you can see, we have a couple of boxes for you to use and your mother's suitcases. When you're ready to leave tell the nurse, and she'll contact me. I have to check and make sure nothing unauthorized is being taken."

I sent her a withering glare. What she meant, of course, was make sure I didn't rob them blind. And people thought I was paranoid.

"What the hell would I take? I'd look a tad suspicious toting the bed down the hall. I wouldn't want any of this crap anyway."

The woman didn't reply, but left closing the door behind her.

I shrugged, yanked open the closet door, and grabbed what little hung there, tossing them on the bed—tops, jeans, slacks, a couple of pairs of sandals, sneakers, and a few t-shirts. I threw them in the luggage then did the same with the items in the dresser drawers. I decided to leave the books in the bookcase. They were all paperback thrillers and mysteries. The tattered and torn covers told me they'd made the rounds of various patients for years.

Just what Mom needed—murder and mayhem. What were these idiots thinking allowing her to read this shit when she has a track record of violence?

I opened the nightstand drawer. It was empty save for a Bible. I was pretty sure Mother had never cracked the cover on that. I double-checked the closet, including the shelves, but found nothing. Then, knowing my mother, I lifted the mattress. I discovered a bunch of wadded up tissues near the headboard, and carefully opened one. Two pills lay nestled in the folds. I counted the bundles—ten in all.

Yeah, Asshole Reynard, she was taking her meds all right.

Even I knew the drill. I always stood by until she swallowed. She'd obviously hidden them under her tongue until the nurse left, and then spit them out. I shook my head. Maybe I *should* sue for major incompetence.

I tucked the pills into a zippered compartment of my purse. If a lawsuit did occur, the DNA would be a clincher. I then raised the mattress further and saw a notebook perfectly centered on the box springs. I slipped it out, let the mattress fall back, and opened the cover. It was a diary of some sort, the last entry being the day before she escaped.

I closed it and dropped it in my purse, too. It was probably something Reynard would confiscate, and I wanted to read what Mother had to say. The notebook wasn't big, maybe six by nine inches, and didn't contain much writing after almost three years. I searched the room again and finally found two more hidden behind the bookcase. They joined the other one in my bag.

Good old Mother. I can always count on her being sneaky.

When I was certain I had all I wanted, I approached the nurse's desk and told her I had finished. She nodded, picked up the phone, and called Mrs. Shafer who showed up a few minutes later.

"I didn't need the boxes. I don't know if the books belong to you or not, but keep them. The other inmates might enjoy them."

"Patients, Miss Ryan. They are called patients." She searched the suitcases, but ignored my purse. Incompetent right down to her toenails. "All right, you may leave. Just sign this."

She handed me a clipboard with a release form saying I had everything that belonged to Mom. I signed eager to finally get out of this dump.

I tossed the suitcases into the trunk of my car and roared out of the parking lot. I wanted to get home and see what Mother had written.

****

I sat at the kitchen table with diary number one,

a bottle of water, and opened the cover. The first entry was about three days after she entered the sanitarium. I skimmed the first paragraph, which gloated at how she had conned the extra notebook from the orderly. Reynard wanted her to keep a journal he could read on a regular basis. Mother had other ideas. That she'd kept a second, more personal diary didn't surprise me in the least.

The written words sent a chill down my spine.

"I blame my thankless daughter for this. First of all she took the gun away from me. I just wanted to scare the stupid asshole who cut me off. I banged his bumper a little to get him to stop. She told the judge I shot at him. Other witnesses said it, too. I didn't. I shot in the air. They're all a bunch of liars, and out to get me. I'll teach them. It may take a while, but I'll get even."

The next passage was relatively calm, describing the sanitarium and her sessions with Dr. Reynard. Another rage filled entry followed. She directed her anger toward some group session member who advocated gun control. Not a good subject to bring up with my mother around.

And so the pattern went—an angry entry, a calm one, and then back to anger again. I'd bet the journal she turned into Reynard didn't read like this. Yet, I noticed that as time passed, the entries were less confrontational.

I spent most of the afternoon reading, then skipped ahead to the last diary. This was the one that would count.

Sure enough, the entries that mentioned leaving began about ten days prior to the breakout. Even her outbursts in group and in Dr. Reynard's office were calculated. She knew they'd sedate her, and outlined a plan for pretending to sleep, and acting groggy in the TV room. The entry also indicated the outside door was chronically left unlocked in violation of the rules. Staff used it as a short cut to the parking lot. She'd even taken the time of day into consideration—shift change.

She was probably out the door the instant the nurse left the room. And the incoming staff wouldn't be aware Mother was supposed to be there.

I had to hand it to her—the damned thing was brilliant. She'd have made a hell of a thriller writer, or an actress, although taking direction wouldn't have been her strong suit.

Mother covered a lot of subject matter in the diaries some of which went back to her childhood. She mentioned her happy places—a tree house, the loft of her grandfather's barn up in Ocala, and her favorite times of the year, which God forbid, included hunting season.

The last tickled a corner of my memory. I remembered my grandmother talking about how every November, my grandfather would take a bunch of buddies up to a cabin in the hills of Northeast Alabama. They'd hunt deer, swap stories, and drink beer for a week. I wondered if Mom had ever gone along, and would she think about those happy places when she finished harassing me?

I made a mental note to call Gran this evening after yoga and find out. I had to tell them about Mom anyway.

"And speaking of yoga, you'd better get ready," I said to myself.

I changed into a pair of jogging shorts and a t-shirt, gathered my mat, and headed for Barnard's School of Whatever. My mini-vacation was over. Liz was due back. I hoped she showed up tonight. Time was running out.

****

I paused at the front entrance to the school and scanned the parking lot again. I didn't see Liz's car. Damn. I walked through the entrance and saw

Corinne in the lobby.

"Hi, Renee, you ready to bend like a willow?"

"Provided the wind bending the willow isn't a hurricane."

She laughed. "The class is down this hallway."

I followed her and peeked through the door of a room with a class already in session, then paused to gape. A woman lay on her stomach, arms outstretched, with her feet flat on the floor on either side of her head. Her body resembled a perfect "O".

"I don't need to be that flexible," Corinne whispered.

"I didn't think that was anatomically possible."

Corinne pulled on my arm. "Come on. My back hurts just looking at her."

We found the classroom, paid the instructor, signed in, and headed for a space in the far corner against the back wall. I didn't want anyone viewing my behind. I spread out my mat and sat down. Corinne did the same.

"What now?" I asked.

Corinne shrugged. "I guess we wait."

I glanced at the door just in time to see Liz walk by.

Oh, thank God, she's here. She got back safe.

In spite of the time factor, a nagging fear the killer might fulfill the contract in Los Angeles had hovered in my mind for two days. Mother's predicament had kept me from obsessing and there had been no news reports of a South Florida socialite dying in California.

Corinne cast a quick glance around the room. "At least Frightful Freddy isn't here."

"She wants to carpool."

"Oh, God. She gives me a royal pain, and I swear if she shows up I'm leaving. Drives me crazy."

"She can get on a person's nerves," I admitted.

"There's something about her that just isn't

right. It's like she's playing a part. I don't trust her."

I laid out my yoga mat. Corinne's words hit a nerve. Freddy asked a lot of questions, and they came in such rapid fire succession I tended to answer just to shut her up.

Could she have ulterior motives for hooking up with us? Maybe she's a thief who chooses her victims from exercise venues. Our presence guaranteed a routine. Maybe a confederate robbed people while she kept him or her up to date on who was where. Hell, I even told her the general area where I live.

I shook off a growing sense of uneasiness. Maybe Corinne was still pissed about her ex, and Freddy had come along at a stressful time.

"I'll tell you something else," Corinne said in a low tone. "I stopped by the bookstore in the Palm Lake Mall, asking if she was there and guess what? They'd never heard of her."

"Maybe she works at another mall. Lotsa Books is also located in a strip mall on Federal."

"Maybe, but I think she's lying."

I ignored the uncomfortable shiver crawling up my spine. So, Freddy might have lied about where she worked. I'd been known to exaggerate my jobs from time to time. And why was Corinne checking her out? I put it down to the fact Corinne just didn't like the poor woman.

Our instructor arrived and stepped onto a small stage at the front of the room. She had short, blonde hair, a wide smile and a boyish figure.

"Hi, my name is Wendy, and I'll be your instructor this evening. How many of you are here for the first time?" Five of the fifteen people raised their hands. "Wonderful! I'll show you the asanas, and you can go at your own pace. Before you know it, you'll be holding those poses for more than two seconds." Her laugh bubbled.

"You know, if she got any cheerier, I'd have to

kill her," Corinne whispered.

I stifled a chuckle as two late comers wedged themselves next to Corinne and the wall. A third woman scrunched into the row in front of me.

"Everybody stand."

Corrine and I clamored to our feet.

"We'll begin with a few breathing exercises."

For the next hour, I learned how to breathe. I wasn't limber enough to do all the poses correctly, but hey, a mountain climber doesn't begin with Everest.

Wendy had names for the positions, but I lost track of them, although we did something called Downward Facing Dog several times, and I thought I might have thrown my back out on a seated twisting pose going by the ridiculous name of Half Lord of the Fishes. I swear to God, something popped, but since I still had feeling in my legs, figured it was nothing serious.

"Everybody stand," Wendy called out. "We will now do a balancing asana, the Tree Pose. Fold your hands, palms together in front of your chest. Stand with your feet under your hips, and slowly shift your weight to the right foot. Now, carefully lift the left foot off the floor. Bending the knee, place the sole against the upper, inner right thigh. Keep both hips facing the front. Beginners, if you can't reach the upper thigh, place the sole on your leg above, but not on, the knee."

I inched my foot toward the upper thigh, but wobbled dangerously and quickly lowered it. I closed my eyes, breathed deeply, concentrated, and tried again. When I re-opened them, I had tilted toward Corinne. Before I could react, my Tree Pose met the Happy Lumberjack.

I fell into Corinne who yelped and fell against the woman next to her. She also cried out and staggered into the lady beside her. Mercifully, the wall stopped the domino effect. The entire class ceased posing and stared.

I lay on top of Corinne, my face radiating heat like a sun about to go supernova.

"Oh, God, I am so sorry. Is anybody hurt?" I scrambled to my feet.

"I'm fine, Renee."

The other two women assured me they were all right, and Wendy quipped, "Guess we'll have to work on that balance thing."

The class laughed and I wanted to sink through the floor.

Wendy clapped her hands for attention. "Our time is almost up. Let's begin the relaxation portion of the evening to allow our bodies to assimilate all the information it has received tonight. If you will, lie on your back and assume the Corpse Pose."

The Corpse Pose? Sounded like a winner to me.

When we finished, I rolled up my mat and apologized to the ladies again, who assured me it wasn't the first time such a thing had happened, nor would it be the last.

With those comforting words, Corinne and I left. In the lobby, I spotted Liz talking with another group of people. Rude or not, I sailed right up.

"Liz, hi, how was Los Angeles?"

"Hi, Renee, Corinne. L.A. was L.A.—crowded and smoggy, but worthwhile. How was your first yoga class?"

Corinne laughed. "Renee and I were just going to have a drink. Care to join us? I'll tell you all about the graceful Renee."

Actually, I hadn't mentioned anything about drinks yet, but didn't begrudge Corinne inviting Liz. The people she'd been speaking to drifted away.

"I suppose I have time for a glass of wine. My husband left for Boston this afternoon, so no one is waiting for me at home."

Her words concerned me. Liz was safe as long as Todd stayed home. According to the conversation I overheard, he'd hit the road to establish an alibi.

We exited the building. Liz stopped and looked around the parking lot, then pushed the alarm button on her key ring. The headlights of her Lexus parked by a light pole blinked.

"Wow, you're careful," Corinne said. "Do you always check out the parking lot before heading for the car?"

"You bet. A friend of mine got mugged about five years ago. She'd parked under a light, but didn't look around. The bastard nailed her before she got to the car. Where did you park?"

Corinne pointed to a space in front of the building, while I had to admit to being in a darker area. It had still been light when I arrived.

"Where do we want to go?" I asked.

"There's a place called Bottoms Up just down the road," Liz said. "It's sports oriented, but nice."

I followed both women to the bar and parked near a lamppost. The Friday night crowd had packed the place, but we found a table.

"I'm starving," I said. "I didn't think it was a good idea to eat before a class." I opened the menu. "What do you recommend?"

"The burgers are good. So are the wings," Liz replied.

A waiter came by and we ordered wine. Liz and I opted for a salad, but Corinne went for the burger.

"So, how did you like your first yoga class?" Liz asked.

"It was all right," I said.

Corinne laughed and told Liz about my gaff. "If she'd yelled 'timber,' I might have stood a chance."

Liz chuckled. "It's happened before."

"That's what the one lady said. It just figures I'd be the one to do it."

Our drinks arrived. We clinked glasses.

"To new friends," I toasted.

"Here, here," Corinne said.

Liz said nothing, but smiled.

"So, Liz, how often do you jog?" Corinne asked.

"Every weekday, weather permitting. When it rains, I work out." She made a face. "I'm not a big fan of the gym, but try not to backslide."

We spent the time until our food was served discussing the merits of gym work outs.

"I need a gym," Corinne said taking a bite of her burger. "What's the name of yours again, Renee?"

"Fitness Forever. It's pretty good. I haven't been a member long."

"I probably can't afford it anyway if Mark the Shark gets his way."

"Who's Mark the Shark?" Liz asked, nibbling on her salad.

Corinne told Liz about her trials and tribulations with her ex while I chowed down. I wasn't learning much about Liz's routine, but she seemed to like being with us and that's what counted. I needed her to trust me—and fast.

"I'm so lucky," Liz said when Corinne finally ran out of venom. "My husband, Todd, is wonderful. He travels a lot, but I think that makes coming home so much nicer." A wistful tone crept into her voice.

I choked and wanted to puke. *Wonderful? The slimy son of a bitch wants you dead.*

I wondered what her reaction would be if she knew the truth. It also hammered home the fact that sooner or later, I had to find a way to inform her. Today was Friday. More than a week had passed since I'd overheard the conversation. How long would the killer wait to strike?

We paid the bill and paused in the parking lot.

"This was fun," Corinne said. "We should do it again."

Suzanne Rossi

"Maybe we can do lunch some day," I suggested.

"Maybe," Liz said, getting into her car.

Corinne and I separated and waved. Liz pulled out first, taking a right. Corinne followed. So did I. A few blocks later, Liz turned left as did Corinne. I had allowed several cars to get between us, and although I should have continued straight, I also turned. I saw the Lexus bear right where the road split. Corinne went left on Plumbago Avenue. It led directly to City Park. I remembered Corinne saying she lived in a condo near there.

Liz's car was almost out of sight, and I had only a couple of cars behind me. Following her would be harder. The stoplight flashed to red and Liz stopped. I accelerated slowly when it went green again, and allowed another car between us. Several minutes later, I had to give up surveillance. Liz turned into a gated community. I headed for home.

Now, I know where she lives. I can hang farther back next time.

Another glass of wine, and an early night was just what the doctor ordered, provided it wasn't Reynard, of course. I opened the front door, juggled the mail, and slipped into the foyer, then flipped on the light in the living room, dropping my purse on the sofa.

My mail contained the usual assortment of junk and magazines. I silently cursed the mailman. Why couldn't he just put the envelopes on top of the magazines instead of inside them? I hated shaking them free from the slick pages. Sure enough several dropped out.

"Dammit," I muttered.

I bent over to retrieve them with an exasperated sigh.

The picture window behind me shattered into a thousand pieces as two loud bangs ripped through the night.

152

Chapter Eleven

Andy, Detective Santos, and several policemen arrived within minutes of my call. Andy and the cops I didn't mind. Given my last encounter at the station when I'd reported the murder for hire plot, Santos gave me a royal pain.

"Are you all right?" Andy asked.

The fear written on his face mirrored what I felt. He immediately gave me a hug and kissed the top of my head. My fear subsided somewhat, but not my trembling. I was both scared by the situation and exhilarated by his actions.

"I'm fine. Just shaken."

His eyebrows rose and his lips curved in a small smile. "Not stirred?"

Oh, I was stirred all right, but chose to go along with his attempt to lighten the moment.

"I am the perfect martini."

He hugged me again and this time his lips found my forehead.

"How many shots did you hear?" Detective Santos asked.

I stepped away from Andy and turned my attention to Santos. "Two, I think, although I don't recall identifying them as shots at the time. It all happened so fast. The window shattered and tires squealed as someone took off," I replied.

"And then what did you do?" He sounded bored, as if he had better things to do.

His attitude pissed me off, so I answered in a tight voice. "I crawled to the sofa for my purse, grabbed the cell phone, and called 9-1-1."

He looked as bored as he sounded, and I expected him to declare I'd shot out my own window.

"Look at this," Andy said returning from across the room. He held two disfigured bullets in his hand. "These are nine millimeter slugs. I dug them out of the wall opposite the window. Wasn't one of the guns your mother stole a nine millimeter?"

"Yes, but that doesn't mean she did it. Lots of people own nine millimeters."

Andy shook his head. "She followed you home from yoga class, waited until you were in the house, cranked off two rounds, and then beat it. She's obviously stolen another car, too."

"Mom may be living in her own little world, but she'd never do this to me."

"You admit you haven't seen her in over six months, and Dr. Reynard said she ranted against you in his office the day she escaped." He dropped the bullets into a plastic bag. "Renee, I'm worried. You say she didn't know about the jogging, the gym, or the yoga, but she knows where you live. All she has to do is park down the street and tail you wherever you go. Did you ever think to look around before leaving the house or the yoga studio?"

Liz's words about being aware of her surroundings beat like a drum in my head. Because I'd followed Liz and Corinne from the bar, I'd never once glanced in my rearview mirror other than for the usual driving needs.

"Okay, so I wasn't as careful as I should have been. I still say this could be random. How many weirdoes are running loose in this city?" He gave me a look. "Other than my mother, I mean. Gangs are always shooting up houses."

"There's been no drug related or gang activity reported in this part of town," Santos said. "For the record, other than your mentally-impaired mother, who else might want to kill you—besides everybody in a two block radius?"

"Stop referring to her as impaired. She's high-strung and has a problem with her temper."

I had a problem with my temper at the moment, too. It took a lot of restraint on my part not to plant my foot up Santos's ass.

"Ease up, Ray," Andy said. "Who else, Renee?"

"Well, there's Joel for starters. He left a nasty message on my answering machine this morning. I got him fired."

"Of course, you did," Santos replied. "Joel who, and how did you get him canned?"

"Joel Wainwright, and I exposed him as the liar and cheat he is to his boss."

Santos ceased writing in his notebook and grinned. "Wait a minute. Is this the guy you chased around the yard with a golf club?"

My face burned. "How do you know about that?"

"I may have mentioned something in passing at the station," Andy admitted with a sheepish expression.

I glared at him while Santos chuckled and resumed writing.

Andy recovered fast. "Do you still have the message on the machine?"

"No. I deleted it. He doesn't scare me. I don't think Joel has the balls to do something like this, but I guess he could have grown a pair."

"Anybody else on the hot seat, Miss Ryan?" Santos asked.

I shifted from foot to foot before answering, "I kind of got fired from my job last Tuesday. My replacement was let go yesterday. She was my boss's girlfriend. I made things difficult for her, too."

"Man, no wonder all your friends are pounding on the door tonight to see if you're okay. I guess it's not a good idea to either date or work with you."

"Santos, why don't you cram it up your—"

Andy cut me off. "Cut it out, Ray. She's the victim here. Go on. Does this woman have a name?"

It was nice to have someone defend me for a change. The fact it was Andy made me feel a lot better.

"Angela Peabody. Carson Electronics can probably give you her address. And while we're at it, my boss, Richard James, was officially reprimanded and written up for not following hiring procedures. I understand he wasn't too happy with me either."

"What about your neighbors?" Santos asked. "You've had several run-ins with them."

"If it was a neighbor, I don't think I'd have heard tires squealing," I pointed out.

"The one you turned into Homeland Security doesn't live here anymore, right? That day in my office, you said he'd moved."

"That's true, and I suppose you can add the guy in the fast food restaurant, and the old dude I pepper sprayed in the parking lot to the list, too."

"That's a stretch," Andy said. "If they were going to nail you, they'd have done it by now through the courts."

I shrugged. "Why bother? I don't have any money. The only thing they'd get out of a lawsuit is court costs." I paused. "I had words today with Dr. Reynard about Mother and the lax security at the rest home. I threatened to report him to the state. I also hinted that Mother might consider him a good bet for target practice."

"Is there anybody you don't piss off, Miss Ryan?"

Andy jumped in before I could give Santos a blistering answer. "Renee, go pack a bag. You can't stay here tonight."

"Of course I can. Once the glass is cleaned up, I'll put the hurricane shutters on the window. Besides, where would I go? I refuse to move in with Katie now. If Mother's following me, she'll follow me to her house, too. Why should she be placed in danger? I have a better idea."

"What's that?"

"I'll make up the spare room in the front of the house. You can move off the sofa and in there."

Santos gazed at Andy with raised eyebrows. "You're sleeping here?"

"Renee is a friend—a stubborn friend—whose mother is an escaped mental patient. She's also a victim. Her house has been broken into, a prowler tried to gain entry, someone is leaving harassing hang-up calls, and now this. I think her mother is responsible. I'm not leaving her alone until the woman is back in an institution." Andy turned to me. "Make up that bed. I'll stick around long enough to help with the shutters. Lock the doors. I should be back around six in the morning. I'll make sure a patrol car comes by every hour."

Andy stalked outside. Santos followed with a smirk on his lips. I'd have loved to give him a good swift kick, but stomped to the utility room for a broom and dustpan instead. Cleaning up the mess would help deflect my anger. At least Andy was staying. That was a plus.

I'd accumulated four large piles of broken glass when Andy returned.

"Where are the shutters?"

"In the shed behind the house. The key's on the pegboard by the garage door. And bring a trash can out front, would you?"

I swept the shards into a wastebasket, and then dumped them in the trash while Andy made short work of boarding up my window.

"I know a guy who replaces windows on an emergency basis," I said. "He used to work with my dad. I'll call him first thing in the morning."

"Might be wiser to leave the shutters up. No one can see in."

"I can't stand living in a dungeon. I need light. Besides, what do I have to fear? You're moving in."

He shot me an exasperated glance and sighed. "By the way, the shooter was most likely in the car."

"Of course he was. Where else?"

"Just thought you'd want to know, forensics didn't find any shell casings in your yard or on the street."

"I thought the shooter used a nine millimeter."

"She did, but my guess is the shots were fired through the passenger's side. If your mother was smart—and she is—she'd have rolled up the driver's side window. The casings were probably ejected inside the car."

"Will you stop assuming my mother did this? My money's on Joel the Lying, Cheating Bastard. You saw how pissed he was when I tossed his ass out."

"I saw how pissed you were, too. After all, you had the lethal weapon."

"I had a golf club."

"You tried to bash his head in with a blunt instrument." He glanced at his watch. "I have to get out of here. Santos is waiting in the car."

"Doing what? He could have helped you with the shutters."

"I told him to stay put. I'm almost as irritated with him as I am with you. Now, lock the doors and close all the windows. Turn on the air conditioner. Leave the front and back lights on. In fact, leave all the lights on except the ones in your bedroom. That should discourage your moth—the perpetrator—from a repeat performance. If you get scared, give me a call. I'll send another squad car right out."

"If I get scared, you'll be the first to know."

He looked around the living room. "I don't like any of this. Are you sure you're going to be all right?"

I heaved a sigh. "I'll be fine. Do you really think I'm going to sleep? Besides, it's like you said, the shooter isn't likely to return tonight. What else could happen?"

As if on cue, the phone rang. With a defiant glance tossed over my shoulder at Andy, I strode across the room snatching the cordless from the holder.

"Hello," I snapped.

Silence hammered in my ear before the caller hung up.

****

Adjusting to Andrew Jackson in my house on a permanent—at least for now—basis took work on my part.

I'd heeded his advice about the lights, windows, and the air conditioner, and sat up until after two in the morning watching movies before finally calling it a night. The last time I looked, my clock read four-fifteen. I awoke around six-thirty to the smells of fresh-brewed coffee and frying bacon. I assumed it was Andy, since I doubted the shooter or my caller would drop in to fix breakfast.

I stumbled out of bed, tossed a robe over my tank top, and staggered toward the kitchen. Coffee is a great motivator in the morning.

"Morning," I mumbled, pouring a cup and inhaling the aroma.

"I take it everything was quiet after I left," he said, slipping two pieces of bread into the toaster.

"Like a tomb—okay, bad choice of words—but it still took a while to get to sleep. I never even heard you come back. Any word on last night's fun and games?"

"No, we'll be checking out the names you gave us as soon as I get some shut-eye. Ray and I have been assigned the case."

"Can't we just push Santos off the Intracoastal Bridge? He doesn't believe a word I say."

"I had a long talk with him. I think I made him

see that while your behavior is sometimes over the top, you don't have a screw loose. At any rate, not too loose," he amended with a teasing smile and a wink. "I have to be back on duty by two this afternoon, but I have tomorrow off. I hope you don't intend to go out today."

The smile and wink gave me an early morning glow inside. "I planned to get the window repaired, and if I had time, on going to the gym."

"Leave the gym until tomorrow. I'll go with you."

"Wow, another exciting date." I kept my tone in the same teasing mode as he had earlier. I suspected he liked me more than he let on. At least, I hoped so.

He grinned and removed the bacon from the skillet onto paper towels, then cracked four eggs into the bacon grease.

"Do you eat bacon and eggs *every* morning? That's not very healthy," I commented.

"I know, but it sure is good. That's why I jog and exercise. Orange juice?"

"Don't have any."

"Look in the fridge. I stopped by a convenience store on the way home. By the way, what's with all the newspapers piled up in the corner of the foyer? Don't you read them?"

"I usually skim the headlines, but things have been a little hectic this week. Maybe I'll read them this afternoon."

I enjoyed sharing breakfast with Andy. Breakfast with Joel had been coffee and little conversation. He'd kept his nose stuck in the sports section of the paper the whole time.

Andy actually talked—and not about sports. He kept me amused with stories about the dumbest criminals in Palm Lake and offered tips on how to defend myself in parking lots.

Even his presence in the guest bathroom turned out to be a pleasant surprise, too. Joel had considered the master bath his personal closet. I had to pick up dirty clothes and damp towels every morning after he left, not to mention putting away the toiletries strewn all over the vanity, before I could get myself together.

"Don't you ever put anything away?" I'd once asked.

"Sorry, babe, I'll try to remember," he'd replied in a bored voice.

He never remembered, and I did the work.

Andy gave me hope for the male of the species. Not only did he clean up after himself, but did it neatly, even remembering to rinse the sink when he finished shaving. Plus his cologne or aftershave, while drugstore variety, smelled a lot better than Joel's expensive designer brand. The last couple of mornings, I'd stood in the bathroom breathing in the clean, fresh scent after he left. Now that he'd moved from sofa to spare room, I looked forward to sniffing a lot more.

With Andy's help, I cleared the table and washed up the few dishes we'd used. He offered to dry, but I shooed him away.

"Go catch up on your sleep."

He smiled. "Thanks. Wake me by noon."

While he slept, I showered and planned a home cooked meal for tonight—well, as home cooked as I could make it since I wasn't any great shakes in that department. Joel had always insisted on the best of everything, so I had a couple of T-bones in the freezer. Not even I could screw up steaks.

While I toweled off, I spotted the scale. I'd avoided the damned thing ever since I went on this diet and exercise thing. Now, the urge to find out if my hard work had paid off was impossible to ignore. I stared straight ahead as I stepped on it, gathered my courage, and then peeked at the digital readout.

Holy shit! Almost six pounds! I dropped six

freaking pounds.

I got off elated, and immediately headed for the bedroom and a pair of jeans I hadn't been able to zip in over a year. The zipper ran smoothly without me having to hold in my stomach.

Well, I'll be damned.

On a weight loss high, I called the window guy. He came out, measured the space, and promised to be back first thing Monday morning with a replacement. I'd have to live in a cave for a few more days.

I made sandwiches for lunch, and then woke Andy. He showered, changed, ate, and before he left said, "I'll be back early. Rogers wants a little overtime and I agreed to give him a couple of hours off my clock. Keep the doors locked and don't go anywhere, okay?"

"I won't even go to the store. You'll have to eat frozen French fries tonight."

He laughed and dropped a light kiss on my lips. As soon as the door closed, I hustled into the bathroom for a deep breath of my much needed cologne fix.

I gathered the unread newspapers and piled them on the kitchen table. An afternoon of lazing on the patio and reading the local news sounded like fun—okay, it sounded boring, but I'd do it anyway.

The phone rang. I was tempted to let the answering machine get it, but decided to give the caller a piece of my mind.

"Hello?" Silence greeted me. "Mother, this is childish and silly. Knock it off, and I hope you're not responsible for shooting out the front window last night. Call your lawyer. Harass him for a change."

The caller hung up.

I stared at the phone, reminded that I hadn't as yet informed my grandparents of their daughter's misadventures. I'd also forgotten to tell Andy about the hunting lodge. But first things first, I dialed North Carolina and talked to my grandmother, giving her the news.

"Has she hurt anyone?"

"No, not yet." I didn't tell her about Mom's possession of the guns or the shooting. That news would upset her, and I didn't believe Mom had done it anyway. "I'm sure they'll find her eventually. I need some information. Mom left a diary, and in it she mentions something about an old hunting lodge in Alabama. Do you think she may have gone there?"

Gran sighed. "Oh, dear, I'm not sure. We sold it over fifteen years ago, and I remember telling her about the sale. I don't see why she'd go there."

"Exactly where was it?"

"A few miles outside of Benjamin, Alabama on the Tranquil River. I can't remember the address anymore, but it was on Hanover Road."

"Had she ever been hunting with Grandpa?"

"Heavens, no. Those hunting parties were strictly for men only. But we did vacation there during the summer. It was a cheap getaway. That's where she learned how to shoot. Your grandfather set up a little target range in the woods and she'd plink away at bottles and cans with the twenty-two rifle he gave her for her tenth birthday. She just loved it."

Yeah. Then she graduated to a thirty-aught and handguns.

"Gran, how long has Mom had this temper thing?"

"She used to have terrible temper tantrums as a child, but show me a kid who doesn't. It wasn't until she met your father that all the trouble started. They brought out the worst in each other."

"Did she ever have counseling or something?"

"Not to my knowledge, but then of course, your mother was never big on words. She preferred action. She wasn't diagnosed with her...illness until later. Renee, should we be worried about her showing up here? Your grandfather and I are too old to handle your mother at this stage of our lives."

"According to the doctors, Mother likes the familiar, so I don't think she'll drive all the way to North Carolina in a stolen car or even take the bus, but if she does show, call the police immediately—for her own safety. My guess is she'll hang around here. For all I know, she'll knock on the front door tomorrow as though nothing unusual has happened."

I spent the next ten minutes filling Gran in on my life—or lack thereof—before hanging up. I believed what I'd said about my mother, but would tell Andy anyway. I shivered picturing Mother busting in on strangers in *her* cabin and threatening them with a deer rifle.

With the afternoon winding down, I grabbed a glass of iced tea, several newspapers, and headed for the chaise on the patio. As usual, I skimmed the headlines before turning to the society pages. It took several days worth of papers until I spotted the picture I'd seen of Liz and her husband. Curious as to why they would run it again, I read the caption.

"The *Palm Lake Courier* wishes to make a correction. The man pictured next to Mrs. Gorman is Mr. Walter Sanger, Miss Hamilton's escort. We regret the error."

Well, nuts. So the little twerp I'd had down as Liz's hubby wasn't. I stared at the photo, still out of focus.

Someone better tell Miss Hamilton her escort looks like a murderous, sniveling weasel.

On a hunch, I fired up the computer and searched the newspaper archives for a photo of Todd Gorman. I found zip. There were plenty of Liz over the last couple of years, but that was all. The online archives didn't go back any further than that. If I wanted to look at anything older, I'd have to go to the *Palm Lake Courier* offices.

Andy got back around seven. I had his fries ready for the oven and the salad made.

"I'll light the fire," he said.

"Fire? I was going to broil them?"

"T-bones require careful grilling. You do have a grill, don't you?"

"Out back." I followed him to the patio. He set the dials and punched the button to light the gas. "Wow, you do breakfast and dinner?"

He grinned. "I am a man of many talents—and quite a catch, too."

I sniffed in pretended distain. "Yeah, right."

I went back inside to uncork a bottle of wine. I had to chuckle. He *was* quite a catch, and I wondered if I'd caught him.

The steaks were done just the way I liked them. Andy and I shared the same medium-rare taste. Joel had insisted on well-done. Should have told me something right off the bat. Never trust a man who chars perfectly good steak into leather.

Over dinner, I told him about my conversation with my grandmother.

"I doubt your mother's on her way to any cabin in the woods. By the way, we found another stolen car. This time out at the airport—hotwired, of course. It was reported missing Friday morning. We're checking it for gunshot residue and fingerprints."

"Let me guess—long term parking?" I asked popping a great tasting piece of meat into my mouth.

"Yeah. I'm sure we'll find she stole another one from the lot. Your mother gets around."

"Any information on the names I gave you?"

"Dr. Reynard was highly indignant we dared to question him and thinks you should be in therapy."

"He would. What about the bimbo and my boss?"

"Miss Peabody called you every name under the sun, but has an alibi. She was at a bar with friends from seven and didn't leave until one." Andy smiled and drank some wine.

"And my idiot boss? Or was he one of the friends?"

Andy grinned. "As of now, Richard James is probably explaining to his wife why he received a reprimand for hiring Miss Peabody. When Ray and I left, he was swearing he only tried to help a friend. I don't think she bought it, but gave him an alibi anyway. He was at home watching TV all night."

I snorted. "A likely story. Anything with the neighbors? What about the Homeland Security guy?"

"Your neighbors are clean as are the people you accosted in the restaurant and parking lot. The other guy, we can't find."

"A-ha! I knew it! He's on the lam. I scared the crap out of him, and he and his terrorist friends split."

I only kidded, but Andy gave me a look of exasperation. I pretended not to notice and finished my Cabernet.

"We just can't find him. For all we know, he's moved out of town. Besides, if I were him, I'd have firebombed your house a long time ago."

"Very funny." I'd deliberately left the best for last. "And what about Joel Wainwright—my number one pick or should I say prick?"

Andy picked up our plates putting them in the sink, and then refilled our wine glasses before answering.

"Mr. Wainwright's first words when we told him about the shooting were, 'Is the bitch dead?' Not the best of ways to start an interview. He described your character in colorful language. Maybe you could introduce him to Angela Peabody. They have a lot in common—unemployment, you, and their vocabulary."

"Yes, but does he have an alibi?"

He raised his glass to his lips and drank. "Actually, no, he doesn't."

My breath caught in my throat. I'd dismissed Joel as a weakling and a coward. Had I underestimated him?

God knows I made a horrible error in judgment when I let him into my life, not to mention my house.

"Did you arrest him?" I demanded.

"We have no evidence to do that."

"But, he has no alibi!"

"He claims to have been home alone watching TV during the time of the drive-by."

"He's lying. I told you he was a liar and a cheat. What kind of an alibi is that?"

"Flimsy, but not enough for an arrest. We did ask if we could check his car. Clean as a whistle. He admitted to having it detailed at a car wash around the corner this morning."

"Did you check for gunshot residue and the casings?"

"We found no casings. The inside had been thoroughly cleaned and vacuumed."

"Damn! Are you keeping a watch on him?"

"Renee, we don't have the manpower for that. Right now, your case is called a random shooting with your mother as the prime suspect. Let's go into the living room and watch a movie. Tomorrow morning, we'll go to the gym and you can work off your frustration."

He picked up his wine glass and walked from the room. I followed and sat next to him on the sofa. He kicked off his shoes and planted his feet on the coffee table, then grabbed the remote. My arm brushed against his.

There it was again. That hot rush of pure lust licking at my soul.

I stared at his feet, then his shoes, and then his feet again remembering my speculations of a week or so ago.

"Uh, Andy, what size shoe do you wear?"

"Thirteen. Why?" he replied staring at the channels whizzing by on the screen.

Oh, wow.

"Just curious. I was thinking of getting a canoe and wondered if you'd mind selling me one of your shoes."

He sent me a sardonic look. "Very funny."

I darted a glance at his thumb. I couldn't very well grab a tape measure, but to my eye it looked two and a half to three inches long. I took a deep breath and unobtrusively wiped the gathering sweat from my forehead, then flapped the front of my tank top.

I wondered if teenage boys spent a lot of time staring at their thumbs and feet.

"You hot?" Andy asked.

"Oh, yeah."

"Turn on the ceiling fan." He continued channel surfing, his gaze fixated on the TV screen.

"Good idea."

I rose, walked around the coffee table, and reached for the chain on the overhead fan. It had broken several years ago and was one of those things I never got around to fixing. I could grasp it by standing on tiptoe, which probably explains why I never fixed it. I pulled the chain and the fan rotated into life.

As I stretched, my tank top rode up my ribcage. I meant to pull it down, but made the mistake of looking at Andy. He no longer stared at the TV, but at my exposed torso. He brushed his hand along his hairline, drew in, then exhaled a large breath, and licked his lips.

"Ah...you're right. It is warm in here. Turn it up

a notch."

I complied before resuming my seat on the sofa. He scooched away, putting a good foot and a half of space between us. I'd survived on fantasies for days and this time I could see them coming true. For a brief moment, I'd seen raw desire in his eyes. The look had gone, and now he was back under control. Dammit.

I cleared my throat. "So, what's on the tube?"

"Uh, is a movie okay with you?"

"Fine."

Get a grip Renee. He obviously doesn't want to start something. At least, not now.

I didn't pay much attention to the movie, and to avoid thinking about Andy, brooded over Joel's non-alibi. He still topped my list of suspects, and friends in the bar or not, the bimbo wasn't far behind. In a crowd, she could have slipped out unnoticed for half an hour. I refused to consider Mother.

But if not Joel or the bimbo—then who?

Chapter Twelve

"Come on, Renee, you can do it. Give me another two."

"No! But, I'll gladly serve up your family jewels on a platter, though." I released the chin-up bar and dropped flat-footed to the floor, the shock running straight up my spine. My arms ached and quivered. "You know, Jackson, when you die, I hope it's because someone drops a fucking barbell on your head."

Andy choked with laughter. "Upper body strength sometimes takes longer. I guess five chin-ups aren't so bad—for a girl."

"You're skating on thin ice, buster."

I brushed a trickle of sweat from my temple with my fingertips and headed for the stationary bike, dialing in moderate difficulty numbers. Andy mounted the bike next to me and cranked it up to the max.

"Actually, you're doing pretty good. I can see you've lost some weight."

I straightened and pedaled faster, keeping pace with my suddenly accelerating heartbeats. He'd noticed. That made all the healthy food and sore muscles worthwhile.

"Hi, mind if I join you?" a woman said from the bike on my other side.

I turned my head and gazed into Marylou Barton's blue eyes. She still looked fabulous, and I could feel those six lost pounds finding their way home again on my butt.

"Sure, but watch out for the keeper of the

dungeon over here," I replied.

She dialed in her numbers and pedaled. "Is Andy harassing you?"

"If he had his way, I'd look like a female Arnold Schwarzenegger tomorrow."

Marylou laughed. "I know. He did that to me a year or so ago. I hit a plateau where I couldn't lose that last five pounds. He hounded me until I did. I refused to speak to him for a month."

"But you lost the weight," Andy said with a grin. His gaze slid up and down her body, giving me a momentary twinge of jealousy. Then he shifted the appreciative look to me. "I'll whip you into shape, too. Can't wait to see you in a pair of skinny jeans."

I forgave him his Marylou transgression and groaned. "Swell, I've hooked up with a sadistic exercise guru."

"Don't let him get to you, Renee."

"Hey, I only harass people I like," he said.

Andy liked me. A warm fuzzy feeling crept out from the pit of my stomach to the tips of my fingers and toes. I wanted to think I was just hot from all the pedaling, but knew better. I liked him, too—a lot more than I should have.

"By the way, Andy, congrats on the law school thing," she said.

"Thanks. How did you know?"

"Katie told me. I ran into her at an art gallery last week. Does this mean you're quitting the force?"

"Not for a while. I still need to pay for all this higher education. I'll go nights and weekends. It'll take longer, but..."

I let their conversation drift over me, impressed by Andy's ambition and work ethic. Nights and weekends wouldn't leave him with any free time. I had hoped he might like to spend a few nights with me. Not wanting to define night, I let my mind wander into erotic thoughts, and then scolded myself.

Get a grip. He's staying with me now only because he thinks Mother's out to get me. As soon as she's caught, he'll go back to busty brunettes and Marylou. Still, there are those kisses.

My timer dinged. As I walked toward the free weight rack a familiar voice said, "Hi, Renee."

"Corinne! What a surprise." She wore a leotard and sturdy running shoes, obviously ready for a workout.

"I joined yesterday afternoon. I'm waiting for someone to show me the machines before I start. And tomorrow I'm meeting with one of the personal trainers."

"Wow, I'm envious. I haven't even thought about a personal trainer yet. Is it expensive?"

"Yeah, but I'll get a routine tailored for me, so I guess it's worth it."

Marylou joined us. Out of the corner of my eye, I saw Andy still pedaling away.

"Boy, I've either got to cut down on my time or lower the difficulty. My thighs are on fire," she said, panting.

I introduced the two women. "Corinne and I jog together at City Park."

"Renee, I can't tell you how happy I am I met you. In less than two weeks, I'm almost back to my full jogging potential, am doing yoga, and now this. A couple of days ago, I was pissed at the world and my ex-husband. Today, I'm calm, and looking forward to getting on with my life. I may even take Jeff's advice about a job." She hugged me. "I'm so glad you're my friend."

I hugged her back and blinked tears from my eyes. A friend. Other than Katie and Andy, those had been few and far between. I had acquaintances, not friends.

A man walked up. "Ms. Vassar? My name is

Mike and I'm here to walk you through your first workout. Are you ready?"

"Yes." She turned to us. "I'm pleased to have met you, Marylou. Renee, I'll see you tomorrow at the park."

"Count on it."

Corinne followed Mike and I picked up a barbell.

"She seemed nice," Marylou said.

"Corinne's terrific."

She selected a free weight and watched Corinne mount the stairs to the walking track on the mezzanine. "No way is that tan natural. I'll have to ask what tanning salon she goes to. She looks great. You met while jogging?"

I gave her some of how Corinne, Jeff, Freddy, and I had met and why we jogged—from weight loss to broken legs to shitty boyfriends and ex-husbands—but excluded Liz's place in the scene.

Marylou worked her biceps. "It's funny how friendships start, isn't it? My best friend in high school and I started out hating each other. We competed for the affections of the same boy. When he chose a third girl over us, we cried, sneaked a cigarette, and ate tons of ice cream vowing to hate him forever."

"Did you?"

She laughed. "Nope. Discovered it didn't matter."

Andy finished with the bike and sauntered over, grabbing the usual fifty pound weights.

"Who was that?" he asked.

I glanced up at Corinne who still talked with her trainer, and then stared into the mirror, a smile on my face.

"A friend—a real friend."

The smile faded as I curled my weights. Something nagged in the back of my mind—some snippet of conversation I should have remembered.

173

Who'd said it? Andy? Marylou? Corinne? I had no idea. And where had I heard it? While on the bike? I didn't know that either. Maybe it was something said between Andy and Marylou that had registered, but because I was in my own little zone at the time, couldn't recall.

Oh, well, I'll remember eventually. Can't be too important.

Since Andy was doing his full routine, I hung around in the lobby to wait for him. I was reading a brochure at the reception desk when someone poked me in the back. Given my experience last Friday, I yelped, jumped, and then turned.

"Surprise!" Freddy said with a grin.

Jeff stood next to her, also smiling. A staff member accompanied them. "Hi, Renee. Didn't expect to see you today. Jim here has been showing us around."

"Are you joining?" I asked, hoping in Freddy's case the answer was no.

"Oh, yes," she gushed. "Jeff asked me to come along and see the place. It's, like, so nifty, and the pool area is far out. Really cool."

I refrained from rolling my eyes. "Glad you like it."

Jeff grinned. "Just plunked down my fee. It's a place to exercise when it rains, or I don't get a chance to jog. You ready, Freddy?"

She giggled. "Ready Freddy. Isn't he, like, a hoot?"

I shook my head as they walked out the door. First jogging, then yoga, and now the gym. Was I doomed to have Freddy Lane as my new BFF? And Corinne would have a cow when she found out Freddy had joined.

Marylou entered the lobby, hoisting a duffle bag higher on her shoulder.

"Well, I'm done. Won't see you for a few days. I

have to go out of town. Have a good one."

She waved, pushed open the doors, and exited. The nagging worry that I'd missed something important returned, but damned if I could figure out what.

****

The next morning, I sat in the car at the park waiting for some of my group to arrive. Andy, back on early day shift, had risen at five-thirty, showered, dressed, and eaten a bowl of cereal. Not wanting to miss spending even a few minutes with him, I also got up.

I yawned and rested my head against the window. I had almost an hour to kill. Might as well catch a few winks in the meantime.

A car door slamming brought me back to consciousness. I glanced, bleary eyed at the dashboard clock. Damn, it was nearly eight. I'd really zonked out.

I saw Jeff, Corinne, and Liz warming up. I searched for my scrunchie, but couldn't find it.

"Can't jog without a ponytail," I muttered to myself.

I finally opened the console and found the damned thing. While I twisted it around my hair, I spied the Lend An Ear—the real catalyst for my jogging mania. Out of curiosity, I turned it on and held one of the headphones to my ear. It picked up a lot of noises, but I was able to single out Liz, Corinne, and Jeff's conversation.

"I thought you seemed a little pissed off at yoga on Friday," Corinne said.

"No, I was pissed off when I discovered I'd have to go to Los Angeles. But Friday afternoon was the last straw. She'd done it again. Had me down for two affairs on the same night at the same time. I fired her," Liz replied.

"So, now who does your schedule?" Jeff asked.

175

"No one, but the position has to be filled soon. I'm too busy to do it on my own. The job opening should be up on the website. And this time, I'll make sure whoever applies can do the job. I've had it with incompetence."

Holy cow, Liz fired her personal assistant? I tossed the device on the front seat and scrambled from the car jamming the baseball cap on my head. What an opportunity. A personal assistant did everything from answering phones—which I could do—to schlepping stuff to and from the dry cleaners—no big deal. Any moron could organize a schedule, and keeping unwanted callers from the boss's ear required a firm refusal and the willingness to lie to avoid hurt feelings. I was great at lying.

I joined my friends at the guardrail. Liz ran in place, a frown on her face. I looked at Corinne and remembered her statement of yesterday about finding a job. Shit. Friend or not, I couldn't let her beat me out. I had to protect Liz, and this job was made to order.

I assumed the warm-up position. "Hi everyone. Running late this morning. How did your session go at Fitness Forever?"

Corinne leaned forward, her leg extended back. "Great. I'm seeing the personal trainer today at one."

"Jeff joined, too." I babbled as I stretched to keep the conversation going until Liz took off. I didn't mention Freddy joining. Corinne might have a heart attack on the spot.

Jeff twisted from side to side, hands on hips. "If they give a discount for finding new members, I'll mention your name," he said.

"So will I," Corinne added, grasping her ankles. "Where's our maven of pop culture from the sixties? I can't understand how a woman who doesn't look a day over thirty can sound so much like a hippie."

"Freddy's not so bad," Jeff said.

"She's pushy as hell, and I think she's stalking one of us. Everywhere we go, she's there," she replied.

"Come on, Corinne, she's shy and insecure. To make up for it, she babbles," he answered. "Give her a break. I like her. In her own way, she's funny."

"In her own way, she's a pain in the ass."

"Let's not argue," I said. "Freddy might be like an over-eager puppy, but she's harmless. Let's jog."

"Well, I'm ready to go," Liz said. "Everyone have a good day." She smiled and jogged off.

"I'm almost there, too. How about you guys?" Corinne asked. Her gaze followed Liz down the path.

Jeff nodded. "I'm ready."

"I need to stretch a little more. Maybe I'll catch up with you."

I was relieved when Corinne and Jeff headed down the usual path, not Liz's. I almost bagged the run to go home and hit the website, but decided that since Corinne jogged, I might as well, too. Plus those six pounds were a hell of an incentive.

Finished with warm-ups, I trotted down the path before remembering the woods and the scare I'd had last week. Today, however, I wasn't alone. Dozens of joggers clogged the trail, and I pushed the uneasiness from my mind.

As I approached the bridge, I saw Sherry coming toward me. I couldn't resist.

"Hi, Sherry." I stopped and leaned on the railing.

She continued to jog in place. "Hi, how are you?"

"I'm fine. I understand Joel is no longer in your employ."

"My uncle got the private investigator's report back, and it was not good. Joel lied on his application about damn near everything from former employment to jail time."

I straightened as shock washed through me.

"Jail time! What for?"

"Assault with a deadly weapon. It was about seven or eight years ago. The repo man was trying to take his car, and he threatened the guy with a gun. Even fired a shot into the air. Can you believe that?"

Yeah, I had no problem believing that what with Mother and all. Still, the similarities from Friday night made my heart hammer harder than any mile and a half run.

Oh, shit! I've got to tell Andy.

"Eventually, the charges were reduced and he only spent a few months in jail, but lying about it was enough to get him canned."

"I had no idea. And to think he lived with me." Nausea churned in my stomach and black dots swam in my peripheral vision.

"And to think he and I were—well, you know."

"Yeah, I know."

"How did you know he got fired?"

I told her about the angry phone call and shooting.

"Do you think it was him?"

"I don't know. I've pissed off a lot of people lately, but he tops my list."

Sherry looked around the trail. "Maybe neither one of us should jog alone. I think I'll find a new place to run tomorrow."

"Probably not a bad idea. Thanks for the information."

She nodded and resumed running, her head swiveling from side to side.

My gaze scanned the surrounding area, too. A shiver raced up and down my arms. Goosebumps formed. I didn't need exercise this badly. I'd go home and check out the job on the Foundation's website. I spun around and jogged back the way I'd come, annoyed when my head swiveled like Sherry's.

I called Andy on the drive home and gave him

the details as Sherry had told me.

"I'll look into it. Did this happen in Florida?"

"She didn't say. But I remember Joel once telling me he was originally from New Jersey."

"That might help. In the meantime, stick around the house, okay? I've got a squad car patrolling the area."

"Thanks. Uh, Andy, what would you like for dinner tonight?"

"I'll bring something on my way home. I should be there around five or five-thirty."

I hung up, wondering if he realized he'd used the word home, and then remembered he'd used it before. I liked the word. It sounded permanent.

I pulled into my driveway to find the window man waiting for me. I'd forgotten he was due. While he worked, I contacted my grandparents' homeowner's insurance company. He left, and once again I gazed onto my front yard, not at a bunch of aluminum.

My gazing didn't last long. I hustled into my office, fired up the computer, and logging onto the Foundation website, clicked the employment opportunities link. The position was listed and I read through it as fast as I could. For all I knew Corinne had already applied.

The job description didn't sound like brain surgery. Taxing and demanding, yes, but nothing unmanageable. I updated my resume stretching the truth only a little. For instance, I wasn't fired from Carson Electronics—I was laid off due to the recent economic downturn. The law stipulated that employers could only confirm a person had worked for them, not the reason for termination or for the employee's attitude.

I also exaggerated my educational accomplishments. I always did that. Employers only check if you claim a degree. I pretended attendance at the local community college for two years following high school. If they asked, I'd say I quit for financial reasons. They never followed up. Besides, after fourteen years most records of that sort are long gone. Satisfied with the embellishments, I left-clicked the mouse on the contact's e-mail, sending what I hoped would be an impressive query and resume.

While awaiting a reply, I re-read the information about the Foundation, paying attention to detail this time.

By the time I finished, my incoming mail alert dinged. I quickly pulled it up. I had an appointment for eleven o'clock the next morning with a man named Stewart. I sighed. It would have been so much easier to simply tell Liz directly I was interested in the job, but then I'd have to explain how I knew it was available. I didn't think eavesdropping was a plus on a resume.

With any luck, tomorrow I would officially be hired as Liz's personal assistant and, unofficially, as her bodyguard. Of course, she wouldn't know that, and Andy would have a cat, but I didn't care. I'd made a promise to myself and intended to keep it.

I turned off the computer and made my way back to the kitchen thinking about lunch. As I passed the phone, I noticed the flashing light indicating a message. Without a thought, I punched the play button.

"You miserable bitch! Not only did you get me fired, but you sicced the cops on me, too. Keep this in mind; what goes around, comes around," Joel ranted. He was either nuts or drunk.

I didn't take a chance, but immediately called Andy.

****

Andy walked through the front door carrying a couple of large bags from a take-out fried chicken place. When he set it on the kitchen counter, I jerked off the lid and breathed in the aroma.

"I love fried chicken. Unfortunately, none of this is on my diet, especially the biscuits and mashed potatoes and gravy."

"Psychologically, it's good to indulge every once in a while. Limit yourself to one helping."

He slipped out of his jacket, hung it over the back of a chair, and then removed his gun and holster, laying them on the counter. I set the table while Andy washed up and changed into jeans and a t-shirt. By the time he returned, questions about Joel burned a hole in my tongue, but I kept still, knowing he'd share when ready.

The meal was one of the best since I'd begun dieting. Or maybe it just tasted that way *because* I dieted. Either way, I tore into a chicken breast with all the gusto of a starving man—or woman in this case—including the extra crispy skin, my favorite part. The creamy mashed potatoes, gravy, corn, and biscuit lived up to their reputations. I followed the advice for only one helping. Andy had three.

"How can you pack all that away and still stay so trim?" I asked.

He shrugged. "I don't know. Metabolism, I guess, plus the workouts and jogging. Haven't jogged since I saw you at the park." He wiped his fingers on a napkin. "I see the window guy got here."

"He was waiting for me when I got home. Andy, how long are you going to avoid talking about Joel?"

"There's not much to tell. You played me the message, and I recorded it, but so far nothing's turned up. I found no Joel Wainwright who was arrested seven or eight years ago on an ADW charge in the state of Florida."

"So? Check New Jersey."

"We are. It takes time."

"Did you haul his ass into the station and grill

him about it?"

"No. We can't do that. I checked, and there's no record of any kind of gun registered in his name in the state."

"Big fucking deal. How many criminals use registered guns?" I asked, thoroughly irritated with his lack of action.

"You mean other than your mother?"

"Leave her out of this!"

"I still say she's good for the shooting."

"You mean, she's pissed and wanted to scare me?"

Andy didn't answer, but rose from the kitchen table, got two beers out of the fridge, and popped the caps, handing me one. I sucked down a large portion and glared.

"Renee, if you hadn't bent over at just the right moment, those bullets I dug out of the wall would have drilled you right between the shoulder blades. She didn't want to scare you—she wanted to kill you."

"That's nuts. Mom may have issues, but she'd never do that."

"How can you be so sure?"

I raised the bottle to my lips and drank again. I wasn't sure at all now. In fact, confusion and fear mingled together until I didn't know what to believe.

"Look, Renee, why don't you get out of town for a while? Forget about Liz Gorman. Let us look after her. Somebody's trying to kill *you*."

I choked on my beer and coughed. "*Me?* Nobody wants to kill me—scare me perhaps, but not *kill*."

Andy took an absent-minded drink and shook his head. "I don't know what it is, but this just doesn't feel right. I'm missing something— something I should see."

I wanted to say "You, too?" He had the same feeling I'd had yesterday at the gym.

"We've gotten off track. Why haven't you hauled Joel in?"

He finished his beer and set the empty bottle on the counter.

"We went by the room he's renting this afternoon to ask about the ADW charge. He wasn't there. One of his housemates said he hasn't seen Joel since our visit Saturday."

"You mean he's flown the coop?"

"According to the guy we talked to, his clothes and personal belongings are still there, so he can't be far."

"He's probably hiding under my bed," I muttered.

"I'm still not convinced he fired the shots."

"Why not? He's got a history of shooting, just like my mother."

"If he's the shooter, why draw attention to himself by calling and leaving a threatening message on your answering machine? It doesn't make sense. And I learned long ago, that if something doesn't make sense, it probably isn't true."

"Oh, come on, I heard that statement from one of those daytime TV judges. She referred to testimony."

"It applies here, too."

"Joel isn't the brightest bulb in the pack."

"Until we recapture your mother or locate Wainwright and confirm the past charges against him, I want you to stay put. Don't leave the house. Read a book, watch TV, write your damned memoirs, I don't care. Just don't go anywhere. I'll pick up dinners on the way home."

"Does that include all my exercise activities?" I inquired in a stiff voice.

"Yes."

In spite of my earlier confusion regarding the

shooter, I still had a gut feeling. "Andy, it's not my mother, I'm pretty sure of that." I ran a hand through my hair, heaving a deep sigh. "And I'll be with people at the park, the gym, and yoga classes. Besides, I have a job interview tomorrow."

He rubbed his forehead. "Cancel it. I thought you were going to sit back and collect unemployment for a while."

"I was, but this came up and it sounds like a good opportunity."

"Another receptionist job will come along."

"This is personal assistant to an executive of a large corporation. It includes a hefty salary, generous benefits, and I'd be insane not to apply. The requirements fit right down to my pantyhose."

"The job of a personal assistant also requires a lot of errand running, which means you'd be out on your own. Forget it." He scowled. "Where is this job?"

"I will not forget it. I've been searching for this kind of opportunity for years. Who knows when the door will open again? I have to jump on it now."

"You didn't answer the question. What corporation and who's the executive?" he asked with narrowed eyes and a suspicious expression.

I finished my beer and carried the empty bottles to the counter next to the back door, still trying to avoid telling the truth.

"What difference does that make?"

"Renee—"

I whirled to face him. "Oh, all right. It's the Susan Richardson Gray Foundation. I used the Lend An Ear this morning and overheard Liz saying she'd fired her personal assistant. When I got home, I applied. The interview is tomorrow at eleven o'clock with a Mr. Stewart."

"Dammit, no! Are you nuts? I can't believe the way you've insinuated yourself into this woman's life." He closed the distance between us with two steps and grasped my shoulders, giving me a shake. "Suppose she's not the woman? I told you we haven't come up with anything on her husband yet."

"Gimme a break! Of course, she's the woman. You know it—you just can't prove it. Sooner or later, you'll find the evidence."

"You're stalking her!"

"I'm protecting her! There's a difference."

Andy took a deep breath, muttering, "Damn you, Renee. You're going to get yourself hurt or worse and I don't want that to happen." He pulled me into his arms, his lips crushing mine.

I stood in shock for all of a nanosecond before parting my lips and clinging to him like a limpet. Searing heat radiated from the pit of my stomach and rolled throughout my body. My heart thudded in my ears and I didn't care whether or not I breathed. My hands slid up his shoulders to his nape where I tangled my fingers in his silky hair. The scent of his cologne made me throb in all the right places.

His lips traveled down my cheek to my neck and his hands wandered under my t-shirt.

"God, Renee, stop me."

"No way," I said, panting.

Nimble fingers unsnapped my bra and pushed it out of the way. His warm palm cupped my breast, the nipple already hard and aching.

We careened around the kitchen banging off the cabinets and the table. I jerked his shirt from the waistband of his jeans and slid my hands up his rippled chest. I'd been dreaming about this moment from the day I'd seen him ninety percent naked in the pool and spa room at the gym.

I moaned and wrapped my leg around his— anything to get closer. He sucked at the pulse point on my neck, sending a zing along my nerves and a strong throb to the one place it belonged.

Suddenly, glass shattered in the living room.

Chapter Thirteen

Andy shoved me to the floor, scrambling to grab his gun from the counter.

"Call 9-1-1 and stay inside," he ordered, and flipping off the kitchen light, jerked open the back door, then slid into the night.

I grabbed the phone and called. More glass broke and something hit the floor with a crash. Then, a familiar voice yelled from out front.

"There, bitch! How do you like that?"

Joel! That miserable son of a bitch. I was furious he'd taken out my brand new window again. I relayed the information necessary to the operator while racing through the house.

Without stopping to think, I dropped the phone, yanked the front door open, and stumbled out onto the porch. Joel stood about twenty feet away, his arm cocked and ready to launch another missile when Andy flew around the side of the house, gun in hand.

Joel took one look, dropped the rock, and ran like a rabbit. Andy caught up in a matter of a few feet, dropped his gun, and brought the stinking asshole down with a flying tackle. He fought, but was no match for a buff cop like Andy, who had him face down and handcuffed in seconds.

"Lemme go! Lemme go, Goddammit! The bitch deserves this," Joel screeched.

My neighbors poured out of their houses to watch the fun.

I screamed like a banshee. "I just got that damned window fixed! What's the matter, run out of bullets?"

"Fuck you!"

"No, fuck you!"

"Shut up, both of you!" Andy shouted over us. Joel tried to kick his way out of Andy's hold. "Knock it off or I'll put the shackles on. Renee, did you call 9-1-1?"

"Yes. They should be here any minute. I told them someone shot at me again and an officer needed help."

Andy rose to his feet and retrieved his gun, keeping it trained on a more subdued Joel.

"I didn't shoot. If I had, I'd have nailed you the first time. I just threw rocks."

"You're still going to jail," Andy told him, and then turned to me. "I thought I told you to stay inside."

"I know, but the minute I heard Joel's voice, I got pissed. What took you so long to get here?"

"The latch on your fence gate could use a little WD-40. It sticks. I thought I'd have to climb over it."

Something was choking me. My bra had wound up in the vicinity of my neck. I yanked it back into place and fumbled to refasten it.

Sirens in the distance told me the cops hauled ass on this one. Sure enough, they took the corner on squealing tires and pulled to a halt, then advanced on the two men with guns drawn.

"Drop it!" one of the cops yelled.

Andy complied and raised his hands, then identified himself. "I'm a cop. ID's in my back left pocket."

Another cop approached, found the case, flipped open the holder, and then re-holstered his gun. The other officers followed suit except for one who kept his weapon trained on Joel.

"What's going on, detective?"

"Miss Ryan and I were in the kitchen finishing

dinner when the front window shattered. Since she was the victim of a drive-by shooting last Friday, I thought it might be a repeat."

As he explained the events of the last few days to the men, two cops pulled Joel to his feet, escorted him to a squad car, shoved him in the back seat and slammed the door. He scowled at me through the window. I flipped him the bird.

"Charge him with malicious mischief, vandalism, attempted assault, and resisting arrest." Andy turned to me. "You are pressing charges, right?"

"You're damned right I am. That window was just replaced this morning. I haven't even had time to clean it yet."

The arrival of the police cars had packed the street with curious neighbors, some from as far as the next block. A few looked concerned, but most just had resigned expressions on their faces. It was embarrassing.

I turned back to survey my battered window. Only a few shards remained hanging in the frame. Even as I watched, another broke free and slammed onto the sill before hitting the hydrangea bushes.

The insurance company's going to love this. And how do I explain to my grandparents their homeowner's rates are about to skyrocket? Insurance in the state of Florida is a crap shoot. Any reason to increase the rates ruled.

My gaze wandered to the border of the flowerbed. Three of the decorative rocks were missing. One lay in the middle of the lawn. The other two no doubt graced my living room floor, along with the glass. I groaned. My trash can was already half full from the other night. Tomorrow's pick up would be interesting.

I turned from the window. Andy had finished with the police and headed for the squad car. I followed. He opened the door, then braced his hands on either side of the frame, preventing me physical access. Probably a good idea. I was still pissed.

"Let's talk a moment, Wainwright. We've been looking for you a couple of days now. Where you been?"

"Around," Joel answered in a sullen voice.

"Around where?"

"Because of her, I didn't get the promotion, my relationship with Sherry went south, and I got fired. It's all your fault, bitch!"

"If you hadn't lied, asshole, you wouldn't be in this squad car now," I retorted.

"Shut up, Renee. You still haven't said where you've been, Wainwright. We know about the assault with a deadly weapon charge. Care to explain?"

Joel shot him a quick look before averting his gaze to the seat in front of him.

"That was a long time ago in Georgia. I haven't had a gun since. And that's the truth. The other night, I got loaded and stayed with a friend. Last night, I went to a bar and got stinking again. Slept it off in my car. When I woke up, I started all over. I was pissed at Renee and left a message on her machine. The more I thought about it, the madder I got, so I decided to teach her a lesson about meddling in people's lives."

"Book him. Miss Ryan will come down and swear out the complaint in a little while." He slammed the door, and the car took off.

With Joel gone and the action over, my neighbors returned home. Eventually, the remaining policemen did the same leaving Andy and me alone on the front lawn.

"I take it the shutters were put away?" he asked in a tired voice.

I nodded. "The window man put them in the shed this morning."

He disappeared toward the back of the house, while I entered from the front to assess the damage. Once again, I gathered the broom and dustpan to clean up the mess. The rocks had also broken a couple of floor tiles. Luckily, they were open stock and readily available.

The shutters didn't take long. When we finished, Andy drove me to the police station where I filled out the paper work for the complaint. It had been a while since I'd done something like this, but it's like riding a bicycle—you never forget.

"So, how long do you think he'll be in jail?" I asked on the way home.

"In case you didn't notice, Wainwright was drunk. He'll be booked, tossed into the drunk tank, and arraigned sometime tomorrow or the next day. He'll probably have a public defender, and make bail or bond out within hours."

"Damn, can't you keep him any longer? I don't buy his not having a gun. He's a liar and a scumbag. I think he's the shooter. He was probably drunk then, too."

"Renee, I don't want to discuss this right now. I'm tired, sweaty, and dirty. We're almost home. When I get there, I plan to have a beer, take a shower, and go to bed."

I bit my tongue to keep from asking, "Alone?" Instead, I sat quietly until we entered the house. He kept his word and had a beer. As soon as he finished, he showered. When he came out of the bathroom, he paused on the threshold of his room.

"Renee, I want to apologize for earlier in the kitchen, before Joel arrived. I was frustrated with you and lost control. It won't happen again." He closed the door behind him.

Appalled, I ripped off my shoe and threw it after him. My aimed sucked. It smacked the wall and bounced onto the floor. A man should never apologize for great kissing, especially if the woman is kissing him back and begging for more. It sends a message to the lady she lacks something. I snatched the shoe and stomped through the house turning off lights. The phone in the living room rang as I passed.

"Hello?" My voice still held anger.

Silence followed by a soft click.

"Goddamn it!" Yanking on the cord, I unplugged the phone and fled to my bedroom, slamming the door.

****

I sat in the outer office of the Director of Human Resources, Robert Stewart, trying not to fuss with my collar. I'd worn a fitted navy blue dress and a matching crop top jacket with white lapels, impressed that it fit again. All the exercise and dieting had paid off. I'd also taken pains to style my hair in a more mature fashion. The Susan Richardson Gray Foundation was founded with old money and demanded a job applicant exude conservatism. I looked like a Republican.

"It'll just be a few more minutes, Miss Ryan. Are you sure I can't get you anything to drink?" Stewart's administrative assistant asked.

"No, thank you, I'm fine. Have you had many applications?"

"Oh, quite a few. As soon as they're e-mailed I print them out." She indicated a large stack of papers in an inbox on the corner of her desk.

Damn. It dawned on me that even though I'd applied and they'd answered quickly, I still might not get the job. In my blind determination to protect Liz, the thought had never entered my mind.

The door to the inner office opened and a man escorted a lady out. Middle-aged and perfectly groomed, the woman had an air of experience and competency about her. I faced stiff competition.

"Thank you, Ms. Hillier, we'll be in touch," he told her with a smile.

She nodded to the secretary, ignored me, and sailed out with a confident stride.

"Mr. Stewart, this is Renee Ryan." His assistant handed him a folder.

"Ms. Ryan, nice to meet you. My name is Robert Stewart. Please, come in."

I rose ignoring the nerves nibbling throughout my body, lifted my chin, and walked into the inner sanctum.

"Please, be seated while I just refresh my memory a moment."

I settled in the cushioned chair in front of his large antique desk with hands folded in my lap as he flipped through the two or three pages in the folder—no doubt my initial e-mail and doctored resume. I willed myself to relax. *Take it easy. Everything will be fine.*

He finished, sat back, and smiled. "Tell me, Ms. Ryan, why do you want this job?"

"It sounds like such an exciting opportunity. I've admired the Susan Richardson Gray Foundation and all it's done for the community for many years. I know the devastation cancer has on families. My aunt passed away at a young age—only forty-two—from breast cancer. I still miss her. Of course, that was before all the breakthrough research increased the survival rate."

Okay, it was a load of shit. I didn't have an aunt, let alone one who'd died of this horrible disease, but if I needed to pile it on, I would. I also hoped the story, which paralleled Liz's mother would strike a sympathetic chord. Stewart's face remained impassive. If my little speech impressed him, he didn't show it.

"Your resume says you've been a personal assistant before. What were your duties?"

"Anything asked of me," I replied with a light laugh. "I worked for a CPA, and during tax season did everything he didn't have time to do—things like personal banking, dropping off and picking up dry cleaning, food runs, and, of course, seeing to it his clients were comfortable while they waited. I more or less ran the office even though I didn't have the title of Office Manager. I supervised a couple of people who did data entry, and several file clerks. I'm proud to say, the office ran smoothly."

I had worked for a CPA at one time in my life, and did do most of what I just told Stewart.

"Why did you leave?"

"I wanted more of a challenge."

Ha! He'd been a cheap son of a bitch who refused to give me a raise to nine dollars an hour after a busy and highly profitable tax season. I'd told him to cram it, and left.

"This job has its fair share of challenges. Are you prepared to work long hours when necessary, Ms. Ryan?"

"Absolutely, Mr. Stewart. I'm single and report to no one but myself."

The truth at last.

"What can you bring to this company?"

I leaned forward. "Dedication and hard work. A personal assistant wears many hats. As a receptionist, I answer the phones and screen all calls. As a secretary, I'm prepared to do all necessary word processing, keep my boss's business and personal schedules, and guard the door against anyone who doesn't have an appointment. Upon occasion, a PA is a detective, making phone calls, tracking down information, or finding that which is lost. And naturally, I'd expect to run the errands a busy executive just doesn't have time to do. And while the titles may not have accompanied the jobs, I've been doing this all my working life. I'm very organized and efficient."

There! I'd made my pitch. Did he accept it?

"You seem to have a good grip on the nature of the job. In this case, the job also requires you to attend various social events. Are you prepared to sacrifice your evenings to keep our CEO on time and at the right event? Occasionally, more than one occurs on the same night."

"Of course, although no one's ever asked me to do that. On the other hand, what woman doesn't like to dress up and look beautiful for an evening?"

"There may also be some traveling involved. Can you handle that?"

"I love seeing new places. I wish I could afford to do it more often. If you don't mind me asking, what is the starting salary?"

He smiled. "Our starting salary is fifty-thousand dollars a year. From that you are expected to pay for any formal wear necessary. Naturally, job related out of town trips are covered by the company, but that does not include first class airfare. If you want to upgrade, you foot the bill. Same with the hotel. The Foundation pays for a room, you pay for meals and the bar tab."

"I'm a light eater, and only drink wine once in a while."

"I see." He made a notation on a pad.

I had no idea how to read him, so played my ace-in-the-hole. "Ah, Mr. Stewart, I'll be candid. I really want this job, and would be willing to take a salary of forty-five thousand dollars a year."

Forty-five grand a year in South Florida is chicken feed, but it was almost twice what I'd ever made in my life. My living conditions kept my head above water. With this salary, I'd practically wade.

Stewart's eyebrows shot up. "Really?"

"Yes. Think of it as five thousand dollars a year that can be returned to the Foundation for bettering the lives of others. What about benefits?"

"Our benefits package is very generous—full coverage including dental and vision." He wrote on the pad again, and then rose. "I'll take everything you said into consideration, Ms. Ryan."

The interview had ended. I had no choice but to leave. He came with me and opened the door.

Now that I had finished, my heart pounded and unanswerable questions flitted through my mind.

Had he seen through my little white lies? Had my request for a lower salary rung true? Did I sound convincing? Too eager, perhaps? Desperate? Just plain crazy? Or worse yet—pathetic?

I straightened my shoulders. I'd done the best I could. Now, I crossed my fingers. We entered an empty outer office.

"Looks as though Mrs. Hardwick is at lunch," he said, escorting me past her desk and to the door. "We'll be in touch, Ms. Ryan."

"Thank you for the opportunity, Mr. Stewart."

As I stepped into the hallway, the phone in his office rang. He turned, crossed the room, and entered, closing the door behind him. My horoscope must have been sensational today. I concocted a spur of the moment plan at the lucky break.

Without hesitation, I snatched my sunglasses from my purse, tossed them under a chair, and made a beeline for the inbox with the waiting resumes. Mrs. Hardwick was scrupulously tidy. The original e-mails and resumes were clipped together. I flipped through them.

The one on top was from a twenty year old. I dismissed it. Too young. The salary requirements for the second in line started at sixty-thousand dollars a year—too much. The third one didn't have the qualifications. The fourth one made me grit my teeth. It was Corinne's. Her resume was as evasive as mine. Without a moment's hesitation, I folded it and stuffed it into my purse. The urge to keep thumbing through the pile was strong, but Stewart could finish his call any second. I needed to leave. I stepped toward the chair when someone entered from the hallway.

"May I help you?" a voice asked.

I whirled, and then gasped. It was Liz.

"Renee! What are you doing here?"

"Applying for a job. How about you?"

"A job? What job?"

"Personal assistant to some executive."

"That would be me."

"You? You're kidding? I had no idea you worked here," I said, feigning surprise.

"Susan Richardson Gray was my mother. She died of breast cancer at a young age. My father and I formed the Foundation."

"Oh, Liz, I'm so sorry, but know about the ravages of this disease firsthand, too."

I gave her the same story about my fake aunt as I'd given Stewart. Talk about breaks. I hadn't imagined Liz would pop into the interview, but now that she had, I took full advantage of her presence.

She nodded. "Cancer has a way of touching everyone's lives, which gives us all a common thread, I suppose. Have you spoken with Bob yet?"

"Bob? Oh, you mean, Mr. Stewart? Yes, I just finished my interview. I thought it went very well."

The door opened and Stewart stepped into the outer office. He halted, staring at the two of us with raised eyebrows.

"Good morning, Liz. Ms. Ryan, I thought you'd left."

"I got to the elevator and realized my sunglasses were missing. I came back to see if they were here and ran into Liz."

"You two know each other?"

"Renee and I jog at the same park and do yoga

at the same studio."

"You didn't mention you knew Mrs. Gorman."

I laughed with pretended amazement. "I didn't know she was connected to the Foundation or that she was the executive in question. Small world. Well, I guess I should be going. Have you seen my sunglasses, Mr. Stewart? Perhaps I left them in your office."

"I don't recall seeing them." His gaze swept the room before settling under the chair. "Could these be what you're looking for?" He bent over, retrieved the sunglasses from where I'd chucked them, and handed them to me.

"Yes, thank you. I look forward to hearing from you." I turned to Liz. "See you tomorrow at the park."

"Thank you for coming in, Ms. Ryan," Stewart said as I headed for the door. "You wanted to see me, Liz?"

"Renee, wait a minute. Yes, Bob, I wanted to see how the interviews were going. Can we talk in your office? Have a seat, Renee. I'll be out in a few minutes."

She and Stewart went into his office and closed the door. I sat, resisting the urge to bite my nails. Maybe they were talking about employment or maybe Liz just wanted to have lunch with me. Either way, the outcome was positive. Fifteen minutes passed before the door re-opened and the two emerged.

"Renee, I read your resume and discussed your interview with Bob. While your qualifications might be on the slim side, I was impressed with your willingness to sacrifice what amounts to a five thousand dollar yearly donation to the Foundation from your salary. I don't know you well, but you seem like you have your head screwed on well enough to schedule appointments and such.

Ordinarily, I would never hire a friend or acquaintance. It's just not a good idea, but I like you. Plus, I'm going crazy trying to arrange my own schedule. So, how about I give you a one month trial? In the meantime, Mr. Stewart will finish out his scheduled interviews in the event things don't work out."

I leaped to my feet. Hot damn! I'd done it.

"Liz—excuse me, Mrs. Gorman—that sounds very fair. You won't be disappointed or regret your decision, and if it doesn't work out, I won't hold a grudge. When do you want me to start?"

"How about tomorrow morning at ten? I'll run you through my routine. And we're very informal here at the Foundation. Call me Liz. Mrs. Gorman makes me sound old," she said with a smile, and then glanced at her watch. "Oh, nuts, I've got to get going. I'm supposed to meet with some potential donors for one of my charities at La Belle Aurore at one and have a dozen things to do before then. Renee, I'm involved in a lot more than Foundation work. So, you're going to have your hands full keeping the appointments straight."

"That's no problem," I assured her.

She swept from the room. Stewart turned to me. "Ms. Ryan, if you'll just come into my office for a moment to sign some papers, I can get things started."

I followed him inside. He didn't smile, telling me he might not have approved of Liz's decision. I scribbled my name on whatever he handed me. For all I knew I was signing over my first born male child to the Foundation. Who cared? I'd accomplished what I'd set out to do—get the job, albeit on a temporary basis. Finished, Mr. Stewart stood, shook my hand, and welcomed me to the company.

In the elevator I contemplated calling Andy to

gloat, but changed my mind. I was still put out with him about last night. I'd spring the news on him later. As for Corinne, I mentally thumbed my nose. *Sorry, babe, but I can't let you steal this from me.*

Back in my car, I laughed out loud and decided to celebrate my two jobs merging into one. What better way than lunch at a trendy restaurant? I started the car and headed for La Belle Aurore.

****

The words trendy and expensive generally go hand in hand and La Belle Aurore was no exception. It sat smack dab in the center of an equally trendy and expensive shopping district known as Vista Del Mar. A few blocks from the Intracoastal Waterway, it contained some of the chicest shops in South Florida. I'd often window shopped, but never had the bucks to buy anything. I didn't have the money to eat here either, but today nothing would stop me from enjoying my new job.

I arrived early and requested a table along the back wall out of sight of the other diners, including Liz I hoped. Slipping the Lend An Ear from my purse, I turned it on. The other noises would probably be a pain in the ass, but I wanted to see who Liz met. A waiter glided over and stared at the device with a frown. I supposed iPods in trendy restaurants were frowned upon.

"May I get you something from the bar, ma'am?"

"What?" I asked.

He must have mistaken Lend An Ear for a hearing aid. I didn't enlighten him. A smile replaced the frown and he repeated the question in a louder voice.

I ordered a glass of wine and sat back to await Liz's arrival. La Belle Aurore had few empty tables. No matter how lousy the economy, rich people always managed to keep places like this afloat. I didn't begrudge them their money—some of them actually worked for it, and if they were lucky enough to have inherited it, I figured that somewhere along the line an ancestor had worked themselves silly to accumulate it. More power to them. I just wished I'd been born lucky.

The waiter brought my wine and since Liz hadn't walked through the doors yet, told him I'd wait to order. He didn't look pleased at the prospect of not turning a single table over quickly, but I ignored him. I was halfway through my wine when Liz and another couple arrived and were shown to a table across the room. Liz sat with her back to me. I turned up the volume and tried to listen to their conversation.

The background noise almost drowned out what they said, but I caught enough to hear Liz singing the praises of The Humane Society. Liz gave a great pitch. Her stories about unwanted and abused animals damn near had me ready to adopt a pet. When she went into the financial aspects of the charity, I turned off the device, pulled the earplugs out, and shoved everything into my purse. These people sounded legit and posed no threat.

The waiter stopped back. I ordered the cheapest thing on the menu—a mixed greens salad with balsamic vinaigrette at an obnoxious sixteen dollars. I refused another glass of twelve dollar wine.

I ate slowly, not because the food wasn't any good, but because Liz and her companions had been served a few minutes after me, and I wanted to make sure they left first. I kept my head low and shot little glances to her table from time to time. My ringing phone stopped conversation at several nearby tables, and I was on the receiving end of some nasty stares. Luckily, the noise didn't carry to Liz. I fumbled in my purse, answering as fast as I could.

"Hello?"

"Hi, Renee," Andy said. "I forgot all about the art showing tonight. Katie just called to remind me. It starts at eight-thirty. We can leave around six-thirty and have dinner first."

I'd forgotten about the art showing, too. It wasn't my thing at all, but if my new job occasionally called for a social event, I might as well use this one for practice.

"That sounds fine, Andy. I don't have a long flowing dress. Will a cocktail dress do?"

He snorted. "You're asking me?"

"Yeah, right, sorry."

"Where are you? I hear a lot of background noise."

"I'm celebrating at La Belle Aurore."

He was silent for a second. "I take that to mean you got the job."

"I start tomorrow morning at ten."

"We'll talk later," he said, and then hung up.

I snapped my phone shut, popped it back into my purse, and shrugged. He could talk all he wanted, I refused to back down.

While I'd been on the phone with Andy, Liz and her party had finished. I resumed eating. She paid the check and rose, shaking hands with her guests, and then left while they finished their coffee. I watched until the door closed behind her, then lifted my wine glass when a man in the bar caught my attention. He slid from a stool and rapidly snaked his way through the crowd, then out the door.

What the hell is Jeff McCarthy doing here? Is he following Liz?

Sure looked like it to me.

Chapter Fourteen

"So, you got the job" were the first words out of Andy's mouth when I exited my bedroom. Not, "How are you" or "Gee, you look great", but a sarcastic comment sure to put my back up. I took a deep breath before answering.

"That's right, I got the job, and don't want to talk about it tonight."

"I don't like it, Renee. My gut tells me this is a dangerous move."

"My gut tells me I'm hungry. Where are we going?"

He shook his head. "The Silver Shell unless you're not in the mood for seafood."

"Seafood is fine."

We rode to the restaurant in an uncomfortable silence. I was irked at his actions, just as he was probably irritated with mine. I wasn't half as ticked off about his sarcasm as I was about his failure to notice the effort I'd put in to looking sensational. A quick call to Katie this afternoon had assured me the affair was not formal.

"A cocktail dress will work. So would a business suit."

I finally settled on the never-fails little black dress. Its soft cowl neckline and swirling chiffon knee length skirt flattered my figure and I was smug in the knowledge that for the first time in two years I could zip it. I not only looked good—I looked damned good.

As we walked into The Silver Shell, I couldn't help but notice Andy didn't look so bad himself. He wore sharply creased khaki slacks and a navy blue blazer with an elegance I'd not expected. The white silk turtleneck under the blazer clung to his lean body making my mouth water.

Those six pack abs flashed in front of my eyes, not to mention the packing in that skimpy swim suit. My hormones played havoc with my internal thermostat, and while he talked with the maitre d', I covertly fanned my face with my evening bag. Once seated at the table, we ordered cocktails.

"Other than that which is not to be discussed, how did your day go?" he asked, not lifting his eyes from the menu.

"Uneventful." I'd not yet decided what to do about Jeff McCarthy's presence at La Belle Aurore. It and his sudden departure just after Liz's raised my suspicious nature to a new level. It bothered me. I fiddled with my napkin and came to a decision. "Andy, that's not exactly true."

He put the menu down. "What do you mean?"

The waiter brought our drinks, wine for me, scotch for Andy, and I waited until he left before answering.

"I wasn't at La Belle Aurore just for kicks. Liz mentioned she had a luncheon engagement there, so I went and kind of hid in the corner."

"Did she notice and fire you before you even started the job?"

His voice had a hopeful tone that matched the look on his face, but I refrained from slugging him.

"No, silly." I told him about Jeff being there and his hurried exit. "It looked odd or maybe my paranoia is getting the better of me."

"Lots of businessmen eat lunch on Vista Del Mar. Did he follow her into the restaurant?"

"I don't know. When Liz and her friends came in I was focused on them, not who may have followed."

"Some bodyguard you are. Did you see him

before he got up to leave?"

"No. And don't be nasty."

"Then it's probably a coincidence."

"But Jeff doesn't strike me as the type to drink his lunch."

"For all you know, he may have finished his lunch already, and probably never even saw Mrs. Gorman. Maybe he rushed because he was late to an appointment."

Andy's explanation sounded logical. I hate logic, especially when it screws my theories. I sipped some wine.

The waiter returned and we ordered—Chilean sea bass for me and grouper for Andy.

"I suppose you're right. Maybe I'll ask him what he was doing there tomorrow at the park."

"Smooth, Renee. Then you'll also be telling your new boss you were there, too."

"I'll be subtle."

"No, you won't." Andy sighed and took a small notebook and pencil from his jacket pocket. "What's the man's name? I'll check him out."

"Jeff McCarthy. I'm not sure what he does for a living—advertising I think, but he's in his late twenties, about five feet, ten inches, and weighs around a hundred ninety pounds with brown hair and blue eyes. I'm not sure about any scars or identifying marks."

"Doesn't matter. You won't be viewing him in a line-up." He returned the items to his pocket. "Joel was arraigned this morning."

"And?" I took another sip.

"He's got a public defender who requested ROR."

I choked and had to clear my throat. "That asshole got released on his own recognizance?"

"No. The judge set bail at five grand."

"That's all? He broke my window—again!"

"We don't know if he's responsible for the drive

by."

"Of course, he is. I assume he put up the money and is now free to further harass me."

"I have no idea. Don't sound so outraged. He's pissed off and hates your guts, but I doubt he's a repeat offender. I had a little chat with him before the arraignment. He said he received six months and time served on the ADW charge in Georgia. It was his first and only offense. I requested the file from the Atlanta PD."

"He's probably lying and in his car fleeing the jurisdiction as we speak."

"I also checked your incoming phone calls. The hang-ups come from two sources. The first couple of days an untraceable cell was used. After the shooting, it's mostly pay phones."

"And what does that indicate?"

"I'd say your mother found a cell phone in one of the cars she stole, used it until the minutes ran out or until the account was cancelled, and then switched to pay phones."

"There aren't too many of those around anymore. Where were the phones located?"

"Public buildings—the library, the bus station, convenience stores, and even the courthouse."

I had to laugh. "What? None from the jail?"

Andy shook his head. "I wouldn't put it past her."

I wouldn't either. It was *so* Mother. If she needed to make a call and the closest phone was in the jail, she'd use it. And how many cops would expect someone with a BOLO out on them to stroll into the police station, drop a quarter in the slot, and make a call?

"I take it you haven't heard any news about your mother," he said.

"Not a word, although another hang-up call came through just before you arrived home."

Suzanne Rossi

He took a deep breath, and then exhaled. "She's checking up on you—seeing if you're home. I really wish you'd leave town for a while."

"And I really wish you'd quit worrying about me and start concerning yourself with Liz. Her husband wants her dead. Somewhere out there, a killer lurks, gathering information on her routine so she can strike. Have you found out anything about Todd?"

Andy finished his drink, and then stared into the empty glass.

"Mr. Gorman has been writing some big checks lately, all to cash and on his private account. He's also covering them with big deposits from one of the Foundation accounts."

"I knew it! The son of a bitch is embezzling. Probably to pay the hit woman. Why don't you arrest him?"

"Renee, this may not be unusual. He may be paying out of town bills with his account and getting reimbursed from the corporation."

"In this day and age of credit cards? Get real." I thought for a moment. "Well, what about his phone records? You looked at mine, why not his?"

"Do you honestly think he's dumb enough to contact a hit person from his personal cell phone? He's probably got one that's untraceable."

Something in his tone and his choice of words told me Andy might not be as disbelieving as he had been earlier.

"That sounds like you think he's up to no good."

"No matter how I slice it, Elizabeth Gorman matches the profile of the victim you gave in your statement. And if that's true, then the part about the husband must be, too. The problem is we have nothing to hang on him."

"But you have me!"

"All right, let's say we arrest the guy. We have no idea who the hit person is, and only your word

206

the incident occurred. And I'm not sure about the legality of that silly device. Plus, a defense attorney would have a field day with your record. The best we can do is to keep on digging. Sooner or later, he'll make a mistake."

"And in the meantime, the killer is out there. How do we know she isn't setting up the hit for tomorrow or the next day?"

"We don't, but you said the killer told the husband she didn't like to be rushed. That tells me she's careful and methodical." He paused for a moment. "You know, we don't have any proof a woman is the hit person."

"I heard them!"

"Did you actually hear the woman say, 'I'll do it'?"

I concentrated on remembering the conversation. Between the background noise and my own fear, I was no longer sure.

"Not in so many words, but it was implied."

"This woman could have been an intermediary, taking the money and making the arrangements. That might explain why she didn't want to be rushed. She needed time to contact the real killer. Brace yourself. We may not be dealing with a woman after all."

Our food arrived. I love sea bass and this was excellent, but I barely tasted it. My mind churned with the implications of Andy's words. If he was right, then the killer could be—well, anybody.

But now, as Liz's personal assistant, maybe I could throw a monkey wrench into Todd's deadly little plans. Perhaps, I could organize her schedule so that it screwed with her routine. Early meetings would force her to change the time she jogged, and late ones might interfere with yoga. And then, of course, I could always keep an eye on Liz—following her from place to place and staying out of sight. I did it today, why not tomorrow?

****

Andy and I walked through the doors of the Rendell Art Gallery fashionably late—after all, this is South Florida. Located on a side street a block or so off Vista Del Mar, it presented only the best, or so Katie told me. Having never strolled inside an art gallery in my life, I wouldn't know, and looked forward to a new experience.

Twenty-five to thirty people milled around viewing, ooing, and ahing over what struck me as little more than kindergarten level paintings. Blotches of pink and red with a couple of stripes of green had the title "Two Roses." Didn't look like any rose I'd ever seen and the three thousand dollar price tag made me wonder who the hell would shell out that kind of money on this crap.

"Do you believe this?" Andy whispered in my ear. "Why did I let my sister talk me into coming?"

"I have no idea. What is *that* supposed to be?" I stared at a fifteen by fifteen inch canvas sporting two shades of blue with a narrow band of tan at the bottom.

Andy leaned closer to read the tag. "It says, 'The Sea' and someone thinks it's worth two grand."

"Isn't this work magnificent?" a pencil thin woman next to me remarked. "Beauregard is so talented. I have several of his works in my home." She sipped champagne from a fluted glass while gazing at the painting.

"Wow, I should tell my sister she has a budding artist on her hands. This looks just like a thing my niece brought home from pre-school last week. It's displayed on the refrigerator," I said, forcing a proud tone to my voice. I love puncturing elitists' balloons.

The woman glared and moved away.

Andy chuckled. "Maybe this affair won't be so dull after all."

A waiter walked by with a tray of glasses. I snatched one and took a sip. I don't really like champagne, but there's something so elegant about standing around holding a glass of it.

Katie sailed up with a man in tow. She air kissed me and patted her brother's cheek.

"Renee, Andy, I'm so glad you could make it. I'd like you to meet Beauregard, our featured artist tonight. Beau, this is Renee Ryan and my brother, Andrew Jackson."

Beauregard gave Andy a limp handshake and in a burst of Continental bravado, kissed my hand.

"So, nice, I'm sure. Are you enjoying the show?"

Diplomatic Andy nodded. "Yes, so far."

Undiplomatic me said, "Who actually buys this stuff?"

Katie rolled her eyes and shot me a 'shut the hell up' look.

The artist's lip curled. "People with good taste and a view toward the future. Art is an investment. Do you plan on investing tonight?"

I sipped some champagne and gazed at the pictures on the walls. "I don't think so."

Beauregard's back straightened and his nose rose in the air. "In that case, good evening." He strutted away, his buttocks—in way too tight pants—keeping time to his steps, and accosted a new potential investor.

"Geez, Renee. Thanks a lot," Katie said. "You just insulted one of the hottest artists on the east coast."

"He's snooty. So are most of the people here. How can you stand to work with these phonies?"

"It's called money. I get a percentage of the gallery's take on whatever he sells. Rendell has already tacked up four sold signs to the tune of over fifteen thousand dollars, and the night is young. With any luck, I'll come away with four or five grand." She lifted a glass from a passing waiter. "Now, wander around and pretend to enjoy it."

"When can we leave?" Andy asked.

"It's polite to look at all the works."

Andy swiveled his head. "Okay, done. Can we go now?"

Katie gritted her teeth and glared at him. "No! I expect at least an hour out of you."

She stalked across the floor to greet a couple coming in the door.

"I guess I've endured longer hours," I said, tugging him toward another painting. "Come on."

"I suppose I have, too, but this one comes real close to being the worst."

"Look at it as supporting your sister's business."

We strolled from painting to painting. They still looked like something out of day care. The champagne helped to keep me from sneaking out the back door. It was a good thing Andy and I had dinner beforehand, because the promised hors d'oeuvres sucked. I'd had better out of a box from my freezer.

"It's been forty-five minutes," Andy declared, glancing at his watch. "Close counts. I have early shift again tomorrow. Let's blow this joint."

I set my second empty champagne glass on a bench in front of one of the paintings.

"Works for me. Do we say goodbye to Katie or just slither out under her radar?"

"Common sense dictates we slither, but I don't want to piss my sister off any more. She's a wizard at getting even. Let's find her and say thanks."

The crowd had thickened in the past hour and it took us several minutes to wind our way past the knots of people singing the artist's praises. They were all nuts.

We finally found her in the middle of the room clinging to the arm of a tall, dark-haired man. The closer I got; the more familiar he looked.

"Okay, Katie, we've done our duty. Thank you for inviting us and I'm sorry if we irritated you earlier," Andy told her.

Katie laughed. Her hazel eyes sparkled. She sipped champagne and squeezed the arm of the man.

"I should have known the two of you in an art gallery would be the equivalent of the proverbial bull in the china shop. I want you to meet someone. This is Barry Blackledge. Barry, my brother, Andrew, and my best friend, Renee Ryan."

So, this was the famous Barry. No wonder he looked familiar. He was just as Katie had described him—tall with dark hair and killer blue eyes. He stared at us with a startled expression for a moment, then smiled and extended his hand to Andy.

"I'm pleased to meet you. Katie's told me so much about both of you."

I also shook his hand. The palm was damp. And I seriously doubted Katie had wasted any of her short time with him expounding on her brother's and my virtues. On the other hand, maybe he was just being polite.

"Barry, Katie's talked about you, too. What is it you do?" Andy asked, while Katie frowned.

"I'm a motivational speaker. I travel around the country giving pep talks to various groups."

"What's the name of the company?"

"Uh, Blackledge Motivational Paths."

"You own it? Anyone work with you?"

"Just me. At times I wish I was a clone. Then, I could spend more time at home and see Katie," Barry said with a light laugh.

"How fortunate you were able to make the showing tonight," I said.

"Yes, isn't it?"

Andy didn't give up. "Do you have a card? I'm a detective with the Palm Lake Police Department. All cops need a pep talk now and again."

Barry's eyes widened as his spine stiffened. He patted his pockets while Katie glared at her brother. Even I knew Andy would investigate this guy down to his toenails from the information on a business card.

"You know, I don't. I got home this evening, changed, and must have forgotten to bring them."

"Never mind, honey," Katie interjected, still glaring at Andy. "I'll give him your phone number and he can call later."

"Great idea." Andy whipped out the notebook and pencil. "Go ahead."

"I said later," Katie snapped. "Barry, have you met the artist yet? He's right over there. Good night, Andy, Renee. I'll talk to you soon."

I turned to stare as she maneuvered Barry through the crowd to the far side of the room. He walked very straight, as though he had a broomstick up his ass. I had the strangest feeling disaster loomed for the relationship.

I didn't like him. And I had no idea why. For a motivational speaker, I thought it odd he'd have sweaty palms. And for an instant when we'd first been introduced, I could have sworn I'd seen fear in his eyes. It crossed my mind that maybe he was married.

"Come on, let's get out of here," Andy said. "Katie isn't going to let good old Barry anywhere near me tonight. At least I have a name. I'll do research tomorrow." We slipped out the doors, walked to the car, and drove away. "What did you think of Barry?"

I shrugged. I didn't want to encourage Andy to meddle in Katie's life, but couldn't really lie either.

"He seemed okay. Good-looking, but not much substance. Of course, we only talked for a whole two minutes."

"I smelled bullshit."

"Andy, you don't like any of Katie's boyfriends."

"True, but an art showing is tailor-made for someone like him to make valuable contacts. Everybody needs motivation now and then. Forgetting his business cards didn't sound right. No one's that dumb." He stopped at a red light. "Are you jogging tomorrow?"

"Of course."

"I wish you'd reconsider."

"Not a chance. What better way to get in good with your new boss than to jog with her?"

"You can't go her distance."

"I can try, and then there's Jeff."

"Renee, I thought I told you not to question him. You'll look silly again."

"It's a park, remember? Lots of people."

"You thought you heard someone in the woods—remember?"

I'd almost forgotten that incident. The creepiness factor still haunted me, but I'd convinced myself it was just an animal, and refused to let it or Andy scare me.

"It wasn't my mother. Drop the subject."

The rest of the drive home was silent.

****

I arrived at the park early, a subtle show for when Liz came that I was eager. I warmed up, my mind on the day ahead of me, and didn't notice Jeff until he stood next to me.

"Hi, Renee, how goes it?"

"Hey, Jeff." Great. Liz wasn't here yet and I could pump Jeff about La Belle Aurore without giving myself away.

"You're here early today," he said stretching his right leg.

"Yeah, I got a new job yesterday. Wouldn't be too cool to show up late the first day. That's what got me fired from the last one."

"Congratulations. Where're you working?"

"At the Susan Richardson Gray Foundation as a personal assistant to one of the execs."

"Sweet." He switched to his left leg.

"I'm excited about it. So excited in fact that I celebrated with a fancy lunch at La Belle Aurore."

"Oh, yeah? Nice place."

"You ever eat there?"

Jeff shot me a glance that suggested the question might not be subtle. Okay, so it wasn't, but I didn't have a whole lot of time. I'd seen Liz's car drive in. She'd be here at any moment. He resumed stretching.

"Occasionally. In fact, I was just there yesterday myself."

"Oh, really? Small world. Shame we didn't see each other. We could have lunched together."

"I was supposed to meet a couple of guys, but the site was switched at the last moment to another restaurant. I'd turned my phone off during a meeting and didn't get the message until late. Had to run like hell to make it."

His explanation deflated my conspiracy theory. Andy was right again, dammit. It had all been a coincidence. Actually, if I stopped to think about it, Palm Lake wasn't that big a city. Sooner or later, everyone ran into everyone else somewhere.

I had almost finished my warm-ups when Liz arrived.

"Good morning, Renee, Jeff. You're up with the sun today."

"Have to get in my morning run before starting my new job. Don't want to be late the first day."

Liz laughed. "I'm sure your boss will understand. Exercise is very important."

"Does that include leaving work early for yoga, too?"

"Sometimes." She braced her foot on the guardrail and stretched. "Within reason."

"I was kidding. I wouldn't dream of leaving until I was finished with whatever I had to do."

"Don't worry. If I didn't think you could do the job I wouldn't have hired you."

"You're working for Liz?" Jeff asked, his eyebrows shooting up with surprise. "Corinne said something about applying, too."

"Oh, really?" Liz said. "I'll tell Bob Stewart to keep an eye out for her resume. We have several positions at the Foundation available."

Corinne's resume had hit my trash can as soon as I'd returned home yesterday.

"By the way, I wonder what's keeping her this morning. She's usually here by now," I said to deflect the conversation away from jobs and resumes.

Jeff glanced at his watch. "I don't know, but she'll jog alone if she doesn't hurry. I'm stepping up my routine. I think I'll try the three mile trail today."

"In that case, why not join me?" Liz said. "I'll step back up to five miles in another few days. How about you, Renee? Ready to go further?"

The idea of Jeff alone with Liz on a jogging trail left me uneasy. Maybe it was a holdover from seeing him at the restaurant yesterday. As of now, I was in no position to increase my distance.

"Not yet. A mile and a half will have to do. Besides, I want to beat the boss into the office. Have a good run."

Liz and Jeff laughed and turned for the longer trail, breaking into an easy trot. They disappeared around a bend. Jeff had picked up his pace from even a week ago and his leg muscles had become sculpted.

Guess diet and exercise are the keys to healthy living and a good physique.

I stalled around for another couple of minutes before deciding Corinne wasn't coming, and then broke into a slow jog down the familiar path. Freddy was also absent. I no longer walked, and chalked that accomplishment up to perseverance.

I had a lot of nervous energy to work off. Liz may have laughed at my jokes about the boss, but if I didn't perform up to her expectations, the job wouldn't last long. In spite of the embellishments on my resume, I had confidence I could do what was required.

I crossed Joel's bridge and entered the wooded area that had given me such a fright a few days ago. Today, no mysterious rustlings or snapping twigs accompanied me. I ran on. The trees on my right thinned into the grassy area I'd run across after my confrontation with Joel and Sherry. In the distance I saw the bench where I'd sat, and more woods beyond.

My pace slowed and finally stopped. For the first time since overhearing the murder plot, I realized the bench was not far from the longer trail where Jeff and Liz jogged. The temptation to cut across and explore that trail was strong, but I decided to save it for another day. I had to get ready for work.

I turned to continue jogging when that eerie feeling I was being watched returned. The wooded area to my left wasn't all that thick, yet I had the impression someone stared. My gaze scanned the trees, but saw nothing unusual. Then I caught movement out of the corner of my eye. Just a blur, and then it was gone.

"Mother?" I took a couple of steps into the woods, peering hard at the foliage. "Mother, is that you?"

Silence answered me. Not even a bird twittered. A brief breeze stirred the branches sending a chill up my spine.

I stepped further in, and then stopped.
Not an intelligent thing to do.
I whirled and took off down the path, my pace faster than usual.

Chapter Fifteen

Angry at allowing my imagination and paranoid tendencies to send me into a panic, I showered, dressed in a conservative business suit, and headed for my new job.

It was a lousy bird, Renee, not some deranged stalker, and certainly not my mother.

Damn Andy anyway for planting the seed of doubt about the hit woman. Now, I had a whole new set of worries. What if the voice I'd overheard was just a middle man—or woman? Suppose she was the buffer between the killer and Todd. That way no one could connect the two, and the middle man—woman—would have an alibi if the murder took place.

I pulled into the Foundation parking lot with the uneasy feeling Liz's time had run out. It had been two weeks since the incident.

How long does it take to arrange a murder?

Old Todd may have been in a hurry, but a meticulous killer would set the pace of the operation.

On that unsettling note, I reported to Mr. Stewart in Human Resources and signed the final employment papers.

"I hope you'll be happy with us," he said as we walked to my new office. "The Susan Richardson Gray Foundation is an amazing combination of a tightly run ship and a family. Personal time off is generous, especially if an employee wants to devote that time to doing something work related, like a 5K run for cancer or volunteering at the hospice."

"I'm not sure I'd make a good volunteer, Mr.

Stewart, but I'm working my way up to the 5K business."

He laughed—an improvement over his frown of yesterday. "It's Bob, and nobody is required to use PTO for company sponsored events. Here, this is Liz's domain."

He opened the door and I entered a spacious outer office. A huge U-shaped work station with the latest computer and accessories dominated one side of the room. Several files cabinets sat next to it. Next to them I spied a small fridge and a cappuccino machine. Mahogany double doors led to Liz's office. A leather sofa with a matching club chair was opposite my desk. An enormous bank of windows allowed the natural light to stream in. A round table with four chairs stood in front of them.

"Wow! I've never had anything this nice before." Plants nestled in corners, on tables, and hung from hooks in the ceiling, including in the windows where they formed a natural valance. "Am I expected to keep this greenery alive? If so, then I gotta tell you I have the kiss of death when it comes to houseplants."

Bob laughed again. "Liz believes greenery is soothing to the spirit. She also believes in the theory that the exchange of gases is healthy—you know, plants inhale our carbon dioxide, humans do the same with the oxygen given off by vegetation."

"I've heard that. I just never knew anyone who practiced it." I gazed at the mini-jungle and hoped my presence didn't do them in.

"Liz has a lot of theories about health, and don't worry, the plants aren't in your care. A service comes out once a week to water and trim."

I walked behind the desk. Never had I seen so much work space available to one person. To show my efficiency, I turned on the computer, sat in the high-backed leather chair, and opened several drawers.

Bob lifted my phone and punched in a couple of numbers. "Hello, this is Bob Stewart from Human Resources. I'm in Liz's office with her new personal assistant. Could Technical Services send someone over to show her the ropes on clocking in and give her the necessary passwords? Thanks." He hung up. "Someone from tech will be here in a minute."

The phone rang and I reached for it. My new job had officially begun.

"Elizabeth Gorman's office, how may I help you?"

"Is Liz in yet?"

"No, ma'am, she isn't. May I take a message?"

"Just have her call Linda over at the hospice when she gets a chance."

"Does she have your number?"

"Yes. Are you her new personal assistant?"

"Yes, ma'am. My name is Renee Ryan."

"I'm Linda Carver, staff director at the hospice. Welcome aboard."

"Thank you, Ms. Carver. I'll see Mrs. Gorman gets your message as soon as she comes in."

I hung up as Liz breezed through the door.

"Good morning, Renee. How was your run today?"

"It was fine. I'm thinking of moving up to the three mile course soon." I handed her the message. "Linda Carver from the hospice called a minute ago."

"Ah, yes. Linda handles the hospice personnel. She and I discuss the schedule of volunteers and patients every morning." She turned to Bob. "Good morning. Is Renee all good to go?"

"I'm waiting for Tech to activate her passwords."

"Excellent. While we're waiting let me give you a hint of what's to come."

"If you're going to be here for a while, I'll return to my office," he said. "I still have several resumes to read."

Was that a subtle hint not to get too comfortable?

I rose and followed her into the office as Bob left. It was twice the size of mine and even more opulent. Bookcases ran floor to ceiling and paintings I knew were originals hung on the walls. The desk was large enough to double as a dining table, and from the massive design, I assumed an antique. Plants sat and hung everywhere. Liz dropped her purse into the bottom drawer, and then turned to face me with a smile.

"First of all, I like the doors to my office kept open unless I have someone inside or am on a personal call. And I must have coffee."

I laughed. "I can relate to that."

"Good. Always keep a fresh pot brewing. Now, let's go over your duties. The scheduling is the most urgent and important. I also have a list of people to avoid, and one for people I'll talk with immediately."

For the next hour, Liz walked me through her day. We stopped just long enough for the man from Technical Services to set up my computer. During that time, I answered the phones three times. Liz took two of the calls.

"Oh, Renee, please answer Elizabeth Gray-Gorman. It emphasizes my connection to the Foundation. Now, put everything to voicemail and I'll give you a tour of the facility."

While Liz's office and reception area was high end, the rest of the three story building was more utilitarian with the exception of conference rooms. They ran middle of the road with wood furnishings. Cubicles, however, were the order of the day for most of the employees. And the people I met welcomed me with smiles.

I quickly learned Liz kept a master schedule of all activities, and smaller ones for each individual charity. She gave me the "always/never" lists, and I noticed her husband topped the always one followed by her father, step-mother, a celebrity conservative radio talk show host, and several names I didn't recognize. The never list included a city councilwoman known for her persistence, a couple of reporters, and a local businessman reputed to have shady New York connections.

I lost all track of time and ate a quick lunch in the cafeteria before hurrying back to my duties. I made several appointments for the coming week, and logged them into both my and Liz's computers. So far, so good. In an effort at super-efficiency, I triple checked each entry. Several names from the always list called, and then came one from the never.

"Elizabeth Gray-Gorman's office, how may I help you?"

"This is City Councilwoman Margaret Matthews. Put me through to Liz."

"I'm sorry, but Ms. Gray-Gorman is on the other line. Would you like her voice mail or may I take a message?"

"I'll hold."

"It may be quite some time. It's a conference call."

"I said, I'll hold. And make sure she knows I'm holding."

"Very well, ma'am."

I hit the hold button, and then proceeded to arrange my desk drawers. Liz emerged from her office, a folder in hand.

"Please file this, Renee." She glanced at the flashing hold light on my phone. "Who's that?"

"Councilwoman Matthews. I told her you were on a conference call, but she insisted on holding. Oh, I was supposed to let you know she was holding."

"How long has she waited?"

"Uh, ten minutes, give or take."

Liz chuckled. "Serves her right. I know what this is about. She wants me to speak at her re-election luncheon. I turned her down last week and the week before that. I never mix politics with the Foundation." She made a face. "Didn't vote for her anyway."

"Shall I try to convince her to use the voicemail?"

"Can't hurt. Put her on speaker."

I did so, and said in my most professional voice, "I'm sorry, but Ms. Gray-Gorman is still on that conference call. Are you sure you wouldn't like to leave a voice mail or message?"

"Do you know how long I've been waiting? Did you tell her I'm on the other line?"

Her angry tone said I'd pissed her off, but then, I was good at that.

"Yes, ma'am."

"Well, tell her again!"

I looked at Liz, who threw up her hands, shook her head, and pointed to her office, whispering, "Put her through."

I nodded. Liz closed the door. I counted to ten, and answered the irritated woman.

"I'm sorry you've been kept waiting. Ms. Gray-Gorman has just concluded her call. I'll put you through now."

"About time!"

I transferred the call and hung up, feeling as if I'd failed to keep a wolf from the door. A few minutes later, Liz opened the door and walked out, purse in hand and sunglasses perched on top of her head. I apologized.

"Not your fault. She's got the hide of an elephant. I should have made my, and the Foundation's, stand clearer a long time ago. I think she finally got the message. Well, I'm calling it a day. Why don't you, too? Put the phone on voicemail, go home, and have a drink. That's what I intend. I'm meeting my father and step-mother for drinks and dinner at the Savoy. See you tomorrow."

"Thank you, Liz."

She swept out the door. I shut down my computer and engaged the voicemail program. Although my ass was dragging, the time had passed swiftly.

Dinner sounded good. Drinks sounded even better, and I wondered what Andy would bring home to eat. Eating dinner with him had become a habit. One I'd like to keep, along with breakfast.

By the time I reached the house, my stomach begged for Italian—something with a thick, rich sauce, and a bottle of Chianti.

The phone was ringing as I dashed through the front door. I grabbed the living room extension.

"Hello?"

No one answered. In the background country music played and voices babbled. It sounded like a bar. A chill swept over my arms and crawled up my scalp.

The caller hung up.

****

Jogging was the last thing I wanted to do this morning. The leaden sky promised rain, and a cooler than usual breeze made me shiver. Jeff pulled into the parking lot as I exited my car. Liz followed a few seconds later.

After exchanging greetings, the three of us warmed up.

"So, how did the new job go?" Jeff asked. "Was your boss happy with your work?"

I chuckled. "I guess so. I haven't been fired yet."

"Yeah, but I hear her boss is a real hard ass," Liz said with a laugh.

Liz made a joke! This was a new side to her.

Humor made her more human...more approachable.

"Actually, I enjoyed it. The day flew by, and I love the challenge of a new routine. Speaking of which, I think I'll give the three mile course a shot today."

"Good for you. I huffed and puffed at the end yesterday, but it was worth it. I could feel myself getting buff," Jeff said.

"Well, between that and yoga I may fall asleep at the computer tomorrow. Will you be at the studio tonight, Liz?"

"I'll say. Even though I now have you running interference for me, I still need to unwind. My husband's going out of town again this afternoon. We have a potentially big donor up in Boston. Wish I could go with him, but I have a luncheon with a corporate donor today."

Looks like I'll be at yoga class. I'd rather skip the damned thing. So far, I hadn't found much relaxing about it. I preferred the gym.

"What's happened to Freddy?" I asked Jeff.

"We had dinner the other night. Her hours have been changed. Until she can get them changed back, she'll have to forgo jogging. Said to tell you hi."

I told him about Corinne's not being able to find her at the bookstore.

He hesitated, but didn't meet my gaze. "I was at the store last week. Corinne must have talked to the wrong person. Maybe someone new who doesn't know everyone's name yet."

His explanation sounded lame, but plausible. Corinne's suspicions stuck in my mind. Was she right? What if Freddy was stalking one of us? Could Jeff be her partner in a robbery scheme? Is that why he had followed Liz and jogged with her?

"Well, I'm about ready. Liz, Renee, how about you?"

"I'm set," Liz replied, running in place.

"As ready as I'll ever be, I guess. Wonder where Corinne is. She hasn't been here in a couple of days."

"Maybe she's having more trouble with her ex," Jeff commented.

"We'd better go if we want to beat the rain," Liz said.

We started off at a mild trot and slowly increased our speeds. Nobody spoke and I let my mind wander to last night.

My desire for Italian had to wait. Andy arrived with Chinese from a take-out hole-in-the-wall place a few blocks from home. While we'd eaten, I told him about the call, admitting that if Mom was going to hang out in a bar, it would be a joint that played country music. The whole evening was unremarkable—TV followed by an early bed time. We could have been any married couple in South Florida. Not an unpleasant thought.

I refocused on my jogging only to realize I lagged several steps behind Jeff and Liz. We passed the mile and a half marker. I concentrated, trying to step up my pace. At two miles, I threw in the towel.

"Guys, I bit off too much today. Go on without me. I'll walk the rest of the way."

"Are you all right?" Jeff asked.

"Yeah, just no more steam left. See you at the office, Liz."

She didn't answer, just waved and increased her pace. Jeff followed her. I slowed to a walk, breathing heavily. I didn't like leaving them alone. My heart pounded, but soon returned to normal. I had no idea where I was until the trees on my right thinned, and I saw the grassy area.

Curious, I pushed through the bushes and spotted the bench a short distance away. Had the killer and Todd been this close to me? I hadn't a clue. Back on the jogging trail, I walked on around a bend surprised to hear traffic sounds from my left. The vegetation diminished, and I saw cars whizzing by on a four lane street. As I stared, a man in jogging gear exited a car parked on the side of the road, cut through the foliage and onto the trail where I stood.

I'll bet this is where Todd parked. No wonder I didn't see a Porsche in the lot.

The pathway was straight as an arrow in this section, giving a good view of anyone approaching. This was where they'd met. I'd stake my first paycheck on it. Had I heard the sound of cars that day? For the life of me, I couldn't remember. So many sounds had infiltrated, and I'd been too horrified at the conversation to pay much attention.

I resumed my walk. It made sense that Todd hadn't used the parking lot. Liz might have seen his car. I estimated the time I listened in as somewhere around seven. Too early for Liz, but why take a chance? The miserable snake had forked over the down payment, and then slithered through the trees to his car. The woman had jogged on. What was one more jogger? Nothing suspicious in that.

Back in the parking lot, I had just pulled out onto the street when a dark gray Toyota flashed by going the opposite direction. Freddy? I was tempted to follow, but didn't have the time. I checked the rearview mirror just as the car turned the corner. An unsettling feeling rolled over me as Corinne's comments echoed in my mind. I glanced at the dashboard clock. Liz should be finished running by now, but I still didn't like any of it.

I hurried home to shower and change. As soon as I got to the office, I'd check Liz's schedule to see where she planned to lunch and with whom.

With my new theory, I needed to be extra vigilant. Todd was out of town again and Liz was going to yoga. Would tonight be the night?

****

Most of the Foundation employees worked the

traditional eight-to-five with an hour lunch and two twenty minute coffee breaks, one in the morning and one in the afternoon. But my position required I follow Liz's hours, which varied from nine-thirty or ten to six or later. I didn't mind, enjoying the flexible schedule.

I looked up Liz's luncheon agenda when I got into the office. She had a reservation at Winchester's on Oceana Drive with two Holland Corporation execs at twelve-thirty.

Swell—Winchester's—an upscale restaurant with a fabulous ocean view. I wondered how much their mixed greens salad with balsamic vinaigrette cost. At this rate, my paycheck would disappear fast. I phoned for a reservation at twelve-fifteen requesting an out of the way table.

The morning sped by. Liz spent her time in a conference room on the third floor talking with lawyers and tax consultants. I took messages and familiarized myself with the files, leaving at noon for the restaurant. The promised rain had arrived in mid-morning, and it still drizzled.

Winchester's was located a good five miles from the office, too far to walk. I finally found a parking spot and hurried in only a few minutes late. A well-stocked bar was located on the first floor with dining on the second to take full advantage of the view.

Once seated, I gazed around, half expecting to see Jeff lurking in the corner. He wasn't. I relaxed and ordered a glass of white wine. Even the house variety cost ten bucks a pop.

Liz arrived with two men in tow and was seated by the window. She sure knew how to set the scene. I was relieved she didn't bother to look around. My table was nestled in a back corner, but with a simple turn of her head, Liz would see me.

The men didn't look particularly threatening, and I didn't seriously expect the hit man to be the executive of a major import-export business. The trips to and from the office concerned me. I might be able to tail her back to the Foundation. With that in mind, I ordered a steak Cobb salad with a low-fat dressing at only twenty-two dollars. I could have gone cheaper, but needed red meat.

My food arrived and while eating, I planned. If I left first, I'd have to pass within a few feet of Liz's table. Not good. That meant leaving after she did. I hoped this didn't turn into a two hour lunch.

I kept my head down and shot little glances toward the window every few minutes. Halfway through my salad, the waiter brought their food. I ate slower and cast a nervous look at my watch. I clocked in and out on the computerized time clock like most of the employees, and while I was sure ten minutes over the allotted lunch hour wouldn't cause a raised eyebrow, an hour and a half or longer would. I should have taken the chance and left my table earlier. I'd forgo clocking back in, saying I forgot. The waiter brought my bill and I paid.

Liz and her party finally left the table at one-thirty. As she disappeared down the stairs, I counted to twenty and followed. The bar was crowded with tourists escaping another shower. I threaded my way through, pushed open the front doors, and collided with someone standing under the awning. It was Liz.

"Renee, what are you doing here?"

Busted! Now, what? This screwed everything.

"Liz, good grief, what a coincidence."

"Yes, isn't it?" She checked her watch and gave me a strange look.

"I'm still celebrating, trying out new restaurants near the office and such. A friend recommended this place. I take it this is where you had your luncheon." I winced inwardly. Was she thinking a good assistant would have known that?

"Yes. The Holland Corporation has agreed to underwrite the Home for Friendless Animals fundraiser this coming year."

"That's wonderful. Are you waiting for a cab? I'm parked nearby. Can I give you a lift?"

"No thanks, I valet parked." She checked her watch again.

"Wise move. Well, I'd better get back. See you in a few minutes."

I didn't wait for a reply, but took off dodging raindrops as I ran for the car. Damn, had I screwed everything?

On the drive back, I did some quick thinking. I'd stick to my plan of not clocking in. With any luck the error wouldn't be noticed by Human Resources until the end of the pay period. By then, Liz might have forgotten the whole incident.

At the office I realized my days of following Liz to lunch had ended. I couldn't afford either the time or getting caught again, not to mention the cost of the lunches.

She didn't say anything when she walked in, just picked up her messages and closed the door to her office. I wondered if she was irritated with me. Half an hour later, she emerged with several file folders.

"Renee, I'm going back into the lion's den with the lawyers and tax guys. If I'm not back by five, go ahead and leave. Are you going to class tonight?"

"I planned on it."

"I'll see you there."

She left and I breathed a sigh of relief. Liz didn't seem too upset about my late lunch at the same restaurant.

I spent the remainder of the afternoon taking messages, entering donors and the amounts of their contributions to the data bank, and filing a mountain of paperwork my predecessor had left behind. It was a few minutes before five when my cell phone rang.

"Hello?"

"Renee?" Katie asked. Her breath caught and I heard a sniffle.

"Katie? Sounds like you're crying. Are you all right?"

"No," she wailed.

"What's wrong?"

"Barry dumped me."

I barely made out the words between her sobs. The news didn't surprise me. "Oh, no! Did he say why?"

"Not really. He just said it wasn't working for him, and it would be better if we split."

"Well, that was cold. And he seemed so attentive the other night."

"I know. I need a friend. How about meeting me at Tootles for a drink?"

Tootles was a bar not far from Katie's loft. I checked my watch. My class started at six. So what if I was late? Katie needed me, and I liked being needed. Besides, my yoga paraphernalia was in the car. I'd change at the studio. My concerns about Liz centered on after the class.

"Sounds good. I'll see you there in a few minutes."

"I'm already here. Have been since four."

I hung up, shut off my computer, not bothering to clock out, and split for Tootles, arriving at the same time as the after work mob trickled in. I spotted Katie seated at the bar holding a half empty martini glass and slid onto the stool next to her.

I squeezed her arm. "How are you holding up?"

"I'm fucking pissed!" She drained the glass and signaled for another.

"What are you drinking?"

"Cosmos." Her words slurred.

"How many have you had?"

She shrugged. "I don't know—two, maybe three. What are you? My mother? Or worse yet, my brother?"

The bartender held up five fingers.

"No, I'm the friend you called. I'll have a Cosmo, too."

The man nodded and left. "Okay, tell me what happened."

"I have decided that Barry Blackledge is a stinking, no account, sniveling rat-bastard, who should be castrated. And if he were here, I'd do it."

She hiccupped. At least she wasn't crying anymore. "I agree. Any man who claims you're not right for him is a louse."

The bartender brought our drinks. I flipped him my credit card and turned back to Katie who'd swallowed a third of her cocktail.

"You're absolutely right. And he's a coward, too."

"How is he a coward?" I asked, sipping my drink.

"The son of a bitch didn't have the nerve to dump me face to face to face or whatever." She gulped some more. "He fucking phoned it in."

"He broke up on the phone? How classless."

"Tell me! Said he was at the airport and wanted to make the break before he returned. Canceled out on a dinner and a play next week, too. Asshole's probably taking someone else."

"Well, look on the bright side. Andy won't have to check him out."

"Whoopee. Is he still sleeping at your place?"

"Until my mother's caught."

"You making it with him?"

"Sort of."

"What the hell kind of an answer is that?"

I told her about the kiss and the interruption by Joel.

"That was days ago," she said finishing her

drink.

"Your brother apologized for taking advantage of the situation and has been a perfect gentleman ever since."

"Oh, my God! He apologized? Geez, are all men idiots? Why do we think we need them so badly?"

"If I had the answer to that, the women of the world would beat a path to my door. I'd charge a dollar a person and retire."

Katie grabbed my drink and downed it, then swayed and grasped the edge of the bar. "I think I might be a little drunk."

"I think you might be a lot drunk. Let me drive you home."

The bartender brought the tab and my credit card. I signed and helped Katie to the car. Her loft was only a few blocks away. I steered her into the bedroom.

"Do you want me to stay?"

She shook her head. "No, that's all right. I'm going to bed. Thanks for being there, Renee." She gave me a hug, and then collapsed on the bed. "You're a true friend, and I love you."

Katie's eyes shut and she was asleep before I cleared the doorway.

In the car, I glanced at the dash clock. I'd be a little late, but didn't care. Nothing was more important than being a friend.

****

I arrived at yoga twenty minutes late and found a spot near the door. Corinne was a no-show here, too, and I wondered if she was sick. Without her phone number, I couldn't even check on her.

The class wasn't crowded. The rain must have kept people at home. The on again, off again showers had made for a dreary day.

I'd left a message for Andy saying I'd be here and not to wait dinner. Maybe I could persuade Liz to have dinner with me. After class, we met in the lobby.

"Dinner?" I asked.

Liz shook her head. "Can't tonight. I have to draft a report. Since we're a tax exempt corporation, I have to justify that status every year to the state. That's part of what the meetings were all about today."

"In that case, I'll see you in the morning."

I followed Liz's example of being aware of my surroundings. I also waited a couple of minutes, and then tailed her.

It was out of my way by miles, but I wanted to make sure she made it through the gate. I assumed the gatekeeper would check everyone who entered like delivery men and yard maintenance crews to make sure they'd also left by the end of the day. God knows I'd never get past him.

I hung back in traffic until she pulled into her neighborhood. The gate opened and she slid through. Having done my job, I drove on past. It was time to head home.

My car clock read seven-thirty. The rain began to fall again in a hard shower. Retracing my route would take another fifteen minutes, so I opted for a short cut on a less well-traveled street.

I had this nagging worry that something was about to happen. Maybe I should have offered to help Liz with the report. That would have gotten me past the gate. I knew Todd wanted her death to look like an accident. Would a home invasion qualify? I imagined the headlines—*Socialite Philanthropist Murdered By Intruder*.

The more I thought, the more I worried. Freddy and Jeff flashed through my mind.

Go back to Liz's. The gatekeeper will call her before letting me through, and I can be convincing. I'll say I feel it's my job to help with the report.

I was in a section of town that catered to self-storage. Warehouses lined the left side of the street, and a canal ran along the right, a small guardrail the only thing separating it from the road.

I looked for a place to turn around. The businesses were closed for the evening. Chains stretched across the driveways barring easy access. I'd been so intent on my mission I didn't notice the pick-up behind me until the lights glared in my rearview mirror. The damned thing was inches off my bumper.

I tapped my brakes and the truck backed off. Ahead I saw an unchained driveway, and flashed my turn signal.

The truck rammed me hard from the rear. I skidded on the wet pavement, frantically turning the wheel to maintain control. What was the matter with this idiot?

Still skidding, I was rammed again in a perfect pit maneuver. I spun and hit the guardrail before I could brake. I screamed and the airbag deployed. My car rose over the barrier, nosing straight down the embankment toward the dark waters of the canal.

Chapter Sixteen

I screamed again certain I'd be a statistic in the morning. Then like a dog racing to the end of its leash, the car abruptly stopped—the momentum sharp enough to give me deadly whiplash if it hadn't been for the airbag and my headrest.

In the distance, the truck roared off. My heart pounded, and I batted the bag out of my face so I could breathe. The wind riffled through the trees, and the rain popped on the surface of the water two feet away.

The back end of the car lurched to the left threatening to barrel roll through the mud and grass into the canal. A massive shot of adrenaline spurred me into action. I needed to get out—now! Sobbing with fear, my shaking fingers fumbled for the door handle. I jerked several times, but nothing happened. My heart hammered in my ears and I couldn't draw enough breath into my oxygen starved lungs. Then, I realized the driver's side window had shattered, the glass crackling into a thousand jagged lines.

I unbuckled my seat belt, grabbed my purse and using it as a battering ram shoved the shards away, creating an opening. Still sobbing, I crawled out head first to the ground below and clawed my way up the embankment to the road where I sat huddled on the shoulder. My mind refused to work. Already two passersby stopped and ran toward me.

"Jesus, lady, are you all right?" a man asked, crouching beside me.

My teeth chattered so hard I couldn't speak.

Rain pelted my body, the stinging pellets soaking my clothing. I shivered uncontrollably.

The man pulled out a cell phone and dialed 9-1-1 giving the emergency operator the location, while another man and a woman joined us.

"She's shivering. Probably in shock. Harry, go get a blanket out of the trunk," the lady ordered. "Come on, honey, lie down and prop your feet up."

I did as she asked on the wet pavement. Her companion brought the blanket and covered me from neck to ankles.

"What happened?" she asked. "Did you lose control in the rain?"

I shook my head and tried to answer. My reply came out in a breathless gasp. "No, hit and run. Rear-ended."

"Can we call anyone for you? A husband?" the man with her said.

The blanket had warmed me enough to get my brain in gear. Andy! I wanted Andy. I wanted his warm arms encasing me in a safe cocoon. I wanted his lips on mine soothing my terror. I wanted to hear his voice telling me everything would be all right. Damn it, I just wanted *him*.

"My—a friend, Andy Jackson. I—I can do it."

The first man handed me the phone, and I dialed Andy.

"Andy?" My breath caught in my throat.

"Renee, where are you? Yoga let out an hour ago."

"Andy, I—I—" The held breath came out as a sob.

"Renee? What's wrong?" His voice had a sharp, worried tone.

I tried again. "I've been in an accident."

"Where? Are you hurt? What happened?" The worry had changed to fear.

"Not hurt. Just shook up. Someone ran me off

the road. I almost ended up in a canal."

"Where are you?"

"Out on Sable Road almost to Whitten Avenue."

"Call 9-1-1. I'm leaving now." I heard the jingle of car keys and the thud of footsteps as he ran.

"Some people have stopped and are helping me. They called."

"Sit tight, honey. I'm coming." The line went dead.

Two police cars and a fire rescue vehicle arrived joined by an ambulance a few minutes later. After making sure I wasn't injured, the paramedics helped me from the roadside and removed the blanket, then wrapped me in some kind of thermal thing that resembled aluminum foil. I may have looked like a Thanksgiving turkey, but I was instantly warm. With the warmth came coherence and I told my story to the officers while seated on a gurney next to the ambulance.

"Did you get a look at the driver?"

"No. The headlights blinded me and after the hit, I had my hands full trying to stay on the road."

"What about the vehicle? Any description?"

I shook my head. "I think it was a pick up or maybe an SUV, but I'm not sure. I have no idea of the color. Sorry."

"Will someone be able to take you home from the hospital?"

"I don't need to go to a hospital, and yes, a friend is on his way." I pulled the foil closer, hoping Andy thought to bring dry clothes.

The cops returned to their cars and huddled, no doubt discussing my report, while the ambulance crew checked my vital signs and swabbed at a few cuts.

Andy arrived. He leaped from his car, showed his badge to the officers, and trotted over. He embraced me, his hard muscles adding to the warmth factor. He was here. I was safe. To my horror, I buried my face in his chest and burst into tears. He held me tight until my choked sobs quieted.

"Are you all right?" he whispered in my ear.

I nodded and wiped my eyes with my fingers. "I'm fine now that my heart's stopped beating like a tom-tom. God, I was scared. I thought I'd bought it."

He gripped my shoulders, kissed me on the forehead lightly, and then on my lips hard.

"Tell me what happened—in detail."

I sighed, but went through the whole thing again for his benefit, his expression becoming grimmer with each word.

"I've got dry clothes for you in the car. Stay put. I'll be back in a few minutes."

He returned to his car, and then to me with a pair of jeans and a t-shirt. "After I hung up, I went back and got these. Thought you'd need them."

I slipped off the gurney and inside the ambulance where I changed while Andy inspected my Honda and the embankment. The rain had stopped, but I wrapped myself in the aluminum foil thingie again anyway. It felt good.

"You were damned lucky," he said when he came back.

"The car stopped so fast I thought I'd break my neck. What caused it?"

"A tree stump. Probably a leftover of one of the hurricanes a couple of years ago. It's about two feet high. Wedged between the frame and your axle just in front of the right rear tire. Were you airborne at any time?"

"I think so. I hit the guardrail and seem to remember a flying sensation."

Andy shook his head. "A foot further and the stump would have missed the axle and hit the gas tank. A puncture could have sent you to not only a watery, but a fiery grave as well."

My stomach turned over and I swallowed hard. Andy was right—I'd been damned lucky.

One of the paramedics walked up. "Ma'am, we're ready to transport. Do you want to lie down on the gurney or sit in the ambulance?"

"I don't need to go to the hospital. I'll be fine."

"Go with them, Renee. Stay there until I arrive. I'm going to talk to the officers for a few minutes."

"But I'm not injured."

"You don't know that! You said the car stopping almost snapped your neck. Get it checked out."

"But—"

"Just do as I ask," Andy said in a sharp voice.

"All right, all right, but why are you mad at me?"

He sighed and ran a hand through his hair. "I'm not mad at you. I'm scared. Humor me, okay?" He dropped a light kiss on my lips.

"Okay." I traced my tingling lips with the tip of my tongue and laid on the gurney. They lifted me into the ambulance. I waved. Andy nodded, and then the paramedics shut the doors, blocking out the view. We rolled for the hospital.

****

I lay with my eyes closed, the sound of beeping monitors creating a rhythm in my head. Someone had drawn the curtains around the bed in the emergency room. Occasionally, people walked by and I'd open my eyes for a moment. The breeze created by their passing blew the curtain apart a couple of inches. No one bothered me. The tests were all finished and the consensus was I'd live. The doctor had given me a mild pain pill for the aches that would soon surface, hence my languid pose. At some point I had scraped my arms, probably when exiting the window, and now sported several bandages.

The curtain rings rattled and someone squeezed

my big toe. I opened my eyes a slit. Andy had arrived.

"'bout time," I muttered.

"What did the doctors say?"

"Just what I said. I'm fine. The airbag and the headrest did their jobs. I'll have some bruising from the seat belt and shoulder gizmo, but that's all."

"Thank God."

"So, am I sprung from this medical purgatory?"

"As soon as I find a doctor to sign you out."

I yawned. "Well, hurry. They gave me something and I might not be awake much longer."

He grinned and left, returning a few minutes later with the doctor.

"Ms. Ryan, if you'll just sign at the spaces marked with an 'X' you can go home."

He disconnected the heart and blood pressure machines from my body and handed me a clipboard with several sheets of paper attached. I scribbled my name and Andy helped me sit on the edge of the bed while a wheelchair was brought in. He and a nurse assisted me into it and wheeled me out the doors. She placed a small bottle of pills in my hand.

"One every six hours as needed. Don't forget to call your doctor in a day or two for a checkup," she said.

"Stay put. I'll go get the car," Andy told me.

Where would I go? I waited a couple of minutes, until he arrived. Settled in the car, I fastened my seat belt and winced as the first twinge of the promised pain nailed my shoulder.

Overhead, the stars twinkled. The rain had moved on and the cool air helped revive me from my drug induced stupor. I waved at the nurse as we pulled away.

"So, how's my car?"

"Pretty banged up. A wrecker towed it to a nearby garage."

"Is it a total loss?"

"Probably. What were you doing on that road anyway?"

I told him about following Liz and my uneasiness.

He scowled. "Damn it, Renee. Didn't I tell you to be careful? What the hell were you thinking?"

"How was I to know some asshole would rear end me?"

He was silent for a minute, and then said, "We got a report of a black pickup stolen from the parking lot of a bar over on Twelfth Avenue between six and seven this evening. It was later found with heavy front end damage abandoned in a strip mall not far away. Both places are only a few blocks away from the yoga studio."

"You think this was deliberate?"

"Too much of a coincidence not to be. I'd have to say you were so intent on being the follower, you never checked to see if you were being tailed."

He had me there. I'd never even thought about it until the headlights appeared.

"Are you saying I'm not very good at this sort of thing?"

"You suck at it. Unfortunately, your mother's damned good at stealing cars and creating havoc. I can't believe we haven't caught her yet."

"Neither can I, because then she could tell you she's not doing these things. Is Joel still in jail?"

"He made bail this morning."

"I rest my case. He followed me to the studio, stole the car, ran me off the road, and split. I don't suppose his fingerprints showed up on the truck, did they?"

"It's being processed, but my guess is whoever stole it wore gloves. You hungry?"

"Starving. What time is it?"

"After ten. I'll swing past a drive-through at the

next fast food joint."

He did and I ordered the largest burger on the menu, fries, and a diet soft drink, which made Andy shake his head.

"All those calories and you get a diet drink."

I ignored him and shoved a couple of fries into my mouth. I'd consumed half the meal by the time we hit my driveway, and didn't miss a chomp or slurp on my way to the kitchen. Andy opened a beer and stared at me with a troubled expression.

"What?" I mumbled with my mouth full.

"I know you take being a bodyguard seriously, but don't do this again. It's only by the grace of God, you weren't injured tonight. Forget the yoga crap. Just go to work and home."

"What about my jogging? And the gym? I'm beginning to see results and don't want to stop."

"It's just until your mother's recaptured."

"That could take a while. She's been outsmarting you for a week." Ignoring his glare, I crammed the last of my sandwich and fries into my mouth and washed them down with the remaining soda. "Look, Andy, Mother blends into the crowd. She's average height and weight, with average brown hair, and average features. There's nothing outstanding about her. For all we know, she's sleeping in the shed out back with the hurricane shutters. And I still say she wouldn't hurt me. Now, if you don't mind, I'm exhausted. I'm going to bed." I patted his cheek. "Go find that son of a bitch, Joel Wainwright."

"Renee, I'm worried. If it hadn't been for that lousy tree stump..." He paused and sighed. "Enough talk for now. You're right. Go to bed. I'll see you in the morning."

Andy ran his knuckle down my cheek to my jaw before kissing the tip of my nose. I tried, but couldn't control the tremors. They started from deep in my gut and radiated to my fingers and toes. God Almighty, just his touch, this simple touch, was not only giving me impure thoughts, but had me wanting to act on them in the worst way—or the best, depending on how I looked at it.

I made my way back to the bedroom, undressed and slid under the covers. In spite of my words, I had to wonder if Andy wasn't right. Maybe my mother had deteriorated under the incompetent care of Dr. Reynard and had crossed that thin line between eccentricity and insanity.

Oh, Mother, would you really be angry enough to kill me?

****

I borrowed Andy's car and arrived at the park early the next morning, limping only a little. As predicted, my left shoulder hurt like hell, and I had the beginnings of a multi-hued bruise forming across my abdomen. I shouldn't have come, but wanted to ease my mind that Liz was all right. Relieved, I spotted, and then joined her at the guardrail. My intuition concerning her safety last night was unfounded. I should have been more cognizant of my own.

"Good grief, what happened to you?" she asked eyeing my gauze wrapped arms.

"I had an accident on the way home last night." I gave her the *Reader's Digest* version of what happened, minus Andy's deliberate theory.

"Oh, my God. Where did this happen?"

I hesitated and winced as pain shot up my leg. Should I tell her where or make up something? I settled on the truth with just a tiny white lie thrown in.

"On Sable Road."

"Sable Road? That's out near me."

"I know. I was half-way home when I decided to see if you could use my help with that report, so I turned around and headed back to your house. It's my job to do stuff like that. I should have offered earlier."

Liz frowned. "How do you know where I live?"

Damn. Major blunder. Come up with something fast.

"Well, I didn't have an address, but you once said you used the gym at the country club because it was convenient. I assume you live in a gated community, and there are only two—one surrounding the club and one just down the road. If I didn't find you at the first, I'd go on to the second." I threw in a small laugh for good measure. "I should have just gone home."

Okay, it wasn't the world's greatest lie, but not bad for spur of the moment, and I gambled Liz wouldn't remember what she had or hadn't said two weeks ago.

"That was dedicated, but unnecessary. It's just a first draft. Don't worry, you'll have plenty to do when I'm finished with it. Is your car totaled?" she asked.

"Pretty much. I borrowed a friend's car this morning. He caught a ride into work with a co-worker."

"Let me call a friend of mine. He owns a car rental agency. He'll give you a good rental at the Foundation discount and deliver it to the office."

I thanked her. Andy had offered to play chauffeur when possible and my budget would stretch to a cab if necessary.

"Take the day off. You must hurt like hell."

Use a sick day on my third day at work? Not a good move. "I'm fine, just a little sore, that's all. I can answer phones and make appointments. Just don't expect me to run up and down stairs too fast, which reminds me, I probably won't go too far this morning, but I wanted to give it a shot."

Before she could answer, Jeff walked up.

"Holy cow! What happened to you?"

I went through the whole story again. By the time I'd finished, Liz was ready to run.

"I'll see you at the office. And if you feel bad, leave," she said and trotted off.

His gaze followed her down the path before transferring to the parking lot. "Wonder if Corinne's going to show up today."

"She missed yoga last night, too. I hope she's not sick. I'd call, but don't have her number." I'd suspended warming-up. It hurt too much. "Corinne's sure made improvement. In less than two weeks she's gone from walk-run to the three mile course. I guess it doesn't take long to get back in shape if you've jogged before."

"From what I hear, even missing a couple of weeks can set you back quite a ways." Jeff paused. "I wonder if she applied for the job you got. Kept asking me questions about how well I knew you and Liz, and if I thought you might be mad if she did. She said she was concerned about how you don't seem to get out of the house enough, and wondered what you did for fun."

"Funny, I had another friend ask me the same question last week. It's true. I didn't do much of anything until I met you guys. Now look, Liz is not only my friend, but my boss as well, and I look forward to my morning jogs for the socializing as much as the exercise."

"I know what you mean." He did a few deep knee bends. I sat on the guardrail with my back toward the parking lot. Jeff's gaze settled over my shoulder. "Well, look who's here."

I turned too abruptly and winced as a shot of pain jabbed my back. Corinne strolled up. "Hello, stranger, Jeff and I were just talking about you. Where have you been?"

"The only appointments I could get with the personal trainer were in the mornings, so I decided to let the jogging slide for a few days until he can squeeze me in some afternoon."

"I was afraid you might be sick or something. You missed yoga last night, too."

She grinned. "Last night I had a hot date."

"Do tell."

"Is this going to get embarrassingly female, because if it is, I'm outta here," Jeff said, laughing.

Corinne also laughed. "My hot date was with my ex-husband. He wants to get back together."

"You're kidding! After he dumped you for another woman, and then tried to screw you out of the alimony?" I exclaimed.

"What did you tell him?" Jeff asked.

"I told him to drop dead, but after I'd consumed a very expensive meal. I'm ready to move on. I've even sent my resume out to a few places."

"Renee just got a new job, too."

Corinne looked at me with raised eyebrows. I wanted to shoot Jeff.

"I'm Liz's new personal assistant."

"No kidding? I applied there, but didn't hear back. Guess I was too late. Boy, you jumped on that one fast."

"Yeah, well, I was surfing job availabilities online when the Susan Richardson Gray Foundation popped up and took a chance. I've had a lot of experience doing that kind of thing. You know, there are several openings at the Foundation. Why not re-apply? It'd be fun to work together."

"That's not a bad idea. Are you guys ready to go?"

"I am," Jeff said. "What about you, Renee? Going to give it a try?"

"I might walk a little ways, but that's all."

"I was going to ask about the bandages. What

happened?" Corinne said.

I kept my answer brief this time around. "I'm fine, just a little sore."

"Well, I hope they find the person who did it. See you later." She waved and Jeff joined her on Liz's trail.

I rose and walked down the beginner's path. I felt guilty about stealing Corinne's resume, and hoped she'd re-apply. Maybe a good word from me or Liz would get her in the door. And it would be fun to work with two of my friends.

And speaking of friends, don't forget to call Katie. She's probably got the mother of all hangovers.

I managed a half a mile before turning around. Time to call it quits and head for home. I hurt, and today I planned to change Liz's routine as much as possible.

****

"Elizabeth Gray-Gorman's office. How may I help you?"

"Is Ms. Gray-Gorman in?"

"No, sir, I'm sorry, she's in a meeting. Would you like her voice mail?"

"Yes, please."

I pressed a button and hung up. That was the fifth voice mail in the last half an hour. The Palm Lake Home for Unwed Mothers annual luncheon was only a few weeks off and I assumed last minute details needed to be ironed out.

A jab of pain stabbed my shoulder, and I rotated it slowly. Since the bandages wouldn't have survived the shower this morning, I replaced them with those extra large band-aids. My suit jacket hid them from sight. They stung a little, but considering the alternative, I put up with it.

Liz had already departed for the third floor and her meeting with the finance people when I came in. She'd left several folders with data entry material and a note saying that if I didn't feel up to snuff to go home. I didn't feel up to snuff, but stayed anyway.

I entered a few items when the phone rang again. At this rate, I might be here until midnight.

"Elizabeth Gray-Gorman's office. How may I help you?"

"Ms. Ryan?"

"Yes, this is Renee Ryan."

"This is Sophia Rogers in Human Resources. You clocked out yesterday at noon, but never clocked back in or out in the evening. Did you take time off? I need to know to adjust the personal time off or sick day schedule."

Wow, that hadn't taken long. "I'm so sorry. I was here, but forgot to clock in and out. I'm still getting used to this method. I went to lunch and returned around one, and left at five."

"It's very important that you remember, Ms. Ryan. Please, leave yourself a note by the computer until you get used to the routine."

"Yes, I will. Thank you for the suggestion."

I hung up and stuck out my tongue at the phone.

A moment later, a man entered the office with several file folders in his hand. "Is Liz in?"

"I'm sorry, she's in a meeting. May I help you?"

"I'm Masters from the Literacy Foundation, and she asked for these files last week. I was hoping to discuss some things with her. Do you know how long she'll be?"

"I have no idea. Would you like to make an appointment to see Ms. Gray-Gorman?"

"I really do need to talk to her, but I'm tied up the rest of the week. What's her schedule look like?"

I pulled up the schedule screen on the computer. "She's pretty jammed up, too. Mornings are full. Nothing in the afternoon until next Tuesday."

"I can't wait that long. I need answers to several questions before then. Is she free first thing in the morning at any time? I could stop by before going into the office."

An idea flashed through my mind. Time to change the routine and I didn't even have to work at it. It had dropped into my lap like a ripe plum.

"Let's see, the Literacy Foundation is on the south side of town, isn't it? That's quite a distance from here. Perhaps, the two of you could meet for breakfast tomorrow."

"That's a great idea. This is important, but won't take much time. Is nine o'clock all right?"

"Let me set it up tentatively, Mr. Masters. How about The Breakfast Bar on Sixth Avenue? If there's a problem, I'll get in touch and we can re-schedule. Would you like to leave those files so Ms. Gray-Gorman can review them?"

Masters clutched them to his chest as if they were of national security importance.

"No, no, that's fine. I'll bring them with me."

He gave me his number and left. I heaved a huge sigh of relief. If Liz didn't object, I had just kicked Todd's ass and that of the killer for at least one day.

I worked on data entry and taking messages until noon when Liz returned. I handed her several slips of paper, and informed her of the early meeting with Mr. Masters.

She frowned. "That means I won't get any running in. What's my schedule like for tomorrow morning?"

I pulled up the screen again. "You have a meeting with Linda Carver at ten-thirty and a conference call scheduled for eleven-thirty."

"Damn. Don Masters is a nice guy, but a fussbudget. He always explains things to me, like he thinks I don't get it. He also has a tendency to just drop in, and then frets when I'm not available."

Disappointed, I said, "Would you like me to re-schedule for later next week?"

"No. Unfortunately, he's right, I do need those files. Naturally, he didn't leave them with you."

"No, I'm afraid not. Clutched them to his chest like a newborn baby."

"That's Don. Call him and change the time to seven-thirty at the Coffee House on Remington Street. I'll jog afterward. I'm expecting some finance files from the hospice. When they get here, please bring them up to conference room four. I'll be there the rest of the afternoon. It's time for the annual Foundation audit."

She glanced at the messages and swept into her office, closing the door. I called Mr. Masters who wasn't pleased with seven-thirty or the change in venue, but agreed anyway, and entered it in the computer. My stomach growled reminding me I hadn't eaten breakfast.

I made my way to the dining hall and ordered a chicken Caesar salad. About half of the dozen tables were occupied. I got a diet drink from the vending machine and gazed around the room. Two women sat at a table along the wall. Never shy, I approached.

"Hi, do you mind if I join you?"

"No, of course not. I haven't seen you before. Are you new?" one of them asked.

"Yes. I'm Renee Ryan, Ms. Gray-Gorman's new personal assistant." I pulled out a chair and sat, unwrapped the plastic utensils and settled the paper napkin on my lap.

"I'm Sandy Hawkins from Finance."

"And I'm Carol Williams, also from Finance," the other woman said.

"So, how do you like working here? This is only my third day, but so far I love it."

"It's a great company. The pay is good, and the hours flexible," Carol told me.

"And the people are so friendly," Sandy added.

I took a couple of bites of salad. Since I had them engaged in conversation, I might as well pump them for information about Todd.

"Yes, everyone seems very nice. I heard that Ms. Gray-Gorman's husband also works here. It must be nice to work in the same place as your spouse. I haven't met him yet. What does he do for the Foundation?"

Carol made a disparaging face. "He's in charge of getting donations, and then distributing them to the various research centers and such."

"He travels a lot and isn't in the office very much," Sandy said.

Well, that was short and to the point. "That's too bad. With Liz's schedule, they must kiss on the fly." The two women glanced at each other. "I'm sorry, did I say something wrong?"

"Todd Gorman is the one person in this company I can do without," Sandy told me.

"Oh? How come?"

"I worked here about a month when the asshole made a pass at me."

"With his wife in the same building? That's ballsy."

"Rumor has it he's had his hand up the skirt of more than one secretary," Carol replied.

"Goodness, does Liz know?"

"She's probably heard the rumors, but she's either in denial or her husband convinces her it's gossip."

Sandy shook her head. "He's damned attractive and with charm out the ass. Turns it on like a water faucet. He told me I could play his game or find raises hard to come by. I told him to fu—er, buzz off."

"He probably doesn't even remember you," Carol commented. "You got a raise two weeks ago. Any way you slice it, he's an arrogant jerk."

They finished and left, while I pondered their comments. Arrogant I believed, but I worried about what they'd said regarding Liz's knowledge of her husband's philandering. If she was in denial, it was deep denial. My guess was the son of a bitch had a silver tongue to go with the silver spoon born into his mouth and was adept at lying his way out of anything.

Then, a chill passed down my spine. I remembered Liz's words about it being audit time. Did Todd know? If he had screwed around with the accounts to pay for the hit, then Liz's time really was running out.

On my way back to the office, Andy called on my cell.

"Just wanted to let you know we only found one unidentified fingerprint on the door handle of the truck. The owner had it detailed two days ago and no one else has driven it."

"Unidentified? That counts out Mother. You have her prints on file."

"Joel's, too. Plus your mother hasn't bothered to wear gloves with any of the cars she's stolen in the past week."

"So, if it's not Mother or Joel, then who?"

"My question exactly. We may have another player in the game."

Chapter Seventeen

"It's the bimbo from Carson Electronics," I said with conviction that night at dinner.

"Either your mother or Joel could have wised up and worn gloves," Andy countered, shoveling lasagna into his mouth.

"This afternoon you said we had a new player in the game. The bimbo is a new player."

"Angela Peabody didn't strike me as the kind smart enough to steal a car."

"So, she had help. Maybe my no-account ex-boss is the culprit. I caused him a lot of grief both at the office and at home. I'll bet he's sleeping on the sofa."

Andy put his fork down and sipped some Chianti, a thoughtful look on his face.

"I'm worried, Renee. You piss people off without half trying. In fact, sometimes I think you do it deliberately." He resumed eating. "Personally, I don't think Wainwright would come after you within hours of posting bail. Being in jail for even a couple of days makes people like him cower under the covers at the thought of ever returning."

"He got a taste of jail seven or eight years ago. I doubt he's cowering anywhere." I ate a bite of some great lasagna. Andy had stopped by Dinners on the Run on his way home. Unfortunately, I was too irritated to enjoy it. "So, if it's not my mother or Joel, and you don't suspect the bimbo and my ex-boss, then who ran me off the road?"

"I can't say if the shooting and this are connected. It's possible someone stole the truck and ramming you was their idea of fun. When you headed for the canal, they panicked."

"Then why mention another person at all?" I ceased eating and stared at him. "You're hiding something, aren't you? What is it?"

He sighed and pushed his plate away. "Both the shooting and this road incident are up close and personal. This is someone who is out to get you specifically, and hates you enough to go to tremendous lengths to do it. I can only think of one person with that kind of determination—your mother. Angela Peabody has an alibi for the night of the shooting."

"Big deal—she was at a crowded bar. She could have slipped out for twenty minutes and nobody would be any the wiser."

He shook his head. "That's not the easiest thing to pull off. You can never be sure someone won't come looking for you. Besides, if Angela wanted to get even, she'd do it verbally with character assassination."

"You're still holding something back. What?"

"Renee, all the stuff that's happened to you occurred after you heard this so-called murder for hire plot. Are you sure you weren't seen running from the area that morning?"

I finished my food and sipped some wine as I thought.

"I don't know. I mean, I heard footsteps—one set running and the other set walking. That's when I took off. But why would either Todd or the hit woman think I'd overheard anything? For all they knew I was a berserk jogger with an iPod."

Andy picked up our empty plates and took them to the sink. He didn't answer as he rinsed, and then stashed them in the dishwasher. I poured another glass of wine and waited. His new theory sent cold chills down my spine.

"I checked out the bench you said you sat on. It's

visible from that path. Either the killer or Todd could have seen you leap to your feet and take off."

So, Andy had done the same thing as I. "But how would he or she know my name and where to find me?"

"It wouldn't be the first time information has leaked from the Palm Lake Police Department."

"Kind of screws your theory about my mother, doesn't it?"

"No, I'm just thinking out loud. I still think she's good for the shooting. Even the canal incident is right up her alley, but if so, she changed her MO and wore gloves. And that's got me bugged."

Andy closed the dishwasher and poured another glass of wine, killing the bottle.

"What about the guy I turned into Home Security? Did you ever find him?"

"He lives in Washington, D. C. now, and works for the government. He wasn't even close to South Florida."

"Jeff McCarthy! Did you get a chance to check him out?"

Andy sighed. "Jeff McCarthy is exactly who he says he is."

"Well, what does he do for a living? I would imagine being a hit man is a part time thing." I told him of my theory regarding Freddy and Jeff being thieves.

"Renee, if that was the case, then why haven't they robbed someone?"

"Then how about—"

"Oh, for God's sake, will you let it drop? I have four open cases at the moment. Technically, I shouldn't even be investigating this since no murder has occurred. Let's talk about something else. I need to think, and I'm tired."

He picked up his glass and headed for the living room. I followed. I needed to think over his new information, too. I couldn't believe I'd been seen at the park.

Andy sat on the sofa, patting the space next to him. I sat and he threw his arm across my shoulders, giving me a hug, and then dropping a light kiss on the top of my head.

"I'm sorry if I snapped, but nothing about any of this feels right. Do me a favor. Don't follow Liz home anymore, and for God's sake, be more aware while you're in the car. I'm not sure how much more of this I can take."

I snuggled into his side. "All right. I'll jog, go to work and come home." I told him about how I would try to arrange Liz's schedule. "And I won't be at yoga again until next week. Liz has a couple of functions on those nights. So far, she hasn't asked me to run any personal errands, so I'm in the office all day."

"I suppose that'll have to do. And I think we're closing in on your mother. We had an unconfirmed sighting at the bus station again. By the time we got there, she'd disappeared. We're checking out motels and boarding houses in the area."

"Good luck. If she spots the cops, she'll be gone." I didn't want to talk about killers or my mother any more tonight. "I do have some good news for you. Katie and Barry broke up."

"That is good news. When?"

"Yesterday. She called me and we had a drink. She was pretty upset." I gave him the gist of what had happened.

"Thanks for not letting her drive home."

"He's one worry you won't have to deal with anymore."

"I did a preliminary check on him and came up dry. No Barry Blackledge, motivational speaker, showed up anywhere in Palm Lake. There's a Barry Blackledge who's an engineer, and I found two people by that name in Orlando—one's an architect and the other's a student at Central Florida."

"I think he was married. He had the funniest look on his face when Katie introduced you."

"Knowing Katie, she didn't even mention she had a protective brother let alone one who's a cop. I'll bet he's some kind of a con artist using my sister to make contact with rich people who can afford to buy bad art. Damn, why can't she ever choose the right guy?"

"You make this sound like its Katie's fault."

"Who else's? She has lousy instincts when it comes to men. I just wish she'd use some sense."

"Yeah, well, it's kind of hard for women to sort through all the lies."

"What do you mean?"

"Men lie. They lie all the time. They tell us they're not married when they are. They claim undying love to get us into bed. They tell us what we want to hear, and we buy it because we hope that, maybe, this guy is the one and only."

"Women lie, too."

"We lie about our weight, natural hair color, and how much we spend on shoes, not the important things."

Andy set his glass on the end table, turning to face me with an irritated expression.

"All right, men sometimes lie, but we do it out of fear."

I drained my wine and set the glass on the coffee table. "Fear? That's a good one. What's to fear?"

"The minute a man enters into a relationship, the woman puts pressure on the guy to live up to their expectations. And female expectations can be damned high. No wonder we don't like to commit."

"Nonsense, you don't like to commit because you're always looking for something better to come down the pike."

His eyebrows rose and his voice took on a

mocking tone. "And women aren't? I'll bet you can find out how much money I make, and my prospects as a lawyer."

I leaped to my feet. "Since when are we in a relationship! Face it. Men are natural born liars when it comes to commitment and sex. Joel lied. He told me he loved me so he could move in rent free and get a little on the side. Guess what? The son of a bitch also romanced a woman at the office to get a promotion. And you lied, too!"

Andy also stood, a scowl marring his forehead. "I lied? How and when did I lie?"

What had been simmering for days finally reached the boiling point. I doubled up my fist and punched him on the shoulder. "You kissed me, dammit! You kissed me, and then had the balls to apologize."

His hands grasped my shoulders, and gave me a hard shake. "Fine! I thought I was doing the right thing. This time I won't apologize."

He yanked me into his arms, and a second later his lips crushed mine. I didn't hesitate, but slid my arms around his neck and gave as good as I got. The argument had been one hell of a turn on. Our tongues danced. I tasted lasagna, Chianti, and that special flavor of Andy.

His hands pulled my blouse from the waistband of my skirt while mine yanked at his polo shirt, then fumbled frantically with the fastening of his slacks. His nimble fingers unbuttoned my blouse, and then unsnapped my bra. He pushed it out of the way and palmed my breast. The center, already erect, hardened further.

Andy bent me back over his arm and trailed his lips down my throat before taking the throbbing bud between his teeth. I moaned and ground my hips against his erection. He sucked hard. I cried out something like, "harder". He obliged, and I emitted a sob.

Fire roared through my veins. I not only heard my heart pounding in my ears, but the crackling of those flames as well. I panted and finally got his pants unfastened, sliding my hand inside his boxers. A large, hot shaft of steel burned my palm. I stroked and squeezed lightly. Andy groaned and nibbled his way up my neck to my lips again.

"I'm not going to stop, Renee," his hoarse voice whispered in my ear.

"You do and I'll kill you," I replied with a gasp.

He pulled my hand from his Dockers, and then picked me up, carrying me to my bedroom.

We stood beside the bed staring at each other for a moment. Then I yanked the blouse and bra from my body, flinging them to the floor. My skirt and panties followed. Andy undressed almost as rapidly.

Oh, my God, his body was magnificent. The skimpy swim suit had hidden the important stuff, and while my imagination had run wild, it hadn't exaggerated. I moaned in anticipation.

"God Almighty, you're gorgeous," he muttered.

No one had ever said that to me. In response, I ripped back the covers and laid down, my arms outstretched. He came to me with a groan, covering my body with his. Lips, teeth and hands kissed, nibbled, and smoothed my skin from the neck down.

I floated in a searing sea, whimpering and writhing, my hands clutching the spindles of my brass headboard as I tried to anchor my throbbing body to the bed. Andy's mouth toyed with my breasts, first gently nipping, and then sucking the overly sensitive tips, while his hand tangled in the hair at the junction of my thighs. He stroked the slick wet heat pouring from me, and then slipped two fingers inside, his thumb massaging the only place that mattered.

Crying out, my hands tightened, and I dug my

heels into the mattress, lifting my hips in rhythm to his caresses. He sucked hard on my nipple and increased his massaging efforts. The burning coil in my gut told me I wasn't far from erupting.

"Andy! I'm coming!"

He ceased and propped his body up on his elbow. "Wait! Condom!" he said with a gasp.

"Nightstand drawer! Hurry!"

I thought my heart would pound out of my chest and couldn't suck in enough breath to fill my lungs. I hung on the edge of a precipice. All I needed to fall was a push from Andy.

He reached over, opened the drawer, and found what he sought. Even without his caresses, the spring coiled tighter and my hips undulated. I couldn't stop the motion. He ripped the foil packet open with his teeth and sheathed himself one-handed, then nudged my legs apart with his knee and knelt between them. With one swift thrust, he slid inside.

The blazing heat melded us into one. I wrapped my legs around his waist, riding the waves of pleasure. Andy stroked like a piston for several seconds, and then pulled almost all the way out. He hesitated before resuming the motion. Three times he repeated the action until I cried out for deliverance. I burned with an intensity I'd never known, and begged for an end to something I wanted to continue forever.

My wish was granted, and I came in a series of hard contractions that threatened to rip my guts out. I screamed. And just when I thought I had nothing left, the spasms returned. I sobbed and pleaded for them to never stop.

Then Andy lunged one final time, his guttural cry echoing my cries for more. He shook as though in a fever and gasped.

Finally, the world ceased spinning. My legs

released and fell onto the bed, limp and spent. Andy rolled to the side. Neither of us said a word. We couldn't. It took a few minutes to regain my breath, and for my heart to return to normal.

"Oh, wow," I said.

"I'll say. And I'm not going to apologize."

I laughed softly. "I don't think that matters anymore."

"I've never made love before because I was angry."

"Who knew arguing was such a turn on?"

He propped himself up on his elbow and kissed me. "Tell me, do you always keep condoms in your nightstand?"

"They're Joel's leftovers. Kinda glad I forgot about them. What would you have done if they hadn't been there?"

"I have no idea." He leaned over, reached into the still open drawer, and grabbed a handful, scattering them on the top of the nightstand.

"What are you doing?"

"Be prepared. I was a Boy Scout." He smiled and kissed me again. "I'm also an optimist."

His erection hadn't withered much and nudged my thigh, giving me hope.

"And how long before you think your optimism is rewarded?"

He pulled the covers over us and smiled. "Not long."

****

"I don't see how you have the energy to jog," I said to Andy as we pulled into the parking lot at City Park.

He grinned. "Great sex makes a man want to go out and conquer the world."

"It makes women want to lay back and purr."

He sent me that lopsided grin. "I have a theory about the generals of the great empires in history."

"And that is?"

"The empires eventually fell because the generals spent too much time on the battlefield. They weren't getting any."

I laughed, exiting the car. Liz, Jeff, and Corinne were already warming up when we joined them.

"Everyone, I want you to meet Andy Jackson. Andy this is Liz Gorman, my boss, Jeff McCarthy, and Corinne Vassar."

Hellos were murmured all around. "Hope you don't mind me joining you this morning. Renee's been talking my ears off about you guys for a week."

"Glad to have you along," Jeff said, eyeing Andy's fit body. "I take it you've been doing this for a while."

"Years. I do five miles. Anyone else go that distance?"

"I can," Liz replied. "I had to cut back due to an injury for a while, but I'm ready to move up again."

"Care if I join you?"

"Be my guest."

"How far do you go, Renee?"

I caught the double entendre along with the twinkle in his eye. "Three is my limit. I need more stamina before upping to five," I said, adding a double entendre of my own. Last night had been busy.

"I found three miles wasn't as hard yesterday as the day before," Jeff added. "Must be getting used to it. I lost another five pounds."

So far Corinne had been silent. "How about you? Are you back up to three miles again?" I asked her.

"Yeah. It felt good."

Her brevity puzzled me until I caught her giving Andy the once over. A little dart of jealousy poked me in the stomach.

"I may move up to five soon," she continued. "Are you going to make this your jogging home,

Andy?"

"I might."

I didn't like the way Corinne smiled and had the strongest urge to bitch slap my new friend.

"Well, I'm just about ready," Liz announced. "How about you, Andy?"

"Just about."

He ran in place, and then bent over grasping his ankles. Neither Corinne nor I could keep our eyes off his sculpted thighs or the jogging shorts molded to his rear end. I shot her a glance from behind my sunglasses, not liking the way she openly admired what she saw or that cat and the cream smile on her lips.

"I'm ready. Which trail do we use?" Andy asked.

"Start on the three mile path. It loops around and eventually joins the mile and a half one," Liz told him.

"See you later, Renee." He and Liz trotted off.

"I guess I'm almost ready, too," Jeff said.

"I've got my legs warmed," Corinne replied.

"Let's do it," I said.

We followed Andy and Liz, our pace much slower than theirs. With my body still sore from the crash and last night's activity, I hoped I didn't wimp out. I focused on Jeff's newly tight calf muscles and Corinne's tanned legs. Three miles was a stretch for me, but if I kept my pace slow enough I might be able to handle it. It wasn't long before Jeff and Corinne pulled ahead of me.

I allowed my mind to wander. Andy's being here this morning was no surprise. During a lull in making love, he'd announced his intentions.

"I'll jog with Liz tomorrow and see if I can strike up a conversation."

"She's not much of a talker," I warned him.

He rolled over and kissed me. "Neither am I."

I forgot about jogging for a while.

Now, as I concentrated on Jeff and Corinne in front of me, the green eyed monster stabbed me again. I'd never considered Corinne a rival until the job thing. And now the rivalry might extend itself to Andy as well.

No way, baby. Friend or not, he's mine.

Making love half the night had given me bragging rights and a certain territoriality. I wasn't about to let her horn in at this stage of the game.

I slowed my pace further, wondering when and how Andy Jackson had become so important in my life.

And how will Katie react? Will she resent her best friend sleeping with her brother?

I'd called her yesterday to find out if she had survived her binge. Other than a hangover to beat hell and residual anger at Barry, she sounded normal, and expressed horror at my accident. I didn't fill her in on the details, just telling her I'd been rear-ended and went into a ditch.

"You be careful," she said.

"I will, and forget Barry. He's an asshole."

"Aren't they all? I think I'll amuse myself by making a Barry Blackledge voodoo doll complete with long, sharp pins."

I jerked my mind back to the present, and realized Corinne had out-distanced Jeff who was only a few yards in front of me. She seemed in a hurry, and it dawned on me that she planned to arrive at the end of the run before or at the same time as Andy and Liz.

Damnation! I picked up my pace and passed Jeff, who did the same keeping even with me. I only had another half mile to go and refused to give up, aching muscles or not. I glanced over my shoulder. Andy and Liz had just entered the path from the longer trail. I slowed and dropped back until they caught up to me, then jogged the rest of the way with them.

Corinne stared with a disgruntled expression when we finished.

"You're making progress, Renee. You'll be fit and trim in no time at this rate," she said with a smirk.

Okay, the first shot's been fired. Look out, honey, you're in the major leagues now. Don't make me angry.

"I sure will. I'm looking better, feeling better, and can swear I've taken off not only pounds, but years as well. And plus, I have a new job. Life is wonderful."

Her smirk disappeared. "Well, I have to get going. I'm meeting with my lawyer this morning. See you tomorrow. Will you be joining us again, Andy?"

I swigged water from my bottle and tried not to glare.

"I plan on it," he said.

"Andy, maybe we should head back to my place. I need to shower and get ready for another day at the office." I kept my tone light. My suggestion brought a nod from him, and a raised eyebrow from Corinne.

Eat that, sweetheart.

Liz finished her water and pulled her car key from a loop attached to her shorts. "I have to get going. My report is almost finished, Renee. You'll get it this morning. What time do I meet with Masters tomorrow?"

"Seven-thirty."

"I'll jog afterward, so I might be a little late."

She moved off with a wave as Andy finished his water.

"Come on, kiddo. I have to get to work also. Nice to have met you, Jeff, Corinne. See you tomorrow."

I eased into the car and cast a glance back at Jeff and Corinne. Jeff was headed toward his car, but Corinne stood and stared after me, a look of anger on her face.

****

Not having counted on sharing a shower with Andy or the consequences of doing so, I was late into work. Liz's office door was closed and her line in use light flashed on my phone, but a thick folder sat in the middle of my desk. After clocking in, I opened it and saw the draft with numerous slash marks and handwritten corrections. I also had seven voice mail messages. A long day loomed.

One of the messages was from the rental agency Liz had contacted yesterday afternoon stating that a Honda Civic would arrive sometime this morning. That was good news. They'd only had high-end luxury cars available the day before. I'd borrowed Andy's car yesterday and used a cab today.

Liz emerged from her office. "I put the finished draft on your desk. It should be pretty straightforward. If you have a problem reading my handwriting, just let me know."

"I'm good at deciphering things like that, and your writing's easy to read."

"Has the rental agency been here yet?"

"The voice mail said this morning."

"Good because I'm going to need you to run a few errands today. I have dry cleaning at The French Cleaners, and need you to run this check out to The Home for Friendless Animals. Unfortunately, they're on opposite sides of town. I'm in meetings with the staff at the unwed mother's home and can't be in two places at once. Oh, and could you call Campbell's and arrange for lunch to be delivered here tomorrow at noon? Keep it simple. Just assorted sandwiches and salads for about twenty. I'll be going over the budget with the hospice people."

I scribbled the information on a pad. "Anything else?"

"Yes, make reservations for two at Martinique tonight at eight. Todd's going out of town again tomorrow morning."

My hand stilled. He would be gone again.

"I thought he *was* out of town," I said, keeping my voice neutral and conversational.

"He's been home for the last couple of days." She sighed. "Sometimes we don't see each other for a week or more. It's rough."

Not as rough as what he's got planned for you.

"That's too bad. Is there ever a lull in fundraising and such?"

"Not often. It's pretty much a year round thing."

"Other than jogging and yoga, how do you spend your spare time? Do you have any hobbies?"

"Spare time? What's that?" she said with a laugh. "I read whenever I get a chance, which isn't as often as I'd like."

"What do you read? I'm thinking Christmas here."

Liz grinned. "I love mysteries. I grew up with Nancy Drew and moved on to Agatha Christie as a teenager. Can't get enough murder and mayhem."

I found her choice of words ironic. *Hope they aren't prophetic as well.*

The phone rang. The receptionist in the main lobby informed me my rental car had arrived. I hurried down, signed the papers, and returned with the keys clutched in my hand.

I opted to run the errands first so as not to be interrupted while writing the draft. After informing Liz of my plans, I headed for the parking lot. Once behind the wheel, I dumped the contents of my purse on the passenger seat to lighten the load. Andy had cleaned out all my personal stuff before the wrecker had towed my car to the garage. Most of the stuff was junk, the lightweight variety found in any console and glove box. The exceptions were a thirty-two revolver—for which I had a permit—pepper spray, a stun gun, and the Lend An Ear.

"Why the hell do you need a gun, a stun gun, and pepper spray?" Andy had asked in an exasperated tone. "Get rid of everything except the pepper spray, and that includes that stupid listening device."

I ignored him, but because it was a rental car, ditched the guns. The Lend An Ear I kept.

The errands didn't take all that long. Since it was almost lunchtime when I finished, I had lunch at a little bistro not far from my house, and then stopped off at the supermarket to pick up the makings for dinner tonight, depositing the groceries at home before returning to the office.

Okay, so it was stealing company time, but I rationalized that everyone did it and who'd know. An inner voice said, *You.* I didn't know I'd developed such a well-defined conscience.

I'll clock out early and stay late to make up for it.

Guilt-free, I tackled my "to do" list saving the draft for last. Liz came and went several times, thanked me for the cleaning, and finally left the office at two-thirty.

"Did you get the reservations for tonight and the lunch for tomorrow all set up?" she asked.

"Done and done. I ordered an assortment of roast beef, turkey, and ham sandwiches with a mixed greens, potato, and tomato salads."

"Good choices. I have a meeting at the bank. Put any calls through to call forwarding. My cell will be on until five. When you finish with the draft, put it on my desk, and then go home. I'll proof it tomorrow. Have a good night."

"Thanks, Liz, and have a good meeting tomorrow morning."

She smiled and exited. The only hitch I saw with her jogging later was that I couldn't join her, at least so she'd see me. Another flaw in another plan I hadn't considered.

I worked steadily for the next hour with no problems. Liz wrote in a concise manner with little rambling. I rested about three-quarters of the way through it and rubbed the back of my neck, then got up to stretch my legs, contemplating going to the break room for a shot of caffeine.

The phones had remained quiet and I walked around the room before finally stopping at the large bank of windows to gaze into the parking lot two stories below. Most of the spaces were filled. A man wearing a suit and carrying a briefcase caught my attention.

I looked away, and then snapped my eyes back and stared harder. He walked quickly, briefcase swinging, his back military straight. My jaw dropped.

What the hell is Barry Blackledge doing here?

Chapter Eighteen

I was certain it was Barry even though I'd viewed him from the back and from two stories up. The straight posture matched that of when I'd seen him at the art show. He stopped by a red sports car, opened the door, tossed in his briefcase and suit coat, then got in and roared off.

I was tempted to call Andy, but hesitated. Barry and Katie were history, so why bother? Besides, he had enough on his plate what with my woes and the rest of his cases.

But still—Barry? Here? I supposed he may have been consulting with someone about motivational speaking. The Foundation did a lot of fundraising, and I could see how a motivational speaker would be a good way to keep employees enthused. Constantly begging people for money was stressful. But what if Barry was some kind of a con man like Andy had suggested? Would he have the guts to target the Susan Richardson Gray Foundation? Or had he dumped Katie because his newest squeeze worked here? I had to find out.

I glanced at my watch—three forty-five. Break time started at three, but I'd seen people in the room as late as four. Without hesitation, I took off for the ground floor, slowing my pace when I entered.

Exactly three people sat nursing either coffee or a soft drink. Not recognizing any of them, I approached a vending machine, and then remembered I hadn't brought any money. I couldn't walk up to a total stranger and ask to borrow money, even a lousy buck and a quarter, much less begin a conversation about motivational speaking.

I left the room empty-handed and walked slowly down the hallway. If he was here legitimately, Barry wouldn't deal with Liz on this. Besides, he wasn't on her appointment schedule. He'd talk to—who? Human Resources?

That seems the most logical answer, but how do I bring up the subject?

What I needed was an excuse to talk to Bob Stewart's assistant, and finally came up with a solution. Even though I loathed using it, I climbed the steps to the third floor and entered the HR domain.

Stewart's assistant, Mrs. Hardwick was at her desk. The door to Stewart's office was open and the room beyond dark. She looked up and smiled as I walked up.

"Ms. Ryan, nice to see you. How do you like working for us so far?"

"Oh, it's wonderful. Liz is super. She's easing me into the position, but even so, I still find it challenging. I hope she's happy with my work."

"I'm sure she'll be pleased. Liz is a very fair employer. She thinks of her staff and employees as family. What can I do for you?"

"A friend of Liz's said she was sending in a resume, and Liz asked me to check and see if it had arrived. She thinks there might be an opening for her."

"What's the name?"

"Corinne Vassar. I don't know what position Liz is thinking about, so I'm not sure I can help in that respect."

Ms. Jenkins flipped through the papers in her inbox, and then extracted one.

"Yes, here it is. It came in this morning at nine-thirty." She read for a moment. "She says she's willing to work part time if necessary. That's a plus.

We always need file clerks and data entry people when the real fundraising season starts in November, but having someone trained and able to do the job prior to that time is always good. She's a little short on recent work experience, however."

"Would you like me to take it to Liz?"

"Oh, no. Mr. Stewart sees all resumes first, but he's out of town today. I'll make a notation on the bottom that she's Liz's friend."

Damn, I wanted to choke and spit, but swallowed instead. I'd deal with Corinne later.

"Thank you." I paused as if thinking. "You know, I was wondering about something. How do you keep people so enthused about their jobs? It must be very stressful to constantly keep asking for money. Do you ever employ someone like a motivational speaker? Because if you do, I know of a man who might fit the bill. Have you ever heard of Barry Blackledge?"

Mrs. Hardwick shook her head. "The name doesn't ring a bell. I've worked here for five years and don't remember a presentation like that. Most of our employees don't need it. Why?"

"Oh, I was just curious. But if Barry were to send a proposal, it would be to this office, right?"

"Yes, I suppose so. Liz might get the initial contact, but she'd route it through here for further discussions."

"Thanks, I'll pass that information along to my friend. Well, I guess I need to get back. I have a report to finish for Liz. I'll tell her Corinne's resume came in."

I waved good-bye and returned to my office. I still had no answer as to why Barry was at The Susan Richardson Gray Foundation. Whatever the reason, it hadn't been to make a pitch for motivation. Katie suspected he had a new girlfriend. *Did* she work here? It was a large company. Barry could have met a woman through social contacts. And Liz wasn't the only female executive. To satisfy my curiosity, I'd investigate more tomorrow.

I finished the report and put it on Liz's desk, then headed home. This time I paid close attention to the cars behind me. A white one stayed two or three cars back for most of the way. I didn't relax until it turned off six blocks from my home.

Even so, I shivered as I entered the house and peeked out the front window. Had I been followed or was my paranoia in high gear?

****

Andy arrived home late and in a sour mood.

"I don't want to talk about it now. What I do want is a pitcher of beer and the biggest plate of nachos on the menu at El Capitan."

That suited me. I wasn't in much of a mood to cook myself. The chicken breasts stuffed with broccoli and cheese could wait another day. Nachos and beer, though not on my diet, sounded like a winner. We were halfway through the first pitcher when he spoke.

"Had a nasty one today. A five-year-old girl riding her tricycle on the sidewalk in front of her house was killed. Got caught in the crossfire from some drug dispute. Naturally, nobody saw a damned thing." His voice turned bitter and he refilled his glass.

"I'm sorry. Her family must be devastated."

"Her mother had hysterics, and fainted dead away. She works two jobs to make ends meet. The grandmother lives in and baby sits. She had a heart attack and is in the hospital."

"And the shooters?"

"Long gone."

Andy launched into an angry diatribe against gangs, frightened neighbors who refused to talk, innocent blood spilled, and the justice system in general.

I let him vent and refrained from offering a shoulder to cry on. Just listening was enough. I wanted so badly to hug him saying everything would be all right and wondered if I was in love—real love.

He ended with, "I'm thinking of quitting and going to school full time. I can flip burgers or work at a nice, quiet bookstore for minimum wage. Anything to never again see what I did this morning."

"If that's what you want, you can stay in the spare room rent free. A little light slavery around the yard would do."

He smiled for the first time since he'd come home. "I'll take it under advisement. I'm sorry. Guess I unloaded on you. Let's order. Want to share a plate of nachos?"

"Get your own nachos, José. I'm starving, and demand calories and carbs."

This time he laughed and placed our order, including more beer. Good thing I decided not to tell him about Barry being at the Foundation today. It might upset him and he'd had enough upset for one day.

"I have some news about your mother. We've been pulling surveillance tape from the convenience stores where some of your hang up calls originated. We hit pay dirt at a Stop 'n Shop on Greer."

"That's only a few blocks from the house."

"I know. The image is typical surveillance camera quality, but it sure looks like her. She comes in and heads straight for the phone at the back of the store. Two minutes later, she leaves. I checked and it coincides with a call you received at five-oh-nine last Monday. Have there been any new ones in the last couple of days?"

"A couple of hang ups on the answering machine yesterday and one live one tonight about five-forty-five. They're so routine I'm used to them."

"I think the sighting at the bus station was mistaken identity. The calls have come from closer and closer to the house."

"I have no idea where she's staying, but Congress Avenue isn't far and it's lined with cheap motels. Have you checked there?"

He nodded. "We just started. Nothing yet. You haven't had any kind of calls at work have you?"

"No, not that I know of. My voice mail had a couple of hang ups, but it could have been someone preferring not to leave a message. You think she followed me to work?"

Andy ran a hand through his hair. "I don't know what to think anymore."

I didn't either. If Mother was stalking me, then why didn't she do something? God knows, she'd had ample opportunity. Maybe she *had* taken a pot shot at me through the window and followed me to City Park that day I'd been so spooked. Off her meds, Mother could be highly unpredictable, but I had trouble seeing her as lethal—at least toward me.

And Joel kept flitting across my mind, too, along with my former boss and his girlfriend. I'd finally decided my Homeland Security neighbor was not in the picture, but what about good old Dr. Reynard? I still intended to lodge a formal complaint to the state about him and his so-called clinic.

Our second pitcher arrived along with the food, and as we dove in I told Andy what I'd been thinking.

"That's why I intend to jog with you and Liz from now on. In spite of what you overheard about the crime not going down in the park, I'm not convinced."

"At least you now admit there could be a crime, but how do you intend to jog with both of us? I can barely handle three miles. Liz just moved up to five."

"You'll be all right with Jeff, Freddy, and

Corinne. Just don't go alone."

Freddy. I hadn't seen her in a while. Jeff had said something about her work schedule conflicting with jogging. On the other hand, if she and Jeff were thieves, she might have moved on to greener pastures.

I shook off my suspicions and replied, "I'm not going at all tomorrow. Liz has a breakfast appointment and said she'd jog afterward. That means she'll be at least an hour later than usual."

"Thanks for telling me. I'll try to re-arrange my schedule by an hour, too."

A tingle tickled the back of my neck and made me shiver. Something hung in the air like a silent warning. I couldn't describe it, but knew time had run out.

"Andy, I'm worried. Liz and Todd are dining out tonight because he's on the road again tomorrow. They're at Martinique. Can we slide by later and see if she's all right."

"We can, but I thought Todd wanted her killed when he was gone."

"He does. And that's what scares me. He's taking off tomorrow morning, and Saturday night Liz is attending a benefit. I saw it on her schedule. It's been there for months. A hit man or woman could crash the party, kidnap, and then kill her." I quit eating and sat up straight. "Andy, I think Saturday night's the night. Maybe he's taking her out to dinner as a kind of final farewell."

"That's macabre."

"Please, let's take a spin through the lot at Martinique. The reservations were for eight. I know. I made them."

"Whose car would they use? You don't know what kind of car he drives."

I waved a dismissive hand in the air. "I overheard the hit woman say something about a black Porsche."

"All right, when we finish here, we'll drive fifteen miles out of our way to cruise the parking lot of an upscale restaurant. Happy?"

"Yes. Let's eat. It's almost eight o'clock."

Andy rolled his eyes, but shoved a fully laden nacho in his mouth. By eight-thirty, we had paid the bill and headed across town to Martinique. It was located near the country club and had received a five star rating from the newspaper food critic. It also had outlandish prices. I'd heard an appetizer started at twenty bucks.

The parking lot was jammed. Andy slowly drove up and down the lanes. I counted no less than twenty Lexuses, several of them black. It was impossible to read the license plates unless I got out, which Andy didn't allow.

We circled three times in Andy's definitely non-upscale Ford Focus before calling it quits.

"This is one restaurant I'll never eat at," he said. "They must charge an arm and a leg."

"So I've heard, but how do you know?"

"Look at the cars. All upper end. And eight of them are Porsches. I can't believe how many sports cars are here. I see Z-4s, Porsches, a couple of Ferraris, and a few I can't identify. The Miata parked on the end must belong to the bus boy. This is useless. Let's go."

"No, not yet. Pull over and wait for me. I'll be right back."

Andy gunned the motor and took off making a sharp right out of the parking lot.

"Hey!"

"No, Renee, you are not going to sneak inside and peek through the fronds of an artificial palm tree to spy on Liz and Todd Gorman. Of course they're here. You made the reservation."

A new thought crossed my mind. "Andy, what if

it's going down tonight? It's supposed to look like an accident or a mugging gone bad. The killing could happen in the parking lot on the way to the car!"

"I thought Todd was supposed to be out of town when it happens."

"Maybe he changed his mind."

"Renee, I'll admit Todd Gorman is hiding something, maybe even screwing with the Foundation finances, but we have no evidence of a murder for hire. We can't just barge in and arrest him. If you'd had a tape recorder instead of that silly device, we'd have leverage."

"I guess you're right, but I can't shake this feeling that it's going to be soon—real soon." The back of my neck prickled as if to lend weight to my words.

Back home, Andy popped the cap on another beer and sat on the sofa. I snuggled next to him. He set the bottle on the end table, and then pulled me into his arms. We necked like a couple of teenagers whose parents had gone for the evening.

He sucked on my lower lip sending red hot lines of fire racing along my nerves. I figured I had only a few minutes left before melting into a puddle of goo.

Andy finally lifted his head, a sexy, lopsided smile on his face, and I swore little flickers of flame danced in his half-lidded hazel eyes.

He nibbled again briefly, and then said, "Wanna argue?"

"Pick a topic."

He rose and pulled me to my feet, his lips fastening on mine again. Warmth radiated from the pit of my stomach and surged throughout the rest of my body. We stumbled through the living room and down the hallway to the bedroom, shedding clothes along the way in a trail even a blind man could follow. I didn't give a shit about blind men—I only cared about Andy.

I ripped back the covers and we hit the sheets in a tangle of arms and legs. Lips, teeth, and hands moved frantically from one body part to another. I slashed his back with my fingernails. He lightly bit my neck. The image of a vampire rolled through my rapidly fogging mind. Two small preliminary contractions throbbed. I pictured fangs sinking into my neck again with the same results. God, I never imagined vampires as erotic.

I couldn't wait any longer. My entire body throbbed and burned, the core of that blaze ready to erupt. My ears filled with the sound of my pounding heart. I reached the mountain top and cried out.

"Now, Andy, now!"

Andy barely had time to get the condom in place. My hips undulated and if he didn't hurry, I'd come on my own. He hurried, and then slid into me with one powerful thrust.

I screamed and climaxed, the spasms like the night before. Strong and gripping, they seemed to last forever. I floated in a sea of pleasure vaguely aware when Andy also reached the heights. His gasp coincided with one last lunge. And still I came, contraction after contraction, until I had nothing left.

Panting, I lay spent, unable to lift so much as my little finger. Andy rolled to the side, his breaths also raging in and out of his chest. We spoke no words. We didn't need them. His fingers twined in mine and I drifted on a cloud, floating in a nirvana I couldn't describe. I think we had discovered a new dimension.

****

Andy's ringing cell phone woke me. I had no idea of the time and didn't care. Satiated and exhausted, I snuggled my head further into the pillow. After allowing our sexual batteries to recharge, we'd made love again, this time slow and sweet.

Andy spoke softly, and then slipped out of bed. A few seconds later, I heard the bathroom door close and the shower come to life. What seemed like a moment later, someone shook my shoulder.

"Renee, I have to go. We caught the guys who killed the little girl. Do me a favor. Just go to work today. No jogging, okay? I'll be in touch."

He kissed my forehead. I murmured something unintelligible and resumed sleeping. The next time I opened my eyes was when the alarm went off at seven o'clock.

I rolled over, patting the cold sheets next to me. How long had Andy been gone? Why hadn't he awakened me? Then my mind cleared, and I remembered the phone call. The temptation to catch a few more minutes of sleep proved overwhelming. I turned off the alarm and closed my eyes.

It was almost eight when I awoke. Sitting up, I forced my feet to the floor. With no jogging today, I decided a good breakfast would hit the spot. I staggered to the kitchen, made a pot of coffee, and poured a glass of tomato juice.

While drinking it, I stared out the kitchen window into the yard, dark with the gloom of low hanging clouds promising rain. Backlit by the kitchen light, I saw my reflection in the panes and the shit-eating grin on my face. Okay, so great sex made me happy. Since when didn't it? I wondered how many other women in Palm Lake were waking up this morning with the same expression on their faces.

Too lazy to bother with bacon and eggs, I dumped a bunch of cereal into a bowl and covered it with milk. I was about halfway through it when the euphoria of the night finally wore off and the anxiety of the evening returned.

That creepy-crawly feeling slithered along my

neck and up my scalp. It had been two weeks since I'd overheard the damning conversation. By now, the hit person had to know Liz's routine, and if her ever-loving piece of shit husband was out of town again, I knew it was time.

I let the spoon fall into the bowl and sipped my coffee, thinking. It was time to take action. I had entered into this bodyguard business to save a woman's life. The fact that I now considered her a friend, not to mention my employer, heightened the sense of urgency.

Reluctantly, I decided to come clean and tell her the truth. Even if she didn't believe me, I'd plant the idea in her mind. She was smart. She'd check it out. It would most likely get me fired and probably cost me a newfound friendship, but it didn't matter. Saving Liz mattered.

I figured Liz would arrive at the park sometime around nine. That gave me a half an hour to get dressed, park, and intercept her. I donned my jogging clothes—I didn't think I'd need business attire after I told her—grabbed my purse and keys, then headed for the park. In my head, I heard Andy's voice from this morning, but ignored his words of warning. I had a job and intended to do it.

****

I arrived fifteen minutes late. A damned slow moving freight train had kept me fuming behind the crossing gate forever. I pulled into the parking lot, noticing Jeff's and Corinne's cars, and then cursed when I saw Liz's Lexus in an end slot. She was nowhere in sight.

Damn and blast. How far ahead is she? And can I catch up?

I contemplated waiting for her here, but what I now simply referred to as "the feeling" had increased on the drive over or maybe it was just the weather. The clouds had thickened and become darker. The urgency to find Liz and tell her what was going down had taken total control. My heart pounded in hard thumps and my legs shook. Without bothering to warm up, I took off at a moderate jog, keeping my eyes peeled for Liz's swaying ponytail. With every step, the feeling of doom grew, settling like cement on my chest. I wanted to scream her name.

At the end of a mile my breaths raged in and out in heavy gasps, and my legs threatened to cramp. I hadn't remembered to bring a water bottle, and was forced to slow my pace.

I was alone on the trail. Due to the late hour and threatening weather, most of the joggers had probably exercised and left. Maybe if I could catch up with Jeff and Corinne, they'd help me find Liz.

On the verge of tears, I gritted my teeth, and ran, but still didn't see Liz or Jeff and Corinne.

Maybe they're at the end of their run. I should have waited in the parking lot.

I don't know why that didn't occur to me earlier. The fact that both Jeff's and Corinne's cars were still here told me they had also gotten a late start. I wasn't happy with my reasoning, but my mind had been so focused on Liz I didn't stop to think. The story of my life.

My left calf cramped. With a cry, I stopped and rubbed the Charlie-horse until it released its grip, then proceeded on as fast as I could, limping.

I passed the two mile marker and came to the fork in the path where the longer trail branched off to the right. Which should I follow? I chose the shorter on the theory that the late hour and impending rain would convince Liz to shorten her run. Plus if she had decided to do five miles and was that far ahead of me, I'd never catch up.

I swung to the left, feet pounding on the asphalt, passing the curve near the little bench. I forgot about my cramp. In the distance, I heard the traffic from the street. Still, no Liz appeared.

Then from up ahead, I heard noises in the brush. I slowed, but didn't stop. An icy finger trailed down my spine and my stomach churned. The sound of breaking twigs made my skin crawl. Whoever was there wasn't being subtle.

Andy's warnings of last night and again this morning screamed in my head. I sobbed and realized for the first time that I might be the one in danger. I bit my lip and put on a burst of speed. A few yards ahead, the bushes parted and Barry Blackledge strode onto the path.

I skidded to a stop and stared in total amazement, frozen like a rabbit hiding from a predator. Then my gaze shifted from his angry, hate twisted face to the gun in his hand.

Chapter Nineteen

I stared at Barry and the gun unable to move or breathe. My mind went numb, and I wasn't even sure my heart beat.

"I thought you'd never show. All right, into the woods, you meddling bitch." He motioned me toward the gap in the bushes where he'd emerged.

My legs went weak, and I thought I would throw up. I couldn't move a muscle, but only stare at that gun, a revolver.

When I didn't comply with the order, he snarled and repeated his instructions. "I said move, dammit or so help me I'll shoot you here in the middle of the path."

I shook my head. If he was going to kill me, he'd have to do it now. I wasn't going anywhere with him.

He walked forward, grabbed the front of my shirt, and lightly tapped me in the head with the gun barrel. I saw stars and sank to my knees. He jerked me upright by the arm, grinding the gun into my back, and then pushed me through the bushes.

It hurt, and my head ached from where he'd hit me. I was madder than hell and wanted to make a grab for the gun, but decided such an action would be stupid. He'd pull the trigger and I'd be dead.

Why he wanted me dead remained a mystery. Did Barry have a connection to The Foundation I had somehow screwed? Was that why he'd broken up with Katie? Something wasn't right, but in my terrified state, my brain refused to work in a rational way. I needed to regain control if I wanted to live.

Clenching my teeth to keep them from chattering, I stumbled past the foliage until coming to a clearing maybe fifteen feet across. A ribbon of old asphalt bisected the space and I recognized it as part of a bike path abandoned when the park had been redesigned several years ago. Tentacles of St. Augustine grass crept across the dark gray surface, and seedlings poked through the cracks.

Barry shoved me hard. My momentum propelled me almost to the other side. I whirled to face him forcing my anger aside. It struck me how silly he looked standing there in designer slacks and a long-sleeved silk shirt. His dash through the woods had caused the vegetation to pull snags along the arms of the flimsy material.

"You just had to stick your nose in where it didn't belong, didn't you? You screwed up everything. I had it all planned, and then you came along."

"I—I have no idea what you're talking about," I said, finding my voice at last. "You're the one who broke up with Katie. I had nothing to do with it."

"Yeah, Katie—good, old, gullible Katie. Easy on the eyes and a damned fine lay. I had it knocked. And then came that stinking art show. I returned to town a day early just to attend and shut her up. Good thing I did. If I hadn't met you, I'd have never known you were friends. She didn't tell me she had a brother who was a cop, or that she knew you."

"So Andy was right—you are a con man. You were using Katie to get to wealthy art lovers."

Even as I said the words, they made no sense. The question of why Barry wanted to kill me hammered in my brain. How did Andy and I fit into the picture? To my astonishment, he laughed.

"Oh, that's good, real good. Wealthy art lovers. That's priceless. Lorraine should have pulled the plug on you last week. You must lead a charmed life."

I didn't understand any of this. Lorraine? Who the hell was Lorraine? My throat closed when he lifted the gun. Then from behind him came the unmistakable sound of someone running through the brush. A second later Corinne trotted into the clearing.

"Corinne! Run! Get help!"

My hope for salvation was short lived. Corinne smiled, and then pointed a nine millimeter at my chest.

"Don't think so, Renee."

My heart plummeted to my feet and my legs threatened to collapse. The pieces of the puzzle suddenly fell into place with a sharp click, and I remembered the conversation of two weeks ago.

Barry Blackledge was Todd Gorman. Corinne was the hit woman. And my interference *had* thrown their plans into turmoil. Liz's death might not take place in the park, but it was the perfect place for mine.

A lot of thoughts tumbled through my mind not the least of which was Andy, but I didn't have the faculties at the moment to sort them out. All I noticed was Todd's look of relief, Corinne's smile, the guns, and the surgical gloves she wore. It didn't take a genius to figure out she planned to shoot me and leave the gun behind—minus her fingerprints, of course.

I had no idea how to get out of this. I wanted Andy. I wanted his arms around me telling me this was all a nightmare. Only it wasn't. It was real and if Andy was here, he'd be in danger, too. And while as a cop he was trained to deal with situations like this, cops *did* die in the line of duty.

I gritted my teeth and tucked thoughts of Andy into the back of my mind. *Think about how to escape.*

He heaved a sigh. "It's about time you got here. I

was afraid I'd have to kill her."

She cast him a contemptuous glance. "Yeah, right. I told you not to come."

"I caught her, didn't I? I couldn't just sit around and let you miss again. Time is running out. The audit is in a few weeks."

"Not my problem. You contracted for one hit. I'm throwing in Little Miss Bodyguard here at a reduced rate."

"It's not my fault we were overheard."

Todd's whining bordered on pathetic. I couldn't believe they argued over money at this time and place. With the two of them distracted, I wondered if I should take a chance and run. The street wasn't that far away, maybe a couple of hundred feet. I still heard the passing cars. By using the trees for cover, I could dodge and weave my way to safety. I took a slow step backward.

Corinne sneered. "Look, dummy, you were the one who insisted on meeting in the park. I told you it was a stupid idea."

"Well, I thought if Liz ran by you could get a good look at her," he explained.

Corinne shook her head. "You stick out like a sore thumb in those clothes. Get out of here. You have a plane to catch if you want to establish an alibi for tomorrow night."

He hesitated, but said nothing, just licked his lips, nodded, and walked out the way we'd come in still holding the gun, his back ramrod straight. I took another step back.

Her gun snapped up. "Don't even think about it, Renee."

Corinne and I stared at each other. The gloom deepened. Thunder rumbled in the distance.

"So, you *did* see me running from the bench that day," I said in a shaky voice.

"I had no clue anybody had overheard us. I

realized it the next day when I arrived to begin my surveillance of Liz. I was on the fringes of the crowd—just another jogger—when you tried to warn that woman."

I don't know why the possibility of the hit woman being in the crowd had never entered my mind. It should have been obvious. Because of what I'd overheard about the killer not wanting to use the park, I assumed it was safe. And by the time I wondered if the hit woman was stalking Liz, Corinne had established herself as a friend. I never suspected her for an instant. Her comments about the hapless Freddy were to draw my attention to another person. And Andy attributed the attempts on my life to my mother, which in view of Dr. Reynard's comments, made sense.

"But how did you know who I was?" I asked.

Corinne shrugged. "I followed you from the park to Carson Electronics."

And of course, I'd told her exactly where I lived when we'd lunched that day.

"I figured you'd gone to the cops. I have a contact inside. He gave me a copy of your report."

"A contact? Inside the police department?"

"I got rid of his ex-wife several years ago. He doesn't dare refuse me a request. I'll admit to being surprised at how much you heard. I called Todd with the news and told him to unload that damned Porsche. If the police or you put two and two together and investigated, he'd have a different car. I also warned him to stay away from his girlfriend. Then, you showed up the next morning all ready to play jogger, and I realized you planned to protect Liz."

"So, you put Liz's execution on hold and stalked me."

"I needed a plan B and you gave it to me on a silver platter."

"You shot at me."

"Thought I'd nailed you, too. Couldn't stick around to find out. And I still can't figure out how you missed ending up in that canal."

"And of course, it was Todd I saw in the restaurant with you."

I hadn't seen his face, but no wonder he'd looked familiar when I met him as Barry at the art show. The posture, and the stride, the swinging briefcase from the parking lot yesterday were all there to see. I just never put the pieces together.

"That scared me to death. He'd insisted on lunching there over my objections. We argued about money. If I was going to kill two people, I wanted more. He left in a huff, but forked it over anyway. I had no idea you were there that day."

"Not only was I there, but so was Katie, his girlfriend. She's a close friend. I wonder what would have happened if she'd seen him."

She shook her head. "I'd have pulled out of the deal."

"Was it you in the woods that day when I was alone?"

"In the woods? Hell, no, but that cop you're living with damn near nabbed me in your back yard. I barely made it over the fence."

So, Corinne had been the prowler, too. It made sense. If she could silence me in the house, my body might not be found for days, and who would connect my death, followed by Liz's a week or so later? A receptionist and a socialite? One deliberate and one a supposed accident. No tie-ins. And since Mother had cleaned me out of guns, Corinne just might have succeeded if it hadn't been for Andy.

More thunder rumbled and the breeze freshened. I smelled the dampness of rain in the air.

"How did you know I'd be late today?"

"Todd told me Liz had a breakfast appointment.

Plus, your comments to Liz after jogging yesterday confirmed it, so we decided today would be a good time to take you out. We met at a fast food restaurant earlier this morning for the final payment. That's also when I gave him the gun and told him to stand by. Liz showed about eight-thirty. Jeff arrived at nine. I dodged them both. I thought you'd skipped jogging. Finally, you pulled in. I called Todd and told him to intercept at the place we'd met for the down payment. Liz finished and left a few seconds after you disappeared."

"So, you're going to kill me, and then snuff Liz, is that the deal? Don't you think the cops will be just a tad suspicious of Todd, given my statement?"

"I'm not going to kill Liz. Todd's head is on the chopping block. He's a loose end, and I never leave loose ends. And he has the perfect motive for your murder." She laughed softly. "You know, I have to admire your tenacity, and your ability to ferret out information. Getting that job at the Foundation was brilliant. When Todd found out you were his wife's assistant, he panicked. Called me practically crying like a girl asking what he should do. I told him to get the hell out of town for a few days, and that I'd take care of you."

"So why was he here today?"

Corinne sighed. "Because he didn't trust me to finish the job. I've already struck out twice. He insisted on showing up to make sure I succeeded. He never realized the gun I'm holding is his. I stole it from his car last night."

"You're going to frame him for my murder."

She laughed. "I even told him where to park, so lots of people will see him go in, and then come out of the woods. And with you dead, he'll be suspect number one. He's not all that bright, you know."

"Why would Todd Gorman want me dead?"

"Because you can identify him as Barry and he

was afraid you'd tell his wife. Keep it simple, I always say."

A flash of lightning followed by a clap of thunder a few seconds later told me the storm was about to break. The wind sang through the trees, rustling the leaves.

"I'd better get this over with. I'm sorry it has to end this way, Renee, I really am. I like you. Another time and another place, we might have been friends."

"Fat fucking chance."

Corinne shrugged and smiled.

It's funny, but with my life about to expire, I was aware of every subtle sight and sound. A bird flew across the clearing, its wings beating in long strokes. The wind blew harder and the tree branches rubbed together, the leaves slapping against each other sounding for all the world like footsteps.

I was going to die. I accepted it and wished with all my heart I'd told Andy how much I loved him. Would I hear the shot? How much pain would there be?

"Turn around, Renee, and lay face down. You won't feel much, honest."

How the hell would she know? And why should I obey? Either way, I'd be dead. Andy's face drifted across my vision, and my acceptance disappeared. Repressed anger surged, sending a flame of heat from the pit of my stomach.

No, by God, I would not go down without a fight. My heart pounded, but whether in the all-consuming fear gripping me or in anger I couldn't tell.

"No way in hell, bitch. You want to kill me? Do it face to face. *Mano y mano.* I will not go like a sheep to slaughter."

I planned to rush her. She stood only ten feet away and would probably shoot before I'd taken a second step, but maybe surprise might distract her aim. I had to try.

"Your call, sweetie." She raised the gun and took aim.

I sucked in a deep breath, prayed, and shifted my weight forward, prepared to duck low and charge, aiming for her knees.

Then, a shot echoed through the clearing.

Corinne screamed. The gun flew from her hand. She fell to the ground where she writhed and grasped her shoulder. Blood pouring from a gaping hole oozed from between her glove clad fingers.

In my angry and terror-stricken state, I thought her gun had somehow misfired. The bushes behind and to the right of me parted, and I gasped in stunned surprise when a familiar figure emerged.

"Mother!"

She ignored me and marched across the clearing to stand over the sobbing Corinne.

"You bitch! How dare you try to hurt my baby!" Mother raised her gun, the thirty-eight revolver, and pulled back the hammer.

I came out of my stupor and rushed forward. "Mother, no! Don't shoot."

"Why not? This miserable bitch has been following you for over a week. I saw her shoot out the front window. I was parked down the street waiting for you to come home, so I could get a good night's sleep in the spare room. When she took off, I followed, but lost her in traffic. You look good, by the way, honey. And what kind of dance classes are you taking?"

It took me a moment to realize she meant the Barnard School. When off her medications, Mother's conversation sometimes jumped from subject to subject.

"Uh, Mom, why don't you give me the gun?"

"No, not yet. I have to kill her first. She tried to hurt you, and no one hurts someone I love. End of discussion."

"Help me. Call an ambulance. I'm bleeding to death," Corinne moaned, rolling back and forth in the grass.

"Who gives a shit?" Mother said, stepping forward and kicking my former friend in her wounded shoulder before once again putting distance between them.

Corinne screamed again and sobbed. I needed to get that revolver out of Mother's hands.

"Mom, I really wish you'd let me have the gun. Maybe I want to off her myself."

She turned to me, a smile splitting her face. "Do you really, dear? I didn't think of that. I can understand how you'd feel the need for revenge. Happens to me all the time."

For someone who'd been on the run for over a week, my mother looked good. Her graying, light brown hair hung in gentle waves to her shoulders and the tan slacks and leaf green top were clean and unwrinkled. Even her running shoes looked new. I wondered how or if she'd paid for them.

"Then we're on the same page." I held out my hand for the gun.

Mother smiled. "No, Renee, I think I want to kill her myself. She pissed me off."

Before I could answer or make a lunge for the weapon, I heard the sound of someone crashing through the bushes in front of us. My heart slammed into my chest.

It's Todd. He heard the shot and returned to view the results. He can shoot Mother and me if he sees us through the trees.

A second later, Andy burst into the clearing, gun drawn, and the Lend An Ear dangling from the headphones around his neck. Never had I been so glad to see a cop. Relief in the form of heat rolled through me. I couldn't believe how much I loved this man.

He took in the situation at a glance, lowered his Glock, and smiled. "Hello, Mrs. Ryan. My name is Andy Jackson. I've heard a lot about you. Glad we can finally meet face to face."

Mother's eyes never moved from the sobbing Corinne. "Are you the young man who's living with my daughter?"

"Yes. I've been protecting her."

"Well, you did a shitty job of it this morning," she snapped. "Excuse me, but I have to shoot this woman again."

"Please, don't do that."

"Why not? And butt out. This doesn't concern you, mister."

"Mother, she didn't actually shoot me, and you did save my life. Why don't we let the police arrest her and put her in jail where she belongs?"

Mother remained silent, her brow furrowed. "Will she be beaten and raped by gang members?"

"Every day," I replied.

"Will there be cockroaches in her food?"

"Without a doubt," Andy assured her.

"Well," she lowered the gun, and then brought it back up again. "No, I want to kill her."

"Mama, please, don't...for my sake? Give me the gun. I love you."

She turned to me, a smile on her face, her eyes brimming with tears. "Mama. You haven't called me mama since you were a little girl. I remember a pink dress with white dots. I think the material was called dotted swiss. It was your fourth birthday and you looked like a princess. Your daddy and I loved you so much and were so proud of you. Where is that miserable bastard anyway?"

"Uh, I don't know, Mama. Could I please have the gun?"

She heaved a huge sigh and handed it over to

me. "Oh, all right, but I still think we should kill her."

I heaved an even larger sigh and passed the thirty-eight to Andy who whipped out his cell phone.

"This is Detective Jackson. I'm on the old bike path in City Park just off Worthington Road. I need back up and an ambulance immediately."

While Andy talked further with the dispatcher, I did something I hadn't done in years. I hugged my mother.

"Everything's going to be all right, you'll see," I whispered. "I promise." Tears streamed down my cheeks.

Mother pulled back and wiped the wetness away with her fingers.

"You're living with a cop?"

"Well, kind of." I didn't think this was a good time to bring up that he thought *she'd* done the shooting at the house.

She popped a glance over toward Andy. "Oh, don't try to bamboozle me. If you aren't sleeping with him, you should be. He's a stud."

Andy hung up and from the look on his face knew he'd heard. He raised his eyebrow, smiled a satisfied smirk, and shrugged.

Swell, just what his ego needs. He'll be insufferable for weeks.

"I'm going to have to go back to that awful place, aren't I?" she asked him.

"Not that one," I said, hastening to reassure her. "Dr. Reynard is an asshole. I think we should sue for negligence."

Mother chuckled. "Maybe I can shoot him, too."

I wasn't sure if she was kidding or not. From the same direction Andy had come, I heard the sound of more footsteps along with a loud protesting voice.

Todd Gorman stumbled into the clearing followed by Jeff McCarthy who held a gun in his hand. This little wide space in the woods had a lot of firepower in it. Then I noticed Todd's hands were cuffed behind his back.

"I demand to know the meaning of this," Todd said, and then saw Corinne on the ground, moaning, her bloody hand clasping her shoulder.

His eyes bugged out and his face turned chalk white. For a second I thought he would faint.

Jeff looked at Andy. "Sorry I'm late. I caught him just before he got in his car. Had a gun in his hand, so I ran over. Then I heard the shot, wrestled him to the ground, and handcuffed him." He passed Todd's gun to Andy.

I stared, unable to take in what I saw. "Jeff?"

"Renee, this is *Officer* Jeff McCarthy."

I gaped, still in a state of semi-shock. Even Corinne stopped moaning for a moment to stare.

"You're—you're a cop?" I said in a high pitched voice.

"Here to protect you," he replied.

"Well, you suck at it, too. If you'd been here, my daughter wouldn't be in this situation. Honey, are you living with him also?" Mother asked with a puzzled expression on her face. "I like to think I'm broadminded, but this is carrying things too far."

Corinne returned to moaning. Everyone ignored her.

I shook my head. Mother broadminded? Oh, brother. Confused, I asked, "Andy, what's going on?"

"I was worried. You warned the wrong woman, and while I wasn't sure what you'd overheard, I didn't want you to get into trouble again. I knew you'd be back trying to find the right victim, so I asked Jeff to keep an eye on you."

"I'm just out of the academy and thought undercover work sounded interesting." Jeff turned his attention to Todd. "Sit down."

"I protest. You have the wrong person."

"I said sit." Jeff forced Todd to the ground.

"What were you doing in the woods with a gun?" Andy asked.

"The gun was for protection. I—I was looking for my wife. She jogs here. I was on my way out of town and forgot to tell her something."

"So you were tromping through the woods looking for her? Why not wait in the parking lot or use your cell phone?"

"I—I was in a hurry. I forgot to charge my phone last night and have a plane to catch. Thought I'd catch up with her on the path."

"In Gucci loafers? You're full of crap," Jeff said.

Sirens screamed from the street. "Jeff, go show them where we are," Andy said. "I'll cover these two."

He nodded and left returning a minute later with more cops and the paramedics in tow. Two of the officers hustled a still protesting Todd away, while the EMT guys worked on Corinne. Andy brought another officer over to us.

"Mrs. Ryan, this is Officer Andrea Hillis. Would you please accompany her to the station and wait for us there?"

"You're putting me in jail?"

"Oh, no, ma'am," the female officer replied in a gentle voice. "You're a material witness. That's very important. We need you to tell us what happened."

Mother eyed her. "That's bullshit and you know it, but because you're nice, I'll go." She turned to me. "Will you come, too?"

"I'll bring Renee by later to see you," Andy promised her.

"Uh, ma'am, I'm afraid I'll have to put handcuffs on you. It's a rule. Think of them as really ugly bangle bracelets."

"Oh, well, if you must, but I am not a criminal." She placed her hands behind her back, smiled as the cuffs snapped into place, and went quietly.

"I like your top," the policewoman said as they walked away.

"Do you really? I got it at a discount store the other day..." Their voices trailed off until finally disappearing.

The thunder, close a few minutes ago, boomed again further away. The storm had missed us. I glanced at my watch—nine forty-five. Only thirty minutes had passed since I pulled into the parking lot. It seemed like a lifetime.

Reaction set in. My knees shook and I sank to the ground. Deep gulping sobs tore from my chest as I cried out the terror of the last few minutes. Andy pulled me to my feet, folding me into his arms. He rocked me back and forth as I buried my face in his shoulder and howled.

"It's all right, baby. I'm here. You're safe now." He murmured the comforting words over and over.

I clung to him until regaining control. He lifted my chin with his finger, and then kissed me.

I clutched his polo shirt in tight fingers and shook with relief. Andy's lips on mine signaled all was right in the world.

Thanks to my mother I was alive.

Chapter Twenty

"We must have looked like the fucking Keystone Cops," I said, taking another large swig of beer. "I was following Liz, Corinne was tailing me, and my mother was stalking Corinne. God!"

I sat at a large table with Andy, Katie, and Jeff in Tootles. I had spent a huge chunk of time at the police station, and then with my mother. Her lawyer arrived and, after she gave her statement, made arrangements for her to go to a sanitarium in Boca Raton—one with excellent credentials from the state. He also filed an official complaint to the state regarding The Palm Lake Rest Home and its incompetent director.

While Mother had settled in, I stopped at the nearest discount store and bought her clothes, toiletries, and books—nice, sweet romances with no violence. We'd had a long talk, the first in years, and I looked forward to the next visit.

"You think you feel stupid? How about me? I'm the cop. I should have realized what was happening from the beginning," Andy lamented.

"If anybody takes the prize for being an ignoramus, it's me," Katie said. "My boyfriend was not only married, but a quasi-killer as well. The son of a bitch didn't even have the balls to do it himself—he hired a woman! And to think I wasted an absolutely horrific hangover on the asshole. If I had seen him at lunch that day, the whole mess would have blown up in his face."

By this time, I had told Katie the whole story, including how Todd/Barry was at the Golden

Hummingbird the same time as us.

"I feel I let you down, too," Jeff said to me. "I'm just glad I went jogging this morning. It was dumb luck that I saw Todd blundering out of the woods. When I saw him stuff the gun in his pocket, I took him down."

I eyed his suddenly svelte physique. "Jogging must work wonders. You look great."

He grinned. "Body suit. I needed to look overweight. Damned thing weighs a ton, but at least I was able to keep my gun hidden."

"I thought your legs seemed well-sculpted for a beginner." A half-forgotten conversation now made sense. "Legs! That's it!"

"That's what?" Andy asked.

"Legs. That day Corinne came to the gym, Marylou made a comment about wondering which tanning salon she used. It didn't register at the time, but now I realize why I felt I'd missed something." I looked at Jeff. "Corinne told us she was recovering from a broken leg, yet her legs were tanned. Only one would be if she'd been in a cast. I even noticed her tanned legs when we jogged yesterday."

"God, you're right. I should have seen it." He gulped some beer. "Guess I have a lot to learn about undercover work."

"I also realize I never told her I had a job, yet when we met at the yoga studio the morning I got fired, she made a comment about why wasn't I at work. I'm sure if I think harder, I'll find other things."

"Like how she moved up to the three mile track so fast?" Jeff said.

"She must have been keeping an eye on both Liz and me. I guess your presence at La Belle Aurore was no accident either."

"I followed you to and from the Foundation expecting you to go home. When you went to the restaurant, so did I. Then, Liz arrived, and I knew why you were there."

"Why did you follow her?"

"I wanted to see if she was parked nearby and if you'd follow. By the time she entered her car, you'd gone."

"I reamed his ass good for losing you, too," Andy said.

"Why did you come to the park?" I asked Andy.

"After finishing with the guys who killed the little girl, I found the results of the fingerprint we lifted from the truck on my desk. They matched those of a Michelle Anderson. She was arrested eight months ago for carrying a concealed weapon up in Jacksonville. I took one look at the accompanying mug shot and damn near had a heart attack. The hair style was different, but the face was Corinne."

"Why did Todd call her Lorraine?"

"Would you give Todd Gorman your real name if he hired *you* to kill someone?" Jeff said.

"No, I guess not. Go on, Andy. How did the Lend An Ear come into play?"

"When I couldn't get you on the phone, I suspected you'd gone to the park. Sure enough, I found your car, unlocked, with that silly device lying on the seat. I figured you were tailing Liz, so I grabbed it and took off. A few minutes later, I heard your voice and enough of the conversation to realize you were about to buy it. The shot almost deafened me, not to mention scaring me half to death." He encircled my shoulders with his arm and hugged me close. "Then I heard you talking with your mother, and finally found you."

"Did you get any information from Corinne and Todd?" I asked, unable to think of Corinne as Michelle.

Andy shook his head and added more beer to his glass. "No, they both lawyered up real fast. Corinne will talk first. She'll want to cut a deal. We confiscated two cell phones from Todd's car and one from Corinne's. One of Gorman's is legit, the other is a non-traceable. Corinne's is also a disposable. We're pulling call records now. Should have the results soon."

"Does Liz know?" I was sorry she had to find out like this. I'd have much preferred to tell her myself.

"She came to the station this morning, and talked to the Chief. I didn't speak with her."

"Must have been a hell of a blow. Imagine finding out your husband who swears undying love, has hired someone to kill you," Jeff commented.

"What did your mother have to say?" Katie asked.

"Oh, Mother was just chock full of information. She said she broke out of the sanitarium because she was tired of all those silly sessions with Dr. Reynard. She stayed at a small motel near the bus station the first few days, and then decided to ask if she could stay with me."

Katie jaw dropped. "You've got to be kidding. Surely, she knew people were looking for her. Besides, she robbed you, didn't she?"

"Mother tends to overlook little niceties like that. At any rate, she was parked down the street when she saw Corinne shoot out the front window. After that, Mother tailed Corinne as much as possible. When she realized Corinne went everywhere I did, she followed me home from the gym, yoga, and the park. She admitted trying to shadow me earlier while I jogged. That's who was in the woods that day."

"She was protecting you, too, in her own way," Jeff said.

"She also made the hang-up calls after the shooting to see if I was alive and kicking." I paused, wiping the cool condensation from the beer glass with my fingers. All these years I assumed she had never loved me. Kind of a shock to find out she was perfectly willing to kill Corinne to show how much she *did*. "You know, it's funny, but in that clearing Mother was angry as hell, but not raging. A little spacey, perhaps, but not out of control."

"Renee, she was determined to kill Corinne. I'd call that out of control," Andy said.

I shook my head. "No, three years ago, she might have pulled the trigger without a word of conversation. Maybe Reynard helped after all." I drained my glass and poured another. Andy pointed out the almost empty pitcher to our waiter. "At least Joel is off the hook for the shooting and canal incidents."

"But he still has to go to court for the malicious mischief charge," Andy told me.

"Maybe we can come to some sort of agreement. He pays for the window, and I drop the charges."

"So, the bimbo and her boyfriend had nothing to do with any of this," Katie said.

"Not unless I include calling me a lot of nasty names."

"Barry—er, Todd—must have had a panic attack when I introduced you at the art show. Imagine coming face to face with the woman who overheard you hiring a hit man, and then discovering she's dating my brother, the cop."

"According to Corinne, he almost wet his pants when he found out I worked for his wife," I told her.

Katie shook her head. "No wonder he broke up with me. Why can't I ever get it straight with men?"

"Maybe you just haven't met the right man, yet," Jeff said with a smile.

"You volunteering?"

"Could be."

"She's too old for you," Andy broke in.

Katie shot him an indignant glance. "Excuse

me!"

"How old are you?" Jeff asked with a laugh.

"Thirty-two—the same age as Renee."

"Hey, don't bring me into this."

Jeff winked. "I'm twenty-nine, and find older women fascinating."

Katie moved her chair closer to him and clinked her glass against his, giving him a sly, sexy smile.

The waiter brought our new pitcher. Andy poured more into his and my glasses. His phone rang and he headed outside to take the call.

"Shall we order?" Jeff asked.

"How about a plate of a hundred wings?" I suggested.

"Sounds good, but what are the rest of you going to eat?" he replied.

"I just love a man with a sense of humor. Are you sure you're a cop?" Katie teased.

We ordered the wings, sauces with varying degrees of heat, and dips. Andy returned, pulled a long drink, and stared into the glass.

"Why so glum? You just caught a killer and a deadly husband," I said. "Or was the phone call bad news?"

"We've traced lots of calls between Todd's and Corinne's disposable phones. That links them. Corinne's lawyer is already asking for a deal."

"What kind of a deal?" Jeff asked.

"I don't know, but it probably involves other unsolved deaths. Officer Bill Sawyer has been relieved of all duties upon further investigation."

"Was that Corinne's contact in the police department?" I asked.

Andy nodded. "So we think. He's been on desk duty for the past year due to a disciplinary charge of striking a fellow officer. We checked out Renee's story about an inside man, and found out his ex-wife died in a hit and run accident four years ago."

"He's probably relieved it's all over. Corinne's been blackmailing him into giving up information," I said.

"You'll also want to know that Corinne's disposable cell number corresponds to the hang-up calls you received prior to the shooting."

"So, she called first to see if I established a pattern, and then Mother took over to make sure I was safe. No wonder we were confused."

"In her own way, your mother did a better job of protecting you than I did," Andy said in a bitter tone.

I laid a hand on his arm. "Hey, you were in the house with me at night when she couldn't be. Don't take it so hard."

"I should have suspected Corinne sooner, but all your troubles began after your mother escaped. It was logical to assume she was the culprit. And yet you were so adamant that she wouldn't hurt you." He shook his head and gulped half his glass of beer. "I was rereading your report yesterday, and that's when it dawned on me that maybe you'd been seen running away in the park. I was so angry with you when you warned the wrong woman I didn't stop to think that the killer could have been in the crowd."

"Andy, it's not your fault," Katie said.

"Yes, it is! I've lost my edge, and in this line of work that can get you killed. It damn near got Renee deader than a doornail. I'm burned out—tired of catching bad guys who laugh at me because they know how to manipulate the system." He drew in a ragged breath. "That's why I handed in my resignation this afternoon. I'll finish my open cases, and then leave."

"Andy!" Katie said with a gasp.

"Hey, man, isn't this rather sudden? Think about it for a while. Don't make any emotional decisions," Jeff added.

"No, I've already thought about it. That's why I

applied to law school. I've got some savings. I'll go full time, and apply for a job in the prosecutor's office. If I can't get in there, I'll try for some other branch of the law that allows me to help people. I might not make a lot of money, but I'll be a whole lot happier."

I wanted to kiss him and did. "That's for following your convictions. Since I'm probably out of a job, I was thinking of applying for student aid and taking some business courses at the community college. I've put it on my resume enough—I might as well make it true for the next time."

Katie laughed. "I'll hire you as my personal assistant. I need one."

"You need a keeper," Andy replied.

"I wonder where Corinne was those days she didn't show up for jogging," I said.

"Knowing what I know now, I'd bet Todd wasn't her only client," Jeff replied.

"Oh, my God, you mean she snuffed someone else?"

"We're checking on it," Andy said.

"She let me overhear her phone conversation to make me think it was about an ex-husband. I'd corroborate her story," Jeff added.

I shook my head and glanced toward the front doors. Freddy Lane walked into the bar and headed in our direction.

"Oh, no, I can't deal with her tonight," I said with a groan.

"Who?" Katie asked, turning her head toward the newcomer.

"Hi," Jeff greeted her. "Pull up a chair."

She did so with a grimace. "Hi, Jeff. Hi, Andy."

"You know Andy?" I said.

"This is Officer Frederica Lane. She was supposed to be Jeff's backup for keeping an eye on you. Unfortunately, she was pulled off the surveillance last week," Andy explained.

"What? You had the whole police force watching me?"

"Damned near. You needed it."

Jeff introduced Katie and Freddy. I wondered how Freddy would take to Jeff's flirting with Katie. He rose and headed for the bar, and then returned with another glass.

Freddy poured a full one from the pitcher and took a sip. "I was having fun with the assignment, too. Shame I couldn't have been there for the take down. Gorman might not have pulled a gun on you with another person present."

"You're speech pattern has improved," I commented.

She laughed. "I got a kick out of sounding like a cross between a hippie and a valley girl."

"You know, Corinne kept trying to convince me you were a threat. When you didn't show up for a while, I started to believe her."

"Probably wanted to throw suspicion off herself," Jeff said before turning back to give his full attention to Katie.

"Uh, you and Jeff weren't an item then?"

Freddy laughed again. "I'm happily married to an accountant, and have three kids, ages twelve, ten, and six."

"Did you suspect Corinne?"

"Nope. Wasn't with you guys long enough. I figured my act irritated her."

"Freddy's role was not to look for a killer, but to make sure you stayed safe if Jeff couldn't be there. My biggest fear was that if you were right and said something to Liz, she'd tell Todd and blow the whole thing," Andy said.

"Gee, I just want to thank everyone for thinking of me in such glowing terms."

Katie looked over and grinned. "Well, you have

to admit, you do have a tendency to act before you think."

The waiter brought our wings and for the next few minutes we concentrated on food. I chose the Destroy Your Tonsils hot sauce. It lived up to its name. The fiery condiment required lots of beer chasers, and I wondered how Jeff and Andy could stand the Nuclear Explosion variety. Katie had chickened out with For Wimps Only *and* ranch dip.

"So," I said gulping more beer to put out the fire in my mouth. "What's likely to happen to Todd and Corinne now?"

"Both are facing charges of solicitation of murder, conspiracy to commit murder, and attempted murder, plus anything else we can hang on them," Andy answered, licking sauce from his fingers.

"Like grand theft auto, hit and run for the canal incident, and just being assholes?" I said.

"Why not?"

"Will Mother have to testify? She might make a shaky witness for the prosecution. I'm sure her past will be brought up by the defense."

He shook his head. "It'll never come to that. Like I said, both Corinne and Todd will cut deals for reduced sentences."

"Will she ever get out of prison?" Katie asked.

"Eventually, if she doesn't buy the death penalty or get life with no parole," Jeff answered. "Although by that time Corinne will be too old and feeble to pull a trigger.

"What about Barry—er—Todd?" she continued.

Jeff grinned. "Todd will be covered with prison tattoos courtesy of his new best friends. Rich and good looking will make him very popular with his fellow inmates."

"You watch. He'll plead his life is in danger and will end up in some kind of minimum security country club prison," Andy said, reaching for another wing. "And you guys wonder why I'm sick of this profession."

I breathed a sigh of relief Mother wouldn't have to take the witness stand. A badgering defense attorney mixing with Mom's temper *and* her slightly skewed logic was not a prospect I wanted to see. The thought of me having to testify was almost as scary. My track record with the law was sure to be brought out also. In spite of my conviction that I was bang on about most of my complaints—shades of Mother—I was still on the right side of sanity to be embarrassed by some of my actions.

But not Joel. Chasing him with the golf club felt good.

"Renee?"

I turned and gazed into Liz's eyes. Surprise rippled through me. Neither of us said a word. We just stared.

Andy recovered first. "Mrs. Gorman, please join us."

He pulled up a chair from a nearby table. Liz sat between us. An awkward silence descended as we all looked at each other.

Again, Andy took charge. "Would you like something to drink?"

She glanced at the pitcher. "Beer is fine."

He signaled the waiter for another glass. He brought one immediately along with another plate.

"How about a wing or two? You have your choice of For Wimps Only, Destroy Your Tonsils, or Nuclear Explosion sauces." He didn't give her a chance to refuse and dumped five wings onto her plate.

"The way I feel tonight, Nuclear Explosion sounds like the best idea." She turned her gaze onto me. "Renee, I—I don't know what to say. And I had a speech all prepared on the way over, too."

"How did you know where to find us?"

"Detective Santos overheard Jeff saying he was meeting you and Detective Jackson here for drinks." She nodded at Freddy. "I understand you're also with the department."

"I'm afraid so. I'm surprised we weren't tripping all over each other."

Silence descended again as Liz nibbled on a wing and tasted the sauce for the first time. She clapped a hand over her mouth, and then reached for the beer, drinking fast.

I touched her arm. "Liz, I'm so sorry about everything. I wanted to tell you, but couldn't figure out how."

She put the wing down on the plate and wiped her fingers with a napkin.

"Don't apologize. I probably wouldn't have believed you anyway." She bit her lip and gazed over Katie's shoulder to focus on the bar. "I'd heard the rumors for a couple of years about Todd harassing secretaries. I chose to ignore them. Call me Cleopatra, but that's the way of it."

"Cleopatra?" Jeff said with a puzzled expression.

"Queen of De-Nile," Katie, Liz, Freddie, and I answered at the same time.

Liz smiled. "I'm sorry, I haven't met you. I'm Liz Gorman," she said to Katie, who shifted uncomfortably in the chair.

"I'm Katie Jackson, Andy's sister."

"Oh, yes."

Katie blushed. "Yeah, I'm the other woman. I swear to God, I had no idea Barry—I'm sorry, Todd—was married. If I'd known I'd have never—"

Liz raised a hand to stop the flow of words. "No apologies necessary. My husband is a very good liar. I suspected his out of town trips to talk with donors involved fewer nights than he said. A three day trip to Boston was really a two day journey. The girlfriend of the moment was blessed with his undivided attention for a whole twenty-four hours."

"I feel like a fool," Katie said.

"Not half as foolish as I do. I married the son of a bitch," Liz replied. "You know, I once found a business card from an escort service in his pocket. When I asked about it, he said a donor had given it to him, but not to worry, he didn't use it. He loved me."

A small sob broke from her throat. I wanted to put my arm around her shoulders, but she brought herself under control and continued.

"I guess I'm to blame for some of this. I was so busy, so involved in other things I took it for granted Todd felt the same dedication for my interests. I never realized he resented me so much."

I remembered the bitterness in his voice the day I'd overheard his and Corinne's conversation.

"You do a terrific job helping people. None of this is your fault, least of all Todd's wandering eye," I said.

"Renee's right," Freddy said. "Don't blame yourself."

"He used to go with me to the fundraising affairs. Then about four years ago, he always came up with an excuse or was out of town. I found out today that he didn't want to be photographed with me and identified as my husband because of the women he had on the side. He gave them phony names and professions."

"I take it you've talked with your husband," Andy said.

"And our lawyer. He said he only wanted this woman he hired to scare, not kill me." She turned anguished eyes to me. "Is that true?"

Her expression plucked at my heart, and my eyes filled with tears.

"Liz, I've lied to you from the first moment we met. I can't lie any more. He wanted you dead. He wanted the money."

She bit her lip and drew in a deep breath. "How silly. Most of my money is in a trust that reverts to the Foundation in the event of my death. He'd get the remainder, but it's not nearly the amount he thinks. Renee, how can I thank you? You saved my life. I'd be dead now if you hadn't heard what you did."

"I did what I had to do. I guess this means I'm out of a job. I lied on my resume and stole Corinne's from the in-basket. It was in my purse when you walked into Mr. Stewart's office."

"Out of a job? Are you kidding? I need you more than ever now. I'm calling an emergency board meeting for eight o'clock on Monday morning. I think Todd's been covering personal expenses with Foundation funds again. I caught him doing that a year ago, and warned him. I suppose that's what put the idea of killing me into his head."

"You want to keep me on in spite of all I've done?"

"Absolutely. It's hard to find such dedication in a person. Besides, I'm getting used to having you around."

"I have to admit, if it hadn't been for you, I'd have never jogged. I kind of like it, but don't expect me for yoga classes. I didn't much care for those."

"I still can't believe Corinne was a professional killer."

"It's going to take a while to sort out who she may have put underground," Andy told us.

Liz looked at Jeff. "I don't suppose you'll be joining us for jogging anymore, Officer McCarthy."

"I jog several times a week when possible. You'll see me."

"I may join the group, too," Andy declared. "Barring hurricanes, I do five miles every day."

"Looks like I have a whole new set of friends,"

she said. "Thank you all for keeping me alive. I'd better go. I'm going to spend the weekend with my father and step-mother in Key West. I have to tell them what's happened. My father won't be too shocked. He never liked Todd. I guess a man can smell a rat faster than a woman. And FYI, I've already consulted a top-notch divorce attorney." Her lips curled into a small smile. "Renee, I'll see you bright and early on Monday morning."

She pushed back her chair and left the bar.

"Well, I'll be damned," I muttered.

"I'd say it's time for all of us to leave," Andy said signaling the waiter.

We divvied up the bill and paused on the sidewalk out front.

"Time for me to go reintroduce myself to my husband," Freddy said. She waved and walked toward her car.

Jeff smiled at Katie. "Have you ever been to a nightclub on the beach called Wanderlust?"

"No, but I've heard of it."

"Wanna go?"

She linked her arm around his. "That sounds like a great idea."

"Ahem! Have I mentioned, *Officer* McCarthy, that I'm very protective toward my baby sister?" Andy said, but with a twinkle in his eye.

Katie rolled her eyes. "Ignore him, Jeff."

Jeff laughed. "I'm not stupid. I know if I don't treat you right, I'll be patrolling a beat in the worst part of town for the rest of my career. I don't suppose the two of you want to join us?"

Andy smiled at me. "No, not my thing."

I read between the lines and remembered his break up with the busty brunette who loved the nightlife. His sexy smile sent a surge of warmth through my body.

"Not mine either, but you two have fun. I'll

314

expect a full report tomorrow at the gym."

They left, and Andy followed me home in his car. Inside, I offered him another beer, which he declined.

"I guess I should pack. No reason for me to stay here any longer."

Now what in hell's half acre did he mean by that? Had I misinterpreted the smile in front of the restaurant? Was I about to get the brush off?

"Um, you know, now that you are soon to be unemployed and in need of saving money, the offer of the spare room is still open. No strings attached."

"Suppose I like the strings attached?"

My heart gave a funny little bouncing thump and my mouth went dry.

"Oh?" For the life of me, I couldn't manage another word. My tongued twisted into a granny knot.

"Renee, I heard that shot today and was terrified. I thought you were dead. When your voice came through on that silly Lend An Ear, I damn near cried. You're a bit of a nut, but that makes you interesting. Somewhere along the line, I fell in love. I'd like to stick around for a while and give this relationship a chance. What do you think?"

"I think I'm withdrawing the offer of the spare room. The master bedroom has a much bigger closet, and my clothes are lonely."

He pulled me into his arms, kissing me senseless. When we finally came up for air, I stepped back.

"Andy, can you handle all the problems I seem to bring down on myself?"

"I can deal with them provided you throw the Lend An Ear away, and promise you'll never be a bodyguard again."

"I'm serious. What about my mother? She may need long term care or supervision. Suppose I turn out just like her? I do have a bad temper. What if—"

He silenced me with another kiss. "No more 'what ifs.' Your mother is in a new facility and if today was any indication, can listen to reason. Once she gets back on her medication and undergoes the right therapy, I have every hope she'll return to society. As for your temper, don't let your fears become reality. And you're not paranoid—merely suspicious upon occasion. In my line of work, a little suspicion is a good thing."

My eyes filled with tears, and I let them fall. "God, I hope this relationship works, because I'm in love with you, too. Today, when Corinne was about to shoot, I thought how I wished I'd told you."

He sobered and brushed a strand of hair from my cheek. "If I'm being honest, I'd have to say I wanted to die when I heard the shot. For the few brief seconds I thought you were dead, my life—my future—looked bleak, empty." He took a deep breath. "Renee, why don't we skip the preliminaries? Let's just call ourselves engaged."

"Are you asking me to marry you?"

He grinned with a lopsided smile. "Yeah, I guess I am."

I shook my head. "Uh-uh. Not good enough. Ask proper."

"Renee Ryan, will you marry me?"

I stood for a moment as though thinking when in reality, my heart fluttered and I wanted to cry.

"Well?"

The tears slid down my cheeks. "Of course I'll marry you. I can't think of anyone I'd rather spend the rest of my life with."

He folded me into his arms and kissed the top of my head. A rumbling laugh echoed through his chest.

"What?" I said pulling back to look at his amused face.

"So, your mother thinks I'm a stud, huh?"

"I knew you were going to be conceited as hell about that."

He swung me up into his arms, heading toward the master bedroom.

"Let's go see if she's right."

I slipped my arms around his neck and kissed him. He'd get no argument from me.

A word about the author...

Suzanne was born and raised in Indianapolis, Indiana, but now calls Ft. Lauderdale, Florida home. She lives there with her husband, Bruce, and 2 lively dogs.

In between books, she likes to travel, especially to visit with her sons, their wives, and her six grandchildren.

Suzanne loves writing and hopes readers find her stories entertaining.